I0822776

THE DARK SIDE

MOROZOV MAFIA SERIES

M.C. RIVERA

The Dark Side

M.C. Rivera

Book Cover by M.C. Rivera

Content Warning

The book contains violence, torture, death, domestic abuse (NOT between MMC and FMC), drug use, attempted rape, bad language, misogyny, and graphic sexual material.

To all the booktokers that want a little taste of the dark side

Chapter One

Shootout

"Crap." Jolie bent down to pick up her keys again. Items fell from her arms, and another curse followed as she balanced a gallon of milk, a box of tampons, a cute pair of flip-flops, and a box of ice cream bars in her arms. The line was five-people deep, with only one slow cashier. She hoped the crowd would have died by this time, but it was a Saturday in Downtown Tampa. People didn't sleep till at least three or four in the morning.

It was her fault for coming so late. If she could sleep, she could have avoided spending money she didn't have, but she was new to city life, and the constant loud sirens and cars from her window gave her anxiety.

Jolie looked at her stuff again, determining what she could put on the gum shelf. The flip-flops weren't necessary, but she'd been eyeing them all week, waiting for payday. Though tomorrow was Friday, her pay hit at midnight. She sighed again, to the annoyance of the man before her. She felt his glare in the mirror tilted on the ceiling. Jolie pretended not to notice, simply so she didn't have to see herself in the mirror. Brown hair in a messy bun, black-rimmed glasses, panda pajamas, and fluffy panda slippers—this was what she usually wore to the drugstore beneath her apartment. No one should expect anything better.

The door chimed, and a five-year-old girl wearing a sparkly pink dress ran through the door, followed by two men in tuxedos. It was nearly one in the morning on a school night.

Why the heck isn't that little girl in bed?

"Oh, man." Jolie dropped her head back. She forgot Tylenol. Abandoning the line depressed her, and for a minute, she believed she didn't need it, but a cramp rolled around her uterus, and she nearly caved in pain. She sighed once more, if only to poke at the man in front of her, before she left the line of hell.

Turning down the candy aisle, Jolie spotted the little girl picking different treats. *Alone*. Some parents didn't understand how easy it was to steal kids. As a teacher of kindergarteners, this fear was a constant reminder on flyers in the break room and *Stranger Danger* posters in random sections of her elementary.

How could her parents leave her by herself?

Jolie could only smile as she passed her, hoping for a wave. She was a beautiful little girl, with curly blonde hair, but the child was in deep concentration, picking between lollipops and chocolate. Life would be a happy place, if only her decisions were so light.

Jolie stuck her keys in her pocket before she grabbed a red bottle with her two fingers. Her hip was out, and her stomach extended, keeping all the items somehow placed just right so her things didn't tumble to the floor.

Jolie heard loud shouting, but everyone in the city was always shouting.

A violent firecracker shocked her, and everything dropped out of her arms as she turned. Screams, cries, and another terrible crack sounded one after the other. As items exploded around her, she only then realized it was gunshots. Jolie dropped to the floor in terror, crawling, searching for somewhere to hide.

The little girl crying caught her attention. She saw the child curling up on the floor as bullets blew items off the shelf. Jolie crawled on her hands and knees across the aisle in mindless desperation, barreling toward her balled, screaming form. She wrapped her up, and the girl's small arms and legs encircled her, not caring that she was a stranger. Jolie clenched her blonde curls, whispering in her ear, "It's okay, baby. I got you. You're okay. Shh…" She kicked all the candy off the shelf and buried herself in it. There was no real hiding place, but it made her feel better. The gunfire continued, but Jolie kept her attention only on the child as they trembled in each other's arms. "My name is Jolie. What's your name?"

Every bullet made her jump. "You know how to sing 'Let It Go'?" She whispered the song into the child's ear while clenching her eyes, begging for the horrible spray of bullets to end.

Then, it went silent.

Jolie could hear her own heartbeat. No one moved. No one dared. Random items fell off broken shelves, and soft whimpering from other customers filled the silence.

"Helina!" a man sounded over the chaos.

The little girl flinched, and Jolie wondered, "Are you Helina?" The little girl nodded.

"Helina!"

"I have her!" Jolie shouted back.

"Who—" Footsteps crunched on torn candy wrappers and a broken bag of pretzels. One of the men dressed in a tuxedo leaned down, holding onto the shelf with one hand while his other arm tucked into his chest. Blood dripped on the floor from his elbow. He had blue eyes, black hair, and a thick face. He spoke in Russian, and the little girl shook her head.

"Is it safe?" Jolie questioned.

The man reached down, and tentatively, she latched onto it, holding tight to the little girl who wouldn't let her go. He lifted her with ease, steadying her when her knees weakened.

"What happened?" Jolie fixed her messed glasses and disheveled hair.

The stranger looked her over, touching her hip. Jolie hadn't even known she got hurt, but she brushed it off. The man rested a hand on the back of Helina, but the little girl only clenched Jolie harder. "She doesn't want to let go."

The man questioned with a thick Russian accent, "Can you watch her for a minute?"

Jolie nodded mindlessly. The stranger stepped away, calling, "Gil? You alive?"

Jolie followed behind him, stepping over broken items on the floor. She was glad she couldn't pay attention to the damage. She was pretty sure there was a body not too far away. "Close your eyes," she told Helina, but she was beginning to doubt the girl understood English.

"Alexei," Gil replied, breathless. "I'm hit."

"Did you see who it was?" Alexei asked.

"No. Ah fuck, it hurts."

Jolie turned the corner to see Alexei squatting down before his friend, the other man dressed in a black suit. Blood was building in a puddle beneath his leg, and he ground his teeth, panting in pain.

Alexei quickly undid his belt and slipped it up his friend's thigh. He clenched his teeth as he tightened the belt. The pain from his own arm didn't stop him. Alexei shoved the pin through the belt, making a new hole. "We got to go."

"Whoever those fuckers are got balls to hit us on our turf. I think I got one, though."

Jolie froze. Did that mean what she thought it meant? Were they the shooters?

"Can you follow me?"

Jolie blinked when she realized Alexei was talking to her. She dumbly nodded, still not wholly working right. This felt like a nightmare. She wanted to help, but her mind wasn't working. Holding the child seemed like the best thing for her to do.

Alexei studied her, skeptical of a stranger willing to help, but the woman wasn't intimidating. She barely stood over five feet tall and weighed less than 130 pounds. And the panda pajamas revealed more about her personality than anything else. With his niece clinging to her, he had no choice.

The sounds of police sirens got Alexei moving. He lifted Gil to his feet, ignoring his cry of pain. "Do you live around here?"

"Why?"

Even though his arm barely worked, it didn't stop Alexei from lifting a gun and pointing it at her face. "Take us."

Chapter Two

Drug Dealers

Jolie led Alexei and Gil behind the alley up the fire escape. The police sirens were now upon them, and she hopped the stairs two at a time, keeping Helina tight in her arms. She thanked God she worked out because the five-year-old wasn't weightless, and she lived on the fourth floor.

Jolie turned at the landing, going up the rickety staircase. She watched Gil and Alexei struggle. They were both losing blood, and it was becoming too obvious. They would be found, but that wouldn't be on her. She was doing what she was told.

Alexei balanced the phone against his ear as he pulled Gil up the stairs. ***"We need a ride at Lexington and Twentieth."*** He paused to listen before loudly saying, ***"Don't ask about the fucking car."*** He shoved the phone in his back pocket, adjusting his brother. The blood was bad, and it was beginning to worry him.

Gil panted, clinging to the railing, ***"We won't make it. The cops are already here."***

Alexei leaned against the railing. Gil weighed more than he looked, and it was slowing him down more than he wanted to admit. In English, Alexei asked, "What floor, girl?"

Jolie glanced up to her apartment window, visible by the numerous plants that decorated the sill. They were close, but she could always pretend she lived on the top floor; ten stories would be implausible for them to climb. "Fourth. That one right there."

What were the pros and cons of having two drug dealers in her house? She was guessing they were drug dealers. Who else would have a shootout in the middle of a gas station?

How did Mom know? It was the first thing her mother said to her when Jolie revealed she was moving to the city. Drug dealers around every corner, her mom claimed.

"Mom's gonna kill me," Jolie said, groaning.

Alexei looked up at her, narrowing his blue eyes on her. "I'm gonna kill ya if you don't hurry up."

Jolie was already going as fast as she could. If anything, he was the one that needed to hurry.

"It's pointless," Gil breathed, sinking to the floor. ***"The cops will sweep. They got our car; they'll know we're on foot. You think Morgan's working tonight?"***

"Can you guys talk in English, so I know you're not planning to kill me when we get to my apartment?"

Alexei eyed the American on the stairs. Sweat was on his brow, and he panted from exhaustion. She was saving their asses, so speaking English wasn't a big request. "We have to keep going. If they catch us, the cops will take Helina." Alexei bent down and threw Gil over his shoulder before pushing up with his knees.

"Oh, great view," Gil sneered, eye level with his brother's ass.

Helina mumbled something off Jolie's shoulder, and instantly, the giant 200-pound killer replied with soothing Russian words that rolled off his tongue with a gentleness Jolie didn't think he could possess. It unnerved her.

She plugged the key into her back door and led them into the house. "Stay on the tile, and don't bleed on anything."

The apartment was barely a livable space. Being in the city was costly, and with a teacher's salary, she was lucky to get this. It was a loft, with her bed behind a screen in the corner, a couch, a bookshelf, and a kitchen. The bathroom was the only thing separate.

The kitchen was an eight-by-eight square, with a tiny two-person table pressed against the wall. The only reason she splurged on this apartment building was for the cute balcony. It was the perfect atmosphere for reading. No one used the fire escape.

Meows greeted them, and two cats jumped up on the kitchen table. "Get down," Jolie hissed, moving to the couch. She tapped on the little girl's shoulder, and with hesitancy, Helina plopped on the sofa, but when she spotted the cats,

Helina squealed and jumped up to chase them. They darted to the bed, squeezing under it, and Helina followed suit, calling them sweetly in a foreign language.

Alexei rested Gil in a chair before turning and reaching for paper towels, just as Jolie had her hand on it. She leaned back. He towered over her by five inches, and his oversized chest was intimidating. Being in a suit didn't hide his muscle. Instead, it made it much more apparent. Her cheeks burned with the uncomfortable thought. "Sit down," she ordered to get him out of her way. She grabbed the roll of paper towels when he stepped back. "Shouldn't you guys go to the hospital?"

Blood was dripping like a leaky faucet, and though Gil's leg was propped on the second chair, there was already a puddle forming. He reached for the roll of paper towels, but Jolie ripped some off and put it on the floor.

Alexei snatched the roll from her hand. "Just stay out of it. For your safety." He began to wrap it around Gil's leg, but the pain in his arm stopped him.

Jolie scoffed. "My safety?" Jolie grabbed the paper towels back. "I was out of it till there was a gunfight while I was shopping." She wrapped it around Gil's leg several times, but he needed something more substantial.

Gil rolled his head back, panting, "I need the Doc. Call them again. Tell them where we're at. I'm not feeling good."

As Alexei took out his phone, it rang. "It's Adrik."

"Shit."

Alexei held out the phone to Gil. "You talk to him."

"He's your brother. You talk to him."

Alexei scoffed. "He's your brother, too."

"He likes you better," Gil pointed out.

"That's why I'm not talking to him."

Jolie held out her hand. "Give me the phone."

They looked at her. Then they looked at each other. The phone continued to ring. Gil shrugged, and Alexei handed her the phone.

"Hello?"

A man sounded off on the other end with, "What...Who the hell are you? Where's Alexei?"

"He's apparently afraid of you."

Alexei scoffed, shaking his head, but Gil nodded with a smile.

"You know what? I don't care. Where's my daughter?"

Jolie glanced around the room. "Talking to my cats."

"And where is that?"

"In my apartment."

"Girl, if you don't start giving me some fucking answers—"

"My name is Jolie, not *'girl.'*"

"Are you threatening my kid?"

Jolie replied, confused, "No? Look, your people are here because they are hiding from the cops. Why is your daughter with them? What is she doing out so late? What kind of parent are you?"

"Never mind. I found you. You better stay the fuck where you are, and don't touch my daughter."

"Like I would." Jolie snapped the phone off and tossed it back to Alexei.

He chuckled. "You are pissing off the wrong person."

"He attacked first," Jolie sheepishly replied. "How can he know where I live?" The guys didn't answer, but she's watched enough FBI shows to know about GPS signals. But what kind of person had that available?

Helina sounded, and Jolie glanced at Alexei for a translation. "What're your cats' names?"

"Ming and Tae-Tae."

Alexei and Gil were silent in the awkward quiet. Jolie avoided eye contact.

Alexei shrugged out of his jacket with enough groans and moans that Jolie's attitude shifted. She moved to help, tucking the material off his ridiculous thick bicep. The sleeve of his white undershirt was red and wet.

"Oh, jeez, hold on." Jolie had to talk herself into going to the bathroom and taking her only towel off the rack. She told herself it was a good thing to do, although she hated seeing his blood destroy it. She wrapped the towel around Alexei's arm, tightening as much as possible and apologizing as he whined.

"Who would attack us?" Alexei questioned, leaning against the wall. "With Helina?"

"We shouldn't talk about that right now." Gil waved to Jolie. "I'm just relieved they missed."

Alexei shifted his blue eyes to her. She stood against the fridge, mindless wiping the blood off her hands, watching them. "You alone here?"

"Why?" she snapped. "So you can rape me?"

Alexei's mouth dropped open. "What?"

Jolie felt stupid for saying it, but it was just another comment her mother made after the drug dealers. Rapists were hiding in every alley. "Yeah. Just me."

"So, all the panda stuff..." His eyes went around the apartment. The panda pillows on the couch. The giant panda-face carpet in the living room. The massive painting of a panda over the TV. Her panda bedsheets. Her panda cookie jar on the counter. The messy coloring pages and panda drawings pinned to the refrigerator were the most condemning. Alexei suppressed a smile. "You don't have a kid?"

"No," she bit with bitterness. "I'm a teacher, and I like pandas."

He flicked his gaze to her pajamas, and when his face went red and his eyes to the floor, she remembered she never wore a bra to bed. She quickly folded her arms across her chest.

There was a knock on the door, and they all flipped to silence, staring at it. "Police! Open up."

Jolie slapped a hand to her mouth. She was going to go to jail. Harboring fugitives was a felony. Would they believe her if she said she was forced? Of course, they had guns! She was a sweetheart. Anyone could tell she was innocent.

Alexei lifted his gun, with a finger on his lips. He waved to Jolie, and with fast understanding, she scooped up Helina and headed for the bathroom.

"Alexei," a whisper came from behind the door. "It's Morgan; I saw your car out front. Your brother sent me your location."

Alexei rushed to the door and quickly let Morgan in. To Jolie's surprise, a cop stepped in, dressed in full uniform and with a hand unconsciously on his gun. "You guys hurt? What the hell happened?"

Gil growled, "Someone made a huge fucking—"

"Don't curse!" Jolie interrupted. Morgan glanced at her with knitted brows.

"Someone made a huge mistake," Alexei corrected. "But we don't know who."

"You think they were after her?"

"Maybe. They certainly didn't give a fuck if—"

"No cursing!" Jolie bit again.

Alexei sighed, and rephrased, "They didn't care if Helina was hurt and killed."

"Alexei?" A voice from the hallway came through the door. It was the man on the phone, Adrik. Jolie clung to Helina as Alexei opened up to let him in. She was curious about what a drug kingpin would look like. He had to be the boss with the way the two brothers were carrying on. What do Dons typically look like?

Was he a Don? What do they call them in Russia? In movies, they were always Italians. They were old and gangster-looking, with tattoos everywhere and gold teeth. Will he be wearing a white jacket like Scarface?

"Where is she?"

Alexei stepped aside, and Adrik entered. Not the kind of drug lord she was expecting. Nearly Alexei's twin, he was tall, thin, and blue-eyed. He was dressed in a suit without a jacket, and a white tailored shirt was open, exposing a clean undershirt. She hadn't expected anyone attractive, so when he turned toward her, Jolie froze like a deer in headlights. Russian poured from his lips as he approached, reaching his arms out. Helina quickly dived for him, and they squeezed each other. Adrik pulled back, looking Helina over, checking for any injury. She shook her head, and he kissed her forehead, running his hand through her hair. His blue eyes drifted toward Jolie, and she sucked in a breath.

He's a model. He has to be a model.

A dozen people piled into the apartment, stretching out along the entire length of her five-hundred-square-foot home. It felt claustrophobic in an instant. Jolie backed into the bathroom as she watched all these men in suits invade her personal space without taking off their shoes.

A young teenager with a tattoo on his face snatched her arm and pulled her out of the bathroom, forcing her to the couch. "Hey!" She yanked and fell on the cushions. When she tried to get up, the guy pushed her back down, and when she tried again, a gun barrel was staring her in the face. It was the second time someone pulled a gun on her.

Mom's gonna have a field day with this.

Jolie watched from over the edge of the couch as two men helped Gil to his feet. He cursed and moaned all the way out of the door. Bloody footprints were growing all around her kitchen; it was only a matter of time before it got elsewhere.

"Can you all be careful? There's no way to get blood out of the carpet!"

Adrik eyed her from over his daughter's shoulder. ***"Who is she?"***

Alexei stayed seated as someone wrapped up his arm. He respectfully replied in English. "This is Jolie. She owns the apartment. She protected Helina when"—Alexei scratched his head, ashamed—"when I lost track of her."

Adrik shifted through the apartment, shooed off the guy with the gun, and stared down at her. Jolie shrunk, unsure where to look. His shoes were shiny; she could almost see her reflection. When she dared to peek upward, his hand was out. "Thank you." Jolie blinked wide before taking his hand. He had star tattoos and religious symbols over his fingers. There was a fat ring on his pinkie, gold, and diamonds wrapped in a heavy outer layer. Just the ring alone was worth more than Jolie ever earned in her whole life.

He detached from her and ran a hand through Helina's hair, turning away as he whispered foreign words into her ear. When he got closer to the door, Jolie jumped up. "Um, excuse me."

Adrik turned to her with knitted brows, almost insulted. Jolie approached, waving a hand. "How do you plan to get the blood off my floor?"

He glanced down before throwing over his shoulder, "I'll send someone up tomorrow."

"You'll—" She coughed, confused by such a statement. "Send someone? What does that mean?"

"Exactly how it sounds. Was that confusing for you?"

"I don't want drug dealers knowing where I live."

He blinked and then fully faced her. A small little smirk teased his lips. "You don't know who I am."

"Should I?"

"No, I guess not."

The look sent a shiver through her unconsciously. She folded her arms across her shirt, praying he hadn't noticed the chill.

Adrik stepped further for the door. "Forgive our intrusion, Miss Bell. Thank you for your hospitality, but mostly for protecting my daughter. Cleaners will call you to schedule a time to clean up this mess. Paid for, of course." He glanced at Alexei. "Give her some money. Maybe then she can afford a bra."

Jolie's face reddened, but she spat, "I don't want your drug money."

Adrik glanced around, and added, "I'm sure a kindergarten teacher living in the city could use some help."

Her mouth dropped open. "How the heck do you know that? Wait, how did you know my last name?"

"I know more than you wish. Where are your contacts? Glasses aren't the best for your small nose."

She narrowed her eyes. "Please leave."

"Gladly."

Chapter Three

Truth

Jolie rested on her hands and knees, scrubbing the blood off the floor. Though she had been assured someone was coming in the morning, waiting around wasn't an option. The longer the blood sat, the more her anxiety rose.

Jolie wasn't immune to the chaos she had endured. It was slowly sinking in, and no amount of disregard could keep it from surfacing. Jolie came from the suburbs of the country. Which was different from the suburbs of the city. Suburbs in the city were wealthy, with their expensive cars and ten-bedroom houses. The country's suburbs were more upscale trailer parks—not dangerous or ghetto, but still making it paycheck to paycheck. A neighborhood watch patrolled the area, keeping teenagers from causing any damage to their old white picket fences and rusted cars that tended to have no alarms.

When Jolie told her parents she wanted to move into the city, they used every guilt trip they could muster, but Jolie was determined. She wanted to help underprivileged kids; it had been her passion since she was young enough to understand the homeless who lived slightly down the road.

She had been in the city all summer, acclimating to the harsh society, and was only a month into teaching.

Now, the dreaded 'I told you so' was in her future. Did she try to keep this incident from her parents? She doubted that was possible. Even now, her hand itched for the phone to tell her mom everything that had happened. She didn't keep secrets from her parents, even when it got her in trouble.

But maybe this one needed to be left out.

Jolie left her parents' house at twenty-three, trying to find a spark to life, and yet, being in the middle of a shootout wasn't precisely what she was looking for.

Jolie squealed and fell when a knock sounded on her door. She held a hand to her chest, her heart racing in terror. The beginning of PTSD was already set in motion. Jolie looked at the time; it was nearly three in the morning.

"Who is it?" she yelled from her seat.

"Tampa Police."

Her eyes widened, and she stared at the blood-smeared ground. She had barely begun to clean and only managed to smear it into a pink circle.

"Hold on," she replied, glancing around, panicking. Jolie peeled off her gloves as she stood, jumped over the area of blood, and grabbed her blanket off the couch, wrapping it around her. No one else was going to notice her braless attire.

Jolie opened the door just enough for her to slide through and shut it tight behind her. She smiled sheepishly at the two uniformed officers in front of her. She tucked a strand of brown hair behind her ear. "Hi." She scanned the hallway and was surprised there were no streaks of blood along the floor.

"Ma'am." Jolie snapped her eyes up. "Sorry for the late call, but were you in the shootout that took place three hours ago at Salem's Pharmacy?"

"A shootout? What?"

The two officers glanced at each other out of annoyance. "We have you on their security camera."

Jolie's face heated up. "Oh, yeah, that shootout, yep." She wasn't always a good liar, but not for the lack of trying.

"We also have you talking to two of the assailants."

"No, I don't know them."

"Why did you leave the store with them?"

"They helped me out."

"They helped you? Or you helped them?"

"How could I help them?"

"You mind if we come in?"

Jolie stiffened and quickly made something up. "Normally, I wouldn't, but um—my dishwasher broke, and I haven't had time to clean, so..."

"Ma'am, you understand that harboring a fugitive is against the law?"

"Yes."

One police officer raised a piece of paper. 'If you are in danger, nod.'

Jolie quickly shook her head. "No, I'm fine. I live here alone. Really, I just don't want anyone to see my mess. I didn't know them. I was scared, and the little girl was scared, so I walked her out, handed her to them, and left."

"You left a crime scene."

That sounded bad. Jolie quickly added, "I'm still in shock."

They clearly weren't convinced. "We'd like you to come down to the station for further questioning."

"Sure, sure. Tomorrow. I have school to teach in the morning. But after, sure."

They gave her a card, and when she reached for it, she noticed the red tint on her hand. She snapped it back. The cop nodded to her hand. "Hurt yourself?"

"Just a little."

"There's a medic downstairs. Why don't we escort you?"

"I'm fine. Band-aid worthy."

With no further questions, they walked down the hallway, glancing back at her as if she was going to cry out for help at any moment. She waved pleasantly and slipped back inside, locking the door closed. "Oh, dog water," she cursed.

Jolie slid down her door, wrapping her arms around her legs. "Why lie?" she asked herself. "Why? They are mobsters. You just lied about the mob!" Jolie cried, dropping her head to her knees. "This can't be real," she moaned.

Jolie was a zombie as she walked into the school the following day. She hadn't slept. With every soft noise, she feared the mob was coming back to execute her. Wasn't that what the mob did? Kill people? Why not kill her? She's a nobody. They could get rid of her body by dropping her in the ocean. Why did she have to live near water?

Jolie sat at her desk, barely blinking. She was going to tell the police the truth. The police could protect her, right? Or did the mob own them, too? There was that police officer that came in; he was a friend of the drug dealers. If she told the truth, they'd come after her.

"Miss Bell?"

Jolie flinched, blinking. All her kindergarteners sat in their chairs, staring at her. They fidgeted uncomfortably, unsure of what to do. She forced a smile. "Morning, class."

Jolie pretended the best she could. They did art projects, but someone dropped their plate of paint, and it slapped on the ground, spraying like a bag of chips blown apart by a bullet. When she got down on the floor, scrubbing the ground, the color played tricks on her, flashing a bright red, like the blood soaking her home. She held her fingers out before her face, blinking, and the dark red transformed to purple.

The students were staring at her again.

Jolie got up on her feet. "Excuse me. Keep working hard, children."

Jolie went next door and asked the teacher to watch over her classroom before she darted to the women's bathroom. She splashed water on her face, staring at her reflection in the mirror. Her brown eyes were bloodshot, with black bags beneath them. She blinked, trying to force the exhaustion and fear from her face. She pressed a wet hand against her mouth, nausea bubbling in her stomach. The fear she had shoved down seemed to take this moment to reignite, and when a toilet flushed, she dropped to the ground, pushing herself under the sink.

A tentative hand reached out. She screeched but saw a little kid looking down at her. "Are you okay?"

Embarrassment crept up her cheeks as she smiled. "Of course. Just taking a break." Jolie slithered out and stood up, forcing a bright grin. "You wash your hands?" she asked before she ran out the door.

As soon as school ended, Jolie didn't stick around to mingle with the other teachers in the lounge. Out of all the days to attempt to make friends, today was not a good day. And besides, the police wanted to talk to her. They had called her cell phone four times and left three text messages. She couldn't avoid them any further.

She got in her car, threw her bag to the side, and sighed.

A knock bolted her in her seat. A young man stood outside her door in a white dress shirt and black pants. She tried to put her window down, but the car wasn't on. With an aggravated sigh, she opened the door, peering up at the guy. "May I help you?"

He took ahold of the door and pulled it wider, holding out his hand for her. "Come with me."

"I'm sorry, who are you?"

He ignored her, snatching her arm and pulling her out.

"Excuse me! Let go." She stumbled, yanking, but when his hold only tightened, she panicked, stomping on his foot. He groaned, releasing her, and she put her hands on her hips. "Who do you think you are?"

"Miss Bell."

Jolie turned to find the mob boss, Adrik, standing beside a black limo, with a humorous smile on his lips. He looked like a bachelor on that stupid TV series, dressed in formal attire. She despised him for it.

"You should teach your son some manners."

The man stifled a cackle, scratching his temple. "Do I look like I can have an eighteen-year-old son?"

Jolie didn't want to tell him what he looked like. She was pretty sure he knew already, and he was baiting her.

"Can we talk?" Adrik gestured to the limo.

She eyed it suspiciously, glancing around the schoolyard. Kids scattered along the grass and sidewalk, eyes on her in curiosity.

Witnesses.

Feeling safer, Jolie stepped forward. Adrik held his hand for her, but she disregarded him as she climbed into the luxurious vehicle.

All fear faded at the awe-inspired sight. She had never been in a limo. She almost had the chance to go to prom in one, but then her boyfriend at the time decided his brother's beat-up jeep was a better alternative. She arrived at prom with her hair in complete shambles and spent the first half hour in the bathroom trying to fix it.

Adrik sat next to her, unbuttoning his jacket. Everything about him was perfect. The way his black hair was gelled. The tattoos were strategically placed. The tailored suit, the gold cuffs, the Rolex watch—all part of perfection. Altogether, he wore more money than Jolie made in a year.

She unconsciously looked down at her clothes. She wore a dress that was covered in paint, and the worst was that she had made it herself and thought it was pretty cool.

We are from two different planets.

"Would you like a drink?" He moved for a wine glass.

Jolie wasn't going to fall for any charms. "What do you want?"

If she knew anything about men like him, which she read enough books to have a hint of the kind of man he was, he'd think she was quickly thwarted. And he may be right. He was not someone Jolie wanted to mess with.

"I heard you have an interview with an FBI agent today."

"So?"

"What do you intend to say?"

"The truth."

"And what's your version of the truth?"

'Her version of the truth.' It was a subtle hint that what she saw and what the police needed to know were two different things. "What do you want me to say?"

"What you said last night to the police was good enough. Simply keep with your story."

Her body stiffened, and she clenched her hands around her dress. "How do you know what I said last night?"

"Miss Bell, you saved my daughter. I am grateful. Take my generosity and my advice. Repeat your story, and all will be well."

As soon as he got a nervous head nod, Adrik got out of the car and held his hand out for her. She wasn't stupid enough to deny him now that she was beginning to understand how dangerous he was. She allowed him to help her to her feet.

Jolie stood in front of him. Their height difference was noticeable; he was six feet, and she was barely over five. He looked down at her. She was sure that intimidation came naturally to him. Or maybe it wasn't intimidation she saw in his eyes but something more treacherous. Something she didn't want in her life.

Jolie bowed her head. "Stay away from me," she ordered, and hurried away with her pounding heart.

Chapter Four

Footsteps

Adrik sat in the limo, fixing his jacket while staring out the tinted window. Jolie stood beside her car, watching them, the fear and curiosity mixing together.

'Stay away from me,' she said. But Adrik suspected that's not exactly what she wanted. He felt a smirk pull at his lips. Jolie usually wasn't his type, but there were always exceptions. Her nipples through her pajamas were still a present image in his mind that he wasn't about to erase.

Alexei rolled down the partition, sitting in the front seat. "What do you think?" His arm was in a black cast, resting on the door. He also looked out the window, watching her. "Think she'll talk?"

"No," Adrik acknowledged. "She understands."

"She didn't cry or beg. You didn't threaten her family. I don't know."

"Sometimes, less is more."

Alexei mumbled, "Guess that's why you're next in line."

Adrik observed the side of his brother's face. Though there was some aggravation, there wasn't any resentment, and that mattered. Alexei was the oldest, but when he turned eighteen, ready to take on as head of the family, Alexei purposely screwed up so Adrik could take over. Alexei never wanted to be the leader. In their line of business, everything needed to be calculated and thought out, and Alexei wasn't a planner. He only knew where he was going once he was already coming back.

"Want me to send someone to Orlando, just in case she changes her mind?"

Jolie's parents lived in Orlando. The implication was clear, but Adrik didn't see the need. "No. Has her apartment been mended?"

"Yep, the cleaners are done."

Adrik closed his eyes. These minor, insignificant problems could become an avalanche if not cared for properly. It was why he took time out of his day to deal with it, but the big situation was the assassination attempt on his child. Nearly eighteen hours later, there was still no claim to the attack. He had gone over every situation, and none of it made sense.

Ten semi-major families were in his control, along with over a hundred gangs and clans that flew the Morozov flag. Any one of them could have done it, but why?

The Morozov family was a million souls strong, with roots in Tampa, Clearwater, Lakeland, St. Petersburg, Bradenton, Ft. Myers, and a slowly developing gang in Miami. They were the most prominent mafia family in Florida. So, who would be dumb enough to go after his child?

Kids were supposed to be off-limits until they were eighteen. It's an unspoken law in their underworld. This was a cause for war, and he had every intention of hitting back as soon as he figured out who it was.

"Who responded so far to the meeting?"

"The Garcia family, Delgado, Utkins, and Kuzmin."

Only four out of the ten. Was there something going on that Adrik didn't know?

"Oh, um," Alexei nervously began. "Papa wants to talk to you."

Adrik curled his hand into a fist. "Shit."

His father went on vacation two months ago to allow Adrik to run the company as a trial. Adrik was fully capable of being the head of the family, but his father was controlling.

"Put him on the phone," Adrik requested.

Alexei grimaced. "He's home."

Adrik sunk into his chair like a troubled teen.

Adrik walked the long hallway toward his father's office. Yakov Morozov was a man of specialized taste. He was fond of a hunter's life, a copy of his father, Adrik's grandfather, who was a great hunter in Russia. Yakov took on all his father's favorites to become the favored child out of ten siblings.

It worked, Adrik mused.

The dark mahogany double doors stood before him, and he took this time to reassemble any anxiety. His father was better at reading people than he was.

With a deep breath, Adrik stepped in.

There were dead animals on nearly every section of the wall. Deer, muskrats, bears, and moose. Behind his father's desk was his most prized kill: a full-bodied lion standing on a shelf. The shotgun he used sat beneath it, always cocked and ready in case of an emergency. The room was a gift Adrik had given his father on his sixtieth birthday.

Yakov sat at his desk, currently on the phone. He put a finger up to quiet his son, and Adrik sat in one of the high-back leather chairs. The office was straight out of a gangster movie, and Adrik sneered at every little stereotype. Yakov was part of the older generation, never conforming to the newest way of things. It's why their ring of business was in decline in Yakov's care.

Yakov hung up, standing, forcing Adrik back to his feet to greet his father with a kiss on the cheek. Yakov held his arms. "How is my granddaughter?"

Though Adrik was relieved his father was here, he worried about what his father would say. For two months, Adrik had complete control over the company. Against his brother's advice to do things the same way they've always been done, Adrik implemented new ideas and improved their resources by thirty percent.

Was his father going to acknowledge the renovation as a good thing?

"Helina's fine, like I told you over the phone. You didn't have to come home."

Yakov sat in the chair opposite of him, offering Adrik to sit as well. "Someone tries to kill my son and granddaughter, I'm stopping everything I'm doing. Don't you want my help?"

Adrik didn't want to insult him. "Of course. Your *sons* and granddaughter deserve all your attention."

Yakov ignored the correction. "Six families aren't responding. That's not a good sign."

"Do you think they are plotting something?"

"Of course. They took advantage while I was out of town."

Adrik withheld an eye roll. Yakov believed he needed his hands in everything, or it went to shit, so he said.

"We need to flush out information. You will stop the fulfillment of all drug orders. We'll see who rats first."

"That's… that's millions of dollars a day."

The idea of stopping the funding of drugs to the populace would have never entered his mind. People relied on their products to survive, whether for money to feed their families or an addiction. To take it away could cause a riot.

Or allow their competition to step up and replace them.

"Yes, is your daughter and brothers not worth it?"

"You're cutting into the livelihood of thousands of people."

"Yes. Again, is your daughter not worth it?"

Adrik had to hold his temper. His father had a knack for pushing the wrong buttons. "Of course she is, but what you suggest is dangerous."

"I give it less than two hours before someone comes with information."

"It's too much of a risk."

Yakov smiled as he leaned against his desk, grabbing a cigar. "What do I always say?"

Adrik watched him cut the tip of the long, fat cigar. He put it in his mouth and looked up at his son. Adrik gave him the answer. "Big risk, big reward."

"That's right. Now, about the shootout. This teacher that was there? What are you doing about her?"

"She's been taken care of."

"She has a meeting with that FBI agent, Mally. The bitch that tried to convict me six years ago. Thought she'd end her career and get pregnant by now. But these women nowadays want to be men."

Adrik reassured, "I took care of it."

Yakov ignited the silver zippo and held fire over the tip of his cigar. The smoke was thick and swirled upward. "Hn," he inhaled, and held it, staring at his son for a moment longer before blowing it out. "I'll leave it alone for now."

Adrik was hoping that was the end of it. And then Yakov spoke again. "Since you're here, let's talk about the changes you've made."

Adrik met his father's gaze. Though Yakov was now an old man, his eyes never changed. They were the same dead eyes he met every day of his life. "What about them?"

"You think you can do this job better than me?"

Adrik chewed the inside of his cheek, looking away. He was disappointed in his father because, for a moment, he thought Yakov would be proud of his actions. But he should have known better. "I wanted to try something different."

"Think I haven't tried different things? The way I operate is the best there is. So, all you need to do is continue in my footsteps. I don't need you to think. I don't need you to question. Just copy. Can you do that? Or should I find someone else to take on the family?"

Adrik snapped his head back to his father. The mere comment made his blood boil. Who else would his father employ? There was no one good enough to handle their family name. It belonged to Adrik. He spent years to gain it, and to threaten him was an insult.

Adrik thought about fighting against it. There was evidence in their profits that Adrik's changes had made a difference, but he had worked too hard to become the heir to lose it because of his pride. He fisted his hand, and said, "I can do that."

"Good."

Chapter Five

FBI

Jolie shivered from the cold sting of the metal chair as she sat at a table in an interrogation room. A mirror revealed her reflection, a detestable sight that proved she wasn't as fearless as she hoped she looked. She took her fingers away from her mouth, sneering at the broken, chewed nails. She could hear the chastisement from her mother since she was in seventh grade.

Jolie watched the clock tick by minute after minute. Her body shivered from the cold and emotional turmoil she was going through. It hadn't even been twenty-four hours, and it felt like a week. More and more images from the shootout were attacking her. She replayed the event over a dozen times. Most of her actions were survival mode, so she didn't hate on herself for hiding cowardly in a candy shelf. What she did chastise herself about was how she spoke to the mobsters.

They could have killed me at any moment.

Jolie didn't know where the attitude came from. She was typically sweet and a friendly person. But in the middle of 'fight or flight,' she lost her consideration for others.

The door popped open, and she flinched. She hated how every sound since the shootout resonated like ground-shaking thunder.

"Miss Bell. I'm Special Agent Mally with the FBI." The fifty-year-old black woman in a gray suit stretched out her hand. Jolie shook it with a forced tight smile, trying not to let the woman's superior title whittle away her courage. "You are the last of my interviews for today," she announced happily, sitting in the stiff chair like it was a throne.

"I'm happy for you," Jolie sweetly said.

Mally opened her folder, sifting through papers, trying to decide where she wanted to start. "I'm sorry that you were involved in this terrible situation. I'm glad you weren't hurt. Many can't say the same." She plopped three photos in front of Jolie. Three dead people were covered in bullet wounds and blood.

Jolie slapped a hand over her mouth and looked away.

Mally sat back and watched, taking in every reaction, trying to assess the truth behind each flinch and emotion. She felt guilty for a moment, but that went away as it usually does. "This was caused by a blood feud between opposing gang members. Do you know which gang members they are?"

Jolie shook her head, wiping a tear from her cheek while she refused to look back at the table.

"These people shouldn't have died." Mally leaned in, pointing. "Xander, 24, buying formula for his newborn baby. Ginger, 33, paying for gas after working at the hospital as an ER nurse. And Paul. A homeless guy who's been a friend of mine for a while. So, I'm personally invested in finding out who did this."

"I'm sorry. I don't know."

Mally hated it when they lied. It was annoying, and it wasted time. "You're a good girl, Jolie. You pay your taxes, obey traffic laws, and you even turned in your boyfriend for robbing a bank. I'm sure he didn't like that. Did you guys break up?"

Jolie didn't want to feed into it, but that situation had escalated and stuck with her for years afterward. It was another reason why she had to get out of that town. 'Snitch' was pinned to the back of her head everywhere she went. No one would have cared if her boyfriend had been anyone else but the star quarterback.

Jolie nodded.

Mally shifted back in her chair with a smug little smirk. "Heard he got eight years. And it looks like parole's coming up."

Jolie didn't understand why the agent was talking about this. Jolie knew about her ex-boyfriend's parole. She was recently contacted to come in to testify against it.

Mally placed another photo on the table. It was a picture of Jolie holding Helina. "That's the daughter of Adrik Yakov Morozov. He will be the next head of a very powerful mafia family that stations here. I've been trying to destroy their illegal corporation for years."

Jolie latched onto anger. She was angry at the woman for bringing up her ex, putting horrible photos in front of her face, and acting like she was guilty. Jolie crossed her arms and met her gaze. "If you know who he is, why can't you go after him?"

"Because, like his father, Adrik does not get his hands dirty. They are untouchables." Mally shifted, sitting with her arms on the table, staring straight at Jolie. "Do you know how the original Five Family Italian Mafia was taken down in New York?"

Jolie shook her head.

"The tiniest listening bug placed on their phones." She placed one on the table. It was no bigger than a thumbtack. "So simple, right? It would be easy to slip one of these into their pocket or drop it in their car. But Adrik, Yakov, and their wives do not go anywhere without an escort. They do not talk to the lower soldiers that do all their dirty work. They are very, very good at staying off the radar. Plus, the county doesn't give us—" Mally took a deep breath, swallowing her words. "It's just impossible."

"Why are you telling me this?"

"You saw him, didn't you?"

"No."

"You held his daughter."

"To keep her from dying. I didn't know who she was."

"He'll thank you. One thing about the Morozovs is their generosity. You see, that's how they reel you in. They go to the poor sections of cities and give out money. They just hand people a thousand dollars. People who have never seen more than twenty bucks in their pocket. They lure them in with promises and then snag them for life." Mally chewed her lip, watching. "Have you gotten money for what you did?"

The untouched wad of cash tucked in a box under her bed flashed across Jolie's mind.

"No."

"Why are you lying for them? Did they threaten you?"

"No."

Yes.

"Then, why not tell me the truth?"

Jolie wasn't stupid. She saw Scarface. She knew what the Mafia did to snitches.

"I can get you in protective custody."

Jolie chewed on her fingernails. *Why didn't I call my mom?*

She wished she had her mother's words to guide her because she was confused. Why didn't she reveal Adrik? She didn't owe these people anything. She hadn't done anything wrong, yet why was she feeling punished? Should she have just left the little girl to her fate? It felt like everything was building into a giant ball, rolling unstoppable down a hill.

'Take my generosity and my advice,' Adrik said. *'Repeat your story, and all will be well.'*

"I don't need protective custody. I saved the little girl, gave her back to her family, and walked away."

"Who walks away from a shootout?"

"I was confused and in shock. I think I still am. I just wanted to go home."

"You said you saved the little girl." Mally straightened, pulling in all her pictures till she only had one: Jolie holding Helina. "Was she the target?"

Jolie's heart pounded in her throat. She tossed a hand, pretending bewilderment, hoping she hadn't just destroyed her life from something she couldn't possibly understand.

Mally stood up and pounded on the door. Another person came and opened it, and Mally whispered, "What if Adrik's control is slipping? What if the other families are going after him?"

The other person leaned into her ear. "Word is Yakov came home from Africa."

"Oh, shit," she cursed. Quickly, Mally swung around and returned to the table, slapping her hands on the metal. "Tell me what you know, or the next shoot-out—and I have a feeling it's going to be big—is going to be your fault."

Jolie sat back and crossed her arms.

Chapter Six

Snitch

Adrik swam to the steps, wiping the water from his face. He snatched a water gun off the rim of the pool and turned, aiming it for Helina, but she dived beneath the water only to come up sputtering and wide-eyed. He couldn't help smiling at her. She always managed to bring out happiness, like the sun in the middle of a storm.

I can't believe I almost lost her.

He dived after her, chasing her, making her squeal and shriek. But, like always, it was interrupted. He rarely had time to be with her. Alexei approached the pool. Adrik tossed Helina again and then waved to the nanny to care for her. Adrik exited the water, running his hands through his black hair to slick it back. He dripped his way over to Alexei.

Alexei cursed, backing up. ***"Don't get me wet."***

"How's the arm?" Adrik snatched a towel from a chair, wrapping it around his waist.

"It hurts," he bit.

Adrik sat and pushed out a chair for Alexei. ***"Drink with me."*** He poured a glass of bourbon and went to pour Alexei one, but the man pushed the glass away.

"I can't. I'm on pain pills. I'm barely conscious as it is."

"Why don't you take a nap?"

"Because my niece was almost killed."

Adrik hardened and pinned his gaze on his brother. It was the same look their father gave, but he didn't realize that. Adrik drowned the glass, swallowing, allowing the harshness to ease the bubbling dragon beneath.

Alexei only hesitated a minute before he broke, saying, ***"It's not that I know you don't care, but why aren't you pissed?"***

"I am pissed. Don't assume to know how I feel. They tried to murder you, Gil, and my five-year-old daughter. There aren't words for what I feel."

"So, then, what is going on?"

"I want to know who to be pissed at. I want to know who I'm going to set on fire. I want to know whose screams are going to go unheard. I want to know who. So, do you have that answer?"

Alexei answered, depressed, *"Not yet."*

Adrik sat back. *"Not yet."*

It would be so easy for him to storm through this house, stomping and shouting, but aside from scaring his daughter, what did that do for anyone? Everyone was working to find out who the fuck was stupid enough to do such a thing. So now, all he had to do was wait. And that was torture, but the answer would come. The answers always came.

"Did you stop production?" Adrik asked.

"Yes. Twenty minutes ago. There are a dozen phone calls already. I'm having the warehouse take the calls, since they're out of work for the moment."

"Father said less than two hours. Then, brother, you will see my rage."

Helina escaped the hands of her nanny. *"Uncle!"* she squealed, running into him. He kept his arm up, saving it from harm. *"How's your arm?"* She reached for it, touching the cast.

"It's okay, sweet girl."

"Can I have a cast like yours?"

"Yeah, I can make you one."

Helina ran her hands along it, envious. *"Hey, can we visit that lady with the cats? She was really nice, and she had so many stuffed animals. I don't even have that much."*

Adrik smirked. Now that he recalled, it was an obscene amount of pandas.

"No, baby girl," Alexei answered. *"She was a stranger. What do we say about strangers?"*

"Don't trust anyone you don't know."

"And what do we say about people we know?"

"Don't trust anyone unless Daddy, Mommy, or you say it's okay."

Adrik looked out toward the sunset. The sky was a dark red, a promise that there would be bloodshed tonight. He curled his fist, containing his anger like a lid to an inferno. "Did the teacher talk?" he asked in English, knowing his daughter didn't understand.

"No. You were right."

Adrik knew people; it was his job to know when to push and back off. It's something Alexei never understood. Despite how sweet he was to his niece, he was a more violent man. It's why Alexei spent the most time building his strength.

"Daddy, what are you saying?" Helina crawled onto his lap, gazing at him with her sweet blue eyes. "Hi," she said in English. "My name is Helina. What you name?"

Adrik ran a hand over her hair, admiring her beauty. She may have gotten the looks from her mother, but he was grateful her personality came from him. ***"Do you want to learn English?"***

"I want to go to school."

The thought had never entered his mind. It wasn't an option for kids of the Mafia. It was never safe enough. ***"I'm sorry, princess, you can't go to school. But I can invite some kids over this weekend."***

"Yes!" She jumped up, running in a circle. ***"Yes, yes, yes."***

Alexei's phone rang, and Adrik's smile fell from his face. When Alexei's eyes connected with his, he knew they had found someone with information. Adrik stood. "Esfir"—he waved over to the nanny—***"take her to her room."***

Helina deflated, but Adrik didn't see it as he left them behind with Alexei on his heels.

The drive to the warehouse was only ten minutes, but it felt like getting his balls waxed. It was stressful and full of unwanted trepidation. His leg bounced uncontrollably. He had taken three shots of whiskey, and it still hadn't stopped his brain. He went over every name, every person that could have done this to his family. And the implications were all the same. He'd have to exert his power. He'd have to remind the low families why the Morozovs were on top. He knew this day was coming, but he hadn't known he'd be the next heir when it hit. Alexei was supposed to be in his seat. Alexei would have probably burned down the city by now.

Adrik didn't wait for someone to open his door; he jumped out when the car stopped and went straight through the parking garage to the basement door. A trail of people was behind him, their footsteps echoed down the long stairway. They stopped at a door that had a big sign that read 'No trespassing.' He barreled through it.

Sitting on a single chair, with a spotlight, was their informant. He was jittery from drug use, the paleness of his skin and the darkness under his eyes a clear sign of approaching withdrawal. Adrik reached back, and Dima, his head guard, put a small bag of cocaine in his hand.

The addict heard them coming and tried to appear steady, but his hands shook as they rested on his lap. "I want protection," he quickly chimed.

Adrik stepped into the light.

The man's eyes widened. "Oh, shit. Look, we didn't know it was your little girl. I would have never killed no little girl! I swear it."

Adrik kept still, the fire he controlled so well was licking at the sides, and the lid began to tremble.

Alexei punched him, and he fell out of his seat. Blood dripped from his nose and mouth, and he groaned as he held his jaw.

Adrik basked in his pain and used it to sedate his temper. He listened to it for a moment more. "Who gave you the order?"

"I want protection."

"You lost that when you aimed a gun at my daughter. Who gave you the order?"

He shook his head and spit at Adrik's shoe. "I ain't saying shit."

Alexei smashed his foot into his stomach, and the man rolled, crying out as he held his ribs.

Adrik held out the bag and waited for the man to notice. When his eyes finally opened, all the pain disappeared, and he stopped whining.

"Who gave you the order?"

The man reached out for it, waiting for Adrik to take it away, but when he didn't, he snatched the bag, sitting on his butt. He rushed to open it, sticking a finger inside it and rubbing it on his teeth. "This guy paid us two grand to shoot up Salem's. He had us waiting and then called when he was ready. I didn't know who was inside, I swear it. I would never go against you."

"Name him."

"I don't know his name. But he had a tattoo, a raven by his thumb."

Adrik looked back at Alexei. There was only one family with ravens.

His wife's family.

Adrik took the gun from his back and pointed it at the man sniveling on the floor. He was thankful for the information, which was the only reason he used the gun. He fired, striking him in the leg. The snitch howled, fueling the fire in his soul. Adrik shot again, hitting him in the other leg. The bone splintered and ripped through the skin. Blood expanded on the floor like a tipped-over gallon of paint. It was beautiful to watch.

Adrik kneeled down to get a closer look, sliding his toes back when the liquid got too close. He observed the pain in the man's face, enjoying it like a kid engrossed in their favorite show. "Did he have a scar on his face?"

The man rocked in agony, crying and screaming, begging and pleading.

Adrik reached out and grabbed the man's shattered leg. The blood was warm on his hand, like touching hot sand at the beach. "Did the man have a scar on his face?" He spoke louder in case it was hard to hear over his bitching.

"Yes!"

Adrik shot him in the head and stood as the body dropped back to the floor, thankfully quiet.

Chapter Seven

Drive

Adrik stood over the body on the floor. The spotlight was on him, casting him in shadows. Alexei stood just outside the light, waiting while the others were sent out.

Being betrayed by allies is one thing.

Being betrayed by family was another matter.

Adrik didn't know why he was surprised. In this business, anyone could betray you, but he had thought his in-laws were more intelligent than that.

"*You want me to bring your wife in?*"

Adrik didn't care for Katia. He'd been married to her for ten years, but no love existed between them. He imagined her trying to kill him, but to go after their daughter didn't seem right. She was cruel, not heartless.

"Not yet."

Alexei was unsatisfied with that answer. He liked swift justice. But the problem with it was that the level of justice needed to match the level of disrespect.

Adrik stared at the body beside him. The blood stopped spreading. He shifted his foot right beside it, nearly touching it.

"The Stephanovs own the dock."

"I know."

"If we lose them, we'll lose our port."

Adrik circled the body as if it held the answers in the mutilation of its corpse.

"Adrik," Alexei called, aggravated.

Adrik lifted his head. *"I think I know the implications, brother. I was forced to marry her at eighteen because of it."*

"Let's tell Dad."

"If we tell him, he'll kill her."

"So? You don't give a shit about the bitch."

Adrik couldn't fight him on that point. ***"She's the mother of my child."***

Alexei sneered. ***"Does that give her amnesty?"***

Adrik kneeled beside the body, a finger stretching to touch the blood. It was cold now. He drew it across the ground, creating an unnatural line. He recalled the early morning when he had brought Helina back. His wife had been delirious, that much had been clear. ***"As much as I hate her, I don't see her trying to kill her child."***

This was a piece of a puzzle, and puzzles were his favorite pastime. He envisioned Tampa in the pool of blood; the unnatural line was the port that the Stephanov family owned. It showed they would lose the lower half of Tampa if he attacked, including the water levy, which would cut their import by a third.

But if he managed to overtake the Stephanovs, he'd gain much more.

Do I have that sort of power?

"How many men do we have on the ground?"

Alexei answered, ***"Sixty thousand."***

"And how many do they?"

"Forty-five, give or take. But it was never about us being stronger. They have more playing cards than we do."

Adrik could see all his cards—the casino, the governor, the hospitals, and the airport. It was a never-ending web of money laundering, drug smuggling, and trafficking that could get tangled if not adequately cared for. It was enough to give him a headache.

Adrik could feel the weight of exhaustion. After finally getting his answer, sleep was sneaking in.

He stood, approaching his brother. They were similar in height and stance. But Alexei was thicker and had more power in his punch, while Adrik had a nicer face. But they still held the family's eyes. Blue like water. He gently tapped Alexei's cheek. ***"Good work. Restart the product line before we have addicts pounding on our doors."***

"What are you going to do?"

Adrik walked away. ***"I'm going for a drive."***

Jolie sat on her couch. Ming was snug in her lap, purring, and it was a pleasant sound in the quiet. The remote was in her other hand, but she had yet to turn on the TV. She feared she wouldn't hear if someone came through her door.

Strangers had entered her apartment and cleaned while she was at work. Now, Jolie was eyeing the lock as if it betrayed her. There was a knife on the coffee table, but it was laughable. What was she going to do with it? She'd never harmed a creature in her life.

The laptop sat next to her, closed and warm from use. She had done the worst thing.

She googled.

Adrik Morozov was the son of the Russian Mafia Kingpin, Yakov Morozov. He was the youngest of six and the current heir to the Morozov kingdom.

There wasn't anything lengthy on Adrik. But his father undoubtedly had a long rap sheet in Russia, including war crimes, sedition, kidnapping, extortion, mass murder, and fraud. No doubt Adrik had partaken in some of those things, or at least knew about it.

There was no pretending that Adrik wasn't a criminal. It didn't matter how nice-looking he was. Attractive people could still be dangerous.

Jolie heard the vibration of her phone, but she didn't reach for it. Her mother was calling. She spoke to her mother every day at 7 p.m. It was now nearly eight and no doubt causing panic, but she didn't know what to tell her mother. She didn't want her to worry, but the moment her mother heard her voice, she would know something was wrong. She always did.

At the last vibration, Jolie reached for it, and then there was a knock on the door.

She stood, the cat screeching as it flew, jumping on the computer before darting under the bed. "Sorry, Ming."

Another small knock.

Jolie tossed the remote on the couch and approached the door. "Who is it?" she called out, afraid to put her face against the peephole. Wasn't that the part in movies where they have a gun, and the person gets shot in the head?

Another soft knock.

Jolie snatched her phone and pre-dialed 911 before she unlocked the door and peeled it open just an inch. Dressed in a bulky black hoodie, Adrik's gorgeous blue eyes greeted her, unsmiling, unfriendly, and totally intimidating. Jolie almost pressed send on her phone, but curiosity got the best of her. "What do you want?"

Adrik put a finger on his lips and put his hand on the door, pushing it gently, asking for permission. He glanced at the phone with the large three numbers reflecting. He waited till she was ready.

Jolie couldn't find any maliciousness in his gaze, but she wasn't naive either. Or she hoped she wasn't. He wasn't so different from her ex-boyfriend, using his looks to get him what ordinary people couldn't. But Jolie allowed Adrik to take the phone from her as he entered the apartment.

Behind him, three people entered in black suits, with odd equipment in their hands. One had a microphone, another was listening on headphones, and another held a metal stick that made a static noise and beeped.

Adrik grabbed the remote off the couch and put on YouTube. He looked back at her quizzically, studying her, before he typed in a song.

Whitney Houston, "I Want to Dance with Somebody."

Jolie narrowed her eyes as the music got louder and louder.

There was no way he just guessed that's my favorite song.

"What are you doing?"

He put a finger back on his lips, passing off the remote and her cell phone to one of his people.

Five little trinkets were tossed on the table: a pen, a USB, and three dime-sized metal discs.

"What the—"

Adrik held a hand up. The soldiers tossed the listening devices in a bag and walked out. He locked the door before he turned back around to her.

"What are those?" she screamed over the loud music.

He took the remote up and turned it off.

"Listening devices. The cops bugged you."

The audacity of police officers coming into her house while at work or during the interview blew her mind. She felt betrayed and dirty. She sat at the kitchen table with her head in her hands, trying to make sense of all this.

Adrik pulled off his sweatshirt, which pulled his undershirt just enough to show her his compact abs and tattoos. She darted her eyes away, feeling the heat in her cheeks. He sat down with a small, secretive smile as if he knew what he had done.

Jolie couldn't understand him. He acted all businesslike the two times she met him, and now, here in her apartment, he was a young college guy hanging out. She didn't like the difference and didn't know which one he was.

Jolie slapped her hand on the table. "Why are you here?"

Adrik didn't know if he should be honest or lie. Because the truth was, he didn't understand why he was here. "Why didn't you tell the cops?"

"Because you threatened my life."

He narrowed his dark brows. "No, I didn't."

"Well," she said, balking, "you would've. I saved us both some time."

Adrik glanced over her shoulder. It was the first time he noticed the alarming amount of panda things on her counter. He looked around, and everywhere, there was a black-and-white bear looking back at him. He spotted the collection of stuffed animals next to her bed, piled in a way that seemed like trophies, instead of play items for little girls.

"My friend's coming over," Jolie rushed out.

"You don't have any friends," he told her, straightening, meeting her gaze again.

"My boyfriend—"

He chuckled, finding her more amusing as the minutes went on.

Jolie felt the insult and retaliated with, "Does your wife know you're here?"

His brows rose in surprise. He hadn't worn his ring in months. Either the FBI agent made her aware, or with the computer on the couch, she found his secret from there.

It meant she was interested enough to find out, which meant Adrik wasn't wrong in assuming she was attracted to him, as much as she tried to hide it.

"We're separated."

"Oh." Jolie shifted in her seat. The information gave her more hope than she wanted it to. Jolie stood. "I'm gonna ask you to leave."

Adrik snatched her hand as she passed for the door. A gentle touch that felt smooth against her skin. But it was unwelcome, and she yanked her arm away.

"You got anything to drink?" Adrik stood and stepped around her, reaching for a cabinet.

"I don't drink."

Adrik stalled and leaned against the counter. "You don't drink," he repeated, the sentence coming off odd on his lips.

"I have milk." She didn't wait for a response, stepping by him to reach into the cabinet. She grabbed two glasses and got the milk from the fridge. After she poured it, she handed it to him. Then she held her own before she put ample distance between them, staying in the living room because the kitchen was not nearly big enough to stop her from smelling his intoxicating cologne.

Adrik drank his milk, swallowed, and licked his lips. The movement sent terribly erotic images through her head, and she twisted away, another foot between them. Any further, she'd be across the freaking apartment.

"My wife's family made the hit," Adrik revealed, placing the cup on the table.

She knitted her brows. "Your wife? But that's her daughter, right?"

"I don't think she was a part of it."

"Wow. That's pretty messed up." She could see the upset on his face even as he tried to suppress it. He was hurt, and that made him a little less scary. She approached the table and sat down. "Your daughter is so cute. How is she?"

Adrik smirked, enjoying how she was losing her fear. "She wants to see you again."

"That's sweet."

But it's never going to happen, Jolie thought.

"What do you think about becoming my daughter's tutor?"

A snicker was muffled as she took a drink of her milk. "Yeah, right."

"I'd pay a six-figure salary."

Jolie gapped openly at him when she realized he was serious. Her reply was quick but honest. "No."

"Why?"

"Because you're a mobster!"

Adrik chuckled, admiring her direct personality. It was something his wife didn't possess. "My daughter isn't."

"She will be."

The thought was poison, and it darkened him. Adrik didn't like Helina's future. He didn't want the mafia lifestyle for her. Maybe if she had been born a boy, it would have been different, but as it were, all he saw for her now was unhappiness. "You teach underprivileged kids. The statistic that they are either dead by eighteen or a drug dealer is high. So, why give them the effort?"

"Because there is always hope. But your daughter has no hope."

It was a terrible thing to say, and Adrik felt the simmering rage inside begin to boil again. It wasn't rage against Jolie. It was anger toward the fact that she was right.

"You'll move into the house," he continued.

"What? I said no!"

"What life do you have here, Jolie? Honestly. Your panda collection can come with you. Or your pathetic amount of stuffed animals."

"My stuffed animals are special, okay? My students have bought them for me over the years."

Adrik knew she was lying. She'd only been a teacher for a month.

"Aside from you being in the *mob*," she stressed, "I have a life, okay? It may not be as insane as yours, but some of us don't believe in carrying our own guns—"

"Oh, don't tell me you're a Democrat?"

"Yes, how horrible to want the world to be a better place!"

"Democrats want to take your control because they think you're too stupid to fix your own problems."

"Republicans want to steal my God-given right to decide what's going on in my body."

Adrik held a hand up. "I'm not touching that."

"Yeah, because you're a man, so stay out of it."

He cackled, watching her with an amused smirk. He enjoyed the small smile tempting her lips, but she covered it by drinking her milk. He bowed his head and focused on the crown tattoo on his finger. It reminded him of his place, who he was, and who he belonged to. It reminded him that he shouldn't be here.

Adrik slipped his hands into the pockets of his black slacks. He observed her, and she shrank under his scrutiny. He liked making her fidget because she wasn't doing it out of fear. She was fighting her attraction for him, and that fed into his ego more than he liked to admit. Jolie stood suddenly, moved to the cabinet next to him, and snatched a bag of chips. He wondered if she ate when she was nervous. He knew about her daily routine at Crunch Fitness, but it didn't mean she was a healthy eater.

Jolie stared at the wall, feeling his eyes boring into the back of her head like he was trying to read her very private thoughts. She didn't want him to see anything. He was sorely mistaken if he thought he could use his good looks to worm his way into her life. She wasn't shallow. She relied on more than just a smile and pretty face to lure her in.

That's not what happened with your ex, her conscience reminded her.

She had a knack for getting involved in bad things. Her ex-boyfriend managed to weasel her into doing messed-up stuff that she'd never have thought of alone. She remembered the thrill, the addiction to excitement, and it was apparent at this moment she missed it.

But this is next level.

There was no way she'd be ready to be involved in such a lifestyle as a gangster's. Not only that, there was no escape. She'd never be able to leave. Isn't there a mob saying? 'Once you're in, you can't get out.'

Or that's a sign on a haunted house.

"Jolie," Adrik called softly.

She didn't turn around. Ming and Tae-Tae took this moment to introduce themselves and meowed at Adrik's feet. He bent down and petted them, making sweet sounds as he stroked their ears. The movement earned him points she didn't want to give.

Why does he have to be nice to them?

Adrik stood up and took his cup off the counter to wash it in the sink. She scrutinized him from the side, chewing on a chip, like a mouse ready to flee when the cat moved. He placed the cup in the dish rack and dried his hands with a paper towel. He leaned against the counter and finally met her gaze.

"What?" she provoked after several moments of ultra-uncomfortable silence.

Adrik glanced at her lips, an irrational movement that annoyed him. She was pretty but average. Adrik typically only went after the best of the best. So, what was it that kept him here?

Her personality? Was he at that point in his life where it mattered? She was interesting in an abstract painting sort of way, like if he stared at her long enough, she'd reveal all the answers to his future.

I should leave, he thought, and even glanced toward the door. He wasn't a little kid anymore. He couldn't do stupid-ass things, like date an American and think there would be no repercussions.

But if he left, he'd regret it.

"I—" Adrik began, but he stopped himself. He was about to say something inappropriate. He wasn't sure how she would take it. He doubted she would respond like the strippers he dealt with or the desperate women who clung to him at parties. No, with her, he'd have to be careful.

"I want hope for my daughter."

Jolie stalled mid-bite, surprised by such a statement. She looked sideways at him, and she could see the anxiousness in his eyes, the desperation that lingered there. What kind of mob boss was he to admit that his world wasn't fit for his child? She thought they were a tight-knit group, faithful and loyal only to each other.

My expertise comes from movies, so what the hell do I know?

Jolie bowed her head. She felt guilty for wanting to say no. And she felt guilty for wanting to say yes. Not every day does someone come up to you and offer a six-figure salary. She knew nothing other than living paycheck to paycheck, envious of people who could afford to pay their bills in advance. If she took the job he offered, she could send her parents money, buy her father a new car, and, maybe one day, buy them a better home.

But it would be blood money.

She shook her head. "I can't."

Adrik stepped back. There was rarely a time when he didn't get what he wanted, but he learned disappointment early on. He knew how to hide it.

He took his sweatshirt off the table and rubbed the chair with the wet paper towel. "Okay." He backed up for the door.

Her eyes widened, and she stepped toward him. "Okay? That's okay?"

"You saved my daughter. We're even." With the fabric of his sweater, he twisted the doorknob.

"Even? How does that make us even?"

Adrik looked back at her. "Because I don't let people say no to me." He lingered, letting it sink in that she had defied him and got away with it. Then he stepped out and shut the door.

Jolie stood there for several minutes, hoping—dreading—that he'd come back, but when he didn't, the last of her strength unraveled. She dropped to her butt, with her head in her hands. "Holy moly," she cursed, squeezing her head in disbelief.

Chapter Eight

Intrusion

Adrik stood outside Jolie's door, hoping—dreading—she'd open it. He didn't know what he was doing here. He wasn't allowed to date her. She's American, and he's married. Their lives were too different. It wouldn't be worth the effort. Nice women typically didn't exist in his world for a reason.

If his father even suspected he was stalking this girl, she'd be removed. He had to stay away from her or risk her life. She was wise to keep her distance.

Still, he was disappointed.

Adrik slipped his hood on and walked toward the elevator. Much to his disinclination, FBI agent Mally stood there waiting with a satisfied smirk on her face.

"Good evening, Agent," he greeted. Adrik glanced toward the corners of the hallway. He must have missed a camera somewhere.

There was no reason to run. Mally was alone, and he had three people with him who could detain her if he needed to escape. But the chance of her actually having anything on him so that she could arrest him was low.

"Surprise, surprise," she cackled. "How'd I know? Is she one of the lucky ladies forced to sleep with you?"

Adrik kept his hands in the pocket of his hoodie, digging his nails into his skin as he held a nonchalant expression over her unpleasant comment. It wasn't abnormal for ugly chicks to be bitter about who he slept with.

Mally stepped forward. "Funny thing. We went searching for one of the assailants from the car that shot up Salem's, and we can't find him."

"That is funny," he replied, tired of this conversation.

"I want to know what you know."

"I don't know anything."

"You think I'll believe that someone tries to murder your daughter, and you just sit back and do nothing?"

"Good thing what you *believe* doesn't hold up in court."

The slight unnerved her, and she bit, "Daddy had to come home, huh? You weren't doing a stand-up job. Does he know about the mess on Martin Luther King? How many of your drug dealers got arrested that night? Five? Six?"

Adrik smiled pleasantly. It did happen to be something he was keeping from his father, but not because he was ashamed. It was because it didn't matter. Drug dealers get caught. They were like front-line soldiers in a war. If they survived, it was luck, and they'd eventually get a raise. But not all soldiers would make it. Some needed to be sacrificed for the greater good.

"I'm sorry, but I have no idea what you're talking about."

"Who was it?" she asked with a hint of desperation. It was delicious to see, and Adrik basked in it. Despite how hard she tried, she'd never succeed in taking down his family.

"Fine," she sneered when she noticed his smirk. "I'll figure it out once the killing starts anyway. But let me warn you, if that girl isn't part of it already, stay away from her. She's a good girl and doesn't deserve to be destroyed like the thousands of others your family has ruined."

Adrik's amusement fell. He didn't like being told what to do, especially by people that didn't understand his life. No matter how much Mally knew about his family, she could never grasp it. And Adrik wondered if sometimes she wished she could. To have such power was godly. "Have a good night." He stepped around her, heading for the stairs.

Mally called after him, "Can I at least get back my bugs? They're expensive."

Adrik waved a hand before shoving the door open. One of his guards turned around and tossed it to her. The broken pieces sounded like a bag full of quarters, and he smiled as her curse followed him into the stairwell.

When Jolie finally collected herself, she grabbed the phone. She was getting in way over her head, and her mother would have good advice on how to get out of it.

A knock flung her around, and her phone flew through the air, smacking against the refrigerator. "Gosh, darn it," she cursed. She hated how afraid she was. Maybe it was time to follow her mother's advice and join kickboxing classes.

Jolie yanked open the door. "I thought we—" She paused at the sight of Agent Mally.

"Can I come in?"

Fearful that Adrik was nearby and Mally might run into him, Jolie widened the door, gesturing her inside. Mally sidestepped and stayed by the entrance, looking around.

Jolie interrupted her search. "I don't appreciate you bugging my house."

"And your car. And your classroom," Mally added. She waved a carefree hand. "I'll take it down tomorrow. Pointless now, anyway. I got to say, I'm surprised. I didn't think you would lie."

"I didn't lie."

Mally twisted her face in skepticism. "You're still lying."

"I don't know them. That's not a lie."

"What was he doing here? Offering a bit of generosity?" Mally glanced at the bed. It was made up nicely, with stuffed animals perfectly placed. No way that was used. But this generation didn't always rely on the bed for lovemaking. "Or something a bit more frisky?"

Jolie sneered at the insinuation. "I answered all your questions. I know my rights."

"I'm sure you do." Mally turned to the kitchen, noticing the bag of chips and the glass in the sink. There's a chance there might be fingerprints on it, but how to look for them without Jolie staring at her? Adrik wasn't careless either. Chances were he had already wiped everything he touched. But there was the moment before all the listening devices were removed when someone put on music. If she could finally get a hold of Adrik's fingerprints, she could go through all the recent murders and see if those match. Or perhaps even plant them if push came to shove.

"Do you have a bottle of water I can have?"

Jolie rolled her eyes but turned for the fridge.

Mally already had gloves on; she didn't come to a scene without them. She picked up the remote, slipping it into her jacket.

Jolie tossed her the water, and Mally took her time opening it, taking a nice long swig as if she were dying of thirst. She was trying to think of anything else Adrik might have touched, but she knew he had already cleaned up after himself, with one cup on the table and the other in the drying rack.

Mally sighed. "That's good."

"Are you waiting for something?" Jolie questioned. "You're being pretty obvious."

"Here's obvious," Mally replied, approaching Jolie. "Adrik is very good-looking, and girls are dumb when it comes to those pretty blue eyes," she mocked bitterly. "He doesn't keep girlfriends. He's not allowed them. But he's into one-night stands, usually with women he's met at a club. The fact that he came here is out of his character. It means he might slip up, and I can finally arrest him. And you should be doing everything you can to help me."

"Why?"

"Why?" She cackled in disbelief. "Because he's evil. A Hitler kind of evil. I can give you a book of everything that he's done, everything his father has done."

"Why can't you arrest them?" Jolie asked, bewildered. "If you know it all—"

"Proof, Jolie. Come on, I know you watch those 'Snapped' documentaries. I need someone to turn on him or have him admit to mass murder. If he's interested in you, it's your law-abiding obligation to use it and get him taken off the streets before he kills someone. All those kids in your school? Thirty percent are gonna end up working for him. Fifteen percent are gonna be dead because of him. Those little girls? Twenty percent will be working the streets by the time they are fifteen and paying money to a pimp. And who does the pimp pay for protection and rights to have a corner?" Mally waited, but she could tell Jolie was finally understanding.

"To him."

"To Adrik and his fucked-up family." Mally approached. "You're a good girl, Jolie. I know it. So, tell me, is he interested in you?"

Jolie didn't know how to answer because she wasn't sure what the answer was. They had just met. Any interest was physical. Maybe Adrik was looking for something different after bedding the same kind of girl. But then he asked her to move in and tutor his daughter. He hadn't hit on her. He hadn't made any indication he wanted to touch her. Maybe he was coming to her as a father desperate for the best for his child and not as a man searching for a bed warmer.

Jolie could hate the kind of man that just wanted to use her.

She couldn't hate the kind that wanted hope for his daughter's future.

"I don't know," Jolie finally managed to get out.

Mally was unhappy with the answer, her brown eyes rolling with aggravation. "Good girls love the bad boys," she murmured. Mally took a pen out of her pocket, holding it up. "This has a listening device inside it. All you have to do is"—she pressed the top—"press that, and it will activate." She pressed it again to shut it off and placed it on the table. "Carry it around with you. It might save your life one day, because—let me assure you—from now on, your life, your parents' lives are in danger. I'll see myself out."

When the door slammed shut, Jolie reached blindly for the chair as her legs weakened. She sat staring at the pen, contemplating all the ways she was going to die.

When the phone rang, she squealed and then cursed.

"Yep," she muttered to herself, "kickboxing classes."

Jolie reached for the phone, putting it on speaker as she dropped her head on the table. "Hi, Mom."

"Don't 'hi, Mom' me. Why haven't you answered the phone?"

"I was busy."

"With what?"

"Classwork."

"You couldn't answer the phone and ease my panic because you were doing classwork?"

"I'm sorry."

"You're sorry?"

"Oh, my God, Mom! I'm a grown adult. If I don't want to answer, I don't have to."

There was a pause, and then—"Where's this attitude coming from?"

Jolie groaned.

Chapter Nine

Marriage

Adrik parked his black Lexus next to the line of cars in the garage under his house. Fifteen vehicles parked in the marble-floor showroom, all exotic and of vibrant colors. His collection was one of the things he was proud of.

Adrik waved goodnight to his bodyguards and took the elevator to the fourth floor of his estate. The mansion overlooked Tampa Bay Harbor, and though most of the house was made of windows, they were bulletproof, and one-sided, so no one could spy on him. Adrik passed his wife's room contemptuously, wondering if she'd pop out to argue or curse him. He didn't want to deal with her tonight, so thankfully, he got by without a problem.

Adrik stopped by his daughter's room, peeking his head in. It was pink thrown-up everywhere, with a Barbie Dream House in the corner, a princess castle against the left wall, a canopy over her massive queen bed, and stuffed animals to keep her from falling off the mattress. She slept peacefully, and it eased his stress.

Adrik went to his room down the hall. He kept his distance from his daughter by choice. He hoped anyone trying to assassinate him wouldn't mistake his room for anyone else's.

Adrik stepped into his room and locked the door behind him. It was a habit he had started when he was younger. Five years ago, someone broke in and nearly managed to kill him. There was a scar on his back where the bullet hit. His father had been the one to stop the intruder. He blew his head off right in front of Adrik with his shotgun. It was a night that stayed with him.

To his disappointment, his wife, Katia, sat on his bed. Adrik ignored her as he removed his sweater and stood before his dresser. He unclasped his Rolex and placed it carefully back in its container. Then he pulled his gun from the back holster and laid it beside a wad of money and his wallet.

"Where have you been?" she asked.

Adrik took out pajama pants and slammed the drawer shut before he went to the bathroom, slamming that one as well. He flicked the shower on to warm it up, then rested his hands on the sink.

Katia was like a honey badger. She was sweet when she wanted something, and if she didn't get it, she became a fucking psychopath.

Adrik had only two regrets, and one of them was marrying Katia. Like any young teenager, there were expectations of what a wife would be like. He thought his mother was a prime example of a perfect partner. She was supportive, encouraging, sweet, and challenging. His father would compliment her constantly on being such a wonderful wife. So stupidly, Adrik believed all wives would be as easy.

Plus, it would be pussy he didn't have to work for.

What was the bad side of marriage?

I was such a dumbass, Adrik cursed at himself before he jumped into the shower.

Katia was from a wealthy military family in Russia. But like his father, her father, Boris, had to leave Russia when things got too hot with law enforcement. By the time Yakov came to Tampa, Boris was already set up nicely with the harbor. To form a positive partnership, they married their children together to keep it. Adrik and Katia had only met twice before they were forced to wed. She tried hard to avoid it. And so had he. But when push came to shove, neither could disobey their parents.

Their wedding night had been horrible. It hadn't been his first time with a girl, but it had been the first time he screwed someone while they were crying. And maybe that put a damper on things between them. But he knew, like she did, that they had to have a child as soon as possible. It was expected.

Days turned to weeks. Every month when she failed to get pregnant was another horrible moment between them. She learned to shut off. And he learned to get the deed done as fast as possible.

Over time, a friendship grew between them, and the sex got better. Adrik even started to feel something for her. He had been so happy when he learned she was pregnant. He recalled how he had lifted her off her feet and kissed her with vigor: joyful, proud, and in love.

Weeks later, he found out Katia was fucking someone else.

Adrik hadn't controlled his temper then. He hadn't known what he was capable of until that night. But he pushed limits he never dared to before. It was the only time in his life when he scared himself.

There was no reconciliation after that.

Adrik got out of the shower. He took his time with his nightly ritual—combing his hair, brushing his teeth, and flexing in the mirror to determine which muscle he wanted to work on in the morning. With slacks on his legs, he walked out.

She was still sitting there.

Katia dropped her phone on her lap. "Your father said you wanted to speak to me. So, speak." Katia sat rigid in a tan Dior dress, with her blonde hair curled and pinned to her head. She had gone out with some friends, or that's what she claimed. He stopped caring about her liaisons when he started his own.

Adrik flicked his gaze away in annoyance. His father was forcing him to face the issue of her family. He was surprised his father hadn't just talked to her himself. Why even bother making it seem like Adrik had any control over what happened in their family?

"We found the assholes that shot up Salem's."

Katia jumped to her feet, hopeful. "Who?"

Adrik clenched his teeth as he watched her. He needed to mark every flicker of her eye, every movement of her hands. If he were to spot her lying, what would he do? Would he be able to hold back, even for the mother of his child?

"A couple of bitches." He used the word 'bitch' as a term for low-level pieces of shit that held no importance. "They were ordered by a man with a raven on his hand."

The color in her face drained.

"No," she whispered.

"Your brother."

Katia collapsed on the bed, wide-mouthed, simply staring at the floor.

It was a good act; maybe he believed it because he couldn't believe otherwise. She loved their daughter as much as he did. He wasn't questioning that.

Adrik snatched his phone off the dresser and sat in a chair, reading and replying to text messages as she recovered. He didn't want to see her tears. They meant nothing.

When Katia stood, Adrik flicked his eyes up. She had pulled her emotions back, leaving behind a stone facade. He didn't expect anything else. She was mafia-born. Tears could only get her so far. She'd go in a different direction when they no longer aided her. "According to our contract, you can't kill him."

Adrik snapped to his feet and was in her face so quickly that she gasped and took back a step. A break in her mask. "Tell me again what I can't do," he threatened dangerously. "Go ahead, Katia. Say it."

Katia, wide-eyed and breathing heavily through her nose, swallowed, bowing her head. "I just meant, in the contract, immediate family—"

"I'll make him suffer for what he's done." Adrik returned to his seat, with his elbows on his knees and the phone in his hands. He wanted a blunt. He wouldn't be able to sleep now with the rage she caused. He sat back, resting his ankle on his knee as he watched her. Katia was a snake, constantly changing her skin. He failed to read her for the years while she was fucking another man. Her lies were plenty and creative. She was able to cover up her moves like a professional chess player. Yet he underestimated her because she was a woman.

"I want you there."

Her head popped up, full of terror. "What?"

"He almost killed our daughter. You deserve vengeance." Adrik observed her eyes flickering in panic. She was trying to find a way out of it, sitting on the bed as if her legs were too weak to sustain her. She knew what it would mean to deny him. It would say she cared more about her brother than her daughter, and Katia couldn't risk that.

"Your parents—" He paused when she looked at him frightfully. "I don't think they knew."

There was relief in the tension of her shoulders, and she nodded vehemently. "They love Helina. They wouldn't hurt her."

"I agree. But because of this oversight, the contract of our treaty is disrupted. We won't be paying forty percent on shipments anymore. From now, it will be twenty-five."

She scoffed; the Katia he knew so well resurfaced. The businesswoman that was built from the moment she knew how to add. "Good luck with that. Your shipments cost us millions because of payouts to the harbor police, the workers, and the senator."

Adrik continued his text before he replied, "Not my problem."

Katia stood with her arms folded, glaring down at him. Adrik pressed on Candy Crush, and the music interrupted the tension in the room. "You have nothing without that harbor."

It was true that seventy percent of his products came through it, but he was diversifying. This past month, he purchased land in Naples to build a small airport.

There was a knock on the door, and Adrik stood up, meeting her. "If our contract falls through, there will be no need for this fake marriage. Perhaps it's what you want." Adrik knew it was what he wanted. He turned to the door.

Katia grabbed his arm. "That's not what I want," she lied. "We can fix this."

When she became desperate, she always resorted to the same tricks. Adrik didn't give her the time to touch him anywhere else. He stepped away, opening the door. Three females walked through, dressed in silk robes. He watched her face, noticed how cold and distant it became, and felt a small victory. The women removed their robes as they climbed into bed, wearing panties, bras, and heels.

Katia moved for the door, but Adrik gripped her bicep, forcing her to look at him.

"If I find out you were part of your brother's plot—"

"That's my daughter—"

"I'll do what I should have done when you fucked another man in our bed." He shoved her out and slammed the door.

Chapter Ten

Invitation

Over a week after the shootout, Jolie thought by now her PTSD would be healing, but instead, it felt like it was getting worse.

She typically parked in a parking garage, but there were too many loud sounds and dark shadows, so for the last two days, she found a spot on the side of the road, but that brought on different fears. The walk to her apartment was longer, she passed more strangers, and there were three alleys where someone could hide. She hadn't yet decided which was worse.

Despite the negative, it was a beautiful September morning. The sun was blaring, and the humid air made her sweat even in the shade of the buildings. There was no fall in Florida. There was summer and then a few weeks of spring, but otherwise, the sun was unrelenting. She had lived here her whole life and still wasn't entirely used to the blistering heat.

Jolie jogged to Crunch Fitness, two miles from her building. It helped relieve the tension in her shoulders. It would be better if she had time to do this daily, but sleep had become difficult. Closing her eyes brought on anxieties, and then sleep brought on nightmares. There was no winning.

The only thing that helped her alter her mindset was when she was thinking about Adrik.

And that's a no-go.

Upon seeing the big sign for her gym, her smile stretched. She was going to have a good, stress-free day today.

A man in a black suit stood in front of her. It took only a second to realize he was part of Adrik's crew. She bowed her head and tried to barrel through, but he moved with her. Jolie spun around to run, and another suit stood there with their hands clasped at the front. The tiny exposure of a gun handle through the buttons of his black jacket reminded her what kind of people they were.

She sunk in defeat.

"Miss Bell. My boss would like to talk to you." Their Russian accent was becoming more familiar than she ever wanted it to be.

What could Adrik want? What if he knew about the FBI agent coming to my house?

Jolie looked longingly toward the gym. If she fought or screamed, she could get away. There were too many ego maniacs hoping to save a damsel in distress. But she didn't want to risk anyone getting hurt because of her.

And she partly wanted to see Adrik again.

Jolie sighed and waved a hand. They took the invitation for what it was and directed her to a building across the street. She felt utterly underdressed as they entered the hotel lobby, with little pocket stores full of glittering accessories and clothes that were more than her salary. It was a side of Tampa she'd never seen. The elevator had a passcode, and it climbed to the roof.

Through double glass doors was an infinity pool that hung off the edge like magic. A little girl was splashing and giggling while her father swung her around. To her surprise, it was Adrik and Helina. Despite his dedication to his daughter, she didn't see him as the kind of guy to pay much attention to her.

Didn't rich people assign others to take care of their kids?

There were guards on the outline of the roof, but oddly enough, they were looking outward and not in. But perhaps there was always the chance of assassination, even from way up here.

This is so unreal. Jolie snorted.

One guard directed her to a chair, and a server quickly asked if she was hungry or thirsty. To each, she said no, landing her attention on Adrik. He caught sight of her, his blue eyes reflecting like the pool, a hypnotic scene that she couldn't break from. Slick, shiny hair dripped in front of his gaze as he looked at her like she was mouthwatering prey he was about to devour.

Helina jumped on his head, and he drowned in the water, breaking the tension, thankfully. Jolie hid her smile.

But the smile was removed forcefully by her conscience.

He is a monster, she reminded herself.

The problem was that Adrik was only showing his sweet side. He was showing her only what he wanted her to see. It was a great way to reel her in, but she wasn't stupid.

"Jolie!" Helina called as her father lifted her out of the water. Her little floaties kept her arms out as she rushed to her, landing in her lap, all wet. Jolie cackled, trying to weasel out of her hold while hugging her. Helina started going off in Russian, and Jolie just smiled, nodding, and searching for Adrik to interpret. He hung out in the pool, with his arms on the edge and his chin resting on them. He simply watched as if the scene was interesting to him.

Helina looked up at Jolie and waited for a response. Then she turned to her father and yelled at him.

Adrik replied in Russian, and it only pissed Helina off even more. She stomped her foot. But with a single sharp 'shh,' Helina stopped moving and stood with a giant pout. Adrik rolled his eyes and conceded. "She wants to invite you to our house."

"She does? How convenient."

Adrik smirked but said nothing in response.

Helina yelled at him one more time and waited.

Adrik reluctantly interpreted, "She thinks you look like a princess, and she wants to dress up."

Helina nodded. ***"Printessa,"*** she repeated. ***"Krasivyy."***

"Krasivyy?" Jolie asked, looking at Adrik.

He paused as he met her gaze. "Beautiful."

Her cheeks heated, and she unconsciously tucked a piece of hair behind her ear. Jolie stroked Helina's arm. "You're so sweet. You're ***krasivyy***." She touched her little round cheek. "But I can't come to your home. I have a busy weekend."

Helina looked back at her father, and he complied with a response. She bowed her head in sadness, and Jolie kissed the top of her head in apology.

Adrik directed Helina to go with her nanny, and they both watched her go with a depressed walk. "She's good." Jolie sat back, feeling the weight of guilt like a winter coat.

Adrik pushed against the wall, floating in the water. "Come in."

She knew what he was doing. His body was a masterpiece of well-tuned muscles and beautifully designed tattoos. There wasn't a spot on his body that wasn't taken care of. His arms were tight, his abs were plenty, and his thighs and calves were shaped like hardened clay. The number of hours he spent in the gym every week was commendable. It made her ashamed of all the days she'd missed because of the anxiousness he caused.

That was something to pay attention to.

I lived in horrible stress this week because of him.

Jolie stood. "I'm gonna leave."

Adrik popped up. "Wait."

She flipped about with frustration, unsure of what she should do. "I shouldn't be here."

Adrik swam to the stairs, rushing out of the water and snatching a towel from a pool attendant. He approached her as he dried his face, rubbing the towel through his hair, noticing how she would look everywhere else except on him. He waited, hoping to catch a glimpse of her eyes to discern why she fought the way she did. Women typically didn't have so much of a problem with him being in the Mafia.

But she isn't the kind of woman I typically deal with.

"Look at me."

"No," she replied with a nervous laugh.

"Why?"

"You're not gonna win me over with—*this*." She gestured to his wet body as she looked at the sky. "Whatever this is."

The comment made him feel like he was desperate, and it pissed him off. "Is that why you think you're here?"

"Why *am* I here?"

"I want you to tutor my daughter. Think I'd waste my time with someone like you?"

Jolie curled her fist as if in victory, gritting her teeth as she finally met his gaze. "Thank you for that. Thank you." It was a good reminder he's a piece of shit, no matter how good-looking. She stepped away, but Adrik grabbed her arm.

"Wait, wait, wait."

"No, I'm good."

"Jolie, can you sit?"

"I'm done talking." She twisted out of his hand and stalked toward the exit. If she let him talk, she'd get sucked in. She knew this game too well. How often had she tried to leave her ex, and he managed to lure her back in every time? They start off sweet, but then they transform into a monster. She was smarter than she was all those years ago. And not nearly so naive.

Adrik contemplated telling the guard to deny her, but he screwed up and didn't want her any angrier. He waved, and the guard opened the door for her.

Adrik sat on the chair, annoyed with himself. He didn't know why he brought her here, just like he didn't understand why he went to her apartment. It wasn't normal. There was an attraction, but not enough for him to jeopardize anything. She was intriguing, like a book he wanted to read, and a banned book was much more enticing. But the risk wasn't worth it. She could be killed because of his interest.

So how to stop it? More women?

It reminded him of the three women he had days before and how he felt afterward. Regret was rare and barely felt, but it sank in his gut like a bad hit of mushrooms.

Adrik got up and ran after her. His guards balked, confused about what he was doing. They scrambled after him, but he got into the elevator without them. He bounced on his bare toes, rubbing his head, trying to think of something he could say to make her come back.

All his life, the women that surrounded him took what they got. Even insulted, they would laugh it off. It was the kind of life they had, fearful of upsetting anyone. They were raised to be compliant and manageable. But Jolie wasn't.

Adrik jumped out of the elevator when the doors opened and ran out of the building. It was careless and stupid, but he didn't think. Jolie was across the street and about to enter the gym when he called her. "Jolie!"

She stopped walking, her head down, but refusing to turn around.

He ran up behind her. "Jolie, wait." He reached for her arm, but she pulled out of it.

"I don't want you to talk to me again. Am I clear?"

"I'm sorry. I'm not used to women like you."

"And what kind of woman am I?"

He stuttered, trying to say it in a way that wouldn't be insulting. "Nice."

The word threw her off. She was expecting a stupid pickup line like 'special' or 'one of a kind,' as if she hadn't heard it before.

"Nice?" she giggled.

Her reaction eased him, and he smiled. "Like grandma nice."

"What!" she squealed.

"No offense."

"Total offense."

The humor in her eyes encouraged him to reach for her arm again. Adrik stepped closer as his fingertips touched her elbow before slipping up her arm. It was a touch that consumed all humor and ignited the fresh taste of desire. He clenched his teeth, swallowing as he looked down into her gaze, noticing how her features changed. He could see it, the want that he was feeling reflected in her eyes. It would be too easy to lean down and touch her lips with his. His gaze flickered to her mouth, her lips slightly parted, a whisper of temptation.

But the risk of denial was too grand. He had to wait till he was sure.

Instead of kissing her, Adrik forced out, "Go out with me."

The sudden topic made her blush, and she backed up, tucking her hair behind her ear, as if the words didn't cause panic. "I thought you wouldn't waste time with someone like me."

Adrik hated how she threw his words back in his face. "I can't, actually," he revealed. "My family has strict rules. Think of it as an interview."

Jolie folded her arms, putting space between them, metal walls for encouragement. She didn't understand him. If he needed a tutor that bad, he could always hire one from some website. Why send mixed signals?

Maybe it's all in my head. Perhaps I'm hoping for more. He's so attractive, and I'm ridiculously desperate that I'm reading into things. Because he's right. He wouldn't waste his time with someone like me.

"I'm being serious when I ask you to tutor my daughter."

Aggravated with herself, she pointed out, "There are tutors everywhere. Why me?"

"Because you put her life first instead of your own. I can't pay enough money for someone like that. You don't even know her and already want the best for her. And so do I. That's why I want you." The way the sentence ended was too much truth. "To teach her," he added.

The guards ran up to them, panting and out of breath. They had taken the stairs down the forty-floor building, and neither were in suitable shape. "Sir," Dima huffed. "Can we take this inside?"

Adrik wouldn't be distracted. "I want to invite you to dinner."

"I'm busy," Jolie shot back.

Adrik cackled. "No, you're not." He held out his hand, and Dima slipped a business card into his hand. He held it out to her. "Get to know me. Ask me what you want. Maybe I can convince you."

Jolie felt defeated. If he wasn't after her sexually, where was the harm in getting to know him? And maybe, if she had the audacity, she could help Mally take down this mafia king. Wouldn't that be an excellent service to all the children he eventually ensnared? She took the card with reluctance. "What's this?"

"Call it, and they'll give you instructions."

"For what?"

Adrik backed away, disregarding her question. "Work out your ass. It needs more shape."

Jolie scoffed, embarrassment creeping on her face. When he entered the building, she turned to look and only ended up cursing. "Jerkface."

Chapter Eleven

Push

Jolie took out her AirPods as she stepped into her apartment. She felt better working out, massaging all the tension in her shoulders. For an hour, she forgot about the shootout, the blood on her floor, and the police station. It felt so unreal that it all happened to her. She reverted to the eighteen-year-old girl who felt lost and scared when she saw her boyfriend rob a bank. Everything about him transformed, and she no longer knew who he was. She had been in denial for most of it until she showed up at the police station, with a statement clenched in her hand.

But I'm not eighteen. And I'm not naive.

Maybe she was a little, but not enough to go on a date with Adrik without backup. She'd have to tell her mother. Not the whole truth, but some of it, so if something did go wrong, she'd have help.

Red flag: needing backup to go on a date.

"Ming! Tae-Tae!" she called out, surprised they weren't mewing at her feet.

The floor creaked just behind her, and Jolie spun around as a man covered in black made a grab for her. She jumped back, slamming into the fridge. She dived for her panda cookie jar, swinging it as he touched her arm. She smashed it into his head. He fell back, holding his face.

Every action from there was purely instinctual.

Jolie snatched the pen off the table and ran, diving into the bathroom, slamming the door, and locking it. She clicked the pen, screaming incoherently into it, but some form of 'help' or 'hurry' got out of her panic.

She flipped her head about madly, trying to find anything to help her. There was no exit in this box. The small window wasn't big enough for her to squeeze through. Jolie flung her gaze around, searching for weapons. There were tweezers, a razor in the shower, a bunch of towels—

The assailant smashed his fists on the door, and it vibrated from the brutal force.

"Get the fuck out of my house!" The curse word felt like a jalapeño on her tongue, but she didn't regret it as she rummaged through the bottom of her sink. More toilet paper, candles, tampons, hairspray, and a lighter.

Relief poured over her, and she took up the hairspray and lighter.

Pieces of wood broke as the man began to break the door down.

Jolie was shaking as she wrapped a towel around her hand with the hairspray clenched in between her fingers. She held it out, stepping into the shower to get as far from him as possible. He peeled back pieces one at a time till he poked his head through, and when he did, his eyes widened.

"Get the fuck out of my house," she repeated before spraying and igniting it. The flame expanded like a growing storm cloud, spinning over itself till it hit him in the face. His scream was gut-wrenching as he fell out of the doorway. Fire licked at the wood where he had been. She dropped the hairspray and tore off the towel, flapping it about to put out any little flames lingering behind.

Jolie didn't know how long she had. Should she call 911 or try to make a run for it? She didn't know if she had done enough damage to keep him from going after her. She knew if she stayed here, she'd be trapped. She wasn't strong enough to do much damage to him, but she was quick.

Jolie took a deep breath and yanked the door open. He had flung off his mask, and his unknown face revealed a snake tattoo on his cheek. It was a millisecond pause that they stared at each other.

Jolie dashed for the door, but in three long strides, he snatched her ponytail just as her fingers licked the knob. He yanked her to the ground. Her back hit hard, pushing air out of her lungs, and she struggled to get it back, coughing. He grabbed her bicep in a painful grasp that made her cry. He hauled her to her feet and tossed her over the couch. Her ribs hit the coffee table, and she fell to the floor, curling in pain and crying.

A knock on the door sounded with a voice yelling, "Tampa Police! Open up!"

The man ran to the open window and dived onto the fire escape, disappearing.

Jolie held the blanket around her as she sat on a gurney in the hospital. She was tired, too drained to do much else than stare. She had spent the first hour shivering. They had given her ice for her broken ribs and medicine for pain. While being looked over, she filled out a police report, and now, after three hours, she was allowed to go home.

But how was she supposed to live there after what happened?

Adrik's card was still in her pocket, and she knew all she had to do was call, but was he responsible? How could she ever trust that he wasn't? He's a mobster, which was too close to the word monster.

Agent Mally approached her slowly. There was a disappointment on her face that annoyed Jolie. As if she was victim-blaming without even saying a word. Jolie already felt stupid enough; she didn't need anyone to say anything.

"What did he look like?"

She didn't want to remember, but his face would be impossible to forget. "Spanish. A tattoo on his face. It was a, um…snake."

"It could be multiple factions that hate Adrik."

"But I'm nothing. I'm not…""You're being watched. That much is real. Did you see Adrik today?"

She swallowed, nervous to answer, before she nodded.

"They think you mean something to him. This was a threat."

Mally pulled up a chair and sat in front of Jolie. "These gangs are very close-knit. They travel like a herd. And the ones that are on the outside get picked off. You aren't in their society yet. You are still weak enough to go after."

Hearing it made it worse. "What do I do?"

"Get as close to the center as you can."

Jolie knew what she was insinuating. But she wasn't the type of girl Mally was hoping for.

"I'm scared. I'm not daring or brave. I'm a coward."

"Not according to the police report."

Jolie shook her head. All of that had been entirely survival. She had been terrified the entire time. There was no bravery in her actions.

"I'm not what you want. Adrik wants me to become a tutor for his daughter."

Mally sat back, thinking. She felt defeated by such a statement. "I don't believe you."

Jolie gaped at her. "I'm telling the truth."

"He could get anyone."

"I know that. I told him that. But he insisted."

Mally twisted her words around, trying to pinpoint where this piece of the puzzle fit. She had worked with this family for years. They were resilient. They'd rearrange the pieces and destroy her progress if she ever got close enough. That's why she was cautious. "He likes you."

"No, he said—"

"I don't care what he said. Adrik doesn't date. He's not allowed. He and his estranged wife have a deal where they can live separate lives but aren't allowed lovers. His wife, Katia, was in love with her brother's best friend, Nikos. And they even were thinking of running away together. But when Katia got pregnant with Adrik's child, he found out what Katia and Nikos were planning. He murdered Nikos."

The word 'murder' doused her in dread.

"How do you know it was him?"

"No proof, but I know."

Jolie shook her head. "I can't do what you're asking."

"This position of being a tutor is huge. You'll earn his trust bit by bit."

"It's too dangerous."

"Only if you get caught."

"And what are your assurances that I won't? You're asking me to risk my life for this."

Mally stood, aggravated that Jolie couldn't see the importance of this position being brought to her like a piece of cake. Mally wanted this, and Jolie was only concerned about *her* life. This could change the future. This could alter so many lives. Including Mally's. If she took down the Morozov empire, all her hard work would finally be worthwhile.

"I'm asking you to think of your students."

Jolie sneered. "That's not fair."

"Nothing in life is. But you have been given an important mission. Do you think heroes sit on the sidelines and wait for something bad to happen to swoop in and save the day? Real heroes, real-life heroes, are out there every day, putting their lives on the line to save yours. What do you think cops do? What do you think firefighters do?"

"I'm a teacher. Not exactly a risk taker."

Mally smirked as she crossed her arms. "I don't know about that."

How she said it unnerved Jolie. "What's that mean?"

A slight shrug. "I've been looking into you," she admits. "And that bank robbery."

Jolie's blood went cold.

A little giggle produced from her pink lips. "Your ex-boyfriend wasn't very smart. But you were, weren't you?"

An instant denial was on her lips. "I don't know what you mean."

"Is that so? I could look into it a bit more. If I can't get into this family, I'll have more time on my hands." The threat lingered as Mally backed up. "Let me know what you decide."

Chapter Twelve

Interview

When Jolie got home, she couldn't force herself out of the doorway. Her back pressed against the wall as she looked around. Her home was a square box. Where had the man hidden? In the bathroom? On the fire escape? Could they be out there now?

Her cats meowed at her feet. They had wisely stayed hidden during the attack, and Jolie thanked God for their fear of strangers. She should have realized when they hadn't greeted her the moment she came back from the gym that something was wrong. She hugged them and cried into their skin, but they were hungry, and Jolie forced herself out of misery and into action. Caring for someone else and ignoring every fear in her body was easy. Her cats needed her.

Once her cats were eating, Jolie could feel the terror creep up inside her again. There was no one else to care for, to take her mind off the horrible intrusion. With shaking hands, she called her mom, Heather.

"Hey, baby, I was just thinking about you."

Tears sprung to her eyes, and her lip trembled, but she didn't want her mom to worry. "Hey, how was your day?"

With her voice sputtering random things, Jolie approached her bathroom. There were broken pieces of the door and charred remains on the wood. Everything was left where she had dropped it.

"—and he thought it was so funny. He's lucky I don't have other options right now."

"Mom," Jolie chastised. "You'd be lost without Derek." Her mother liked to talk a big game, but Jolie's stepdad was her foundation. They had married when Jolie was five. Derek was the only father she remembered, while her biological father had been killed in a car accident.

Jolie attempted to clean. She turned to her broken coffee table, pieces shattered from where she landed. The pain in her ribs amplified, as if it knew what had happened.

"I might make it on my own," Heather responded. "Think of how much time I'd save not picking up the towels off the bathroom floor every day. Or cleaning his coffee mug every morning. Or not having him ramble on about the stock market. I could have a whole garden by now."

Jolie got a garbage bag from under the sink, waving it open. Her movements were slow. Her body didn't want to move, and yet, she couldn't leave all the broken pieces lying on the floor, reminding her of what happened.

"Did you get to work out this morning? It's so good for you. My yoga class is amazing, and I'll never miss a day."

On and on, she went, saying things she'd already said earlier this week, but that was the thing about her mom. Whenever Jolie talked to her, Heather never made her feel like she didn't have time or that she was busy. Jolie felt wanted, and the fear began to fade away. She rested her burdens in her mom's hands even though she didn't know it.

"I'm going out tonight," Jolie cut in.

"With who?"

"A guy I met at the gym."

"A guy you met? Why am I just hearing about this now?"

"Because it just happened. And it's not what you think. He wants me to tutor his daughter."

"Well, that's a new one."

Jolie rolled her eyes. "How can you hate him already? You know absolutely nothing."

The protective mother in her faded, and she said, "Okay, you're right. Tell me about him. What's his name?"

"Well, um—" Jolie contemplated, needing to be very selective with her words. "Adrik. He's very nice. Well-mannered. Married," she stressed to relieve her. "So this isn't a date. It's an interview, I guess."

"Uh-huh. Will his wife be there?"

"Well, no…"

"Can you admit that you are a little gullible? I mean, Vincent was able to convince you—"

"I don't want to talk about Vincent. I was a teenager!" Jolie exasperated. "Can I get some leeway, please?"

"You are smart, and you still fell for his charms."

Jolie bitterly fought back with, "I'm a grown woman now."

"With minimal experience. I'm just saying thousands of men out there will treat you well, and they have no agenda and aren't married."

"This isn't a date!" She winced, holding her ribs. Water stung the back of her eyes, and she fell on the couch with little energy. The noise didn't go unnoticed, and Jolie was quick to assure her. "I hurt myself at the gym. I'm fine."

"Okay, I'll back off. It's just going to dinner with a nice, well-mannered married man. Nothing wrong with that."

Jolie dropped her head on the couch. "You know, sometimes you are more cynical than I like."

"A personal flaw, but you love me anyway."

Jolie fidgeted in her seat in the limo. She was in pain. Every breath she took was like a sledgehammer to her ribcage, and it didn't seem to matter how she sat; nothing eased it. But she had to pretend. She wasn't a hundred percent sure that Adrik wasn't to blame for her attack, but it didn't make sense. He wanted her to befriend him.

Mally said it was Adrik's enemies, and if that were the case, if Adrik found out, would he want to retaliate? She couldn't have any blood on her hands. The police were doing their job, and she trusted in the process. She'd have to hide it from him and pray he never found out.

Jolie was sure what she was wearing wasn't good enough: a *Friends* T-shirt and jeans with flip-flops. But when she asked the odd person on the phone what she should wear, they replied with "casual," and this was her casual. Her lack of pretty dresses with sleeves showed she had lived in Florida her whole life. Wearing anything sleeveless wasn't currently an option, because of the massive welt on her bicep. Even now, it threatened to poke through under her shirt, but she couldn't find an excuse to wear a sweater. The heat was near a hundred, and the humidity made the air barely breathable.

It's not like I'm dressing to impress anyway.

Jolie had standards, and Adrik didn't fit those guidelines despite how gorgeous he was and how he looked at her with promises of a long night of porn-rated lovemaking.

Love making, she belittled herself for the romantic in her. *That's not what he does.*

Jolie repositioned herself for the fifth time. "How much longer?" she asked the driver. It had taken her some time to get into the car, but they all insisted they drive her. With the pen in her purse and a silly pocketknife, she felt that there was some defense against him if something were to go wrong.

These guards tried to take her cell phone, but she refused that request. There was no way in hell she would journey into *hell* without a phone.

She texted her mom. 'The driver is about five foot ten. Russian. With a beard. A fat nose.' She was relaying everything that was happening, and it helped ease her fear. But she had still gotten in the car.

Why? Why am I risking my life?

Her mother texted back. 'Pull out a piece of hair and put it under one of the seats.'

Jolie giggled at the absurdity. But found herself rubbing her hands through her hair.

Beneath the fear, there lay the excitement she was trying to suppress. The wonderment of what's gonna happen next. And the very plain fact that she'll be able to talk to Adrik again, because despite how much she didn't want to, she really, *really* enjoyed listening to him talk. His accent was like butter on a cinnamon roll. It's not everyone's taste, but she couldn't get enough of it.

The car stopped, and the driver got out. Jolie sat there and took a deep breath, wincing, blowing out regretfully.

You're fine. You're going to do something for your country. They'll write about you in history books. You'll write an autobiography for your kids that will be worth reading.

The door opened.

If you ever have kids, and don't die a horrible and utterly preventable death.

Jolie got out and deflated at the sign: TGI Fridays. She looked at the driver and watched him lead her to the front door, where he held it open for her. She was still unsure even as she peeked her head inside like it would be radically transformed into expensive dining.

Adrik sat at a barstool and smiled wide, waving her in.

She approached cautiously, and he got up to greet her, moving in to kiss her cheek. "Sit. Sit. What would you like to drink?" He guided her to a booth, and Jolie had to think about how she would sit without pain showing on her face. And then a great excuse came to her lips as she sat, taking huge breaths. He watched her, and she quickly answered his unasked question. "The gym. I think I hurt my ribs somehow."

"You need a proper spot."

When the waitress popped up, Jolie asked for a Coke.

Adrik chided, sitting across from her. "Come on. You are out, and you don't need to drive. Have a drink with me."

"No, I'm good." Aside from her not liking any liquor, mixing it with painkillers didn't sound like a good idea.

He conceded, ordering a beer. "I'm happy you came."

"Me too. I love TGI Fridays." She propped her purse beside her, sticking her hand in to flick the pen on. It kick-started the fear in her heart. She was grateful when the server brought her drink. She took a long gulp of it and then ended up burping. She covered her mouth in embarrassment and quickly sipped her soda to stuff it down.

Adrik pointed to her shirt. "I know *Friends*. Chandler's my favorite."

"Phoebe's mine."

"I know why you like her."

"Oh?"

"She's odd. Like you."

"Excuse me, I'm not odd."

"It is good to be odd."

Food was brought over by the server, surprising Jolie. It was a ton of appetizers, from wings to quesadillas to mini burgers. Adrik watched her. "I didn't know what you liked."

Jolie nodded. "So you ordered everything instead of waiting. Makes sense."

He popped a fry in his mouth as he chuckled. "I like to impress."

Jolie suppressed a laugh, a hand to her rib cage as she fought it.

"If you came to my gym, you wouldn't be hurting."

"Which one is yours?"

"My house." He smirked.

Jolie rolled her eyes, sinking into his charm like a dinosaur in tar. She hated how good he was at making her forget he was a mafia member. TGI Fridays didn't help either.

He's not an ordinary man, she reminded herself. *Average men don't kill people.*

On crutches, the man she met at the shootout came toward them. Adrik shifted over to let him sit, and he groaned, stretching out his leg as he propped the crutches against the table. Gil held his hand to her in greeting. "Miss Bell."

"Gil, right?"

Gil had acne scars on his face and messy blond hair. He was skinny, like Adrik, but not as fit. Compared to Adrik, he looked homely, even in a suit.

Gil kept a bright, obviously fake smile even as he mumbled toward Adrik in Russian. Jolie knew he was talking about her and watched them in a vain effort to figure out what they were saying.

Adrik didn't like what Gil said, picking at the fries on the table like a chastised child. Jolie could feel the tension and nervously shifted in her seat, groaning as her ribs burned intensely. She didn't know how much longer she could sit. And she didn't think she could eat either. She was too nervous with the pen recording their conversation. How far away were the Feds? Were they close enough to stop Adrik from killing her if he caught on to what she was doing?

That's when the guilt trickled in.

Why does he have to be nice? Show me your mean side.

Jolie forced a bite of food. "You guys are brothers, right?"

"It's questionable," Adrik bit.

"Yes," Gil answered, nudging him. "I was orphaned at four, and Adrik's parents adopted me."

Boy, was she a sucker for adorable stories like that. "That's really sweet."

"Yes"—Gil glanced at Adrik—"sweet."

She felt like he was making fun of her, but she wasn't ashamed of being a softy. She enjoyed that about herself. There weren't many people left that cried at romcoms anymore.

Gil spoke in Russian again, more annoyance in the sound of his voice.

She watched Adrik and met his aggravated gaze, slightly hoping to see the madman beneath, to stop herself from liking him. But she also prayed he continued to show this version of himself—a controlled, level-headed, sweet man. Maybe instead of Agent Mally trying to go after Adrik, she could convince her that Adrik was innocent and everyone around him was the terror.

"Khvatit," Adrik hissed in Russian, turning his head to Gil. There was a staring contest that made her nervous. She hugged her purse, as if the touch would warn the FBI.

Gil slapped a hand on Adrik's neck, squeezing slightly, and laughed as he said something else.

"Forgive him," Adrik said, returning his attention to Jolie. "He isn't around Americans often. He forgets it's rude to speak in another language."

Gil held up a hand. "Yes, Miss Bell, I apologize."

Jolie shook her head. "Well, I'm twenty percent Russian if that makes you feel better." She was hoping to ease the tension. Adrik appreciated it as he smiled at her.

Gil nodded in approval. "Blood is critical in our family. Our DNA makes us who we are. And who we are loyal to."

Adrik chewed the inside of his lip, staring out the window. There was discouragement on his face, but he said nothing, and Jolie sipped on her drink, unsure what to do now.

Thankfully, Jolie's phone rang. "Sorry. It's my mother." She clicked it off.

"How do you know without looking at it?"

"Because she's waiting to make sure I haven't been murdered or sold."

Adrik laughed, and Gil sneered, shaking his head.

"You are very close with your parents," Adrik pointed out. "I am, too. Close with my mother and father."

"I think it's family that makes us who we are. Not our blood."

"Yes." Adrik proudly nodded. "Yes, good point."

Gil was gonna reply, but Adrik's phone rang. He took it from the inside of his coat pocket. Gil cut himself off to watch Adrik, confused about who was calling. "Morgan." He glanced at Gil, as if it was a surprise. He put it to his ear. "Go.

Jolie watched with interest, wondering if he'd give himself away. She didn't know if the listening device could hear the conversation. But she hoped the agent got everything she needed because Jolie didn't think she could do this again. She could barely swallow her drink because of the amount of worry in her throat.

Adrik's gaze flicked up to her, and Jolie went cold.

He murmured something in Russian.

Jolie felt her body begin to tremble.

He passed the phone to Gil and simply sat and stared at her.

She couldn't take her gaze away from him. He found out about the listening device. She should have known he'd have people to check her over. She should have never thought she could get away with something like this. He's been in the mafia world since he was born. He was too observant, too calculating.

Jolie couldn't remember how far she was from the door. Where were the guards? There were always guards.

Adrik sat back. "You lied to me."

How did she fight her case? Did she try, or should she simply run?

"Adrik—"

"Show me."

Tears burned in her eyes. He wouldn't understand. He wouldn't see the position he had put her in. She wanted a future for the children at her school. She put so much time and effort into their well-being, and to know that so many of them would be snatched away had gotten to her.

Adrik ground his teeth. "You told me it was the gym."

Her brows knitted, and then she realized he had found out about her attack. She didn't know which was worse. Now, instead of her dying, would someone else be killed? How was that any better? A tear fell from her cheek, and she didn't know if it was from relief or stress.

"Show me."

With a shaking hand, Jolie lifted her shirt. The welt expanded across her ribs, black and purple, like someone tossed paint on her white skin.

He didn't show any reaction, not that she could see.

Adrik nodded, chewing his lip and looking out the window before coming back to her. His blue eyes were dark in disappointment.

Jolie quickly fought. "I didn't want anyone to get hurt."

"So you hurt me instead. Lies to me are like knife wounds. They are a reminder to trust no one. Is that how you want to start this off?"

Tears dripped down her cheeks. She hated how clear he was with his pain. She hadn't expected that from him.

Adrik stood with Gil. He threw two hundred dollars on the table, refusing to look at her. "Edik will take you home."

With her purse over her shoulder, she shifted in the seat, wincing with every movement. Adrik hated it and clenched his fists as he watched her. She used the table more than she needed to. Unable to stop himself, he grabbed her arm to help her stand, but she squealed in pain, and he released her like he touched a hot pan. The guilt on her face made him reach for her sleeve. A bruised handprint marred her skin. It was another dose of lighter fluid to a building inferno.

Adrik turned away from her, no longer sure he could hide what was happening inside him. He approached Edik. "Take her home. Inspect the house. Stay with her until I call."

Adrik walked out of the restaurant even as he heard Jolie yell his name. The door to his car was already open, and Gil was on his way to the passenger seat.

"Adrik, please." Jolie rushed to him, diving in front of him, with her hands on his chest. "It doesn't matter. I'm fine, I'm fine."

He kept moving. "You are not fine. Do not hurt yourself. Go with Edik." He went to get in the car, but she grabbed his arm.

"Don't kill anyone." She wrapped her arms around him, and he stopped. "Please, please. Don't. I couldn't live with myself."

Adrik kept his hands at his side as he stared outwardly, unable to give in to her demands even while knowing if he didn't, there was a chance she would never forgive him. It was too early in this budding 'friendship,' but how could he let anyone get away with hurting what belonged to him?

"Live with me," Adrik found himself saying.

Jolie pulled back, tears ruining her eyeliner.

"Be a tutor for my daughter."

The ultimatum was clear. Immerse herself in his life, or someone dies tonight. It wasn't an option. There was no choice, because the latter was too much. She felt defeated that he had snagged her, like a fish that had been swimming along enjoying life when a net wrapped around them and yanked them from the water. She felt like that fish, struggling to gasp for air.

Jolie could only nod.

"Edik will take you home. Rest. Someone will come tomorrow."

"And you promise, right? You aren't going to hurt anyone."

Adrik was hesitant, looking her over. He wasn't a liar, but he learned to skirt around the truth long ago. "I will leave it for the cops."

What she didn't understand was the police were in the palm of his hand.

The stress in her shoulders fell away, and she smiled. "Thank you."

Adrik dropped in the car and shut the door, watching as Edik directed her to the car. He didn't want to let her go, but he had no place by her side. Not when he was trying to pass her off as a tutor. He would have to pretend he didn't know her, if only to keep her safe.

Adrik waited until her car pulled away. "Drive."

Gil sat beside him. ***"Am I calling Morgan?"***

Morgan was their partner at the police station. ***"Make sure they make it look like an accident."***

"And what should we do about the Toxins? Why did they go after your girl?"

The Toxins were a small 200-person group that dwelled between Orlando and Tampa. They had their own company, selling guns to pimps and drug lords.

Why was a good question. Perhaps they saw Adrik and Jolie talking outside by the gym. But as far as he knew, he hadn't upset anyone in their gang, so why would they risk retribution?

"Interrupt their weapon distribution without looking obvious. A lost shipment or a missed payment. A turf war with the Garcias will kill them off."

"And you can continue to pretend with this woman."

Adrik curled his fist. ***"I heard enough at dinner. I won't hear anymore."***

"Be reasonable, Adrik. You know what you are risking."

There would always be a risk. No matter what he did. But there was no reward without risk.

But what was the reward?

Being around a woman I cannot have.

It was stupid and childish, and yet it hadn't stopped him.

He had gotten what he wanted.

As he always did.

Adrik picked at his lips to hide his smile.

Chapter Thirteen

New Life

Jolie didn't pack when she got home. She curled into her bed and cried herself to sleep.

Her life had been stolen from her. This stranger, Adrik, was coming in and destroying everything she worked for. She felt angry at him for making her choose. How could he take away her control so smoothly?

Jolie tried to look on the bright side. She was going to help bring down the Mafia. But that kind of evil was bigger than her. She could help the world little by little with recycling, planting trees, and joining a community service at the local church. These were conceivable actions she loved to participate in.

But taking on the Mafia?

If she had never saved Helina, she would have been left alone, struggling with PTSD like any normal person. And yet here she was, about to lose her whole life.

Jolie wanted to call her mother, but she knew what she would say. Her mom would tell her to go to the police and return home. But Jolie knew, deep down, there was nowhere to go.

He'd find me.

Jolie remembered how easy it was for him to find her house, to know all about her. He had power she couldn't fathom.

A phone rang, forcing her awake. The noise hurt her sleep-deprived headache. She held up her own phone, which was currently off. Jolie sat up, searching, finding a small black flip phone under her pillow. She didn't even know they made flip phones anymore.

"Hello?" Her voice was groggy and terrible.

"Is there anyone there with you?" It was Agent Mally.

"How did you get a phone here?"

"When we were inspecting your place after the attack. Is there anyone there?"

She collapsed against the pillow, too tired to care. "No. A guy is outside the door."

"Turn some music on so he can't hear you."

She hadn't been able to find the remote for the past couple of days and glanced around lazily. She knitted her brows when it was plainly on the couch's armrest. There was no way it had been there this whole time. "Did you find my remote?"

Jolie attempted to get up, but there was too much pain, and she decided against it, putting a pillow on her face. "He can't hear."

"After we finish this phone call, throw the phone in the trash. Bury it and then take the trash to the dumpster. Don't wait."

Jolie wanted to suffocate herself. Was this the kind of life she was going to have now?

"I was going over the recording last night. There isn't anything we can use."

That depressed her. She had wasted so much energy and nerves, and they had gotten nothing. "I can't do it again," Jolie admitted breathlessly.

"You got into the 'lion's den, Jolie," Mally celebrated. "This is our chance."

Jolie was less than enthusiastic. "They have ways to find listening devices."

"If you get caught, just say I slipped it in, and you didn't even know. You have the upper hand here. Adrik will believe you."

After he learned she lied about the attack, the look on his face was enough to keep her from ever betraying him again. It wasn't fear he provoked. But guilt.

"I believe," Mally continued, "Adrik really likes you."

Those words made her sick to her stomach. Jolie stressed, "He wants me to be a tutor." This was complicated enough without someone putting ideas into her head.

"The conversation with him and Gil says differently."

Jolie's interest perked. She had listened to their Russian argument like she could interpret little sounds, but it had been impossible.

Trying to push her curiosity out of her voice, Jolie asked, "What did he say?"

Mally hesitated. "I don't think you're gonna like it." Papers shifted, and Mally cleared her throat. "Gil-'You go out of your way to keep her hidden, make us eat at this odd place, and she dresses like a boy.'"

Jolie sneered. Her outfit hadn't been that bad.

"Gil-'She's like freaking Snow White.'"

"Gil-'You are risking your reputation by humoring this goodie-two-shoes. She is American. If you want virgin—there's a word I'm not going to say. You can use your imagination—I can find you a—' And then Adrik cuts him off with 'Enough.'"

'Khvatit,' he said.

Jolie removed the pillow from her face to breathe and stare at the ceiling. A smile was creeping on her face. He did like her, or at least Gil seemed to think so.

"Jolie, Adrik is not husband material. You know that, right?"

Jolie scoffed. "I know." But the words sounded pointless.

"Tell me you don't like him."

"Look, ma'am, I'm a grown woman. I already have a mother. Was there anything else to this phone call?"

"Be careful. When you think you're the safest, you are in the most danger."

What the hell does that mean?

A knock on the door stopped her from replying, and she shut the phone and shoved it under her pillow. It took an unbelievably long time for her to get to the door, as her body seemed in more pain than it had been yesterday, which was impossible. They knocked again and called for her. She slapped it open. "Yes?"

Edik stood there. "I thought I heard talking."

"I was watching TV."

He glanced at the TV, but it was off.

That doesn't mean I wasn't, Jolie defended mentally, hoping it was believable.

Edik didn't care. "Movers will be here at 9 a.m. Boss doesn't want you to do anything, and he encourages you to rest."

"I have a lease on this apartment."

"Not anymore."

Jolie hesitated. How was that possible?

"My job—"

"Has been notified, and a substitute teacher has already been selected to take your place on Monday. Plus, there was a donation of five thousand dollars for the kids to have free breakfast and lunch."

She stood there, lost in space.

Edik grabbed the doorknob and shut the door for her.

Jolie turned around and sat at the table. She couldn't understand how Adrik had such power. It could be seen as magic if she didn't know that beneath the mystery and the awe, there was blood and bodies.

When the movers arrived, she was getting dressed. Edik was nice enough to open the door and let them in, and she screeched as she ran to the bathroom.

"Sorry." His muffled Russian voice came through the door. "I am not used to houses with no rooms."

She glared at him through the wood, feeling the insult in his backhanded apology.

Jolie tried to help pack, but anytime she reached for anything, someone took it out of her hands. They divided her stuff into necessities and things that would be stored. The workers were primarily teenagers, young boys with tattoos on their arms. A warden was among them, keeping them moving, shouting Russian words with gusto.

The older man pointed to her collection of stuffed animals. "I know an orphanage that would appreciate these."

The sentence seemed rehearsed, like Adrik had talked to him. Of course, she couldn't say no to an orphanage. She grabbed two from the pile of thirty: a panda her mother had given her as a little girl and a graduation dog her stepdad got her when she made it through college. Also in her arm was a frame of her parents, her, and Princess Cinderella at Disney World for her tenth birthday. They had saved for years to take her. She dressed up as a princess every Halloween till she was thirteen. And then, she turned to saving the planet and was a recycling bin for the following years.

Jolie turned back to her empty apartment. It hadn't meant much to her, since she hadn't had time to fall in love with it. Her neighbors were too loud, and the elevators were permanently broken. Homeless people hung out by the front entrance, asking for change.

But it had been a gateway to a new life.

Now, she was stepping foot into a whole new world that she didn't want to be a part of.

So, why am I excited?

Chapter Fourteen

The Castle

"I don't like this one bit," Jolie's mother reported from the cell phone speaker.

Jolie kept the phone on her lap so she could pick at her nails. It had been a habit she broke back in high school, and for a while, she had manicured fingers that she was proud of, but now, she searched for ways to rip the nail, if only to distract her from her thoughts.

"It will be fine," Jolie vaguely responded, with absolutely no conviction behind those words.

"You had an interview yesterday, and now you're moving in with him. Did you even google him? What's his full name?"

Jolie winced and skirted around the request. "I googled him already. It's real."

"And how do you know they will live up to their side of the bargain? A six-figure salary is nice if it's real. You know people scam."

"It's not a scam."

"It sounds like a scam. What are their jobs that they can afford a full-time, live-in tutor?"

"Mom, rich people do this all the time. This isn't some out-of-this-world idea."

"What do they do?"

Kill people? Jolie struggled with a response. Lies weren't easy to make, especially toward her mother. "Finance."

Her mother mumbled to her stepfather for a minute, and their bickering became annoying. Then she returned to the phone. "Your father wants you to sign a contract with a notary. And we want a copy."

Just to get them off her back, she replied, "Sure."

The car turned into a driveway, and her attention deviated. She pressed her face against the window as the single road traveled up between palm trees and beautiful red and white crape myrtles. "I think I'm here," she whispered.

"What's the address? We'll look it up on Google Maps."

The road seemed never-ending, twisting through a rainforest of plants. And then, there was a clearing, and they pulled up alongside the mansion. "Oh, my God."

"What?" Her mother panicked. "What happened? Are you okay?"

"It's massive."

Her mom whispered to her husband and then asked, "How massive?"

"It's a castle."

"A castle? Who the heck has a castle in Tampa?"

It wasn't a literal castle, but Jolie didn't feel like explaining right now. "I gotta go. I'll send pics." And though her mom protested, Jolie shut the phone off as the driver opened her door.

Jolie looked down at her clothes. She was utterly underdressed, and the comment about looking like a boy filtered through her head. She wasn't the type of girl who dressed sexy for no reason. She liked jeans even in the hot Florida sun. It meant she didn't have to shave her legs as much. It's not like anyone was looking anyway. And the T-shirts were fun. She only chose the ones that made her smile. Bob's Burgers always managed to get her out of a bad mood; why wouldn't she buy their shirt?

Jolie shut her mouth, stuffing down negative thoughts. She wasn't going to feel bad about herself, especially at a time like this.

Jolie got out with flip-flops between her toes, holding her purse to her side. She felt like a baby bird that fell from its nest. She didn't belong here; she knew that on every level. But yet, there was no way to get back to her perch. This was the future, and she needed to embrace it.

A woman approached her, speaking Russian in such a hurry that Jolie couldn't even tell her she didn't know what she was saying. So instead, Jolie smiled and followed every gesture the older woman made as she was brought up the marble stairs and into the house. Jolie wanted to stop and take in every sight, but the woman had her by the arm, pulling her along with foreign words spilling from her mouth.

A bulky guard stood at the door, with an earpiece and a gun exposed at his waist. Jolie attempted a shy smile, but the guy didn't look at her. Stepping into the house, a grand chandelier draped from the twenty-foot ceiling, hanging over an ornate round carpet.

A servant stood at the door and reached for Jolie's purse, but she politely waved her away. The woman wore a modernized servant dress—a white top that hung off the shoulders and a black skirt that went to the ankles. A male servant rushed by, dressed in a suit like a butler.

Jolie kept tripping on her feet as she tried to walk and look at her surroundings. Inside, the dual staircase to the second floor was made of white marble and a pale egg-white carpet. Russian artwork decorated every wall, and a dozen statues sat on pedestals.

It was a palace fit for a czar.

The woman stopped before a door and shoved it open, gesturing.

"This is my room?"

The woman latched onto her arm, confusion on her face. "English?"

Jolie bowed her head in apology. "Yes."

She sunk with annoyance and pointed to herself. "No English." She put up her hands, a gesture to stop. "Okay?" With a heavy sigh, she walked down the hall, leaving Jolie to herself.

Jolie stepped into the room. Ming and Tae-Tae ran to her feet, meowing in confusion. She kneeled down, scratching their ears, giving them kisses before she looked around. The room was massive compared to her apartment. The walls were white and striped black. A hint of dark green in the decoration went with the bamboo color taken from the giant piece of art above her bed: a panda in its natural habitat. It was a beautiful piece that nearly made tears come to her eyes. The bedsheet was white, with a mix of pillows on top. Against the side wall were floor-length windows and a sitting area of dark green chairs, with a white carpet beneath them. She touched the sheets of her bed in fascination. She had never seen anything so extravagant.

A few of her belongings were on the dresser. How the movers had beaten her here and managed to put away all her stuff was insane to her. She didn't like how they had touched all her clothes. She found her underwear folded and neatly placed. She sneered at the thought of all those boys touching her things. The walk-in closet had her clothes hung and organized by color. There was depressingly plenty of space left over.

She sat on the bed, overwhelmed.

What am I doing here?

A different woman stood in the doorway, and Jolie popped back up on her feet. This woman was intoxicatingly beautiful, with blonde curls. She stood in an elegant skirt and blouse, with heels.

"Esfir says you only speak English."

"Yes, sorry."

"No need to be sorry. You are my daughter's English tutor."

Jolie's smile faded. *Adrik's wife. Why does she have to be so pretty?*

"It will just be difficult for you. The staff only knows Russian." With her hand out, Katia stepped into the room. "I'm Katia, Mr. Morozov's wife."

Jolie shook her hand, trying to not feel self-conscious. "You're beautiful."

Katia smiled. "I didn't know my husband was looking for a tutor." She drifted, looking around the room. "How did he find you?"

Katia wasn't as stupid as Adrik hoped she was. They had never talked about a tutor for Helina, and yet he hired a young, pretty, big-breasted American and brought her to their home. No other servant had gotten such a nicely decorated room. Whatever game he was trying to play, he failed. There was no keeping this woman a secret when he was obviously trying hard for her affection.

But why?

Adrik never needed to try. Women flock to him like bugs to light. Katia had once admired him from afar. She had been bitten by his charm, but she learned her lesson early that men like him were never worth the trouble.

Katia felt pity for her. If Adrik had feelings for this girl, then her world just got a little bit darker.

"I was at the shootout at Salem's. I helped Helina."

Katia turned to her, wide-eyed. "You're the girl my daughter is obsessed about."

Was that what ignited Adrik's affection? It would make sense, because otherwise, he would have never noticed her. Jolie was too simple. Too common.

Then, perhaps the feeling was temporary, and it would wear off as soon as he got his fill of her, Katia mused. "I'm sorry. The way she described you, I thought you would look more…angelic."

"Kids have extraordinary imaginations."

Jolie had wholly missed the insult, and yet, it made Katia happy. She was naive and dull. She would never last long here. Katia rushed over to her, embracing her, acting the part. "Thank you. You will forever be in my debt."

"No, it's fine."

Katia touched her brown hair, invading her space. "We must be the same age."

"I'm twenty-three."

"You and I are gonna be best friends," Katia declared. "I'm so excited." She parted and headed for the door. "I will leave you. If you need anything, press one." She tapped the intercom on the wall. "Food, bedding, cleaning, help with anything. You've been in a hotel before?"

Another jab at this pincushion of a woman, and she was ignorant.

"Yeah, when I was ten."

The response made her laugh, but Katia stifled it, hurrying out of the room.

Chapter Fifteen

Bad Things

Jolie lay in bed, resting on her side to ease the ache in her ribcage. Her cats were curled around her as she stared out the floor-to-ceiling windows. In the distance, across the bay, she could see the twinkling lights of the city of Tampa. It was indeed a different view from her apartment's. The stone wall building beside her hadn't been nearly so pretty.

There was a never-ending ache in her belly, and she didn't know if it was fear or nerves. Or being in a strange place with no friends, cut off from the world. What was she allowed to do? Was she a prisoner here? Because so far, she felt like one. No one had come in to tell her what she was going to do. She had been left unsure if she was allowed to step out of her room.

And too afraid to figure it out.

It is fear.

The thought was a depressing one. How was Jolie planning on living if she was in a constant state of worry?

Jolie shifted, laying on her back, twisting her face in pain with every movement. The ceiling was even nicer than her whole apartment. How was that possible?

She knew this was a mistake, but what had been her other option? Adrik might have hurt someone or perhaps even killed them. He hadn't given her a choice. He trapped her.

And that would be the kind of relationship we'd have.

Jolie knew Adrik's type; she knew what they did, how they smelled sweet like roses only to ensnare you like a Venus flytrap, draining your life little by little till you no longer existed.

Her first boyfriend had been such a man. At one point, she felt so enraptured by him that she believed his happiness was more important than her own. It wasn't until he robbed a bank that she realized he wasn't a good man and she deserved better. Jolie turned her boyfriend into the police, and guilt swallowed her for years after. Only after leaving her small, judgmental town did she finally feel okay. And now here she was, once more put in a horrible position that would damage her.

Regret after regret piled on her like dirt on a grave.

A knock yanked her from a panic attack. She struggled to sit up, pain hindering her as she searched for the noise. It was the door that connected Helina's room to hers. It was too late for Helina to be up, but then again, she had no idea what time that child went to bed. She hadn't even been able to see her yet.

Jolie unlocked the door and peeked in, looking downward for her little form. Instead, she found a man's legs. She snapped her eyes up, and Adrik was smiling at her in the dark. Jolie stepped back, running her hands through her hair subconsciously. She was in her panda pajamas, with panda socks, and couldn't be more embarrassed.

"Hi," Adrik greeted, dressed in jeans and a dark-gray Armani shirt.

"Hey," she breathed out. How did he manage to look good in everything?

"Can I come in?"

"It's your house."

Jolie shifted through the room aimlessly. There was more than enough space to put between them, and she went over to the bed, standing on the opposite side. Aside from the lights outside the window lighting up the pool area, the room was dark. Jolie glanced toward her purse, sitting on the dresser. Could she get to it and turn on the listening device?

Adrik knelt down to greet her cats, an action that would have melted Jolie if she didn't have walls in place. His fingers scratched their ears as they cried at him.

"Do you like everything?"

"Yes, thank you." She crossed her arms, feeling betrayed by her cats.

Adrik rushed to the windows. "Look." He pressed a button, and the windows darkened, making the room black. "Oh, shit," he whispered, fumbling in the dark for the lamp nearby. "Got it." He flicked it on, exposing her face. He was surprised by her expression of anger. "What?"

"Am I a prisoner here?"

His brows knitted. "We had an agreement. I thought that was understood."

"Yeah. You don't kill anyone, and I move in. Do I need to worry about you killing me?"

Adrik slipped his hands in his pockets as he watched her. "You can leave anytime you want."

"Can I?"

"If you check your email, a contract was sent. Read it carefully. I have a lawyer if you want to talk to someone."

"I'll get my own lawyer."

"If you can afford it."

"Shut up; you don't know how much money I have."

Adrik gave her a side look as he shifted through the room.

"You saw my bank account."

"I know everything, Jolie."

"How is that fair? You know everything about me, and I know nothing about you. You like this power, don't you? You like making people feel inferior."

Adrik sat, resting his ankle on his knee as he folded his hands in his lap. "Why am I in charge of people's feelings? If you feel inferior, perhaps it is a problem within you."

"Screw you. Why are you here?" She cackled. "How many times am I gonna ask you that?"

"I wanted to see you."

The simple reason smacked her like a semi, silencing her. She folded her arms over her chest, unsure where to lead with that. She didn't want to be unfriendly while he was being nice.

Jolie caved a little. "You come off as a stalker, you know that?"

Adrik cackled. "Yes. I'm sure I do. It's for my protection and has nothing to do with you."

"My bank account is for your protection?"

"When people are desperate to pay rent, they become dangerous."

"I wasn't desperate."

"I know."

Jolie didn't know why that made her feel good. But it didn't disregard the fact that he invaded her privacy when he could have just asked.

"Will you sit with me?"

Jolie was hesitant for obvious reasons. She didn't want to be his friend. She didn't want to get closer. She needed the distance to remind her of the destruction he could cause. But yet, her feet moved of their own accord. She took a deep breath and sat, nearly crying out from the pain.

Adrik observed her, curling a fist against the armrest. Her pain was a thorn in him that needed to be eradicated, and the only way to get it out was revenge. Any moment now, someone would text him and let him know that the culprit was caught. And from there, Adrik could have his vengeance.

"I can get you some pain pills."

"Tylenol is fine."

"That doesn't do shit for a broken rib."

Jolie was adamant. "I don't want anything."

Adrik chewed the inside of his cheek. Her pride was frustrating. She stared at the dark windows that now reflected them in the panels. He wanted to break into her walls, but perhaps it was better that she remained distant. It kept him in reality. "I want to go over how things will be here."

Jolie mumbled, "I'm sure Esfir will give me the rundown. I'll just use Google Translate."

"What I have to say is different."

Jolie glanced toward him. His countenance altered, like his words caused a burden on him that he didn't want to deal with.

"I brought you here to teach my daughter. To be a friend to her. To help shield her from the world I live in. This alone is a problem for my family. My father would have put a gun in her hands on her first birthday if he had his way. The Mafia is indoctrinated. It is grooming to create carelessness for life. I do not want that for Helina. It is why I keep her here in the United States. Katia, my wife, and my parents want me to send her to my uncle in Russia, and I will not do it. So, thank you for agreeing to come here. I am forceful when I shouldn't be. But I am a spoiled man. I get what I want."

Jolie scoffed, rolling her eyes.

"Why do you do this?" He rolled his eyes, copying her dramatically, making Jolie hide a cackle behind her hand. He smiled. "I am honest, if nothing else."

"You're full of yourself."

"No. I am proud. And rightly so."

Jolie positioned herself to face him. "You want honesty?"

"Yes. I beg for it."

"I'm scared of you."

Adrik played with a ruby ring on his finger, twisting it. It was a good thing to be scared of, and usually, a bit of fear was precisely what Adrik wanted. Even his brothers had a tiny shred of apprehension in them. But from her, it was annoying. "Fear is good. It will keep you wise. But respect is better. Respect me, and you will have no reason to fear me."

"And you will do the same? Respect me?"

"Have I not shown respect?"

"Going through my things is not respectful."

Adrik shifted uncomfortably in his seat. She was laying into him like a mom catching their teen kid sneaking out. It wasn't like he didn't want to talk, but he was hoping for this conversation to be going in a different direction. He had come late at night to her bedroom. There was always a bit of hope that their situation would change to a more horizontal position.

But that is not going to happen. Adrik reminded himself, even if she looked amazingly sexy with her messy hair and awkward pajamas. What woman could rock panda socks?

"My men were helping you move. I personally have gone through nothing."

"Not the point," Jolie sneered.

Her audacity was humorous, and he hid his smile behind a finger, playing with his lips. He didn't know whether she was completely devoid of feeling or, more logical than he hoped, that she didn't find him attractive or desire him in any way. She did not indicate that she would fall for his charms if he tried.

Could he try?

Not yet. She is injured and too skeptical of me.

It was the long game, then.

No game. Adrik sighed in frustration, hating the argument going on inside his head. She was off-limits. He brought her here specifically for his daughter. Not to dangle fruit in front of his face like in the Garden of Eden.

"You met Katia?" He brought her up to remind himself that another woman would not be tolerated.

"Yes. She's beautiful."

Adrik sighed. "She is."

"Are you working on your marriage?"

Adrik didn't know if she was asking as a friend or from a different desire. But he took it as a sign. "No. There is no working on it."

"Then, why not get divorced?" The words came out faster than Jolie meant for them to, and then she bowed her head. "I'm sorry. That's none of my business."

Her reddened cheeks humored him and reassured Adrik she had some interest in him.

"Our marriage is connected to a treaty for our families. If we divorce, the treaty ends, and there will be much bloodshed. To avoid it, we pretend."

"That sucks. I'm sorry."

Her sympathy was a salve. No one had said that before. "I am, too."

Adrik had wanted his marriage to work. He wanted a relationship like his parents, but Katia had destroyed it from ever happening.

Is that what I see in Jolie? The wife I should have had?

But it was a stupid thing to think because she was American. She was too sweet, too innocent. She would break if she knew even a fraction of what he'd done for his family. He should send her away now.

But he was a selfish man.

"You said you know nothing about me. Has Google not answered your questions?"

"It's like looking at a blueprint of a house," she replied. "It's an outline and not all that you are."

Adrik could only stare at her, with a finger against his temple. Her innocence was everything he needed in his life. His daughter brought him happiness, but there was always a hole inside him that was missing. And Jolie was too close to finding it.

Adrik stood up. "I'll leave you."

"Oh. Okay," she stammered.

When Adrik heard her slight disappointment, he almost sat back down. He'd gladly spend the rest of the night here in her presence, but he knew how bad that would be.

Adrik went to the side door, turning toward her. She approached with her arms across her chest to hide her breasts. She truly hated bras, it seemed. Something they had in common. "I came through my daughter's room for a reason. You and I do not know each other. Do not talk to me unless I talk to you first."

"Are you serious?"

"If my father thinks you and I are fucking, he'll try to get rid of you."

Fear spread on her face. "What?"

Adrik cackled, resting a hand on her arm, incapable of resisting touching her when she was so close. "Do not worry. We are not fucking."

She cringed and yanked out of his grip. "No, we're not."

The way her cheeks reddened in the light provoked him. "I have a question."

"How is there possibly anything that you don't know?"

His smile grew. "You aren't going to like this question."

"Say it already."

"I overheard my men talking about your belongings."

Jolie hid her face. "Oh, God. I already know. Not every woman wears thongs, okay? It's not like I go out to the club or anything."

Adrik knitted his brows with a grin. "So, granny panties are a thing?"

She pushed him. "Shut up." Jolie grabbed the door, shoving him through it. He was laughing every inch.

"But wait, wait, that is not my question."

Jolie pressed her forehead against the door.

"You don’t have a boyfriend, and yet, there were no devices—" Jolie slammed the door in his face, humiliated.

Then the door popped back open, and Adrik was there again. "I feel this will work. You teach my daughter. And I teach you."

"Teach me what?"

Adrik gripped her arm and pulled her close till his lips were on her ear. "Bad things." He heard her quick intake of breath and bit his lip to stop himself from tasting her skin. He let his nose tickle the hairs on her skin and felt the shiver it induced. A smirk twisted on his lips. He yanked himself away and shut the door behind him.

Chapter Sixteen

The Family

Morning couldn't come soon enough. It was a dreadful night, with only Adrik's voice to soothe her. She went through their conversation with a fine-toothed comb, searching for the toxicity she was familiar with, and was discouraged to notice there wasn't enough to fortify her walls.

I like him.

She groaned in self-loathing.

Jolie forced herself up, using the pain as a distraction. She wasn't going to allow herself to dive any deeper. She would find all the bad things about him, of which there should be plenty for a mafia boss. She was being thrown off because he seemed more likable than she imagined killers to be.

Yeah, so was Ted Bundy. That's how he was able to ensnare all of the women he raped and murdered.

"Good point," Jolie muttered to herself. "He's Ted Bundy."

Now, with a suitable headspace, Jolie got herself dressed. She found the pen in her purse and debated taking it. What would happen if someone found it on her person? Could she act confused, or would that not matter?

The sooner I get the information the FBI needs, the sooner I can get out of here.

Jolie slipped the pen into her pocket before she moved to the door. Adrik said she wasn't a prisoner, yet she didn't feel right leaving her room without someone telling her she could.

That's ridiculous, she motivated herself. *I live here now.* She glanced back toward her cats for encouragement, but Tae-Tae was currently licking his privates, and Ming was staring out the window, watching a bird twitter in a palm tree.

Jolie stepped out into the hall.

She flipped her head each way down the long, elegant hallway, having no idea which direction to go. Lights were bright. with LEDs in the ceiling reflecting against the white tile on the floor. Her black flats tapped against the shining ground with every step she took, and no matter how light she was on her feet, it echoed.

A door at the end of the hallway whipped open, and Katia stepped out. Her brown eyes widened at the sight of Jolie. "You're up early."

"I didn't know what time we were getting started." Jolie noticed the outfit Katia wore: yoga clothes that were tight in all the right places, exposing the plumpness of her breasts and the perfect shape of her ass. It was intimidating and discouraging. What could Adrik ever see in her if he had Katia to compare her to?

"Cute dress," Katia commented as she approached, her high heels hitting the ground like anvils.

Jolie wasn't sure she was being truthful. Her dress was decorated in multicolored letters and draped down to her knees. It was one of her favorite teaching dresses, but now she felt ridiculous.

"Helina usually wakes around nine. Would you like to join me for breakfast? The family is promptly fed at seven."

Jolie took a deep breath and followed behind. "That would be great."

"You can meet my husband."

"We've met."

"Oh. What a surprise." Katia glanced over her shoulder. "My husband and I talked about your schedule last night. Monday through Friday, ten to four, with an hour's break for lunch. Esfir will take a list of any supplies you need. Please do not be shy. Spare no expense for my daughter's education. She might be a bit behind. We'd hoped she would've returned to Russia by now, but plans have changed."

Down the double staircase and into the main foyer, their movements sparked a wave of attendants rushing about, as if they'd been caught idling. To the left, they went through a sitting area but kept traveling through another set of double doors into a dining room. There was a long table meant for twelve, but it was empty. Opening up with glass doors was the pool area, and they stepped out onto the terrace where the family sat in the early morning humidity. The house gave them adequate shade, and a nice breeze came from the harbor.

Jolie tucked her hair behind her ear and nervously approached.

Adrik sat with his back to her while Alexei sat at the end, and his mouth dropped open upon seeing her.

Jolie's attention, however, was on the old man sitting at the head of the table. Yakov, the leader of their mafia family. Gray hair, gray facial hair, dressed in black pants and a white button-up shirt, he was slightly heavy set, with a bulging belly, but his blue eyes were as bright as ever when he looked up to greet her. And though he smiled wide and greeted her with delight, all Jolie saw was his mugshot and the cold, malicious look in his dead eyes. His misdeeds were proudly posted on the internet, as if he had done an interview about all the atrocious things he committed. She hadn't thought she'd ever come in contact with someone so dangerous.

Jolie slipped her hand in her pocket, clicking the pen, hoping against all hope that he'd reveal something terrible and she'd be free to leave this place. If he caught on to her deception, would the police be able to save her in time?

Jolie strengthened her back, trying to erase the trepidation in her soul.

Russian broke out on Katia's lips as she greeted the table, and everyone turned to look at her. Adrik's gaze passed over with quick indifference, his attention on his phone.

"Miss Bell?" Alexei stood up. "What are you doing here?" He approached. He wore a light blue suit, but his arm was tucked against his chest with a sling.

Katia answered before she could. "She's the new tutor for Helina."

"Tutor?" Alexei looked to Adrik and quickly stated in Russian, ***"You didn't tell me you were hiring a tutor."***

"Me either," Katia added as she sat across from Adrik, staring expectantly at him, but he promptly ignored her.

Jolie kept her fingers connected in front of her, trying not to pick at her nails. She felt intrusive and completely out of place. Alexei had been at the shootout, held a gun to her, and forced her to take them to her apartment. Was that erased? Did he think it was a common thing to have gun in her face?

"Come sit," Alexei offered, pulling out the chair next to him.

Jolie's knees almost gave out. She was swallowed in fear and wished she could return to her room and pile all her furniture against the door.

Oh, God, if they could hear my thoughts, they'd skin me alive.

Alexei waved to a servant to bring her some food. He turned to his brother with Russian on his lips. ***"You had a background check done on her?"***

"Gil hired her; ask him," Adrik carelessly replied.

"I usually do the hiring."

"You were busy."

Alexei didn't believe him. Why wouldn't Adrik involve him in who was teaching his niece? *"Does she even know Russian?"*

"Ask Gil."

Alexei sneered. *"I understand you were grateful, but she is not material for this family."*

Adrik was getting aggravated with the questions, and he met his brother's gaze. *"She nearly got killed saving my daughter. That is enough."*

Yakov said from behind his newspaper, *"Do not question your brother."*

Alexei swiftly replied, *"I will if I think he's being stupid."*

Yakov laid the paper on the table and met his son's gaze. *"Why do you worry so much?"*

"She's not the kind of person we have here. If she goes missing, people will take notice."

Adrik popped a grape in his mouth. *"She will not go missing."*

"Until you scare her, and she runs away. Then I'd have to kill her."

"Why am I scaring her?"

"You're an ass to people."

"Some people," Adrik specified.

"Most people," Alexei corrected.

Adrik held up a finger. *"But not all."*

Alexei rolled his eyes. He glanced at Jolie and noticed her struggling to understand. He switched to English. "Sorry, family discussion. Nothing about you." She smiled sweetly and nodded. Alexei switched to Russian, muttering, *"God, she's like a mouse."*

"Certainly dresses like it," Katia nipped.

"She's a teacher," Adrik replied. *"Not a call girl."*

"It is questionable," Yakov added. *"If you were so grateful, why not give her a few thousand? It is probably more than she's seen in her whole life."*

Adrik rubbed his mouth with a napkin, slapping it down on his food before he leaned back. *"I didn't think we were in the business of insulting people who did us a favor. And by favor, I mean saving your grandchild from being riddled with bullets."*

There was quiet after that, and Alexei kept his head bowed. He always knew when Adrik had been pushed too far. But what confused him was why Adrik felt as strongly as he did. There have been people in the past who accidentally got caught in their lifestyle and suffered because of them. They were paid extraordinary amounts for it but never brought to the house.

Yakov sipped his coffee. ***"Whatever you see fit."***

"Thank you." Adrik glanced toward his brother. He hadn't thought Alexei would put up such a fight. What did it matter who he hired?

"This is a big mistake," Alexei muttered, unwilling to let it go so easily. ***"What makes you think she won't report anything she sees to the police?"***

"I made her sign a non-disclosure agreement. If she talks, nothing she says will be admissible in court. And once again, Agent Mally will lose."

Yakov cackled, saluting. ***"She will always lose. But just to be safe, no company conversations around the teacher."***

Adrik was annoyed by the insinuation. ***"She doesn't speak Russian."***

Katia interjected, ***"You suddenly know so much about her. You aren't sleeping with her, are you?"***

The three men turned their attention to her like a spotlight. But Katia wouldn't cave from the intensity. She was smug, as if she had caught him in the biggest lie right in front of his father. Despite how much he claimed 'gratefulness,' there was nothing that Adrik was grateful for. He believed God started the day for him. His ego was brighter than the sun. And if she could crack him, just a splinter, she'd regain all the confidence he destroyed in her.

Yakov cackled, and it sprung a smirk from Adrik. ***"My son has better taste than that, Katia. Jealousy is an ugly color on you, my girl. Try to do better."***

Katia stood roughly. ***"I'm not 'your girl.'"*** With that, she fled the table.

Jolie turned with wide eyes, looking at the three men with confusion. Alexei sent her a reassuring smile and shrug.

Yakov picked up the paper again. ***"Is there a chance she's pregnant? Her temper as of late has been odd."***

Adrik bit, ***"How the fuck should I know?"***

"She is your wife."

Adrik shifted, relieved this conversation was in Russian. He twisted his head as if he was looking for a servant, holding up his half cup of coffee. Jolie and Alexei was sitting close together, talking. She giggled, shaking her head. It unnerved him.

"You need an heir."

Adrik waited for the servant to fill his cup before he sat back and grabbed his phone.***"I have Helina."***

"Don't be foolish. Even in this odd generation, a woman cannot run a mafia family. She'll be good for developing a partnership. Perhaps with a cartel in the south."

Adrik could feel the boiling of his temper. He rolled his fist, clenching his teeth to get his voice under control. ***"You sold all my sisters like cattle. I will not let you sell my daughter."***

Yakov folded up the newspaper and held it out for a servant. They came quickly and replaced it with a cigar. It was already prepped, and he put it between his lips as the servant lit the tip. He took a drag and blew it out toward his son's face. Adrik turned his head away like he had been slapped. ***"Watch your tone."***

Alexei got up, sensing a building argument. He pulled on Jolie's arm even as she tried to eat. "Let's see if Helina's awake. She'll be thrilled to see you."

Adrik dropped his phone on the table as they escaped and used the time to calm himself. He couldn't allow his emotions to build. He had to dismantle it like a Jenga tower, one piece at a time. He glanced behind him, making sure they were gone.

Yakov began, ***"I'm allowing a tutor, but if you think she has any other purpose, you fool yourself."***

Adrik looked at him. ***"You aren't allowing anything. If I want a tutor for my daughter, she gets one."***

Yakov leaned forward. ***"Son, I understand you cherish Helina. I do as well. And if this world was different, I would be encouraging. But this is the life we have."***

"How can I accept anything but the best for her?"

"I'm not saying she won't get the best. She will have everything. She can learn languages, art, and any instrument she wants. I want only a smile on her face. But she is no heir. So, if you want her to be able to choose who she marries and the kind of life she wants, then you must get your wife pregnant with a boy."

The thought made him sick. ***"I don't want to touch Katia."***

"She is a beautiful woman. Where is the problem?"

Adrik chewed the inside of his cheek as he stared out at the pool. His father knew what Katia did and still acted like nothing was wrong. Adrik's disgust for Katia was more than just physical. It was in everything she said and did. It was in her looks. In her personality. In her smell. In the way she dressed. Her existence was a reminder of her betrayal. He couldn't let it go, even years later.

"Marriage comes with plenty of problems. I hear therapy works wonders."

"I wanted a marriage like you and momma."

"You think your mother and I don't have problems? Where is she now? In Russia because she's upset with me. Women are emotional and too much work. I did not enjoy your mother's presence until she produced me a son."

"Do my four sisters account for nothing?" Adrik bit, disgusted by the insinuation.

Yakov cackled. ***"It was a joke, boy."***

If his father wanted a joke, Adrik would provide. ***"If I kill you, I can do whatever I want."***

Yakov cackled adoringly. ***"Perhaps now you stand a chance, but that is why I married you off so young."*** Yakov winked at him with a proud grin. He slapped his son's shoulder, squeezing, ***"Put a bag on her head if it helps. But I want her pregnant by the end of the year."***

Adrik remained there long after his father left. The walls felt like they were tightening around him, and he was struggling to get out, but no key would work on the locks. He thought by becoming the heir, there would be fewer chains strapped to his wrists, but instead, they kept piling on. How was he supposed to make a better life for his daughter if he couldn't even make a better life for himself?

Yakov wanted Katia pregnant.

Adrik shoved his plate off the table, and it shattered on the floor.

Chapter Seventeen

Unavailable

Jolie looked over her shoulder at Yakov and Adrik as Alexei kept a hand on her back, guiding her through the house. She could feel the tension worse than the summer heat. What had gotten them to that point? Was Adrik okay?

Alexei tried to assure her with, "My father's a rough guy. Probably better for you to stay away. He's a little racist."

Jolie focused on Alexei, noticing for the first time how much he and Adrik looked alike. They have the same jawline, the same eyes, and the same kind of hair. Slick, black, and short. Alexei's body was thicker, like he had drunk more milk as a kid. He definitely focused more on upper body strength than his brother. "How's your arm?"

"It's fine, thanks." Alexei led her to the living room, sitting on the opposite side of the couch. He stared at her, the same kind of stare Adrik had, but it wasn't nearly so intimidating. She fixed her dress over her knees, looking around the room. It was as elegant as the rest of the house, with the white furniture and a pop of red in random spots. There was a grandfather clock in the corner and a beautiful white piano. Alexei cleared his throat. "I guess I should apologize. The shootout and forcing you to take us to your apartment probably gave a bad impression."

Jolie appreciated the apology, but it wasn't enough to erase it.

"Though I'm thankful for what you did, I don't think this is a good fit. I'll talk to my brother."

Could Alexei convince him to change his mind? Did Jolie want that?

"Are you twins?" Jolie said, deviating.

The question paused him. Did she really not understand the kind of danger she was in? Did she believe they were the typical run-of-the-mill drug dealers, living in a house like this? Perhaps from movies, she assumed those types of gangs were rich—when in reality, they knew nothing about business.

Alexei scratched his head uncomfortably. "No, but we are ten months apart." He leaned in and whispered as if it was a secret. "I'm older."

Jolie smiled. "Shouldn't he be taking orders from you?"

"I'm more muscle." He shifted his arm to expose his bicep. Even in a suit, it was noticeable.

Jolie giggled, shifting her gaze away.

Alexei couldn't figure out why his brother brought this woman here. But he wasn't that upset about seeing her again. She was impressionable. She tried so hard to fit into the background, but by doing so, she stood out. Perhaps it was her quirky dresses or her fearlessness, but whatever it was, he hadn't forgotten her. "So, you're going to tutor Helina?"

Jolie popped right back up with a smile. "Yep, that's the plan."

"I guess there's nothing wrong with that. She should be up. Do you know how to get to her room?"

Jolie stood, "Yeah, thanks. See you around."

Alexei watched her walk away, her ballet shoes tapping against the tile differently than high heels. He dropped his head. He was never good at talking to women. His good looks got him a seat at the bar, but then he'd always screw up. Now, Alexei had gotten to the point where being drunk was the only way to get laid.

A crash from outside got him to his feet. Servants raced out in front of him, cleaning up the mess Adrik made as he sat in his chair. Alexei rested his hands on the empty seat of his father's.

Adrik glanced at him for half a second, telling him all he needed to know before his gaze went back to the pool.

Dealing with Yakov was another reason Alexei gave up his seat as heir. He wasn't nearly so willing to obey their father as Adrik was. Too many times, he went against Yakov and paid the price for it. If he had kept the position as heir, he would have killed his father or been murdered in his sleep.

"I don't think this is a good idea," Alexei began. ***"This tutor."***

Adrik stood and threw back the rest of his coffee before slapping it on the table. ***"It's done."*** He turned to leave, but Alexei moved in front of him.

"Why? Why her? You're gonna ruin her life, Adrik."

He scoffed, stepping around him. ***"Dramatic as always."***

Alexei latched onto his bicep, forcing him around. Adrik's temper ignited, and he stepped up to Alexei, getting in his face. But Alexei wasn't stepping up to the plate. ***"You're mad at Papa."*** He pushed his brother back. ***"Do you want to fight? Let's go get gloves on. I don't want to mess up my pretty face."***

Adrik huffed a barely there snicker. Alexei suppressed his smile, relieved he got Adrik off the edge. It wasn't always easy. Alexei approached, with his hand up before resting it on his brother's shoulder, ***"What did he say?"***

When no answer came, Alexei nodded, understanding the silence. Their father required sacrifices, and it never mattered what it was. It still took a toll.

If Adrik ever asked him, Alexei would kill Yakov in an instant. He had no love for that psycho of a man. And though it would be against their code, and he'd be cast out, he'd do it for his brother.

But until then, he pretended to be a good son.

"Papa knows what he's doing. You got to trust in it," Alexei said with bitterness, words that had been forced down his throat.

Adrik stepped out of his brother's hold. ***"You don't believe that."***

Alexei kept his eyes on him, searching for any sign that Adrik wanted what he couldn't say, but Alexei wasn't sure and wouldn't risk being wrong. Adrik loved their father still. He couldn't lose Adrik because of their differences. ***"About this girl."***

Adrik rolled his eyes. ***"She stays."***

Alexei rushed after him, grabbing his arm and pulling him to the side. ***"And she is just a tutor?"*** he asked.

Adrik slapped him on the arm, the casted one—***"Yep"***—and smiled as his brother winced.

"Then, I could ask her out?"

Adrik snapped back around, brows knitted.

Alexei shrugged and explained, ***"She's got nice tits."*** It was an off-the-cuff comment, unwilling to admit he was attracted to such an odd woman.

"She's not really your type."

Alexei tilted his head as he thought of all the women he'd dated. They were primarily oddballs, some of them downright ugly, but a sense of humor usually got him. ***"She kind of is,"*** he corrected. ***"You remember Melissa?"***

Adrik looked down at their feet in memory. Alexei was a late bloomer. He didn't get his first girlfriend till tenth grade, three years after Adrik. And even then, he didn't lose his virginity until senior year, which Adrik made sure to make fun of him for every chance he got. And the girl he finally gave his cherry to was Melissa. She was an anime-lover with pink hair. She carried a Naruto backpack and dressed as the female character with pink hair for fun.

It was the first and last time his brother had been in love.

"How could I forget?" Adrik stepped back, crossing his arms, trying to figure a way out of this mess. He couldn't date Jolie, but he sure as hell didn't want his brother to. So, how did he make her unavailable? ***"I hear she's a lesbian."***

Alexei blinked. ***"You think?"***

"Yeah. Yeah. That's what I heard, anyway. I could be wrong."

"I don't know. I flexed earlier, and she liked it."

Adrik cackled to hide the jealousy inside. If Jolie liked Adrik, there was no certainty she wouldn't want his brother. They looked alike enough despite their personalities differing on many points. Alexei might even be a better match for her than he was.

"Alright," Alexei conceded. ***"That sucks."***

Adrik slapped him on the shoulder, ***"Sorry, brother."***

Adrik turned away, and his smile fell as he moved through the house to find Jolie. What if she realized he was off-limits and directed her attention to his more available brother? He'd hate them both for it, and it wouldn't even be their fault. He needed to ensure she knew her purpose here: to teach his daughter. Nothing else. She stayed without a boyfriend for the past few years, so she could go a little longer.

Adrik could hear his daughter's giggles from down the hall, and it eased his upset. The anger dripped out of him like candle wax. He stopped in the doorway, watching Helina run about the room, with a princess costume on, as Jolie sat in the center, trying to get her to stop. But with zero communication, Helina ignored her.

Adrik hissed, and Helina stumbled when she noticed him. She stood still, putting her head down.

Jolie smiled with relief. "Ah, thank you. I think she thinks I'm here to play."

In Russian, Adrik explained what Jolie was doing here, and when she found out she was learning English, she jumped in Jolie's arms. Jolie held her, kissing her forehead. "Let's learn."

Adrik was about to speak to her when Katia suddenly came up behind him from the hallway, touching his arm. He moved out of her way, with disgust on the curve of his lip. He couldn't stop himself from chastising her. ***"Your outburst at breakfast was petty."***

Jolie and Helina looked at him, and though he spoke in Russian, he was sure his tone didn't go unnoticed. Katia always managed to bring out the worst in him.

Katia smiled back. ***"You're just mad I'm not as dumb as you think I am."*** She nudged her head toward Jolie. ***"Are you her bad little student?"***

Adrik slipped his hands in his pockets to stop himself from laying hands on her. He had only done it once, and Helina had been there. It was enough to keep him back, even when he only wanted to hurt Katia as much as possible. His words would have to be enough. ***"You weren't this ridiculous when I brought three women to my room. Are you intimidated by her? You think she can replace you? Because chances are she'd be a better mother. Hell, Esfir is a better mother."***

Helina latched onto her mother's leg. ***"Daddy, Mommy, don't fight."***

Katia changed her language. "Say it in English," she goaded. If he didn't give a shit about the teacher, he'd say whatever he wanted loud enough for her to hear.

When Adrik turned out of the room, Katia knew she had won.

But it wasn't victory she felt. This new strange woman would be around her daughter. Was Adrik hoping to find a mother for Helina because he was going to kill her? Panic made Katia pick up her daughter. "Get out," she ordered Jolie. "Get out!" she yelled again, and the woman rushed out of the room as Katia stood there, squeezing her daughter as if she'd never get to hold her again.

Chapter Eighteen

Contract

Jolie sat on her bed, scared and confused. Katia kicked her out of the room after she fought with Adrik. Not knowing Russian was becoming a huge inhibitor. She was gonna have to make an effort to learn.

If I'm choosing to stay, which still hasn't been decided.

Jolie stared at the clock. It was nine in the morning—when she was supposed to start her new job.

This isn't working.

Jolie took the pen out of her pocket. It was still activated. "I need to see you," she spoke into it. "I want to get out. I'm gonna go for a run. Find me." She rushed through her drawers, searching for her yoga pants, and slipped them on, changing out of her dress. She found her running shoes in the closet. Everything was lined up nicely. Someone had come through her room again to clean what was already cleaned. Her bed was made. Her dirty clothes were gone. Everything she had touched had been put back at a precise angle.

She couldn't live like this. There was no privacy. Nothing went unnoticed.

Jolie slipped the pen into her sports bra. No way was she going to leave it behind.

To her surprise, there wasn't a problem with her walking about. The house was quiet, aside from the servants dusting, sweeping, and washing the floor. Jolie went out the front door and stood on the steps, stretching, looking all around, searching for an exit out of the compound. A driver was standing next to a black Lexus, waiting for her, but when she jogged down the steps and turned left, he stared after her in confusion. She set off into a run, going down the elongated driveway till she reached the gate, waiting for it to open. An intercom came on, and Russian flowed through the speaker. She could only guess what they were asking.

"I'm going for a run," she said into the stone pillar. "I'm allowed to leave," she put out there, more of a reminder to herself than them. She blew a breath of relief when the gates opened.

Running down the sidewalk, the neighborhood was for billionaires, every house as lovely and massive as the last. The street was done in cobblestone. The trees and grass were trimmed and aligned. She didn't have any idea where she was, but she kept running, hoping to find something familiar.

Another runner was coming toward her, and she tried to move out of their way. They tried to move out of her way simultaneously, and they bumped into each other. "Sorry."

"Go to Starbucks."

"What?"

The woman bent down to tie her shoe that was already tied. "Starbucks." Then she bit, "Keep moving!" And the stranger got back up and raced away.

Jolie forced her feet forward. Would it be a good idea to follow such an instruction? Maybe it was a trap? Or perhaps it was Agent Mally.

Jolie found Starbucks on the corner and went into it with a bit of hesitancy. Mally wasn't around, and without knowing what else to do, she ordered a coffee. When her name was called, she grabbed her cup, only to find a message written on the cardboard. 'Go to the bathroom.'

Finding all this clandestine activity over the top and kind of funny, Jolie suppressed her smile as she went into the restroom.

Agent Mally stood there with a finger on her lips, like Adrik had done the first time he came to her house. She waved a wand over her body, down to her feet, but when the only sound came from the pen, Mally stood up. "He still trusts you."

"Was all this necessary?"

"Yes. And the fact you can't see that just tells me you're in over your head."

Jolie narrowed her eyes. The only reason she was there was because of the damn cop. "Of course, I am!" Jolie snapped. "I don't want to be here at all. I want to get out."

"It's too late. It would be too obvious."

Jolie nearly broke. "I don't care! It's scary there."

"Jolie, all you have to do is get Adrik to say he killed someone. That's it."

"That's harder than you think. He watches what he says all the time."

Mally leaned against the counter, and casually said, "Maybe find a way to make him relax."

The insinuation wasn't lost, and Jolie's mouth dropped open. "I'm not a freaking hooker."

"He likes you, and you like him. Nothing wrong with getting to know each other better."

Jolie couldn't believe her audacity. She wasn't at all what she perceived FBI agents to be. She thought they would be all for protecting people like Jolie. Not trying to get her into terrible danger.

"I'm not doing this. I want out. I want protection."

Mally crossed her arms, "You aren't getting it. You haven't done anything for us. If you want protection, then get Adrik to talk. Get Yakov to talk. Get Alexei to talk."

Jolie had never wanted to punch anyone in the face, but the more Mally spoke, the more Jolie could feel her fist ball up. Jolie asked, "What about breakfast?"

"Nothing we can use. Alexei spoke about killing you."

Her shock pierced through her throat. "He what?"

"These aren't normal people, Jolie. It's what I'm trying to show you. They get by because they start off nice. They start off by handing out money or gifts. They lure you in, and by the time you realize what's wrong, it's too late to get out. Thousands and thousands of people fall prey to them every year."

Alexei apologized for putting a gun to her head and then talked about killing her in another language. How much of him was real? She'd have to be careful around him. He was easy to talk to and came off like a friend, but he was far from it. It was disappointing to learn. But it helped Jolie solidify her role. She needed to get Adrik to admit to something so she could get out.

"I don't know how to flirt," Jolie admitted. "I haven't had much practice."

"YouTube has got everything nowadays. I'm sure you can find a way. And be careful with that pen. If they find it on you, I don't know if I'll be able to help."

Jolie's mouth fell open at the admittance. Mally told her from the first day that she could protect her, and now she's claiming she can't. How was Mally any different from Alexei?

Jolie leaned against the counter after Mally left. She'd dug herself into a hole she didn't know how to escape. She felt just as trapped as she did when she was a teenager. She had gone to her parents and relied on them to guide her. But here, she knew that wasn't possible. Her parents couldn't help her now. She was a big girl. She'd have to figure it out on her own.

As Jolie finished her late morning jog, she returned to the front gates, only to find it overrun by men in black suits. They were searching for someone.

This is for me, isn't it?

Mally's warning about the pen was fresh in her mind, and she dug into her bra, removing it. But she didn't know what to do with it. There was a bush beside her, and in a moment of terror, she flung it into the trees. Then regretted it. She was about to reach for it when one of the guards noticed her, and she heard their Russian call. "Crap," she cursed as they approached.

The beast of a man spoke into a walkie-talkie before he greeted her in a harsh accent, "Miss Bell, please follow me."

"Am I in trouble?"

He took ahold of her bicep roughly, and she stumbled beside him, intimidated by his strength. There was a bunch of people walking around, teenagers and adults alike. They glared at her as they passed, murmuring in their rough language and spitting at the floor.

The man brought her into the house and down a hallway. Stepping from white marble flooring onto dark mahogany wood floors made her heart drop. She felt like she was descending into hell. "I'm sorry. I just went for a run," she pathetically whimpered as he pushed her toward double wooden doors. The soldier pushed them open and pulled her to the center of the room, only to abandon her there. The doors shutting vibrated in her chest.

Jolie hugged herself. The room was every bit of an office belonging to an ancient vampire king. It smelt of cigarettes and stale liquor. She wondered if he stowed bodies in the floor-to-ceiling wooden cabinets. Dead animals on the walls might as well be human carcasses. Her animal rights activist badge was burning against her chest. The terror transformed into anger.

What kind of man hurts these creatures just for the thrill?

Yakov came from a different door, greeting her with a pleasant enough smile. However, she couldn't take the ick off her lips as she watched him. He poured himself a drink, "Welcome back."

"I just went for a run."

Yakov smiled, cackled lightly, and nodded. He took up his small glass and moved from his desk to a sitting area beside a massive fish tank. There were beautiful fish inside, exotic and colorful.

More than likely illegal.

"Sit. Chat with me. Tell me about yourself."

Hesitantly, she stepped up to the red leather high-backed chair. As silly as it sounded, she was searching for a weapon. Would Yakov have one on his person? Would one be in the floorboards or behind the walls for easy access? Jolie sat. Yakov stared at her in wait, and finally, she focused on him, remembering his last comment, "I'm from Orlando. I moved here to help inner city kids."

"That's wonderful. I've built four schools downtown, and I pay for after-school programs for over two thousand kids. Teachers are in desperate need."

Jolie shouldn't be shocked. Mally told her they were generous. But still, she was impressed. "Wow."

"I've been lucky. I am fifth-generation wealth. I haven't had to scrimp and save. But I appreciate those who do."

"Wish you were that generous to the animals," she smiled, hoping it came across as playful, yet still wanting to get the point across that she was disgusted by his collection.

His expression tightened, and she wished she could take it back.

Yakov looked around the room, loving every trophy like they were his kids.

Jolie interrupted his reverie. "I didn't know I couldn't leave."

"You can leave, but please, make sure there is a guard with you next time. The world is dangerous, Miss Bell, and you are now part of this family. We can't have you hurt on our watch."

Jolie nodded, pretty sure he could care less about her safety. "Um, can I go?"

"How's Agent Mally?"

Jolie was drenched in terror, and her body went cold. There was no trying to save face; she could feel the look on her features, the shock, the worry, the fear. She struggled to speak and make an excuse, but what could she say? No lie was good enough.

Yakov eyed her proudly. Emotions were easy to manipulate, and now, he's got her right where he wanted her. Fearing him.

The problem with many people was the lack of self-awareness. They believed no one was watching. But eyes were everywhere. Especially now in the time of technology. It was so much easier to find a rat in the sewer. And there was no doubt in his mind Jolie was vermin sniffing for a scrap of rotted meat. Women typically were the worst of them. Men at least had pride and dignity, whereas women tended to give up such things only to get what they wanted. It made them tricky but not impossible to figure out.

"My son feels gratitude toward you. And I am thankful as well. If not for you, I would have had to plan a funeral for my granddaughter last week. So, tell me about your conversation with Agent Mally the other day, and we will be even."

Jolie clenched her teeth. 'The other day,' he said. Which meant he wasn't talking about her meetup at Starbucks. He didn't know. Jolie swallowed and relaxed in her chair. "She told me you were dangerous."

He smiled, taking a sip. "She's not always wrong."

"She told me to stay away from you."

"And why haven't you taken this wise advice?"

She could lie here, and he might see through it. Or she could tell the truth, and he'll see what she wants him to see. "I need money."

Yakov sucked on his tongue, observing her with the same intense stare as his sons'. Now she knew where they got it from. It was less intimidating. "Money," he said, chuckling. "Now I understand you. Now we can work on our friendship."

Jolie didn't like that. She nervously twittered, wishing she had the recorder. She felt suddenly unprotected and in the eyesight of a dangerous beast.

"I'll keep you in mind for jobs."

She vehemently shook her head. "I am not… I'm—I like honest work."

His big brushy brows knitted, asking, "Do you? Yet you are willing to take money from me?"

She stuttered. She unknowingly backed herself into a hole.

"We all start off honest, sweet girl."

Yakov took this time to eye her up and down. She wore a training outfit that she more than likely got from Walmart. 'Eat, Pray, Run' was written on her shirt, summarizing everything he needed to know about her. Now that he thought about it, he doubted a job would ever come his way for someone like her. "And my sons are of no interest to you?"

"No," she answered too quickly, and nervousness spewed from her.

He nodded, pretending to believe her. "Good. You were hired as a tutor, and that is what you will do. Anything else will violate your contract, and I will turn you out faster than I gutted that lion." Yakov paused, enjoying the apprehension on her face, and then added, "You understand, Miss Bell?"

She swallowed and nodded. "Yes. Yes, sir," she corrected, and he liked that immensely. Even wild boars could be trained if struck with enough fear. With a dismissive wave, Jolie bolted out of the room and didn't breathe again until she was safe in her room.

Chapter Nineteen

Swimming Lessons

Jolie watched Helina write her letters from over her shoulder. The little girl was so eager to learn that after a week of tutoring, she was already reciting the English alphabet. Jolie was proud of her, and this was a feeling she loved. It's what got her into teaching. She wanted to build a healthy foundation on positive energy and positive reinforcement. Jolie clapped her hands when Helina finished writing her name.

Helina jumped out of her chair and spun in a circle before plopping back down. Her excitement was palpable, and Jolie admired it. In this awkward world where Jolie felt more fear than ever before, Helina was her shining star. And though it might be odd to say, she was definitely Jolie's only friend.

At lunch, Helina pulled at her hand to join her. Jolie hadn't spent much time out of her room other than tutoring and morning runs. She had found the pen still hidden in the bushes two days later. She pretended to fall into the bush because of the escort behind her. It wasn't one of her proudest moments.

But what was her purpose for the pen? Jolie still hadn't figured it out. She wanted to bring down Yakov but didn't want to hurt Adrik. But the reality was they were entwined. There wasn't a way to do one without the other.

It's been a few days since she had seen the mysterious mafia man. She hoped she'd stop whatever was developing inside her by keeping away. Yet, she prayed Adrik would stop by every night, but he never did.

Jolie told herself it was for the best despite how disappointed she woke up every morning.

Helina disappeared into the kitchen, where Jolie was sure she couldn't go. Instead, out the window, she noticed Adrik and Alexei at the pool, and her heart started to pound in her chest.

Adrik stretched out in a lounge chair, dressed in a swimsuit and Bentley sunglasses. He looked everything like a *Playgirl* model. His tattoos hugged every muscle. His arms, his chest, his back, and his legs—there wasn't a place that hadn't been touched. And with a terrible yet stomach-dropping thought, she wondered what she'd find beneath his swim shorts.

Stop it! she scolded herself. *Ted Bundy. Murderer. Bad. Bad. Bad.*

Jolie forced her eyes off him, and they fell on his brother. Alexei sat on the edge of a chair, with his phone in his hands. He wore workout shorts and a tank; his muscles were as built as a bodybuilder's, with pulsing veins. He must have just come from working out because his skin shined from sweat. Unlike his brother, Alexei had no tattoos on him that she could see. He was just as gorgeous, but his strength made him scarier. Even if he was nicer to her.

Jolie found her eyes gravitating back to Adrik. There were dozens of people on the pool deck, but she only wanted to look at him.

Helina popped back into the room, and Jolie jumped with a little squeal, a hand quickly on her heart.

Still got that PTSD. Good to know. Jolie smiled reassuringly and took Helina's hand, leading her to the lunch table where their sandwiches awaited.

Alexei hated this heat. Even with an umbrella hanging over him, he was sweating. Alexei took the edge of his shirt and rubbed his face. It was days like today he wished he still lived in Russia. The sun was barely visible half the time and typically matched his mood. But going back without Adrik was not an option anymore and hadn't been for the last few years.

Alexei held his phone out, rereading the text message from their father. ***"'We will be celebrating Adrik's twenty-eighth birthday. Make it extravagant.'"***

Adrik groaned from the chair beside him. ***"I'm not a fucking kid."***

Alexei shrugged, trying to be encouraging. ***"It will be fun."***

"And it's a month away. Why is he even talking about it?"

Alexei glanced back at him, and playfully said, ***"Maybe he's got a surprise for you. What if he wants to give you the keys to the kingdom?"***

Adrik snapped his head to his brother. Was that a possibility? It's something he's been waiting years for. But there was plenty of doubt. His father was too controlling to give anything up willingly.

Adrik noticed movement in the house, and as Jolie walked up to the window, he saw her. His sunglasses were too dark for her to notice him staring right at her. He spent the last five days away from her, and now, finally seeing her face brought a fresh wave of hunger that couldn't be sated with food.

"Mama's coming." Adrik vaguely said, ***"Ask her to plan it."***

"What's the tutor doing?" Alexei casually questioned, looking up at her room. ***"Maybe she'll like to do it."***

Adrik smirked. ***"You got a hard-on for teacher, don't you? Lesbian and all."***

"Just because I don't want her to die doesn't mean I want to fuck her."

"But you do."

Alexei shrugged, ***"Why not? Pussy's pussy."***

Adrik mentally winced. He knew when his brother was putting on a show. Alexei was clearly starting to like Jolie, which made his stomach turn. Adrik tried to keep Alexei away from her. All this past week, they were busy tracking rumors about Katia's brother. But the moment he was able, Alexei's thoughts returned to her.

And so did Adrik's.

"She's right there," he heard himself say. Alexei snapped his head to the house just as Jolie was pulled away from the window. ***"Call her out,"*** Adrik tempted, noticing how Alexei struggled with the phone. He didn't like it. How could he make her more off-limits other than calling her a lesbian? ***"She's a Democrat, you know? Can tell just by the way she dresses."***

Alexei scoffed, sitting back. ***"Don't say that."***

Adrik smiled, proud. He knew his brother too well. Her political standing would be a definite turn-off.

"Okay, why not?" Alexei texted Esfir, telling her to bring Jolie out here.

Adrik's smile faltered. That plan backfired.

Alexei looked down at his shirt, brushing off some lint. A pathetic attempt to look better. He shifted, straightened his back, and tried to figure out how to sit like he suddenly forgot.

"What are you doing?"

"Shut up," Alexei bit back. ***"Can you tell everyone to clear out? I don't want to spook her."*** There were women in thin bikinis sitting at the pool. Wives, girlfriends, and their friends floated around, wanting attention from wealthy individuals. Their most profitable drug dealers were invited on weekends to the house for parties and to talk business. There were always ways to improve, and Adrik constantly looked for the best ideas.

Not that Father will do anything with the information, Adrik bitterly thought.

Adrik was against kicking everyone out. Jolie needed to be exposed to their world if she was living with them. But maybe it was too soon to start. ***"Everyone out."***

There was a grumble of discontentment, but they collected all their stuff and got out. The last of the single women were leaving as Jolie came out of the house. Her eyes were wide as she approached, dressed in jeans and a T-shirt. She was gorgeous even in the stupidest things. He hated her shirt, but it was everything she was.

'Coexist' was written in rainbow colors.

He could hear Alexei curse out, ***"Oh, hell."***

Adrik chuckled.

"Hi!" Jolie approached eagerly, like she was dying for some conversation. "Oh, my God, it's so beautiful out. I feel like I haven't been out in weeks."

Because she hadn't been. Adrik kept tabs on her, hoping to find more about her quirks, but she never left her room. Part of him was glad for it; he could keep his hands to himself if he didn't see her. But not seeing her had brought unwanted erotic thoughts that came barreling into his brain at this moment. One of those thoughts wondered what she would look like in a bathing suit and soaking wet.

"Join us," Alexei invited, moving slightly for her to sit on the same lounge chair. "You got a suit?"

"Actually, no. I don't know how to swim."

Adrik wondered if it was a lie, simply to hide her bruises. They should be on the verge of healing but still visible. He wanted to see them to assure himself she was getting better. "You're a Floridian who doesn't know how to swim?"

"Yeah, I know. I got made fun of enough, thanks," Jolie bit back, making his smirk widen.

Alexei interjected, "How has your stay been?"

Jolie shrugged. "Great, I guess. You guys live like kings here; I'm not used to it. I kind of miss baking."

Alexei wondered with excitement, "You bake?"

"Yeah, like cupcakes and cookies. My mom and I would always bake on the weekends and give them out at church."

Adrik was glad the sunglasses hid his face. She was too much in her good ways; he almost couldn't stand it. But it made him wonder. No one was perfect, so what were her flaws? Why did it intrigue him so much to find out?

Adrik cut in, "Religion is for the weak-minded. A way to control the masses."

Jolie shrugged. "It works. And it gives people confidence, security, and hope. What a terrible thing."

Alexei snickered, but the glare from his brother snapped him shut, and he coughed.

"Is this what you guys do on your days off? Bask in the sun and enjoy beautiful women?"

Alexei quickly sputtered. "Oh, no, no, I'm not for"—he waved a hand—"all that. Adrik's more…" He glanced toward him, and Adrik waited for what he was 'more' of. Alexei finished with, "For that."

Jolie giggled. "Okay."

Adrik wanted to change the subject and asked what he'd been dying to know. "What did you and my father talk about?"

The happiness on her face drifted, and she turned away, avoiding his gaze. His fist tightened at his side. He avoided Jolie all this past week. He knew if he found out Yakov threatened her, he'd do something stupid.

Alexei cut in. "Don't mind Papa, okay? He's a bit"—he paused and thought of a word—"um, paranoid?"

"And a hunter, apparently," Jolie nipped.

Alexei sneered. "Yeah, I never enjoyed hunting. Animals are so much better than people."

"I know, right! My cats are my best friends, literally."

Alexei chuckled, and Adrik could tell he was enjoying her in the same way that he was, but Alexei was much more obvious about it. There would be no doubt that if things kept going in this direction, Jolie was gonna fall for his brother. They were clearly a better fit.

Am I jealous?

Adrik stood, gaining her swift attention. He didn't need to look at her to know her eyes were on him. He worked out two hours a day to have a body like this and used it now. He stretched unnecessarily. "I'm going in."

Adrik jumped in the pool to clear his head. He didn't fight for girls. Girls fought for him. That was the way the world worked. Alexei had a lot more practice fighting for girls because they were always choosing Adrik. Even though they looked similar, Alexei didn't project sex appeal as well as Adrik did. He was less confident, more in the background, fearful to look a woman in the eye.

Adrik swam to the pool's edge, putting his arms up as he looked at the two of them talking. He didn't know how to interrupt without it seeming obvious, but he wanted her to look at him.

And then she did, with no incentive. Her eyes slipped over to him for just a fraction of a moment, and though it could have meant nothing, he didn't believe it did.

His confidence was restored, and Adrik threw himself on his back and stared at the sky with smug satisfaction.

"We own an animal shelter," Alexei told her.

Jolie couldn't stop her gaze from going over to Adrik. With every move of his muscles, it was like artwork. The water glittered around, reflecting off his smooth, hairless skin like a snake slithering in the water. He was beautiful, and it was hard not to watch or feel something in the middle of her belly. "That's awesome," she replied, focusing on Alexei. He was way better at conversation than Adrik was, and he didn't make her nervous.

But Alexei was not a friend. Every word out of his mouth was fake. Mally said he talked about killing her, and from there, any bridge they could have built or any friendship that could have formed was impossible. Despite Adrik being a womanizer, he hadn't threatened to harm her.

Just forced me to live with him so he wouldn't kill anyone, Jolie reminded herself. "Who were all those people?"

"Workers," Alexei quickly answered. "Some family."

"Do you have a lot of family?"

"Oh, yeah, we're pretty big. You still haven't met our sisters. They live in Russia with all my nieces and nephews. My father's parents had nine kids, and my mother's parents had ten. From there, everyone had six, seven. So, I have over a hundred cousins."

"Oh, God. Christmas must suck. I don't have any family. I was an only child, and my parents' parents are dead. My father had a brother, but he died. My mother's brother lives in Texas. I've never met him."

Alexei pitied her. "That sounds lonely." He looked over his shoulder at his brother. "I couldn't be without my family. Especially my brother."

Jolie melted under those words. Nothing was more adorable than sibling adoration. "You're not married? No kids?"

"No, no. I'm..." Alexei stifled his words. He wasn't about to say he was waiting for the perfect woman, because that sounded too much like a line, despite it being true. Unlike Adrik, he was allowed to marry any person he wanted. As long as they were Russian. Alexei shifted uncomfortably, and said, "I'm selective. What about you?"

Jolie took a breath, sighing out, "No. I can't seem to find someone worth my time."

Alexei cackled, "Yeah, I get that, too."

"Hey." Adrik broke in from the side of the pool. He had his phone in his hand. ***"Did you start up distribution for the Toxins?"***

"Yeah."

"Why?"

"Because it was causing problems." Alexei glanced at Jolie before switching to Russian, ***"There were three murders this past week."***

Adrik dropped his phone, glaring at Alexei. ***"You should have fucking talked to me. I talked to you about doing shit without me."***

"I'm not gonna come to you with every little problem. I can handle shit on my own."

"That's the problem, Alexei; you can't handle shit, because you aren't in charge. You talk to me or Papa. They fucked us, and I don't want to deal with them anymore."

Alexei got up, approaching. ***"What did they do?"***

"They pissed me off."

Alexei threw a hand in the air. ***"You'd destroy our family if someone pissed you off. You got to grow the fuck up."***

"You piss me off."

"Yeah, same."

Jolie stood, hoping to stop their argument, "You guys okay?"

Alexei shook his head, stomping away into the house, leaving Jolie bewildered.

She looked down at Adrik and accused, "What did you say?"

Adrik lifted himself out of the pool, and her question was instantly forgotten. Water dripped around him as he stood. The sun shined like a spotlight, his skin sparkling like a marble statue. Jolie couldn't close her mouth as he approached, his blue eyes on her, pinning her where she stood. This last week, she was desperate to lay eyes on him but was too paranoid to go to breakfast. The pen was starting to feel like a hot poker in her pocket, a constant reminder that she was playing a dangerous game.

When Adrik leaned in, her heart pounded in her throat. She could scarcely breathe, watching with parted lips, noticing how the closer he got, the more she leaned in.

Adrik snatched the towel off his chair and swung it around his shoulders with a grin. "You okay?"

The tease broke her, and Jolie forced out sarcasm. "You are a bigger ass than I can handle."

"That's probably true." He rubbed his face dry, running the towel through his hair and spraying her with water.

She flinched with aggravation, "Would you stop?"

Wrapping the towel around his waist, he asked casually, "What did my father say to you?"

Jolie bowed her head, afraid he'd see the fear in her eyes. His father was way more frightening than any of them. Adrik knew it, or he wouldn't be so concerned. She didn't want to cause a problem, so she answered with a light response, "To not leave the house without someone. I specifically remember asking if I was a prisoner here."

"You are not a prisoner, but you need an escort."

"Yeah, thanks for the email, even if it is a few days late."

"I aim to please."

"I doubt that." Jolie went to step around him, but his hand rested on her wrist, stalling her. She stared down at it, at his fingers. There were so many tattoos she didn't know where one began and another started. She wanted to know what each one of them meant. Why had he suffered such pain for them?

His fingers drifted up her arm, shifting the sleeve teasingly before he dropped his hand. Her bruises were still heavily visible. "Did he threaten you?" Adrik turned his attention to the water so she couldn't see the aggravation on his face. What made it worse was the fact the Toxins weren't admitting to anything.

Jolie shrugged, "Not badly."

He nodded, clenching his teeth.

Jolie's stomach was in knots. His touch caused a shiver up her spine that she didn't want to confront. His father's threat came to her then. It was another sign that whatever was forming between them wouldn't ever be more than a dream. "You shouldn't be talking to me," she whispered. "Your father wouldn't like it."

He knew she was right. There was no telling who was watching. But he never liked being told what he could and could not do. The temptation to touch her was right under his fingertips. If he was daring enough.

Adrik reluctantly stepped back. "Get a suit. I have much to teach you." He backed up and waited for the blush to cross her cheeks before turning away.

Chapter Twenty

Father's Orders

Adrik sat in his room, with a drink in his hands. A half-empty bottle of vodka rested on the nightstand beside him. The effects of the liquor were starting to make the room spin, and he enjoyed the numbness of his body. If he could function like this, he would be drunk for the rest of his life. All the thoughts in his head that blared with a red flashing light were now loose pieces of paper flying in the wind above him, and he had no desire to reach for them, to keep them in order, or to find solutions to each problem. He laughed instead, letting the wind blow away all of his stress.

He stood, and the world wobbled.

Adrik held onto the nightstand. With more focus than he should need, he made it out the door without hitting the wall and down the hallway. It was dark, with only a dim nightlight against the wall to guide him. His hand dragged across Helina's door until he stood before Katia's. He didn't bother knocking. He pushed his way in and shut the door behind him.

Katia sat in bed, holding the blanket to her chest. The only light came from the backyard.

"What are you doing here?"

Adrik leaned back against the door, staying in the dark. It's been a few years since he came into her room.

Resentment was impossible to quell as memories assaulted him.

They got married at eighteen and struggled with infertility for years. Adrik shared Katia's bed every night till she was six months pregnant. He had known no other woman, staying loyal to her, helping her through emotional upheavals and uncontrollable fears when she thought the baby wouldn't make it. He had been present at every doctor's appointment. They had the beginnings of a beautiful family.

Until a simple text message on her phone made him realize she was cheating on him the entire time.

It shattered the future, shattered his heart and any chance at healing. And because of her actions, he hadn't bonded with Helina when she was first born. He had to wait for a DNA test to confirm she was his. Only then did he allow himself to hold her. Two months of her life he missed out on because Katia couldn't keep her legs shut. Her cheating not only denied him a future with a wife and daughter at his side. It denied him the ability to connect. He felt like he was holding someone's kid for a long time. It wasn't until she called him 'Papa' that the world righted itself, and he'd been addicted to Helina ever since, trying to make up for the years he was indifferent to her existence.

"Father wants another kid," Adrik said, putting his hands in his pockets and resting his head against the door. He thought it would be possible to touch her if he drank enough to forget, but the memories were resurfacing like a sunken body that escaped its chains. He closed his eyes, swallowing.

This bedroom reminded him of their first night together. The bedsheets and furniture were the same. It was like entering a portal going back in time.

Her whimpers echoed in his ears.

Adrik had never forced himself on a woman. And Katia hadn't fought him. But she didn't want him, and it had been apparent how she trembled.

"You still beat yourself up." She brought her legs into her chest. "I've let it go. You should, too."

He forced a bitter chuckle. He doubted she let anything go. Katia was a vengeful woman despite how hard she played perfection. "I'm not a fucking…" He couldn't even say the word. It was ridiculous, he knew. He killed, tortured, and did other horrible things, yet this gave him PTSD.

"You did what you had to. Just as I did."

It was a different way to make rape sound less rape-y, but it didn't fix it.

Katia straightened her back. "But if you touch me now, I'll fight you the whole fucking time."

Adrik met her gaze. Her features were hardened, and there was a knife in her hand. She must be sleeping with it. He almost wanted to fight her just to fight. Maybe in the effort, he'd kill her, and then he wouldn't have to fuck her.

"I'm not having another baby."

"What am I going to tell my father?"

"I don't give a shit. Tell him I'm barren. Tell him you can't get it up. I don't get you sometimes, Adrik. You act like such a badass, but then Daddy says something, and you become a little bitch."

Adrik stepped forward, and she quickly moved to her knees, both hands on the hilt. He thought of how he'd snatch it out of her hand, press it against her neck, and make her regret ever challenging him.

"You should know by now he always gets his way."

"You are more powerful than him."

Adrik shook his head. "That's what he wants us to think." Dizziness overcame him, and he stumbled back till he hit the door.

"You can't fuck anyway. How much have you drunk?"

He couldn't remember.

"I'll pretend." She lowered the knife back beneath the blanket. "I'll say something tomorrow about being up late. We can pretend."

It sounded nice. And if it worked, that would be great. But it had to be convincing.

Adrik pulled his shirt over his head. Her eyes were wide, panicked. Despite how she said she would fight, if he attempted, she'd have to cave. It was part of the contract. She wanted to act like he was the only one who followed orders.

Adrik tossed his shirt on the floor.

Taking his lead, Katia got up and messed up the neatly made bed, pulling all the sheets into a big pile. With the cover of her nightgown, she pulled her panties off and left them on the floor. She looked at him, hoping that was enough.

"You better put on a good show. Or I'll have to."

She nodded, trembling.

Adrik stayed for five more minutes before he left, shutting the door. It was a relief and a brand-new stress all at once. He didn't know if getting it over with was better. What would the punishment be if his father found out about his lie?

Adrik walked down the hallway, sluggish, with a hand on the wall to help keep him steady. His feet stopped of their own accord when his fingers dragged across Jolie's door. He stared at the doorknob, imagining what would happen if he were to go inside. Would she welcome him to her bed? With a single touch, she'd heal all the damage inflicted on his soul. He'd be brand-new again, unsoiled by the sludge. She'd find the parts of him buried beneath his father's world. He'd be different somehow in her hands. Better.

Adrik glanced behind him and found Katia standing in the doorway. She met his gaze, reading him in an instant. Katia knew what he was feeling even though he still wasn't quite sure. She knew because she had felt it once.

Adrik realized then that she'd never forgive him for killing her lover. And in the unstable mess of his mind, he wondered what she would do to exact revenge.

Adrik turned away, too tired to think more of it.

Chapter Twenty-One

Two Years

Adrik took a seat at the breakfast table, with his coffee and cell phone. He scrolled with his thumb, searching for anything interesting in the news. Sometimes, the media was faster than his own people. It was because of the chain of command that kept information slow. Like the military, there were levels. The lowest soldier could only speak to the next in command, and so on and so forth. To the lower levels, he was a ghost, a figment of their nightmares, the god they worshiped, and the devil they feared.

That being said, news sometimes took time to pass through the ranks, making the media outlet the second-best thing.

He was searching for Katia's brother.

Zinof Stephanov was the third-born son of the Stephanov family. He was insignificant, aside from being very protective of his younger sister. He had been against Katia's marriage, even insulting them by refusing to come to the wedding.

And now, he tried to kill their daughter.

Zinof's life was forfeited. He knew it, which was why he went underground.

The thing about guys like Zinof was they wanted attention and to feel important, which meant he wouldn't hide for long. The ache for the spotlight would drive him to the surface. All Adrik had to do was pay attention to the tide.

"Good morning."

Adrik snapped his head up as Jolie sat at the breakfast table. He was becoming desperate to see her. She was dressed in a tight maxi dress that exemplified her bust and the shape of her hips. It was a modest dress, but she looked amazing, nonetheless.

Six days had passed since he last saw her. He wanted to talk to her for no reason but to get her attention, but sneaking into Jolie's room wasn't as easy as he hoped.

Katia had conveniently slept in Helina's room last night, like a sentinel guarding Jolie's door.

The fading bruise on her arm distracted him from her gaze. It was discolored now, lighter, but so clearly a handprint. A wave of disgust rolled through him, and he quickly turned away with a muffled, 'Good morning.' He put his attention back on his cell phone. Anything else would be questioned.

Finding Jolie's attacker was another added weight, but this was more difficult. Adrik was using most of his force to find Zinof, and Alexei was in charge of it, so Gil was the only person currently searching for the man who had hurt Jolie. And Gil tended to get sidetracked with drugs and women.

Yakov joined the table and began speaking with Jolie about stupid shit. His father didn't even mention the bruise, not caring about who would harm a woman. His attention was on shopping and inviting her to go out with Katia for dresses for the family dinner on Saturday. She was surprised she was invited and expressed excitement.

A smile pressed on his lips, and he covered it by leaning on his hand. Jolie didn't know the kind of dinners they hosted. Adrik stuffed any humor down his throat and mumbled in Russian, ***"She's not ready, Papa."***

"Nonsense," he replied in English. "You want to go, yes?"

Adrik flicked his eyes toward her, and Jolie nodded with enthusiasm.

"Then, she shall come. I want to show off this girl who saved my granddaughter's life. Katia! We were just talking about you."

Adrik glanced at Jolie again, and her eyes touched his for a moment, but she bowed her head, leaning down to take a bite of food.

"Good things, I hope." Katia rested her hands on the back of Adrik's shoulders. He gripped her fingers and brought them to his lips, playing the role. She leaned down and gave him a soft, sweet kiss on the cheek. ***"Good morning, my beast."***

Yakov smiled wide. ***"This makes me happy. Even on a troubled ocean, come calm seas."***

It was the fourth morning they showed such nauseating affection, and Yakov was eating it up. But with Jolie at the table, he nervously fidgeted, hoping she didn't take their actions seriously.

Katia walked around Yakov and kissed his cheek, too. He tapped her hand and waved for her to sit. "I was telling Miss Bell that you would take her shopping for a fine dress. One to match you in beauty."

"Of course, Papa." Katia raved, turning to Jolie, "Our dinners are extravagant but entertaining."

Adrik flicked his narrowed eyes over his phone and met her condescending smile.

Katia continued, "I would love to take out Jolie. Perhaps tomorrow."

"Of course, of course."

Alexei arrived, greeting them all a good morning. He took the chair beside Jolie, leaning in to get her to smile at him. "Hey, I was hoping I'd see you."

Jolie's face reddened, but she enthusiastically greeted him. "You work so much. I thought you would have more fun than this."

Alexei chuckled. "Nope, I oversee a lot of different things. Plus, I have to babysit my little brother."

Jolie glanced at Adrik. He sat back with his arms crossed. "You babysit me? Were you doing so two nights ago when I dragged your drunk ass out of a casino?"

Jolie put a hand over her mouth. She had never experienced sibling rivalry but knew how to spot it a mile away. It was similar to kindergarteners trying to top each other.

Alexei quickly changed the subject, asking Yakov, "What time will Mama be here on Friday?"

"Four, but I'm sure she will want to rest. You'll see her Saturday."

Alexei moved in to whisper toward Jolie, "You are going to love Mama. She's over the top. One time, she..."

Adrik wasn't listening as he watched his brother and Jolie. They were so comfortable around each other, like they were friends, yet Alexei had been just as busy this past week as far as he knew. They didn't get any extra time together.

But they also didn't have a wall between them like he had with Jolie. Alexei could hit on her in front of their father without risking her life.

It was a depressing thought. But Adrik had to keep his distance. It was better for both of them. And if she fell for his brother, he'd have to accept it and move on.

It didn't stop Adrik from doing what he could to keep them apart. ***"Perhaps it is a good chance for Alexei to meet someone."***

Yakov glanced at his son and shrugged. ***"Can't rush love."***

Love, his father said, like it's a realistic goal in their world.

For Alexei, he was allowed to be picky and wait around for it because he was no longer heir to their father's empire.

Katia whispered, hiding her teasing smile, ***"He does seem smitten with our teacher, doesn't he?"***

Adrik glared at her from across the table, and she hid a giggle behind her hand.

Alexei glanced at them angrily. ***"I'm just trying to make her feel welcome."***

Yakov scoffed, taking a sip of his coffee. ***"Even Alexei wouldn't be dumb enough to go for an American."***

The insult was straightforward, and the warning was blatant. Adrik felt guilty for bringing it up. He didn't like his father taking potshots at his brother. Despite being younger, Adrik protected Alexei against his father since they were kids. Alexei had a softer heart than most, and it always irked his father.

"But you're right," Yakov said, decided, setting down his mug. ***"We must introduce him to someone."***

"What?" Alexei straightened.

"Katia, you know some women. Bring them."

"Of course," Katia smiled lovingly to hide her humor.

Alexei sneered. ***"I'm good meeting girls on my own."***

"It's just for options, son," Yakov assured. ***"I want more grandchildren. God knows your sisters are working hard, and Katia and Adrik are doing their part. You have to pull your weight at some point."***

Another jab agitated Alexei. He excused himself abruptly, and Jolie, having no idea what was going on, looked after him in bewilderment.

"He's fine," Katia reassured Jolie. "What kind of dress are you thinking of?"

Adrik moved to follow his brother, but his father stopped him.

"You haven't finished your breakfast."

"I'm not hungry."

Yakov looked up at him. ***"I haven't finished mine."***

Clenching his teeth, Adrik plopped back down and concentrated on his cell phone. It was this controlling attitude that Adrik had followed his whole life that had him bucking in his restraints. He was tired of being leashed. He was so close to the finish line. Only two more years till his father claimed he would retire, and Adrik would take over the company. Two more years to follow every rule and unspoken law, and then he was free.

If I kill him, I could be free tomorrow.

It's a distant, unthinkable thought, yet it waved in the back of his mind like a white flag on a body-filled field.

Killing parents was against the Mafia code, and he'd be shunned. But if he could make it look like someone else did it, he could get away with it. The problem was trusting someone with such a task. Failure couldn't be an option, because the ramifications would be too terrifying to think of. Who had enough confidence to believe they could kill a king?

As soon as Yakov took the last bite of his toast, Adrik excused himself from the table.

He found Alexei in the gym at the punching bag. His hands were wrapped in thick tape, and he was railing on the bag with his right arm, keeping his left back. His injured arm was healing but couldn't withstand punching just yet. The person holding the bag was struggling to keep it still. When Alexei took a small break, Adrik dismissed the help and took hold of it.

Alexei paused at the sight of him. He rubbed the sweat from his brow and adjusted the tape. The words in Alexei's mind weren't something he could share, but he struggled to keep them to himself. There was a dark place inside him Alexei was worried that Adrik wouldn't approve of. He hit the bag once, twice before he huffed, ***"I don't know how much longer I can put up with him."***

"I know."

"He acts like I'm choosing to be alone when he forced me to shove Melissa out of my life."

Adrik kept quiet. He hadn't known about what happened between him and Melissa. Alexei had been infatuated with the anime oddball for years, and then suddenly, she was gone. Alexei said he broke up with her and got drunk for a few days before he went back to work. That was the extent of the conversation.

But as Adrik thought about it, after Melissa was gone, two months later, Alexei gave up his seat as heir.

"When we were younger—" Alexei took up a bottle of water, swallowing some before he questioned, ***"Did you ever think about leaving?"***

Adrik had always wanted to be better than his father. He couldn't do that if he ran away. He knew where his place was. The only way to protect his brother, to help this family, was to be the one to lead it. Adrik shook his head.

"I almost left a dozen times."

"He'd find you, Alexei. You know that."

Alexei distantly nodded. He knew there was no escape. But he hoped by now things would be different. He didn't want to have his pride taken from him daily. He didn't want to be forced to live the way his father wanted. He was nearly twenty-nine-years old, but life hadn't changed all that much from when he was a ten-year-old helpless boy.

"Two more years," Alexei murmured, lightly hitting the punching bag. He met his brother's eyes, hoping he'd find something there. A silent request to do what they both wanted.

But Adrik only whispered, ***"Two more years."***

Chapter Twenty-Two

Touch

The Toxins had called a truce. Adrik stared at the picture on his phone. On the screen was the man who attacked Jolie. He was handcuffed, with a gag in his mouth. He was bleeding in several places. Under the picture was a text message. '*At the dock. Though we weren't aware that girl was part of your family, we apologize. Let this rectify our disagreement.*'

Adrik bit his lip as he clicked off his phone and tossed it on the table. *'Weren't aware the girl was yours,'* he repeated. If the Toxins hadn't gone after her because of Adrik, why did they target her?

Was it simply a hit-and-run?

Had he gone there to rape her?

Adrik shifted uncomfortably as a roll of hot rage spiraled down into his stomach.

"What is it?" Gil wondered, sitting on the other side of Adrik's desk. He played with a squishy, tossing it up in the air and then squeezing till the beads nearly broke through the skin.

Adrik leaned back in his chair, gesturing to the phone, and Gil took it up to look. He smiled and nodded. ***"Good stuff."***

"Why did they go after her?"

He shrugged. ***"Young girl, living alone, new to town. Perfect pickings."***

"The Toxins don't deal in human trafficking."

Gil paused, racking his brain. But one thing about Gil, he didn't like to think. ***"Don't know. Have you asked her?"***

Adrik looked around his office. The room was three floors up on the opposite end of the house, furthest from his father's. He liked the sunlight and had glass walls leading to the rooftop terrace that overlooked the pool. There were three men in here, two of them playing pool. 'Friends,' they would call themselves, but

Adrik kept everyone at arm's length. A *friend* had tried to murder him three years ago. The scar on his back was covered by a Grim Reaper tattoo.

Adrik stood, and Gil nearly dropped the ball as he watched him. ***"Where you going?"***

"To ask her."

Gil jumped to his feet, cursing, nearly falling before he snatched his crutches off the floor. He used every muscle to sway his body forward as fast as possible to catch up. ***"You know that's not a good idea. You need to stay away."***

"Avoiding her like the plague is just as obvious as pursuing her." Adrik stood before the elevator doors, glaring at his reflection. ***"Meanwhile, my brother is moving in on her."***

"Then, let him." Gil snatched Adrik's arm. ***"Adrik, think about this."***

Adrik fisted his hands on his side, and calmly said, ***"I am simply going to ask her questions. I'm not going to fuck her."***

Gil scoffed. ***"You think I don't know you? You need to stay away from her."***

Adrik stared at the open elevator. He knew he should listen, but he didn't want to. He stepped into the elevator, and Gil was shaking his head.

"Try not to get caught."

Adrik could at least follow that advice. He shut off his phone, unsure if he was being tracked or not. He fixed the collar of his shirt in the reflection of the elevator doors, flicking some black hair back into place. He cursed himself for doing something so trite. He actually felt nervous.

It's just questions, he reminded himself, but he knew going to her bedroom always ignited a flame of hope for something more.

Adrik had kept as busy as possible this past week. He packed his schedule with the stupidest shit, hoping to avoid Jolie at all costs. And the one day he gave himself to relax and regroup, he found himself heading to her door. It was pathetic. But it didn't seem to stop him.

Adrik dived into his daughter's room. Helina was at her desk, writing while Jolie stood behind her. She still wore the maxi dress from this morning that amplified all her curves with insane accuracy. He could see the outline of her 'grandma' panties, and it did nothing to cripple his attraction.

Adrik cleared his throat and spoke in Russian. ***"It's time for a break. Go find Esfir."***

"Yes!" Helina squealed, darting out the door.

Jolie crossed her arms. "We still have twenty minutes left. Where did she go?"

Adrik shut the door behind him, and he met her eyes. "You shouldn't come to breakfast."

Jolie leaned back on the table. "I learned that on my first day. But your father requested it. Should I ignore it?"

Adrik slipped his hands into his pockets to keep him from approaching her. Distance was his friend. "Why?"

She shrugged. It made him go over every moment of the last two weeks. There was no way his father would suspect anything. But it could be more about getting her and Katia together. "Do you plan to go dress shopping with Katia?"

"I don't think I have a choice. I'm beginning to see why you guys walk on eggshells around him."

The insult nearly choked him, and he nipped, "I don't walk around on eggshells."

She winced with a suppressed smile. "Sorry. I hit a soft spot."

He sneered. "I can rule this family without him."

"Okay!" she squeaked. "I'm sorry. You're the man." But her smile only got bigger.

Adrik realized then what she was doing. "You're teasing me."

She proudly smirked, her hands resting on the table. "A little payback."

Adrik ground his teeth. It wasn't anger he was feeling. It was something much more primal than he wanted to admit. He kept still and glared, because anything else would give away exactly what he was feeling.

Then a smile slipped on his lips. "I can see your nipples."

With incredible speed, she slapped her arms over her chest. Her smug expression turned horrified. "You're an ass."

He chuckled deep in his throat. "Don't play a game if you don't want to be beaten."

"Was there something you wanted?" Jolie left then, heading into her bedroom through the side door. He followed behind, quiet, observing. She dug into a drawer, pulled something out, and disappeared into the bathroom.

Adrik sat in the chair, hating how her bed was the most significant and noticeable thing in the room. "I wanted to warn you about Katia. She isn't exactly trustworthy. Don't believe what you hear."

When Jolie came out again, she stood before him boldly, with her hands on her hips. It was almost a dare to look at her breasts, and he had no problem taking it. He flicked his eyes to her bosom but was disappointed that her nipples were no longer so prominent. As much as he enjoyed nipple pasties on a naked woman, it was discouraging that she took away one of her best features.

Jolie smiled, fake and forced, before she sat down. "She's been super nice so far. And the only person that talks to me," Jolie admitted, avoiding his gaze. She didn't want to sound pathetic, but the truth was, living here was incredibly lonely. And this came from someone who had lived alone in a strange city for the past three months, with no friends. She felt unwanted and discarded. Mostly because Adrik had been completely avoiding her.

Jolie knew life here wouldn't be easy, but she had never imagined it to be boring and depressing. The only purpose she had was to get up and teach Helina. After four o'clock, Jolie dived into her room and didn't return until the following day. All her meals were brought to her. If she didn't have something to read, she'd have gone insane by now. She felt too afraid to go for walks. She felt too intimidated to ask to go anywhere. If she needed anything from the store, she handed a list to Esfir, and the items would be delivered an hour later. She missed all the mundane chores that she used to hate, like cleaning and reorganizing. Everything was taken care of by someone else.

And on top of all of this, there was the stress of helping Agent Mally.

Jolie needed help figuring out how to get her the information she wanted. And she was afraid to try. She wasn't used to this type of betrayal. She was a nice person, someone people trusted, and she didn't know how to be a spy.

Jolie peeked at Adrik, but he was currently picking lint off his pants. What did a mafia ruler care about her living situation? She was quick to brighten herself up. "Helina's so smart. She's gonna be speaking English in no time."

Adrik folded his hands in his lap. "Regardless, Katia is not your friend. Don't be fooled."

Her brows knitted. She felt like he wasn't listening to a word she was saying. "Okay."

"And my brother. He is not who you think he is."

Jolie let her aggravation shine. "Yeah, none of you are; you're mafia." Jolie stood. "Like, what am I supposed to do? Not talk to anyone? I already have no one here. Stop trying to take away the only people that will talk to me."

"I'm talking to you."

"Yeah, the first time in days. And according to you, you're the only person I can trust. Great."

Adrik hated passive-aggressive attitudes. It was a pet peeve. "I'm not paying you to have friends."

"I'm doing my job, but you can't control how I live despite how hard you try."

He paused, trying to figure out why that hurt him. "Is that what you think? I'm trying to control you?"

"Yes," she sighed.

Adrik looked out the window. This wasn't the first time someone accused him of being controlling. It was a trait he had gotten from his father and one he was desperate to destroy.

But there was a reason he was the way he was. "Perhaps I am. But it's for your safety."

"Why? Am I too stupid—"

"Not stupid," he cut her off, refusing to let her put words in his mouth. "But ignorant. Unless you've suddenly educated yourself on the culture of the Russian Mafia." He stared at her and waited for a battle, but he knew he was right when she bowed her head. "I understand this life is an adjustment. But focus on the benefits."

Jolie nodded, blinking back the tears. She didn't know why she hoped he'd fix it, break this weird wall between them. She wanted the man who first came in with a smirk on his lips. Not this emotionless husk. "I am," she murmured, if only to appear grateful. "I'll be able to save. I can pay back my student loans. I can eventually send my parents some money, and they can get a new car. Maybe even get them to Disney; they've always wanted to be one of those old couples that go all the time. This is just a momentary sacrifice." She sniffed, clearing her head, and pushed back all the sadness. She needed to focus on the ultimate goal of why she was doing this.

I'm not here for a relationship, she reminded herself. *It doesn't matter how he treats me. I'm a tutor. Nothing else.*

Adrik suddenly changed the subject. "The police are having a hard time finding your attacker."

Her smile drifted.

"I thought perhaps I could help."

Her fingers reached for a chair. "He's still out there?"

She didn't know why she believed the police would have no trouble tracking down her intruder. It seemed like such an easy thing to do. She had given them a description of his face. She had done her part. So, why hadn't they done theirs?

Jolie sat down, holding her ribs as if the pain suddenly escalated. It had been two weeks, and she was just now able to breathe without a problem. Her bruises were slowly fading, and the nightmares weren't as intense. But it was under the belief that her attacker was off the streets.

"Can you think of any reason someone would attack you?"

She scoffed. "Aside from knowing you?"

"The Toxins had no reason to come after me."

Her brows knitted, and she shook her head. Her thoughts were weaving all through her features, but she stayed silent, staring at the ground.

"He came from the window," she suddenly began. She cleared her throat, forcing out the terrible emotions the memories stirred. "He could have shot me, but he didn't. He wanted to hurt me. I ran to the bathroom, but he started beating the door down. I set his mask on fire with hairspray and a lighter."

Adrik smirked and repeated, "You set his mask on fire?"

Jolie could see the humor in his face. It made her proud. "Yeah."

"I'm impressed." Adrik rested his elbows on his knees, two inches from her, and if he dared, he could reach out and touch her hand. "Maybe your thoughts on gun control—"

"Haven't changed!"

He chuckled, his eyes light, and he admired the smile that graced her lips.

Even as the seconds ticked by, simply staring at her, Adrik felt no need to be anywhere else. In her presence was enough. He soaked her in like a wet dog in the sunlight. She warmed him to his core.

He tried so hard to remain distant, but he was losing the fight. He could only pretend not to care for so long until he broke. Now, Adrik found himself saying, "Go out with me tonight." He didn't regret it. He had spent weeks apart from her already. He needed a recharge before he forced himself to go any longer.

"Okay."

A finger stretched, touching her knuckle. Adrik kept his eyes on hers, suddenly desperate to get her to understand how much he was hiding, how he was pretending. Her cheeks reddened, but the desire was very much in her eyes, and she swallowed, parched, as her heart rate escalated.

Adrik added a second finger, a feathery touch across her knuckles. He couldn't believe such a small action would cause him to lose his breath. It was dangerous, but it was the kind that excited him. He wanted to feel her skin atop his, with her lips at his ear.

But a reminder came swiftly through the fantasy. If Katia or a servant came in right now, it would be over. She'd be taken from him.

Adrik sat up suddenly, breaking from her. "Wait for a text." He dived out of the room, feeling like a fucking coward.

Chapter Twenty-Three

Courage

Jolie stared at her reflection. She wore tight jeans, a nice blouse, and decorative sandals. She was going for a less 'boy look' while trying to be casual. Her hair was curled and layered, with just a bit of eyeliner to help her brown eyes pop. And though she appeared calm and collected on the outside, she felt out of breath as her heart pounded excitedly. She didn't know if this was a date or something else, but it certainly made her stomach twist like it was.

Stop it, she chided herself. *It's just lust. It's desperation. It's his undeniable sex appeal.*

There were so many reasons to be attracted to Adrik.

And so many reasons to be afraid of him.

Jolie attempted to cover the bruise on her arm, but the coverup only made it look like a bruise with makeup on it.

A knock on her door made her jump, and she spun toward it. A voice on the other end muffled through. "Miss Bell, I'm here to take you to your parents."

My parents? Who said I'm going to my parents?

Then it dawned on her. It was code. Adrik was not taking any chances.

Jolie snatched the listening device off her dresser and slipped it into her purse. She wasn't going to use it, but there was always an underlying fear that something terrible could happen to her at any moment. She hoped Agent Mally didn't put much stock in her ability to get good information. Jolie wouldn't know even if she succeeded. They spoke Russian more than sixty percent of the time.

A text message beeped on her phone, and she clicked it. *'I'll meet you.'*

It was from an unknown number, but she knew it was Adrik. Though it made her smile, it didn't last long. The extent he's going through to keep anyone suspecting was disconcerting.

It brought Yakov's warning to her head. '*You were hired as a tutor, and that is what you will do. Anything else will violate your contract, and I will turn you out faster than I gutted that lion.*'

Another text binged, but this was from her mother. '*Where is this man taking you? I need the exact address.*'

Jolie texted back, '*Can you not be so paranoid?*'

'*You're my only child. I will be paranoid even when I'm dead. Address.*'

Though her mother's overprotectiveness was annoying, Jolie was used to it by now. '*I'll send it once I know.*'

There was another knock, and Jolie was out the door, following the foot soldier, trying to even out her breathing as she went. She felt giddy, like a kid the night before Christmas.

"Jolie!" Alexei called from the living room as she passed. She spun from the front door, hoping to have an innocent, not caught-in-the-headlights look, but she was sure he saw everything in the reflection of her eyes. Alexei slipped his hands into his pockets. With an unreserved look down her form, he said, "You look nice; where are you headed?"

"Um, uh, oh, am."

Alexei cackled. "Oh, interesting place."

Jolie cleared her throat and flushed with embarrassment, forcing out, "My mom's, sorry."

"Oh, good. Alright. I was going to ask you out for tonight, but you're busy."

The confession was announced so casually Jolie almost didn't catch it. It took a second for her mind to fully process, and then she blinked. "You were?"

Alexei smirked, an exact replica of Adrik's that nearly melted her. It was a sin how much they looked alike. "I was. But, uh, I'll let you go. Maybe we can go to my mom's dinner together."

Panic clogged her thoughts, and she mindlessly responded, "Maybe."

Alexei backed up. "Alright." His smile never faded. "Have fun." He watched as she left the house. He bit his lip, proud of himself despite it taking over two weeks to gain the courage to do it. He realized he hadn't felt like this in a long ass time. Denying it only worsened it to the point where Jolie consumed all his freaking thoughts.

It reminded him of what he felt when he was with Melissa.

At sixteen, Alexei was innocent in everything except death. He had seen his father murder people in front of him and had become immune to the violence. Alexei was known for getting into fights and coming out the winner. And though he had seen his fair share of porn and knew the kind of women his father brought to the house, Alexei was always too shy to pursue anyone. He was never like Gil, who took any random girl to bed, or Adrik, who preferred high-end beauty.

He was selective, as he told Jolie. And though Adrik and Gil called him a pansy every day for years, it never caused him to change. They wouldn't know love if it smacked them in the fucking head. But Alexei had known it once, and perhaps he was trying to find it again.

He met Melissa at sixteen. She was the one who came onto him, stalking up to him at the end of class, asking him if he wanted to hang out. Until that day, he had never noticed her, but after that day, he never forgot her. Alexei had kept her a secret at first. Like a trinket he stole out of Walmart. But his father knew by the end of the first week. Alexei had yet to learn the art of lies. Yakov had acted like it was the best thing: Alexei finally popping his cherry. But a year later, when Melissa was still hanging around, Yakov shared his concern. Alexei was the heir; no unworthy female would take on the Morozov name.

It was this that ended many things for Alexei. It ended his love for his father. It ended his desire to be a boss. It caused a rift in their family that couldn't be mended.

Melissa was married now, with two kids, living in England. She was an illustrator for children's books. He saw her randomly without her knowing, keeping in the back of the crowd at book fairs. It was never a regret breaking up with her, despite how difficult it had been. He saved her life, but the hole she left had never been filled.

Except maybe Jolie could fill it. Alexei was older now, more prepared to deal with his father, more willing to fight. And less caring if his father approved or not.

"Alexei," his father called. ***"Come here, please."***

The muscles in Alexei's jaw clenched, and his eyes darkened. Every part of him wanted to deny his father, but an invisible chain tied to his neck pulled him into the living room. His father sat on the couch, drinking his glass of scotch and reviewing business reports. It was his common end-of-the-night routine. The TV was on, with Judge Judy, the only thing Yakov liked to watch.

Alexei stood behind the couch, with clenched fists. He had purposely asked Jolie within his father's hearing. It was a not-so-subtle dare. Yakov wouldn't do anything but make snide comments. The punishment was worth it. Jolie was worth it.

Yakov leaned back and looked behind him. ***"Do you know why you and I have a problem?"***

"You want to control everything I do."

"I want the best for you, and you don't."

Alexei snickered, shaking his head. It was typical of his father to make him always right and his sons always wrong.

"You have been this way your whole life. Thinking you know better than me. But I've been around a lot longer than you. Your attitude is rubbing off on your brother. He dared to change things while I was away. I've been cleaning up his mess for the last two weeks."

"Adrik knows business, Papa. You should listen to him."

"He listens to podcasts and thinks he's a businessman. But he's not. And neither are you. You make sure to keep Adrik in line, or I'll ship you back to Russia."

The threat was nothing but annoying. ***"Adrik won't let you do that."***

"Last I checked, I am the boss in this family. It sounds like you need a reminder." With a flick of his finger, one of Yakov's soldiers came from the hall. Alexei stepped back, shifting away as the soldier approached. It was Li-Choy, a fighter his father won in a poker game. It was unusual for a Russian mafia to own a Chinese foot soldier, but Yakov had come to like the talented beast. Behind him, Alexei realized his path was blocked by more soldiers.

Alexei ground his teeth. ***"I haven't let you beat me in years; what makes you think I'm going to let you now?"***

Yakov watched his son over the rim of his glass as he sipped his scotch. Alexei curled his fists, refusing to cower as the soldiers stepped closer. ***"I will say this once."*** Yakov placed his glass on the table. ***"This teacher is beneath you. You want to fuck her, fine. But you will not present her to your mother. And you will keep your rebellious attitude to yourself. Adrik is to walk in my footsteps. Not yours. He needs me."***

"He needs you, or you need him?"

Yakov sneered, and with a wave of his hand, he turned back to his paperwork as Li attacked.

Chapter Twenty-Four

Bowling

It took an hour for the driver to bring Jolie wherever Adrik decided for their 'non'-date. She thought for a moment she was actually going to see her parents until they passed the 1-4 interstate and kept heading north. She'd never been up toward Ocala. There were plenty of empty landscapes and cows. It was a different kind of pretty. If she ever had the ability to travel, she'd go north. She always wanted to see mountains and snow.

They pulled into a nearly empty parking lot with only one car, and Adrik leaned against his black Lexus. He looked incredibly sexy, wearing black shoes, light jeans, and a dark shirt. The shirt was tight around his chest and arms, amplifying the muscles. He pushed off the car and approached her door. She took a deep breath to calm her shaking.

Adrik held out his tattooed hand, and she took it. His grip was firm, and it caused sensations down her spine. "I'm surprised," he murmured as he leaned in to kiss her cheek. "You know how to dress sexy."

Her knees wobbled. She swallowed before she replied. "I have many skills," she quipped.

He led her to his car, and replied, "I hope bowling is one."

"Bowling?"

"I like to bowl."

Jolie sat in his car on his leather seat. The interior was personalized with a dark blue. The car smelled like him, his cologne filling every nook. She wanted to drown in it.

Adrik sat beside her, starting the car. The engine vibrated like a purring tiger. He was clearly proud of his car, watching her expression as he revved the engine. She knew she had to compliment it. "Pretty car."

"Pretty? No. Fucking gorgeous."

Jolie shifted, clenching her thighs tighter. She didn't know what about him made her so turned on. Every word out of his mouth could ignite dirty thoughts. She never had this problem before. It was almost unfair how much he clouded her rational thoughts. She could forget the real reason she was here. She could forget how he's a murderer. She could forget that he's supposed to be evil.

But it wasn't right.

He's not a good man. No matter how he treats me. He kills for a living.

Jolie reached into her purse and clicked the pen. It made her nauseous. She didn't want to do it, but her conscience told her she had to. "You've been pretty busy the last couple of weeks. What do you do?"

Adrik shrugged. "Boring shit."

Adrik didn't know how to talk about his work without lying. And one thing he was realizing was that he didn't want to lie to her. He wanted to have someone to talk to without a wall up constantly. And as stupid as it sounded, he found himself trusting her.

Adrik looked at his hand on the steering wheel, once more searching for any sign of blood. He had come from the warehouse at the dock. The man who attacked Jolie had been left in handcuffs for over twenty-four hours. He had been lying in his own shit and piss. He was shivering and desperate, terribly dehydrated and hungry. At first, Adrik thought he had enough torture, but then the man spoke. Talking about Jolie, how she screamed and trembled. He made shit up, talking about fucking her and enjoying it.

The monster in Adrik, the one he tried so hard to conceal, seeped out of him. He had not been kind or gentle. He took the man's hand and broke all five of his fingers one by one, enjoying every cry from his broken lips.

Torture wasn't necessary, but Adrik enjoyed it like a hobby. He had gotten good over the years, learning how to extract the most pain. He found it humorous how some of the smallest actions can cause the biggest cries, like pulling fingernails or flaying skin. The speed at which it's done causes the best reactions; slow and steady were the common denominators.

And by the time he was done, there was only blood and broken bones. It wasn't until the end, till the man was already dead, that Adrik forgot to ask him why the Toxins had targeted Jolie.

Gil took him to a getaway house to shower and find clothes. He had barely managed to meet Jolie in time.

Now, guilt was burying him. He couldn't be honest with her about what he did. She would never talk to him again.

"You're always gone."

"Yes. I own a few dozen businesses. I make my rounds throughout the month. I've been trying to update, but my father believes the old ways are best. Even though I made us more money." Finances was one of the things he didn't mind talking about, and he was eager to share with her the problems he was facing. It was something she would understand better anyway.

"Then, show him that."

"He doesn't listen."

Jolie frowned. "That must be frustrating."

"Very. He never listens. It's why my brother and my father do not get along. I've learned to deal with it. My father won't be around forever. I just have to wait."

Jolie joked, "Why not get rid of him?"

Adrik snapped his head toward her, but seeing her smile, he realized she was playing around. Little did she know that he thought about it more than he wanted to admit. "Funny."

She shrugged. "I told you I have many skills."

"I would love to learn more of these 'skills.' Can I have a breakdown of your talents?"

Jolie loved the banter and fell into it naturally. "Well, we've covered a sense of humor and how to dress."

"And an excessive reader."

"Excessive sounds negative."

"But accurate."

Jolie shrugged. There was no denying that.

Their witty back-and-forth continued as they got to the bowling alley. Jolie wasn't used to someone opening her door, and he sat her back in the car to make her wait for him to do it for her. It was another addition to her attraction. He was checking every box, and she hated it.

Adrik tried to get her to drink, but she refused again, so he bought her a Coke instead, setting it on the table. He hooked up the bowling lanes as she tied on her shoes. She wasn't blind to the two men in the back against the wall. They stood out like sore thumbs, and people passed them with skeptical gazes. "Do you always need protection?"

Adrik glanced behind him. "I don't even know they are there most of the time. You'll get used to them. Dima" —he pointed to the one on the right—"has been with me since we were kids."

Jolie met Dima's cold, empty stare. Though he was a beefy guy, he didn't bring her any sense of relief. "But why do you need them?"

Adrik shrugged, fitting his fingers into the ball. "Never know. Now, I should warn you. I'm good."

"Is it possible for you to be bad at something?"

Adrik thought for a moment. "No."

She giggled as he grinned.

Wings and pizza were put on the table, and Adrik's vodka and soda never went empty for long. Jolie was sure there was no waiter here, yet whatever she wanted was provided without her having to go up to the counter.

Jolie went for a ball, and Adrik stepped behind her. She tried to suppress her smile. "What are you doing?"

He leaned over her shoulder, his lips near his skin. "I said I had things to teach you." He took her hand in his. "Now your fingers," he whispered as he slipped them slowly into the hole, "should go in like this."

Jolie giggled, full of embarrassment, the insinuation too obvious to be ignored. "Oh, my God."

"Don't be ashamed. Everyone does it." He positioned her finger and poked it into the hole till she was laughing so badly she fell against him. He chuckled, watching how she hid her face. "It's better when it's wet."

She dived away from him, collapsing into a chair.

"What?" He called after her, joining her at the table. "I was helping."

Jolie kept giggling, her face as red as a tomato. Her stomach twisted, and she couldn't will herself to eat another bite, so she sucked on her straw.

"Is that a skill?" Adrik wondered. "Sucking?"

Jolie choked and spat, slapping a hand over her mouth too late. The spit had flown.

Adrik took a napkin and wiped a few sprinkles off his face.

"Can you stop with this?"

"With what?" he asked innocently.

"Talking like that?"

"About sex?" He popped a fry into his mouth. "Say the word. Sex."

"No. I don't want to."

"You scared?"

"I'm not scared."

"You sound scared."

"*You* sound scared."

Adrik eyed her, and she bowed her head, ashamed of her childish reaction. Jolie didn't have many conversations about sex and definitely never joked about it. The whole thing made her super uncomfortable as much as it turned her on. She turned her attention to the game, noticing his score was nearly over two hundred, and she was almost breaking eighty.

Adrik allowed the change of subject. "Think I won."

"Oh, you think?"

He smirked. The movement caused her to remember Alexei. Should she tell him what happened with his brother? She didn't want to come between them, but that sentence sounded so egotistical. Like she could come between brothers.

"I wanted to let you know," she began tentatively. "Your brother asked me out today."

Adrik paused in his movements. "He did?" He sat back. "And what did you say?"

"That I was busy."

Adrik nodded, taking a fry and twisting it between his fingers. He didn't think his brother was going to do it. But then again, it's been a couple of weeks. He finally gathered up the courage.

"Then he asked me to dinner for your mother's arrival."

His brows rose. A date was one thing. Going with her to a family event was another matter altogether. To be so bold wasn't a characteristically normal thing for Alexei to be.

"He likes you." Adrik accepted it despite how much he hated it. "How do you feel about him?"

Her brows knitted. The question was like a slap in the face. Here she was, going on a date with him, knowing full well his father wouldn't like it, and he dared to think she felt something for his brother? And then to ask her about it?

But when has she ever been vocal about her feelings for Adrik? She barely wanted to admit it to herself. Was it so impossible for him to be unsure of how she felt? How could she say it without actually saying it?

His attention shifted from her to behind her, and his facial features altered dangerously. She was so confused by it she turned around to look. A pack of men with tattoos was standing in the middle of the foyer, a frightening bunch of bikers. They were all looking at Adrik.

Adrik's two guards approached him and whispered something in his ear. Adrik nodded and stood. "We have to go."

Jolie glanced at the board. "We have two rounds left."

He grabbed her hand and pulled her along anyway. "But my shoes!"

Adrik kept a tight grip on her hand as they approached the group. He maneuvered her behind him, keeping her nearly flushed against his back. As they got closer, she noticed the guns at their hips. She stopped fighting after that and tucked into his shoulders. Her thoughts went right to the pen. Should she call for help? Or did Adrik know what he was doing? She clenched her fingers around his shirt, holding his hand tighter. Jolie put her life in his hands.

Adrik kept his head high, moving toward them, moving through them. They parted, keeping their narrowed gazes on him as he passed by, going through the exit. He pulled Jolie forward, putting her in front of him and pushing her to the car.

"Russian," one of the men called.

Adrik spun around, but Jolie clung to his backside, desperate to keep him from attacking.

The man wore a thick leather jacket over his body-building muscles. He was nearly fifty, with a thick beard stretching down to his belly button. "Leave the girl."

Adrik snickered. "Not happening."

"Hey, girl," the biker called.

Adrik glanced behind him, watching as she peeked out.

"You need help?"

Jolie shook her head.

The biker's gaze dipped to her arm. "He do that to you?"

She looked at her bruise. The light from the alley shined on it. She shook her head, but there was skepticism in his eyes as he analyzed Adrik. "You know pussies hit women."

Adrik clenched his fist.

The biker stepped forward, while the rest of his pack kept their distance. "What are you doing out here?"

"Just wanted to bowl."

"Far from the nest. Your kind isn't welcome here. But she can stay."

Adrik bit, "Keep her out of your mouth, or we are going to have a problem."

"She know what you are? A Russian bitch?"

Jolie felt the insult and came to his defense. "I'm with him."

The man spat on the floor, and his friends sneered at her. "Then, you betray your homeland. No more than a Putin whore."

Adrik flinched, but he stayed put, with Jolie digging her nails into his back. He was outnumbered and too far from home. A hand at his side motioned for his two guards to take their hands off their guns. He wasn't going to start anything. They were right. He shouldn't have come here. But there were only so many places he could go with Jolie that his father wouldn't discover.

"We're done," Adrik announced, turning and directing Jolie into the car. He shut it and faced the biker one more time. "You made your master proud. Go tell Benny what a great job you did. He might give you a treat."

Adrik ignored the curses and the threats. They were full of it. They couldn't touch him without permission, and it was clear they weren't given that kind of leeway. He got into his car, revved the engine more than necessary, and sped off.

Chapter Twenty-Five

Logical

Adrik didn't know what to say. Jolie wasn't speaking. She sat shivering for the first ten minutes and was now staring out the window, too quiet.

Having a gang come up on him in the middle of a bowling alley wasn't something he wanted her to experience for their first date. It had been going so well up till that point. He was sure he could get her to ignore his mafia life and simply surrender to the attraction growing between them. And now, all he did was reinforce her fears. Any advancement in their relationship was looking more as an impossibility. He should just give up.

Maybe it was the mafia in him, but he refused to do so.

"You suck at bowling, by the way," Adrik cut into the silence.

Jolie snapped her head toward him. He met her gaze, humor dancing in his eyes, hoping to weasel her out of the bubble she put herself in. And though it took a minute, a soft smile danced on her lips. "Not one of my skills."

He grinned, reaching for her hand. She allowed it, and he tied his fingers in with hers. Such a simple action that he wanted to do every day.

"Does that happen often?" Jolie finally wondered.

"No," Adrik admitted, wishing to change the subject, but he couldn't. He needed to explain. "I didn't know that bowling alley was tied with any gang. But there aren't many neutral places. Everything I own is tied in with my father. Someone would report back to him."

She paused as those words rolled in her head before she whispered, "And you can't be seen with me. Because your father will hurt me."

Adrik clenched the steering wheel. "I won't let him."

"He told me to stay away from you. Both of you."

He nodded, more out of frustration. His father was a gnat that wouldn't get out of his face. Yakov saw everything as a threat. Even someone as harmless as Jolie was dangerous to his empire. When Adrik was younger, he thought his father was smart to see the world as an enemy. But now, he realized it was a weakness to be afraid of everything.

"You should slow down," Jolie whispered, squeezing his fingers to get his attention. He was nearly over a hundred, lost in his head somewhere.

Sirens kicked up behind them, and Adrik cursed, stealing his hand from hers to grab his phone. As he pulled over, he texted someone before dropping it in his lap. Resting his head back in his seat, he stared at the roof. This night kept getting worse. Adrik glanced at Jolie and gave an accusing look. "You jinxed us."

Playful outrage burst on her face.

Adrik rolled down the window as the police officer came to the window. "Step out of the car, please."

Adrik looked at the man with an odd expression. "Good evening, officer. How is your night?"

"You were speeding in a construction zone." He gestured to the one orange cone half a mile down the road. "Get out of the vehicle and put your hands on the hood."

Adrik tapped a finger on his thigh. Being arrested was not in his best interest, but running with Jolie in the car wasn't ideal. He looked at Jolie and the panic on her face. He would have to play nicely. "Stay in the car." Adrik got out with his hands up, knowing the routine well enough. "I have a gun and a permit to carry." As the police officer felt him up, removing his weapon, Adrik watched his movements, studying him. "Officer Jameson," he read his nametag. Adrik didn't know Pasco's police as well as Tampa's, but most were corruptible, if not corrupted already. But Adrik knew the signs to look for, and this man was determined to do his job well. "New to the force?" The new ones always had the attitude to save the planet. The drive would fade in ten years, and that's when people like Adrik snagged them for personal gain.

The officer didn't like the insinuation and shoved him down on the hood of his car. Adrik chuckled but took it with grace. He wasn't going to lose his temper on a police officer. It typically wasn't worth the aftermath. When the officer removed his wallet and took out his ID, a foreign name was read back to him. But Adrik responded to 'Mr. Judds,' nonetheless.

A black SUV squealed their brakes beside them. The police officer put his hand on his gun, turning to the car while keeping his other hand on Adrik's back. Jolie was wide-eyed, terrified of what was happening. But out of the SUV was Adrik's police friend Morgan, dressed in jeans and a T-shirt.

"Get back in your car," the officer warned.

Morgan held up his hand with his badge at the ready. "I'm the chief officer for Tampa Police."

"Tampa? You don't have any jurisdiction here."

Morgan glanced wearily at Adrik, "Boss, you okay?"

"Perfect," the sarcastic reply came muffled against the hood of the car. This wasn't the first time he dealt with law enforcement, and it wouldn't be the last. It never bothered him much before, but with Jolie watching the scene unfold, he was pissed.

"Can we please talk, Officer Jameson?"

There was a silent pause before the man said, "Let me put him in the car."

Morgan rushed forward. "No, no, no, friend, you don't want to do that. Let's talk. Please, please, let's talk." As Morgan led the other officer away, Adrik stood, flexing his back muscles. He caught Jolie's deer eyes through the windshield, and he winked, smirking. It took her a minute before a giggle broke out, and she covered her face with her hands.

Jolie didn't need to be told what was happening. He was getting away with an arrest so effortlessly it was ridiculous. It was another example of the power he had. He was a god here, with friends in valuable places. So, not only did he have money to move the world, but he had connections that made anything possible. He was magnificent.

It made her realize he could actually protect her against his father. But then the question wasn't if he could. It was, would he?

It took two minutes for the officer to come back and uncuff him. "This is bullshit," the man admitted. "I'm gonna talk to my superior about this. Don't think I'm not coming back."

Adrik nodded as he rubbed his wrists. "Do you like your job?"

The officer sneered, "Yes."

"Then, let this go, and I will, too," Adrik said, spitefully slapping him on the arm as he passed. He got into his car and slammed the door. He looked at Jolie, ignoring the officer as he cursed and stomped back to his vehicle. "Do you like gelato?"

Jolie huffed. She couldn't believe him. All of this was normal to him. An inconvenience, yes, but typical. What was she doing here with him? This was too insane. She didn't reply, staying in her thoughts as Adrik spoke with Morgan in Russian, keeping her solely out of the conversation. Not that she was paying attention to any of it.

Jolie clicked off the pen and thought about throwing it out the window. She fully understood what kind of man Adrik was, and being against him wasn't a wise place to get caught in. Her heart pounded like a drum in a rock band, thumping harder than she could handle.

This was a mistake.

After Adrik began driving again, Jolie found her voice. "What am I doing here, Adrik?"

Adrik rested his head back against the seat. He clenched his teeth, unsure what he was supposed to say. It wasn't common for him to date. He fucked and walked away. Being in a relationship wasn't anything he wanted, but here he was, attempting to start one.

Adrik turned the car down the road, finding an empty parking lot in a half-finished construction site. Out here, away from the city, there were many places to get lost and go unnoticed. He could only imagine how many bodies were buried out here. How many he had killed.

It was a full moon, and they were illuminated even though there wasn't a streetlight around. He stopped the car and got out. His bodyguards kept in a distant vehicle, shutting off their lights. They had wisely stayed back when he was being accosted by the police officer. They knew better than to murder law enforcement.

Adrik opened Jolie's door, held out his hand, and waited. She needed to learn to trust him, and though she was confused, she put her hand in his.

Jolie rested against the car, with her head down, as he stood in front of her. "I like you," she whispered. "But I don't know if I can do this."

Her admittance to how she felt was all he needed.

Adrik stepped into her space, a foot between her legs. A hand rested on her hip as the other traced the curve of her jaw before resting under her chin, forcing her head up. She almost refused to meet him, but he was insistent. He needed to see what was reflected in her face.

When her brown eyes finally met him, the desire was too pronounced to be overlooked. All these things that they worried about didn't matter. He wanted her, and she wanted him. It was intuitive. It was instinct.

Adrik leaned down, brushing his lips against hers in the gentlest of touches. So soft, it was barely there. Again, he kissed her, just enough to entice her. And when she pushed herself up on her toes, pressing her lips in desperation against his, he devoured her. He pressed her against the car, her lips tangled against his. The darkness made them appear as one shadow; no space separated them. Her hands were on his shoulders, gripping his shirt. Adrik took hold of her hips, lifting her, and her legs wrapped around his waist. A moan escaped her mouth when she felt his excitement, his desire for her unprotected, hard against her. The kiss was everything she dreamed of and more.

But then she broke from him. "No." She weaseled out of his hold. "No, you can't touch me," she said as she backed away. "That's not fair."

Adrik ground his teeth in disappointment, his fingers dancing across his lips. He rarely dealt with being turned down; it was a bat to his pride. Adrik stepped back, putting even more space between them. He wasn't a pathetic pubescent boy who couldn't control himself. If she wanted space, she'd get a whole mountain of it.

"I'm not the type of girl that just sleeps with anyone. I'm not a one-night stand."

Adrik knew this and would have been insulted, but his reputation preceded him. There was no doubt she knew about his past. Katia was more than willing to reveal all his flaws.

"You can't be seen with me, because you don't want your father to find out. We came hours away just to see each other. Gang members kicked us out of a bowling alley. You evaded arrest! That's insane to me."

Adrik let her rant. He realized it was a lot to take in for someone like her. There was little he could say to help her accept it.

Jolie groaned. "You're married, Adrik."

Adrik acknowledged how it looked, but she didn't understand what happened between Katia and himself. There would never be reconciliation.

"Are you having sex with her?"

"No. I haven't touched her in years."

Though there was slight relief, she didn't quite believe it. Jolie crossed her arms, her thumb going to her lips to nibble on her nail in obvious worry. "You're a criminal."

Adrik brows knitted. "Am I?"

She scoffed. "Don't be an ass."

"I don't follow the nonsensical rules of your corrupt government. So what?"

"I don't even have a speeding ticket." She laughed at the ridiculousness of her statement.

"Neither do I." He smirked.

Jolie eyed him, not humored at all at his attempt to joke. She swung around, walking away, and then came back with wide eyes. "How is this supposed to work? Am I supposed to be hidden away? What kind of life is that? What kind of future?" She slipped her hands into her crazy hair. "This just sounds impossible. We're just too different."

Adrik was disappointed, watching her. All her words, all her fears—they were so trivial in the scheme of things. He liked her. He wanted her in his life. All these things she talked about could be worked out eventually, but she was focused entirely on how it could never be. If she couldn't even get past the beginning, there was no way she'd make it to the end.

She isn't strong enough.

"I'll have you returned home."

"What?" Jolie stepped toward him as he went for the car door.

"I'll find someone else to tutor Helina. And you can go back to your stuffed animals and cats."

Jolie pressed against the door so he couldn't open it. "Wait, wait, wait," she begged, with her hand on his forearm.

Adrik looked past her as if he couldn't see her. All her excuses were signs of her weakness.

"Let me think."

"About what?" he asked, annoyed.

"You are asking me to become a fugitive for something I don't even know what it is. Just because I'm attracted to you and like you? I don't know you that well. You can't expect me to jump in your boat when you're still a stranger. Please. Just give me time."

It sounded like a reasonable request. But time was a scary thing to give her. The more she found out, the more it would reinforce her fears.

Adrik gripped the side of her face. "Look at me," he ordered, and waited till her eyes were on him. "You want to be rational. Then, the answer is easy. Leaving is safer, smarter, and easier for you. I'm not going to convince you to ruin your life. So, let me take you home."

Adrik opened the door for her and waited. She stood there like a lost tourist, unsure of which direction was home.

"What if," she murmured, "I want more than you can offer? If I get involved with you, I will want a future. And I know it's so new, and we've only had our first date, if that's what this was. But I know what kind of person I am. I don't date just for fun. I'll go all in." Jolie looked up at him, desperate. "Is that something you can give?"

Adrik shut the door and leaned against it. She faced him, her fingers going to his, and he watched as their hands entwined. Her touch was everything. It held a future that he always wanted. But being in his life would open her to a new and dangerous world. Did he want to expose her to it? Did he think she could last?

That was why the words out of his mouth felt like knives in his gut. "I don't know," he admitted.

In a moment of clarity, the relationship would cause him so many problems. It was a reason he never allowed himself to date. It was a headache he didn't want. But as a tear slipped down her cheek, and she nodded, full of misery, he couldn't let her go. When her fingers loosened on him, he only tightened his hold. He wasn't giving up.

A car door opened. ***"Excuse me, sir."***

Adrik rolled his eyes in aggravation and turned his attention to his bodyguard. "It better be good."

"It's Alexei."

Chapter Twenty-Six

Mama

Adrik sat beside Alexei's bed, staring at his face. There was swelling over his eyes, and his lips were torn. Beneath the covers were more bruises. His father was careful not to break anything, as if that made a difference. Broken bones were harder to heal from and needed more care, while bruises could be ignored and forgotten. But all of it was an insult.

Yakov's audacity was breaching Adrik's patience. The only thing keeping him from attacking was the lingering anchor of love between a father and son.

When Adrik was young and not in line for the position of heir, Yakov had been a doting father to the point where it became apparent that all his love and attention was on Adrik, while none of it had gone to Alexei. Adrik hadn't noticed it for a long time, not till he was ten years old and watched Alexei get beaten again. He finally faced the reality that he'd have to protect his brother from his father's hatred. He'd throw himself in front of Alexei, and Yakov would stop his strike in mid-swing. He'd call a guard, and someone would grab him, kicking and screaming, pulling him out of the room.

Adrik hadn't dealt with Yakov's cruelty until he gained the ring to be next in line for the Morozov family. When Yakov forced him to marry a woman who didn't want him and expected a child, while he struggled to touch her.

When Katia cheated on him, Adrik wanted nothing more to do with her and went to his father with the divorce papers. Yakov only laughed at him. *'You are not getting a divorce,' he chastised. 'No one can know the embarrassment you've caused this family.'*

'What I've caused?' Adrik had been so incredulous he couldn't breathe.

'Is she not yours? Then, control her. Chain her. Do what you have to so that it never happens again.'

Adrik rubbed his face to push away the memory. It wasn't helping.

Gil sat on the other side, tapping his crutch against the chair. "I want him to have soldiers with him at all times."

Adrik vaguely nodded.

"Why wasn't he with you? Why wasn't he with me?" Gil rolled his eyes. "I've always hated your fucking father. You know that? This is stupid. Why don't you kick him out of your house, Adrik? This is *your* house your father's invading. You built him that office as a courtesy. You allow him here as a courtesy. And he's taken advantage of that."

Adrik didn't want to hear Gil right now. As much as he was a part of this family, he wasn't blood. He couldn't understand.

Alexei groaned as he woke. Adrik quickly got him a glass of water, knowing well how dry the mouth gets after a night of suffering. Alexei could barely reach for it without wincing. He laid his head heavily back on the pillow. Only one eye could open, and he peaked at Adrik. A smile was attempted on his swollen lips. "I'm still better looking."

Adrik choked on a laugh-sob and hid his face, hoping his brother couldn't see the unhindered wave of emotion. This was different when Alexei was shot. Adrik had been so focused on his daughter that he couldn't mentally handle his brothers being in danger. But now, it was all about Alexei and their father's overreach.

"I'm fine, Adrik. I've been through worse."

Adrik clenched his teeth and folded his arms, staring at his brother and seeing every time their father hurt him. It started when Alexei was five. He'd get beat for everything, even if it was Adrik's fault. Alexei had been bigger since they were kids, making it seem like he could handle pain.

Gil leaned up, greeting him, "I think I could still find someone to fuck you if you need it. Might have to pay her a bonus fee."

Alexei smothered his laugh because it hurt too much.

"What happened?" Adrik broke in, fighting the monster in him that was begging for revenge.

Alexei tried to shrug, but he winced instead. "He thinks I'm rubbing off on you."

The answer wasn't what Adrik wanted to hear. "I've been compliant."

"I know. But I guess while he was away, you changed some things."

"Because they're better."

"I know, bro. I know."

Adrik snapped to his feet. "He's so full of himself. The numbers are there! We doubled in nearly every way. And he's had me reverse it. Do you know how stupid it made me look in front of our workers when I told them to go back to the old ways? They all said the same thing: it works. I reorganized our shipments. I've put in so many fucking hours to better our way of life, and it's not enough. It won't ever be enough."

Alexei tried to sit up but surrendered with a sigh. "Adrik, it's fine."

"It's not fine!"

Alexei watched him as he paced. Was this the moment he'd been waiting for? Waiting for Adrik to snap, to tell him that it was time they killed their father? He desperately wanted to say something, but he feared a response. Once he said it, he couldn't take it back. "Adrik, come here."

Adrik collapsed on the chair, resting his head in his hands.

Alexei glanced at Gil, and Gil shifted uneasily in his seat, slightly shaking his head. Alexei and Gil wanted Yakov dead. For Alexei, it was because of the abuse, but for Gil, it was because of vengeance. Gil had learned a few years ago that Yakov was responsible for his parents' deaths. It was guilt that brought the four-year-old boy into the Morozov home. And it was guilt that made them care for him. When Gil found out, he moved away from the family, but never too far from his brothers.

Yakov had given Gil an ultimatum: keep the Morozov name and receive an inheritance. Or try to kill an unkillable king.

Gil chose money because of Adrik and Alexei. But he never stopped thinking about Yakov's death.

Alexei knew this, and if there was ever an attempt to kill Yakov, Gil would be right by his side.

But Adrik? He was the baby. He was the most loved and protected. All the siblings knew this and kept Adrik out of their problems because Adrik was the most loyal. There was always concern he'd rat them out to Yakov.

Alexei leaned over, grabbed Adrik's arm, and pulled him closer. "You know you can rely on me for anything, right?"

Adrik lifted his blue eyes, confused. He flicked his gaze over his brother's malformed face. "Of course."

A knock on the door interrupted, and Alexei laid back, relieved and disappointed that he'd lost his chance. Perhaps Alexei needed to realize there would never be a good time to talk about murdering their father and just do it, like ripping off a Band-aid.

A surprising face stepped in the doorway. "Mama."

Their mother, Tatiana, was a beautiful blonde of sixty. Though she had six children, she was thin and petite, sporting fake boobs their father bought her ten years ago. She never wore anything unfit for heels or less than a thousand dollars.

Adrik got up and was instantly in her arms, like a little boy lost in the woods. She gripped his dark hair with her pink fake nails. "My baby," she whispered. But she detached quickly and came to Alexei's side. Her hand on his forehead felt like heaven, and Alexei basked in her attention. She leaned over and kissed his cheek. "Mama's here." She reached out to Gil, and he put his cheek in her palm, kissing her wrist. "My boys."

Tatiana had been gone for six months. She left one day to go shopping and never came back. She called from the plane, shocking them all. Whatever happened, they knew instinctively it was caused by Yakov. There was a long list of possibilities stemming from cheating, lying, or just because he was an ass.

"I thought you weren't going to be here till tonight?"

Tatiana sat back, motioning Adrik to approach, and he sat on the chair, pulling it in to hold her other hand. "I actually came back this morning."

"You did?"

She shifted uncomfortably, her blue eyes darting from each child as she built up her courage. "We'll talk later, but right now, I want to take care of my sons."

Adrik eyed her, concerned. Something was off. He talked to her two to three times a week. Even though she was gone for six months, he didn't feel distant or as if he didn't know her. That's why the way she was acting was strange. Maybe it was because of Alexei. She avoided the topic of his assault. But that was normal. Whatever bruises the boys received, she would never ask or get upset. She would baby and help them heal, but she never defended them or stopped Yakov. Adrik quit expecting her to do something years ago.

Whatever she was hiding, it was big enough for all of the boys to feel it. They looked at each other, searching for answers.

Chapter Twenty-Seven

Shopping

Jolie paced in front of her floor to ceiling windows. A finger was caught between her teeth but every few seconds she remembered and snatched her hand away. But less than a minute later, it was right back in her mouth and she gnawed on the broken nail. Adrik had ditched her last night, placing her in the hands of his bodyguards before he rushed off to attend to Alexei. There was no information otherwise. All night she waited for something, but nothing came, leaving her with not only anxiety about Alexei's safety, but also leaving her with the last moments of their conversation.

Jolie kept telling herself this attempt at a relationship was a bad idea, but the excitement, thrill, and exhilaration that kept her heart pounding gave no mind to the negative thoughts. If Adrik wanted to try, than she could too. She was constantly wondering why a man like him would want her. It was clear he had options, and she was far from good enough for him. But those gloomy thoughts dissipated every time they spoke because it didn't matter why. He wanted her.

Her cats zoomed around the room, running into walls and freaking each other out. Despite it being annoying, it actually reassured her she wasn't alone. She sat to gain their affection and they were quick to jump on her and give her headbutts. She smiled into their sweet attention.

He's killed people, the logical part of Jolie reminded. But it didn't compute. How could Adrik be a murderer and be as sweet as he was?

What if, one day, she saw him kill? Would it then make a difference? Would it then make her realize what she's doing?

It would be too late then.

Jolie held the pen in her hand. If she decided to be with Adrik, could she come clean about Agent Mally? Would he be forgiving? Understanding? Or would it destroy whatever is developing between them?

A text spooked her, making her jump. With annoyed frustration at herself, she grabbed it.

'Shopping today. Ten minutes.'

She mentally groaned. No part of her wanted to go shopping with Katia. She liked the woman enough, but Jolie could only handle Katia in small doses. Spending hours with her did not sound appealing.

Jolie redressed three more times before another *ding* told her she was late, and she rushed out the door. She was fixing the fat belt at her waist when Alexei's door popped open, and to her surprise, Adrik stood there. He was wide-eyed, meeting her face. She had time to sleep and shower while he still wore the same clothes as yesterday. Exhaustion riddled his face.

"Hey—"

Adrik walked right by her; with enough space between them, another person could have walked through. She stared ahead, slightly numb. She had forgotten about the world around them, and for half a second, she felt discarded and hurt. But then it poured into her, reminding her he couldn't talk to her.

With his disregard, the doubts returned like a Ferris wheel going round and round.

Jolie sat in the limo. She had been a minute late, but Katia's look of annoyance greeted her as she climbed into the limo. Helina's full grin made her feel better, and she sat next to the little girl and played with her on the iPad. She enjoyed the break from her thoughts, diving into a five-year-old's silliness. Helina was more than willing to teach her words for things and less willing to learn the English form of it, but with a few tickles and giggles, Jolie was able to teach her a couple new words.

Her phone beeped with a text, and Jolie couldn't stop her smile when she noticed the unknown number. Adrik wrote, *'Let's finish our conversation tonight.'*

Such a simple message that wreaked havoc on her heart.

"I hope you will let me pick out your dress," Katia interrupted, dropping her phone in her lap. There was something about Jolie's happiness that annoyed her. Perhaps because she knew who was texting her. With unhindered distaste, Katia eyed Jolie's clothing. "We have certain requirements." Katia forced a loving smile. She wasn't doing it for Jolie. She was doing it for her in-laws. It was bad enough that the Americans had to attend. Jolie needed to fit in at least, and wearing cats on one's dress wasn't currently trending.

Jolie nervously fidgeted. "I'm not sure I'll be able to afford the kinds of dresses you're talking about."

Katia giggled and reached for her purse. She pulled out a black square credit card. "All expenses are taken care of. Welcome to the Mafia."

Jolie nodded quietly, moving her eyes to the window. She was using blood money. In fact, ever since she came to Adrik's estate, Jolie had unconsciously been surrounded by things they had gotten because of drugs, murder, and prostitution. Even this car was paid for by it. She shifted uncomfortably. How did she think she could be with Adrik when his life was drenched in blood? She rested her head against the window.

It's not going to work.

This shouldn't be difficult. Adrik was an evil man and should be in prison. It didn't matter how nice he was. She was pretty sure Hitler was nice to a few people. He still deserved to die a horribly gruesome death.

The drive was thankfully short, cutting off her misery as she got out of the car. Katia kept hold of Helina's hand as they stepped up to a blank store with black and gold trim. At the entrance were two bodyguards and, surprisingly, Gil. It's only been three weeks, but he stood on his leg, with a slight limp and a single crutch, as he pulled the door open. "Good afternoon, ladies."

Jolie stopped and smiled. Gil clearly hated her, evident by their talk at TGI Fridays, where he tried to talk to Adrik about her 'boy' look. Since then, Jolie decided she would try to win him over. And kindness was the way to go. "It's good to see you. How's your leg?"

Katia stopped and looked between them with an odd expression. She met Gil's gaze, but he stuttered in response, "I'm good, thank you."

"I'm glad," Jolie didn't think her words were so terrible, but the awkwardness was apparent.

"Me too," Katia added patronizingly.

Inside, a man at the front desk, with painted pink nails and gold bracelets, gushed over them as he brought them to the other side of a wall. A dozen dresses were on a rack, and two or three dressed mannequins, but it was otherwise limited. The selection was bare, and Jolie almost wanted to tell her that the superstore, Ross, wasn't too far and had plenty more options.

They spoke in Russian, leaving Jolie to her thoughts as she moseyed over to the rack, checking for a price tag. To her confusion, there were none.

"Jolie, Miss Lacy has a dress for you in the back."

Jolie quickly followed the path to the open curtains where Miss Lacy stood. She was an old Russian beauty, with eyes like crystal. She didn't know English, but she understood the gestures well enough. Jolie undressed and stood awkwardly in the middle of the changing room while the woman stared at her.

"Off," Miss Lacy ordered.

Jolie looked down at her undergarments.

"Off." The woman flicked her hand again.

"Um." Jolie fidgeted and then turned around and undid her bra.

"Off, off," Miss Lacy instructed as Jolie stood in her panties, covering her breasts with her arms.

"No. On," Jolie fought back.

"Off."

"On."

"Jolie," Katia sang, "listen to Miss Lacy."

Jolie narrowed her eyes. For some reason, she had an inkling that Katia was enjoying this.

With aggravation, she pulled her panties to the ground. Miss Lacy was quick to help her into her dress, and it was then she understood why she needed to be completely naked for it. The dress dipped so low in the front that it almost touched her belly button, and then there was no back to it. Jolie could feel a draft in her butt crack. Only two strings kept it up.

It was beautiful, what little there was of it. Glittering red fabric went down to her ankles, with a slit riding up to the top of her hip.

Miss Lacy had shoes ready and slipped the tallest stilettos in existence on her feet. It was like walking on twigs.

"There's no way." Jolie cursed as she held Miss Lacy's arms.

Katia's voice came through the curtain, "Well, let's see it. We don't have all day." She snapped the curtain back. A smile started on her lips until a choked laugh came through, and Katia slapped a quick hand over her mouth. Jolie glared at her, her knees shaking from the awkward, steep hill her feet were camped on. Katia put up a hand in apology, ***"Maybe something not so revealing. She is still a virgin."*** Katia then joked in English, "Can't risk your virginity, can we?"

Jolie leaned over, gripping Miss Lacy's hand as she reached for a chair and roughly collapsed. "I'm not a virgin."

"Oh." Katia perked, quite surprised. "Sorry. I just assumed."

Jolie flung off the death trap of a shoe as Miss Lacy went in search for something else.

"Who was the lucky man?"

Jolie ripped off the other shoe. She thought about lying, but she was already struggling with enough lies that it didn't seem worth it. And she still wasn't sure if Katia was trying to be her friend and gossip or make fun of her. "A high school boyfriend."

Katia adored the look of embarrassment on her face. If this woman provided nothing else, at least she was entertaining.

"I think that is sweet," Katia admitted. "Do you still love this man?"

Jolie winced, thinking of it. "No. He wasn't exactly my type. I know that now."

"Yet you slept with him. I don't see you as the kind of woman to sleep with just anyone. And believe me, that is all the women I encounter in my world. You should see how they throw themselves at my husband. It is disgusting." Katia could have patted herself on the back for that little zing. She wanted this girl to realize Adrik was off-limits. Instinct was a woman's greatest defense, and she felt the need to get Jolie out of her life and Adrik's as quickly as possible.

Jolie stood as Miss Lacy brought in another dress. This one had more fabric to it. Katia closed the curtain so she could change.

"He was the first boy to look at me in high school. I wasn't exactly cheerleader material. I was a book nerd."

Katia rolled her eyes and mouthed the word, '*Shocking.*'

"But he was sweet initially, and I kind of just went with it. He was the quarterback but a delinquent. You know, smoking, a skateboarder. I thought I could fix him. Get him on the right track."

"Did you manage it?"

"Not even close."

Jolie peeled the curtain back and stood before Katia, even more unsure than the last one. There was more fabric, but it sucked around every curve. It was a short long-sleeved black cocktail dress. There was no bending over in this.

Katia grinned. "Perfect. You can wear high heels, correct?"

"Yes. Just not Eiffel Tower heels. But this is too revealing."

"For our dinner, this is perfect. And you do want to fit in, yes?"

"Of course."

"Then, it is settled. Alexei will fall over when he sees you."

Jolie blushed. Not exactly the brother she was thinking of.

Katia nudged her with a smile. "Do you like Alexei? He has the heart of a kitten. You pet him, and he'll mew at your feet for a lifetime."

Jolie turned to the mirror to analyze her dress as she thought of that horrible comparison. What man would like to be compared to a cat? As much as Jolie adored cats, it didn't sound appealing.

"Alexei's nice."

Aside from the fact that he said he would kill me.

She would love to ask what happened with Alexei last night, but she wasn't supposed to know about it.

"You never told me your lover's name; what is it?"

"Vincent Ortez. I'm pretty sure he's still in prison."

"Prison?" Katia stood behind Jolie, fixing her stale long brown hair, trying to decide if she should curl it or just let it hang. But it was a distraction as she thought of the name. Ortez sounded too familiar. It wasn't a family name or Russian, but why would it spring out at her?

"He robbed a bank when we were together. I turned him in."

"Oh." Katia feigned heartache. "How brave."

And terribly stupid, Katia thought. *Why would Adrik bring a narc into our world? Is it possible he doesn't know?*

"I'll be back." Katia stepped out, leaving her alone.

Jolie needed help getting the dress off, and she wondered who was going to help her put it on for the party. She never understood why women dressed to the point of being uncomfortable. Feeling pretty was a state of mind and had nothing to do with the makeup or the outfits. She learned to love herself in high school even when others clearly didn't. She was made fun of by the girls with self-esteem issues, but their words didn't outweigh her own thoughts.

Jolie felt relieved to be back in her own clothes. She stepped out, finding Helina sitting on a couch, with a lollipop and her iPad. Jolie searched for Katia and heard the distant whispers of Russian. She peeked behind the wall and saw Katia and Gil arguing. It was intense and full of hand movements that expressed the vital upset. Gil reached out to her, touching her arm, but she snapped it away before turning around.

Jolie was too slow to hide, but she rushed over to sit next to Helina, her heart pounding as she heard the sharp clip of Katia's heels. The woman stomped toward them. "Let's go," she ordered.

"Is everything alright?"

Katia narrowed her eyes. "That is clearly none of your business. And just so we're clear, eavesdropping could get you killed." She pulled Helina up even as the little girl protested and yanked her to the door.

Chapter Twenty-Eight

Glance

The ride home was unpleasant. No amount of apologizing got Katia in a good mood, and it became a point to Jolie that shutting up was better for both of them.

But it did leave Jolie with questions.

Why were Gil and Katia arguing?

What's their relationship?

And did that touch seem more of an apologetic movement as opposed to an aggressive one?

Gil was family. He was like a brother to Adrik, but 'like' a brother wasn't one. He didn't live in the house, and he was clearly a soldier. Maybe he got more privileges than others?

When they got home, Katia didn't leave the limo. She dropped Jolie off and then left with her daughter. It was a relief. Jolie didn't like when people were upset with her. Chances are she'd start baking brownies, cookies, cakes, and strudels just to get back on Katia's good side.

Gil's car had been behind them. He stepped out of the car, watching Katia's limo drive off. Then he turned to Jolie. She attempted to give a supportive smile, but he shook his head and slipped back into the car, driving after her. As her escort, he had no other choice.

With enough drama today to exhaust her, Jolie headed to her bedroom, but a woman was coming down as she was going up.

This person was amazingly immaculate; from her nails to her hair to the inch-thick of makeup, there was not a strand of her that wasn't planned. Behind her, Adrik walked, and though it was clear the woman had Botox and other cosmetic surgeries, something in her face exposed her.

Adrik's mother.

Jolie leaned against the wall even though there was ample space for them to walk down while she went up. But the thick feeling of intimidation and how Adrik ignored her earlier broke her confidence.

Jolie could feel the woman's ice-blue eyes on her. Not wanting to expose her lack of a backbone, Jolie lifted her head and smiled sweetly, "Hello."

In Russian, the woman looked over her shoulder, speaking to her son, ***"Who is this?"***

Adrik replied in English, "Mama, this is Helina's tutor, Jolie Bell. Miss Bell, this is my mother, Tatianna."

Jolie straightened her back, sparking to life like a cat getting attention. "Hi." Jolie put out her hand. It's a pleasure to meet you."

In Russian, Tatianna replied, ***"An American?"*** She gently rested her hand in the girl's, but it was brief, and she took it right back, her fingers rubbing together to wipe off any germs.

Feeling his mother's disapproval, Adrik whispered, "She saved Helina, Mama, at the shootout."

The tension disappeared, and instantly, Tatianna grinned so lovingly. "Oh, my girl!" she squealed in English, rushing to take Jolie into her arms. "You are a prize. Thank you so much for what you did for my family. You are forever my hero. Are you being well taken care of? All your needs must be met. Adrik?"

Adrik answered, "Esfir is in charge of her care."

"Esfir, that beady-eyed old woman. She's still alive? If Esfir gives you any trouble, you come to me. Understood?"

Jolie grinned, red-faced, "Yes, ma'am."

Ma'am! Wonderful manners. I hope you are teaching my stubborn little cookie such manners. Where is Helina? I must see my granddaughter."

Adrik clenched his teeth and revealed, "Katia took her to her parents."

A sneer was unnatural on Tatianna's artificial lips. "Of course. Tell her to return as soon as possible. I've been without my sweet nugget for too long. It was wonderful to meet you, and I hope you will join us tomorrow for my dinner."

"Yes, ma'am, I'll be there."

"Oh, love you!" Tatianna touched Jolie's cheek before continuing down the stairs.

Jolie was grinning; the woman's energy was like a bomb of glitter and sunshine. She flicked her eyes to Adrik, and he hid a little smile, keeping his eyes from hers as he descended the stairs. She stood there and watched him, hoping for a moment of his attention, but he walked by, and her shoulders slumped.

Just before Adrik stepped around the corner, his blue eyes slid toward her. A hand fell to her stomach as a wave of emotion drowned her.

Jolie fled to her bedroom, locking the door and resting her head against the frame. She bit her lip, his daring glance replaying before her eyes, devouring doubt like a tidal wave. Ming and Tae-Tae mewed at her feet for attention, and she slipped to the floor, allowing them to crawl into her lap. It was a devastating reality that she was already too far gone to turn back. Adrik was bewitching her, and she was powerless to stop it.

And I don't want to.

Ming left her and jumped on the bed, rubbing her head against a white box. Her brows knitted as she stood, Tae-Tae meowing at her with dislike. The box had a red satin bow and a small square envelope. Jolie quickly opened it.

'Meet me tonight in the movie theater. Find a movie. No romcoms. Until then, enjoy.'

"Enjoy?" Jolie knitted her brows as she reread the message. She dropped the note on the bed and unwrapped the box. She imagined chocolate or candy. He'd know which was her favorite. He knew everything else about her.

And then the lid came off, and her eyes widened.

A massive hot-pink dildo sat in the center of white silk.

Jolie stepped back, slightly frightened by such a thing. She rushed to slap the lid back on, a hand pressed against her mouth as she sat on the bed, too shocked to move.

What the heck am I supposed to do with that?

It had to be ten inches long and two inches wide.

She shook her head, unable to believe women could fit that anywhere.

He's not…

Jolie slapped her hands against her face to stop her crazy thoughts.

But what if…

No!

Jolie stood and took up the box, crazily searching for a place to hide it. She felt the same panic when her ex-boyfriend brought weed into the house, with her parents in the next room. Jolie couldn't have the maids find something like this, but where could she put it that they wouldn't look? If she tried to throw it away, they'd see it. She couldn't put it under the bed; they cleaned it. The box felt hot in her hands, like the sinful object was burning her. She darted to three different places before the only other location she hoped they never went was her underwear drawer.

But the box didn't fit.

She would have to take it out. She would have to touch it.

With a shaking hand, Jolie reached in. She folded the silk around it and squeezed her eyes as she wrapped her hand around the pole. It sent shivers up her spine; disgust and curiosity tangled together like a tornado. It was surprisingly heavy, like a fat stick of salami. She shoved it in the back of her underwear drawer, piled all her panties around it, and then slammed the drawer shut, wishing there was a lock on it.

No way a man has something like that.

Jolie's experience may not be top-notch, but she knew what could and couldn't fit, and that monstrous thing was a negative. If Adrik had something like that, their relationship really wasn't going to work.

But she was getting ahead of herself. They weren't going to have sex. They were just trying to figure out if they liked each other. She clarified that she didn't have sex randomly, and so far, Adrik seemed to understand that.

But if he bought me that, it's clearly on his mind. And I'd be lying if I said it wasn't on mine.

Jolie moved to the bathroom, splashing water on her face. She thought of taking a shower and shaving her legs but refused. It would be admitting that sex was an option, and it wasn't. She wouldn't give up her standards. Everyone had desires, but it was better to wait. She wasn't a loose woman, giving it up to any cute boy who looked at her.

How long had she made her ex-boyfriend wait? Jolie didn't have sex with Vincent for over a year. Why had it been so easy to deny his advances, yet all Adrik had to do was look at her, and she was fighting her resolve like some horny dog in heat?

Think about the disappointment, Jolie told herself. Vincent had lasted two minutes the first time. It was miserable, painful, and horribly unsatisfying. He had talked about all the ways he'd please her and how much she'd enjoy it. She thought her first time would be different from all the others out there who said it was the most awful experience of their life. Instead, she joined the long list of women unprepared for the night.

Then it took him a month to talk her into it again.

Vincent got better as time passed, but she no longer expected him to help her get a release. She began to believe that women in the books she read were lying because it didn't seem to matter what Vincent did, he never got her to completion. Not that he knew that. For all Vincent knew, he was the best she'd ever have.

Jolie shook her head. She was comparing an eighteen-year-old virgin to a man with experience. No doubt Adrik knew ways to please without even trying.

As a shiver of anticipation ran through her, Jolie hardened herself. *It doesn't matter. I must be as logical as possible about our situation, and sex will only hinder my decisions.*

A text message sprung hope in her, but it was only her mother. *'How was bowling?'*

'I lost.'

'Obviously.'

'I don't appreciate your lack of faith.'

'I have faith in God; that is all the faith I need.'

Jolie giggled, adoring her sarcastic mother. The weeks here at the Morozov mansion were only bearable because of the hour-long conversations with her mother every night. Sometimes, they didn't even talk; they shared the quiet together as Jolie read a book and her mother made dinner. Simple things like that made Jolie feel a little less alone.

It was then Jolie realized where most of her hesitation was coming from.

Her mother's approval.

Chapter Twenty-Nine

Poker Night

Adrik glanced at his watch. 11:25 p.m. He put the cigar back in his mouth, puffing as he held his cards. He hadn't thought he'd be caught in a poker game at this time, but here he was. A random party had popped up when Gil brought in a group of women. He was slightly drunk, really high, and looking for a good time. Now the girls sat at the bar, getting drunk, while some got naked and were twisting on the stripper poles, gyrating to the music. The lights flickered in colors with the music, and it vibrated the floor, making his drink of whiskey ripple. He tossed a card, and the dealer handed him a new one. The five of clubs only pissed him off. He was gonna lose the round *and* miss his meeting with Jolie.

Alexei sat next to him. He asked for this impromptu gathering. He was covered in black and blue and moving hurt, but he wanted to get drunk and forget that his father had beaten him the night before.

His mother and Alexei both asked Adrik not to do anything in revenge, and though he assured them he wouldn't, there were little things he could do to fuck over his father. Subtle things that could be deniable. The shipment of his father's cigars would be lost. The whiskey he loved would disappear. The sugar-free donuts his father adored would go out of stock. It was petty, perhaps, these silly little ramifications. But it would prove to Yakov one thing: Adrik had control of this company, not him.

"Game's rigged." Alexei cursed, unimpressed with his cards.

Adrik hid his amusement. His brother was never good at bluffing. He was too honest. A woman passed by, a hand on Adrik's shoulders. She smiled and winked before sauntering over to the stripper pole. Adrik humored her because he had to. She didn't know that after years of this shit, it was boring. It had nothing to do with her, because she was a beautiful woman. But it didn't matter. Adrik was no longer interested in what she had to offer, and he didn't want to pretend to be.

"Want the last hit?" Gil nudged his head to the final white line on the glass tray. Adrik shook his head and watched him take a glass straw and stuff it up his nose.

"Take it easy, brother," Alexei chastised. "You want to be alive tomorrow?"

"It's the weekend," Gil fought. "Besides, I've never had an apology taste so good."

Alexei chuckled as he held his ribs. Yakov's apology came in the form of an ounce of cocaine and a new Rolex left on his bed while he slept. It was an empty gesture, put there out of obligation and fear of Adrik's retaliation. He did admit that the Rolex looked great around Gil's wrist.

Gil flexed his arm, pulling the sleeve up to expose the watch. "And it's never looked so great either."

Though Alexei and Gil found it amusing, Adrik was far from allowing humor to ease his anger. If Yakov believed he could do something like that, what else did he think he could do? He thought his father would have limits when it came to his kids. But the evidence was proving otherwise. Yakov was more daring than Adrik ever hoped to be.

"You should get beat more often, Alexei," Gil joked, high as a kite. "This is a great fucking night."

Alexei took a big swig of his whiskey and sighed, "I'll try."

Adrik bit the inside of his cheek to keep quiet. He wasn't going to ruin his brother's high. But the more the night wore on, the more the petty shit wasn't good enough.

"Oh, shit," Alexei cursed.

Adrik looked at him, only to see his eyes at the doorway. Jolie stood there, frozen with her mouth open. She saw the bar full of women, the stripper poles where naked girls danced, and the bowling alley full of people smoking weed and sorting out a line of cocaine. Guns were out on the table, watched over by a guard to ensure no one popped off in a fit of anger after losing a stupid game. Alexei stood, and it broke Jolie out of her stupor. She ran from the doorway.

It was Adrik's fault. He asked her to the movie theater that was three doors down. No doubt she would have gotten lost.

Alexei sat down and glanced at him with a glare. ***"She doesn't belong here."***

After last night, Adrik spent all day thinking about their words to each other. The one conclusion he came to was she was too good for him. She deserved more than he could give her. And though he wanted to try, there were certain things he knew he couldn't give. One of them was marriage. As long as Katia was alive, he was bound to her. And there was no killing the mother of his child.

Adrik took the cigar from between his lips and set it on the ashtray. ***"I'm thinking of getting rid of her."***

"What?" Alexei paused. ***"No. There's no need to kill her."***

Adrik tossed a poker chip to the center of the pile. ***"Did I say that?"***

"I never know with you."

When Adrik lost his hand, he tossed the cards, glancing once more at the clock. 11:45 p.m. He didn't know if it was a lost cause if Jolie had returned to her room, too shocked to handle it. He almost felt resentful. His world wasn't apple picking and scrapbooking. If they were going to attempt to be together, it was something she would have to accept. And he didn't know yet if she was capable of it.

"I'm done," he announced in English. "Party's over." There was a look toward him, incredulous gawking as they paused whatever they were doing. While it was true he never ended a party before three, it didn't stop him. "Get out," he shouted with a little more demand. There were whispers as they slowly gathered their things.

Alexei tried to keep the peace, "He just lost twenty grand. He's a little moody." A small collective chuckle eased the tension.

Adrik didn't care about their upset. This was his house, and he could kick them out whenever he wanted, but he allowed his brother to ease their tempers. Drunks and druggies tend to have attitudes when you take away their free supply.

Gil gathered the chips, stacking them with a grin, ***"You are always trying to piss someone off."***

"What do I care?" Adrik provoked. He was pissed at Jolie for the judgment he saw riddled on her face. Picking a fight was probably for the best, so he didn't go look for her and say things he shouldn't.

"Don't get an attitude with me. I've had to deal with your wife all day. I was a fucking escort today."

Adrik's brows knitted. Only low-level guards did shit like that. Not something his adoptive brother was supposed to be doing. ***"Why?"***

"Filling in. Your dad went out to meet with some people, and we were short-staffed."

Adrik shifted his gaze to Alexei, accusing, *"You gave him a guard job?"*

Alexei held up his hand. *"I didn't. I was in bed all day. Dad must have scheduled it. We've been short-staffed for a while. He might not have had a choice."*

"Then hire people. Isn't that your job? Maybe if you weren't focused on this fucking teacher, you would have noticed a problem. He is family. He doesn't do bitch work."

"Watch your fucking tone," Alexei bit back. *"I don't need your shit right now."*

Anyone hanging around began to panic and swiftly moved to whatever exit they could find. Gil sat nervously, darting his eyes between the two brothers before he reached out. *"Adrik, it's fine. I didn't mind it."*

Adrik ground his teeth, tapping his fingers on the green velvet of the table. He knew he was overreacting. He was pissed about his father, about his mother's awkwardness, about not being good enough for the one girl he wanted. Everything was piling on, and he knew it was only a matter of time before he snapped.

"That teacher, by the way"—Gil grinned, avoiding Adrik's eyes, talking to Alexei—*"got some nice legs. The girls were trying on dresses. Think you're gonna like the one she picked. I know I did."*

Adrik straightened his head, glaring at Gil, but the guy knew what he was doing.

"I asked her to Mom's dinner," Alexei revealed casually, as if it wasn't a big fucking deal.

"Oh, yeah?" Gil laughed, eyeing Adrik and enjoying his brother's reaction. *"That's fucking hilarious."*

Adrik never wanted to shoot Gil in the face so badly.

"Gil!" Two girls stood in the doorway, their long hair hanging over the shoulder, with their boobs nearly out of their shirts. "We're lonely."

Gil smirked and stood. "There's enough for all of us."

Alexei got up. "Gonna head to bed."

"Alexei, do you ever just fuck to fuck?"

"It's funny you ask that. How many STDs have you had?"

Gil shrugged, confused about why he would ask. "I don't know."

Alexei laughed. "Yep, that's all I need." He dropped a hand on his brother's shoulder, as a way to apologize. ***"I'll hire more people on Monday."*** He slapped Adrik's cheek affectionately, but he turned away, unmoved.

Adrik continued to sit there as the boys left. He rubbed his fingers over the felt of the table, unsure if he should be stupid enough to show up in the movie theater, just for it to be empty. He should just go to bed. It was time to end what could never be. He glanced at his watch. 12:01 a.m. Adrik got up and took a last gulp of his whiskey before he moved out of the room.

Chapter Thirty

Risk

Adrik leaned against the doorway of the theater. It was a thirteen-seater, with big reclining chairs on an elevated surface. The screen was the entire width of the wall, and a movie played. A pathetic romcom that annoyed him. But he knew she'd pick nothing else.

Jolie sat in the center, curled up with a blanket. He stayed silent as he stared at the back of her head.

When he was away from her, the reasons for ending their budding relationship were apparent. He could name a dozen off the top of his head in seconds. But the moment he saw her face, all those logical facts disappeared.

It fucked with him because he wasn't the type of man that questioned himself. He chose with confidence and never second-guessed. To be a leader, he had to make difficult choices with conviction. Otherwise, his enemies would see a weakness in him and exploit it.

So, why couldn't he make this decision to leave her with just as much certainty?

"I didn't think you'd stay." Adrik slipped a hand in his pocket, keeping his distance.

Jolie paused the movie and didn't speak for a moment before a small whisper escaped, "Me either."

Adrik pushed himself into the room, moving forward till he stood behind her. She didn't turn around, her eyes dead set on the screen in front.

"Let's hear it," he said.

All her judgments would no doubt spew forth, only to confirm what he already knew. It would help him to end this doomed relationship. He needed to hear her call him a cheater. It was a pet peeve, and getting pissed off might be the only way to walk away from her.

Jolie whispered, "Why do you want me?"

His brows knitted. That wasn't an accusation. It wasn't a judgment.

"You are surrounded by beautiful women all day. Any one of them would bend over backward for you. Your father would approve, I'm sure. They would accept your lifestyle. There would be no risk. And you wouldn't have to choose. You can have all of them. It doesn't make any sense."

Everything she said was true.

But it sparked no desire in him.

A hand lowered to her hair. Adrik touched her scalp, tracing down her ear and along her jaw. Her head tilted back just a bit for his hand to cup the bottom of her jaw. A thumb brushed her lips.

This simple act ignited a storm in his gut.

Adrik swallowed and pulled away. "What movie did you pick?"

Her cheeks were red, and she watched him sit beside her, keeping his eyes on the screen. She didn't know why he wouldn't look at her, but if he felt even an ounce of what she did, then he was keeping distant because it was getting harder to stay away. She fought a smile, touching her lips where his thumb had graced her skin. "*50 First Dates*."

"Adam Sandler. I love this man." Adrik pushed the button on his chair and leaned back, putting his feet up. "It is funnier in Russian."

Jolie sat there with a weight in her stomach that made her twist. She didn't know how he could act so normal when all she could do was fantasize. His touch was like fire, and it burned her cheek and lips, and she wondered if it would have the same effect if he touched other parts of her. "Is your brother alright?"

There was a stiffness in his reply. "He's fine."

With no other explanation, Jolie let the conversation drop. She saw Alexei sitting at the poker table, but it was dark, aside from the strobe light above the stripper pole. Too many distractions to really pay attention.

Jolie didn't know what to feel about it all. She knew his life would be different, but that was intense. She'd rather not think about it.

'Ignorance is bliss,' her mother said. *'But stupidity is dangerous.'*

Adrik broke the silence. "Did you enjoy my gift?"

"No!" Jolie bit back in a shriek, hating how he cackled. "It was frightening." That made him laugh more.

"Not big enough? I fear we will have a problem if that doesn't satisfy."

Jolie buried her face and groaned, "Shut up."

Oh, he enjoyed this too much. Embarrassing Jolie exposed how much she didn't know about everything he could show her. Everything he could teach her. Adrik bent his knees, hiding the growing excitement. There were too many thoughts that he couldn't control and too much liquor in his system to stop him.

"Tell me something," Adrik ordered. "This boyfriend you had. What did he do for you?"

Her brows knitted at the question because it was hard to answer. "I don't know." She concentrated, trying to come up with a response. "He was fun."

Adrik chuckled, and rectified, "I meant in bed."

She flushed and hid her face. "I'm not gonna talk about that."

He grinned, adoring her embarrassment. "I can't imagine much. He was eighteen at the time, yes? So, this is why you have a problem with my gift."

"I have a problem with your gift because it is terrifying."

Adrik conceded, "Perhaps a little over the top."

"You think?"

"I can buy a smaller one—"

"No, no, thank you."

Adrik cackled, his hands linking behind his head proudly. "You had sex with him, didn't you?"

"Yes, not that it's any of your business."

"It is my business."

"Why?"

"Because when I take you to my bed, I need to know how rough I can be."

Jolie buried her head into the chair. She didn't know how he could be so confident about something so intimidating. It brought back waves of nervousness and tension. She remembered the pain of sex and the uncomfortableness. Despite the excitement in her, she mentally knew it wasn't as pleasant as she wished it was. And the word 'rough' frightened her. Her boyfriend had been all kinds of gentle, and it still hurt.

"If," she enunciated, her voice muffled by the armrest, "we"—she stuttered—"do *that*, not very."

Adrik watched her, trying to understand her movements and her words. Until it hit him. "Did he hurt you?"

Jolie's head popped up. "No, well, not on purpose. It was just painful. Every time."

"He was that big?"

Jolie choked. This conversation was worse than getting a pap smear. "No. And that's all the information I'm giving you."

A smile once more crept on his lips.

Jolie's brow knitted. "Why are you smiling?"

Adrik shook his head, shrugging, momentarily speechless. It was exciting, in a way, all that he could give her. Not only would he bring her up out of poverty, provide medical care for her parents, and allow her to fulfill her dreams in ways she never imagined, but now, along with all of that, he could expose her to a world of sexual pleasure. He turned his attention to the movie, soaking it in, and even though he could tell she was still confused, he kept it to himself. Their situation was new, and how he felt about her was overwhelming.

The movie continued to play, and she made little comments about the film, telling him memories from her childhood. Adrik found himself indulging in every word she spoke, the way she ran her hands through her hair when she couldn't handle his stare, or the way her cheeks reddened when her gaze would drift down to his lips in the middle of her speech, and she'd stutter, trying to find the sentence again. All his negative thoughts about their future were now about ways to combat it. Would there be a way to divorce Katia? With her brother nearly killing their kid, he should be able to maneuver out of it. Her brother was still missing, and for all he knew, Katia and her parents were hiding him. That would give him leeway to get out of the contract.

Then there was his father.

When the movie was over, Adrik glanced at her, against his will, but found she had fallen asleep. It allowed him to look at her when no one was watching, and he found himself drowning in her. She had perfect eyebrows, which was insane, because they weren't drawn on or colored in. She wore little to no makeup, except around her eyes, which didn't need much help. Her thick black glasses rested on her small, perfect nose. She only wore her glasses at night, and he had rarely seen her in them, yet they fit her, were a part of her. Her brown hair lay against her cheek, and he almost reached out to move it, but it looked like it belonged there.

Jolie questioned the women in his life. It would be a lie if he didn't admit they were all beautiful. They had perfect bodies that only money could buy. They knew how to please and strived to do so. They had talents that could only be learned from years of sexual conquests. But Jolie failed to realize that none of them even compared to her.

And he barely even knew her.

How could he let her go?

Adrik pushed his seat back up, planting his feet on the floor. The movement woke her, and she stretched, moaning. A sound that he'd loved to provoke one day.

It was nearly two-thirty. He still needed to visit Katia to keep up the act of their coupling. "It's late."

Jolie smiled at him. "I enjoyed *this,*" she emphasized.

It's funny because he figured she would. Unlike all the other women, it didn't take much to impress her. Material things were barely on her radar. He would have to change his entire mentality to make her happy. Was that something he could do?

Adrik stood and held out his hand. She was hesitant, but only momentarily, before her fingers slipped into his palm. He pulled her to her feet and stood her in front of him. She was half a foot shorter, and though she tried to bow her head, he had a hand on her cheek, lifting her face to meet his eyes.

He was never good with words. Emotions were another thing altogether. But showing physical affection was something his family never had trouble with, and he hoped if they continued this forbidden affair, she'd learn that his touch held all the words he could never say.

Jolie struggled to make eye contact. "Don't look at me like that."

"You cannot control how I look at you." His thumb brushed her lips, and she leaned into it, closing her eyes. The movement nearly broke him. "All day today," he began in a whisper, "I've been thinking of everything about us that would not work."

Her eyes snapped up to his in a sudden panic.

"But I don't care. I want to try."

Her brows knitted, and the yearning returned to her gaze. She gripped his wrist, the other hand resting on his chest. Then she dropped her eyes. He attempted to get them back onto him, leaning down, but she refused.

"It's easy for you to say that," she murmured. "You aren't the one going against everything you've ever learned. You aren't betraying your morals. You aren't risking your life."

"I think we are more alike than you realize."

"Then, why are you choosing this?"

"There's a saying in my family. Big risk, big reward. There are no small bets in my life. Everything is a big risk. It makes what I do worth it. *This* will be worth it."

Jolie clenched his shirt. He was so sure and confident that fighting it was hard. But what if she didn't fight it? What if, instead of going against the current, she allowed it to take her away? It may drown her, but it could also bring her to land.

"Okay," she found herself saying.

A smile flashed on his face before it faltered. "Are you sure?"

She shook her head. "Big risk, right?"

Adrik felt a flash of pride in her words. It made him believe she could handle everything that came their way.

He leaned down, his eyes on her lips, unable to stop himself. "Big reward," he finished as he graced her skin. Their lips collided like a gentle wave against the shore. It was unsure at first, concerned she'd change her mind, that he was dreaming. But then her fingers clenched the back of his head, pushing him against her, and he wrapped an arm around her waist, aggressively pulling her to him. The speed of their kiss intensified as the desire swallowed them. He could feel the rate of her breathing rapidly increasing, and every time they broke, the desperation only got stronger. There would be no waiting. He was going to take her here in the fucking theater.

"Wait, wait, wait," she panted as his lips traced her jawline. "I'm not ready."

Adrik's lips descended down her collarbone. "Yes, you are." He didn't need to slip his fingers in her pussy to find out, but it didn't mean he wasn't going to.

"I…umm—" Jolie struggled with words as she fought herself. A curse was on her lips. "Crap, I'm sorry. I didn't shave."

Adrik chuckled against her skin. Like that mattered to him. She could be hairy as a wolf, and it still wouldn't stop him. A hand slipped down her ass, a place he'd been dying to touch, and gripped the fat, shoving her against him so she could feel what awaited her.

"Adrik," she panted. "There's one thing I need you to do." Her fingers dived into his hair to bring him back to her lips, and she found his tongue with hers, surprising him in the best way.

Adrik shifted, sitting in a chair. "I already know," he revealed. She stood above him, her cheeks red, her lips swollen, her gaze full of want. He held her hips and kissed her belly over her shirt, her big breasts like mountains from this angle. The one thing she needed was an orgasm, and he had every intention to give her more pleasure than she could handle. He bit the hem of her pants, ready to pull them down to her ankles.

"I need you to meet my mother."

Adrik paused. "What?"

A gasp escaped her lips, and she stepped out of his hands. He looked up at her, but her gaze was on the doorway. Adrik turned his head and found Alexei.

Adrik stood, but Alexei only shook his head before he backed out of the room.

Chapter Thirty-One

Brothers

Adrik ran down the hall after his brother. "Alexei!" When he reached the garage doorway, Adrik seized his brother's arm. "Alexei, stop."

"Get in the car," Alexei ordered, grabbing a pair of keys from the panel. The beep echoed as he unlocked his white Porsche.

Adrik didn't hesitate, diving into the passenger seat. He rubbed his face, cursing his stupidity. It was only the first day of his affair, and he was already caught. How in the world would he keep anyone else from finding out? It was only a matter of time, and then what?

Fucking disaster.

Alexei got in and started the car.

"Alexei—"

"No." Alexei stopped him. He backed the car out of the garage and drove up the driveway with the speed of screeching tires. It wasn't until they were a mile down the road that Alexei finally spoke. "You're a fucking dumbass. You had your phone on you. You know you have a locator app, right? Why the fuck would you bring your goddamn phone?"

The topic threw Adrik offbeat. "You're mad you caught me?"

"No, I'm mad that you're fucking dumb. The tutor, Adrik? Really? Why the hell did you let me go on about her, man?"

"I told you she was a lesbian."

Alexei rolled his eyes, "Yeah, great cover story. What the hell are you doing? You bring her to the house? Why would you do that? You want to get this girl killed?"

"I brought her because I could protect her better."

"Who's gonna protect her from Dad?"

The very mention of the old man brought fury to his lips. "I am."

"Oh? Like you protected me?"

Adrik clenched his teeth, looking out the window. There were words on his lips that couldn't be said. Not even to his brother.

"This is so fucking dangerous. What about Katia? If she finds out you're in love with this girl—"

"I'm not in love," Adrik bit.

Alexei cackled. "Yeah, okay. You think I don't know you well enough? You wouldn't do this for some chick you wanted to fuck."

It was hard to fight that. Love wasn't exactly what he was hoping for. Infatuation, maybe. Unhealthy desire, maybe. But not love.

"Where's the future in this? You can't marry her. You can't have kids with her. Dad can never know. And if it's not because you are stupidly in love with her, end it."

Adrik held his face in his hands. All the words he didn't want to hear said out loud like a wailing siren. He tried to ignore it, not give it time to manifest into reality. But it was reality already.

"I'm fucked," Adrik admitted, sinking into the chair.

Alexei pulled to the side of the road. He kept the car running, letting the air conditioning cool his temper. He wasn't mad at his brother for lying, though it would have stopped him from thinking about Jolie in his spare time. He was angry because of the danger Adrik put himself in. Adrik didn't realize how bad things could get with their father. He had been sheltered. He didn't want what happened with Melissa to happen to Jolie. "Answer this before anything else. If you weren't married. If Papa wasn't around. If you weren't in the Mafia. Would you be with this girl?"

It's crazy because all those things he mentioned were the only things stopping him from pursuing her already. He couldn't say it, because he knew what it meant. But he nodded, as terrible as it was.

Alexei sighed, loud and long. "Okay. You've known this girl for a month, and you already know. Mom always said when you know, you know. And I guess, you know." Alexei cut off his monologue and tapped on the steering wheel. "Any chance this is just lust? I mean, you've fucked her, right?"

"No."

"No?" Alexei said incredulously, hiding a wave of selfish relief. "Then, maybe you just got to get her out of your system."

"She isn't like that."

Alexei fought a smile. He agreed that Jolie wasn't like that. It's one of the things he liked about her, too. It was one of many, many things.

Jealousy popped up, and Alexei sat silent, staring blankly out the window. Of all the girls they've ever encountered, they've never gone after the same one. Adrik liked porn stars, and Alexei was into the 'housewife' type. So, what changed? He was so blown away by his brother's interest in Jolie that he couldn't grasp it.

Why this one?

Jealousy was an emotion Alexei dealt with a lot growing up. He had to watch his father dote on Adrik with gifts, with hugs and warmth, while Alexei was ridiculed if he had a wrinkle in his shirt.

"I'm not gonna let you hurt this girl, Adrik. So, are you sure, beyond a doubt, she's what you want? She's nothing like the girls you've been with." The words came from a place of resentment despite how he tried to make it seem selfless.

"Don't you think I know that?" Adrik bit back. "She's a mouse in a snake pit. I've tried talking myself out of it, but I can't." Adrik pulled a paper from his pocket, slapping it on his brother's leg. "Wrote a whole damn pro-cons list. And none of it fucking matters."

Alexei could hear the turmoil in his brother's voice, but it didn't stop the evil smile as he unwrapped the paper to check it out. A dozen cons were on the list, all reasonable and valid, with only one pro. Of course, he had to read it out loud. "'Pro: she's perfect.' Awww."

Adrik snatched the paper from his brother's hand, slapping him in the face with it.

Alexei cackled, hiding his head. "Okay, okay, I'm sorry."

Alexei watched him, his smile slowly fading. There was no denying it then. Adrik was in love with Jolie. It was rough to accept because he began to think he was feeling the same damn things. She was perfect in every way that other women weren't.

His jealousy was fading. Adrik was his best friend, and despite always getting everything Alexei wanted, Adrik cared for him when no one else did.

Alexei swallowed any spite and became the big brother. "Alright. Here's the plan. One, you can't look at her. Even side glances. She doesn't exist. She's beneath you in every sense of the word—"

"No, she's—"

"She's beneath you. Everyone sees it. She is a schoolteacher. She is a cat-loving book nerd. A Democrat. American! She is completely out of your realm. She might as well be on a different fucking planet."

"Okay."

"Okay." Alexei rubbed his face, trying to organize the jumbled mess of his thoughts. "I'll get you both burner phones that you can use to talk to each other. But you have to delete your messages every night. Keep the phone in your safe. I'll get her a safe. But number one, the most important, you can't fuck her in the house."

Adrik wanted to fight. He tried to pretend that it wasn't a big deal and that it wouldn't matter if he made his way to her room. Or if he snuck them into private hallways or closets where his father's cameras weren't watching.

"If you guys get caught, her life is in danger. Dad will kill her if he realizes what's going on."

Adrik knew this; it had been the one thought to keep him from going after her, but how was he supposed to keep them a secret? It didn't seem possible.

"Does anyone else know?"

"Gil."

"Gil?" Alexei huffed. "You told him before me?"

Adrik scratched his head, feeling guilty. Gil was the one who harbored all the taboo secrets of the family. But telling Alexei made it real, and up till this point, Jolie was a secret in his closet. Now, there was no going back. "I knew you wouldn't approve."

"I don't approve. I most sincerely do not approve. This is stupid and dangerous—"

"You've said that."

"And I'll say it again. This is *stupid* and *dangerous.* But"—Alexei stalled, shaking his head and looking around before he forced his head toward his brother—"my little brother's in love." He dropped a hand on the back of Adrik's neck, squeezing as he grinned. "It's great. I'm happy for you. And I'll do whatever I can to help. But you have to understand the risk."

"I do."

"Does she? Have you explained your situation?" A nod eased him in one direction but depressed him in another. "I can't believe she's willing to do this. She must be in love with you, too."

Adrik kept his gaze on the window, but a smile teased his lips. That may be true.

"And I fucking asked her out like a dumbass. Did she tell you?"

"You didn't just ask her out," Adrik bit. "You asked her to a family dinner."

Alexei tried to defend himself, and admitted, "Just to piss off Dad. It worked, apparently."

Adrik snapped his head toward him. Though it was dark in the car, he could still make out the bruises. "You provoked him," Adrik sneered. "Damn it, Alexei. That's your fucking problem, you know that? You fucking push."

"I'm not going to be controlled like a little fucking puppet."

"Is that how you see me? Look at me, asshole. Is that how you see me?"

Alexei turned his gaze to his brother. He ground his teeth, unsure of what to say. Honesty was the go-to. "A little."

"Oh, fuck you."

"Everyone knows that Papa is past his prime. The whole fucking family is waiting for you, and you just sit there as he fucks shit up. You know he lost a case of cocaine? How does someone do that? How do you lose a million dollars' worth of supplies? Where the fuck did it go?"

Adrik rolled his eyes. "No, he didn't."

"Adrik, you don't see it, because you're so far up his ass. He's been making mistakes. Why do you think he left for those two months?"

"Because he nearly had a heart attack."

"Fine, believe what you want, but don't come after me because you are too busy being daddy's little bitch."

Adrik bit the inside of his lip. He had half a mind to break one of his brother's fingers, just to sedate the rage inside him.

"Oh, God." Alexei rubbed his face, setting panic in Adrik as he watched him.

"What?"

"Mom. She'll see it the moment you look at Jolie. You can't look at her, do you hear me? Or she'll know."

"I won't look at her," Adrik agreed, but he didn't know how much of not looking he could do if Jolie were in his line of sight. What was the alternative? Stay out of her reach. Stay out of the house.

Looking for a distraction, Adrik asked, "Any luck finding Katia's brother?"

"That's what I was coming to tell you. I have a lead. Think he went to Puerto Rico. Gonna head out there on Sunday after the dinner. See if I can't flush him out."

"I'll go."

"To Puerto Rico?"

"Yeah." Adrik needed the trip. Needed to get away because his brother put into words every fear he had. There was not going to be a happy ending for them.

Unless he could prove that Katia knew the hit on their daughter was coming. Part of him wanted it to be true simply to be rid of her, but the other part prayed it wasn't. Helina deserved a mother, and though he hated Katia, he didn't want her to be absent from his daughter's life.

A trip to Puerto Rico was the only way to help him stay away from Jolie. But that was one day out. Twenty-four hours to not fuck it up. Why did it suddenly feel like an impossibility?

Chapter Thirty-Two

Meeting the Parents

Jolie had barely slept, and though it was the weekend, and she didn't have to wake early, she was still up before the sun. The lack of sleep filled her brain with fog, making thinking difficult, yet that was all she could do.

Adrik had left her to chase after his brother, and just like the night before, he sent her no message to ease her worries. His lack of communication was gonna have to change. She wasn't the kind of woman who just went about knitting as the world blew up around her. She was proactive, but she could only react to the information she had, and if she had nothing, then she could do nothing.

Facts. Start with the facts, Jolie attempted to focus her brain. Alexei knew about them now. What would he say? How would he react?

That's not facts! she scolded herself.

Ming and Tae-Tae followed her around the room, trying their darndest to rub against her legs. Tripping her was a consolation prize. "Would you get out of my way!" she barked with annoyance before she plopped into a chair. They promptly jumped at the invitation and meowed in her face.

Dropping a hand on their furry heads helped relieve the stress, and she sighed, lowering her head back.

Alexei's face, she mused. *He was beaten. Why did Adrik tell me he was okay if he wasn't?*

"Because he keeps freaking walls higher than China," she answered herself, but Ming thought it was praise and meowed in affection.

Jolie stared at her phone, telling herself to let it go while getting up simultaneously, hoping for some sort of text message. She was afraid to message him, but she pressed his number anyway. She hadn't added his name. She hated how, even with her own phone, she didn't know if she could trust anyone looking at her call log or somehow finding out.

Jolie began to text, writing a single letter before erasing it and starting over. It took her ten minutes to find a way to say what she wanted without really saying it. "Everything okay?" It was a blank question; if anyone read it, they wouldn't think much of it.

She was surprised when dots showed up on her phone, and she sat up, suddenly eager.

Seconds ticked by. It felt like an eternity until the text came from Adrik. "Fine."

It was so anticlimactic Jolie got frustrated. She wanted answers. She wanted to know when she would see him again. She wanted to talk to him, to understand what was going on. But this was something she would have to learn to suppress.

Was she going to have to wait on pins and needles all day until he deemed to bless her with his presence? Was that the kind of life she was gonna have?

I can't keep going back and forth. I need to make a final decision and be done with it.

And that one decision waited on one person: her mother.

Jolie texted, *'I'm going to my mother's.'*

She waited for a reply, but when none came, she left the safety of her room. It was early in the morning, so it wasn't a surprise there was no one out except for the maids. She told the front doorman where she wanted to go, and a car was brought around immediately. Though it was so easy, she didn't know why she always felt anxious when leaving the property, like she was doing something wrong.

Her mother was beyond excited for her to be coming home. She hadn't been back to the trailer park in months. Leaving the small town of Geneva had been difficult. It was all she had known for so long. There wasn't any chaos or crime. It was always quiet. Of course, it was only in her part of town. A charming little neighborhood that had its own neighborhood watch. Across the street was the 'riffraff' her mother deemed unworthy. Jolie was never allowed outside the gates, even when Vincent wanted to bring her to his house. He was part of the 'west side' her mother disapproved of.

Jolie was nervous. She knew Vincent was still in prison, but his cousin lived in their old place and absolutely hated her.

For a reason, Jolie knew. When she turned Vincent into the police, she made plenty of enemies.

Jolie smiled upon pulling up to her parents' trailer. There were so many plants, gnome statues, bird feeders, and windchimes it looked like a store. She hopped on the little round footpath, and the door swung open. Her mother greeted her with her arms open.

Heather Bell was a fifty-year-old retired schoolteacher, part hippy, part human rights activist. She used to have beautiful brown hair like Jolie, but gray hair had started back in her forties, and she didn't do anything to stop it. Now, she was entirely gray and proud of it. She wore a flowery dress, with a dozen bracelets on each arm. "My baby came home!" Heather embraced her, and whispered, "I didn't know you were bringing a guest."

"A guest?" Jolie responded with confusion. As her mother pulled away, she found Adrik standing in the living room.

Her heart nearly burst.

"What—" She stumbled as she took a step forward. Adrik reached out for her hand, trying hard to suppress his smile. He enjoyed surprising her more than he thought he would. Jolie stuttered, "What are you doing here?"

Adrik leaned in, kissing her cheek, "You said you wanted me to meet your mother. So, here I am. She and I have been talking for a few minutes."

Heather came up behind her daughter. "Yes, can I borrow her for a moment?"

Adrik released her and sat back on the couch.

Her mother had her by the arm, and she tripped over her feet, interrupting her wild stare. Adrik looked entirely out of place on her mother's 1940s floral couch. He was a building in an enchanted forest. She never really appreciated how tall he was, how his muscles were shaped against his white shirt, how long his legs were in his tight jeans, and how big his feet were in their white Nikes.

Heather shut the door to the bedroom. "Where did you find that Greek god?"

Jolie giggled, shrugging.

"He's beautiful. And so charming. That accent is every fantasy I've ever had—"

"Okay, Mom."

"But the tattoos. You know how I hate tattoos. Does he smoke?"

"No."

"Alright, redeeming quality. Is he the brother of the guy you are working for? Because that other guy was married, right? It's their daughter you are tutoring, not his?"

Jolie hesitated. She had been given half-truths since she first started working for Adrik, but here it was presented in a way that would be a full-out lie if she said yes. The last time she started lying to her mother, she was dating Vincent, which turned into a disaster.

She needed to be honest if she was seeking her mother's approval. "It's his child."

"But you told me he was married."

Jolie was able to stretch the truth with this answer. "They are separated and about to get divorced."

"Oh, okay. So, he's the one with all the money." Heather peeled open the door, looking down the hallway to watch him. Adrik was nervous, his fingers tapping on his thigh as he looked around. There were dozens of photos frames hung up, covering nearly every inch of empty wall space. Jolie winced, remembering all her school pictures since she was in kindergarten were in those said frames.

"You said he was in finance?" her mother questioned. "Doesn't quite fit the corporate look. He looks like he's in a gang."

Jolie vehemently shook her head but couldn't deny it, so she casually agreed offhandedly. "Yeah, I know."

"Jolie." Heather turned to her, grabbing her hands. "This isn't the kind of guy I was hoping you would bring home. What kind of wedding photos are you gonna have?"

Jolie's cheeks burned. "We just started dating."

Her mother looked out the door again and sighed. "I guess there's Photoshop." Heather dived out of the room. "Adrik, what do you know about plants?"

Adrik and Jolie waved as they moved off the front porch. Heather and Jolie's stepfather watched from the doorway, with bright smiles and high aspirations in their glittering eyes.

Adrik had a hand on her back, guiding her toward the car. But when Adrik saw the man who was driving, he pulled Jolie behind a tree. It was one of his father's lackeys. Jolie questioned it, but he changed the subject. "Do you believe I have your mother's approval?"

Jolie leaned against the tree trunk, with a massive smile. "When you broke out about annuals and perennials and the kind of sunlight certain plants require, I think she thought about divorcing my stepdad for you."

He chuckled, smiling, shrugging. "Might have done some research."

The reveal overwhelmed her. What kind of man puts so much effort into meeting parents?

Adrik stepped up, a leg between hers as he rested a hand on her hip. "You didn't sleep," he noted.

Jolie hung her head, ashamed of her overthinking.

Tears stung her eyes, and Adrik's brows knitted as he watched her bow her head, hiding the emotion. He quickly gripped her jaw, forcing her to look at him. His thumb wiped across her cheek. "What?" he asked.

"I'm scared. Alexei caught us—"

"He won't say anything."

"But how long until your father finds out? I'm terrified of him. If we do this, he's going to find out, Adrik."

Adrik slipped his hand to her neck, holding her still as he rested his forehead against hers. He knew she was right. He'd have to tell his father at some point. But he was more concerned about whether Jolie wanted to be in his life. He wasn't about to start a battle if Jolie gave up at the first sign of trouble.

"And what about Katia?"

"What about her?" The words came out crisp. Jolie continued to add to their problems, pointing out the flaws. And it didn't help that she brought up the same things even after he reassured her they weren't a problem. "I've told you; Katia and I have nothing to do with each other."

Jolie's cheeks heated up. "I've seen you kiss."

"Yes, we perform. We pretend. But that is all."

She nodded, but it was clear she didn't quite understand. He didn't know what else to say, however.

Jolie touched his chest, fiddling with a frayed edge of his shirt. "And the girls on the stripper poles?"

Adrik chuckled. "I was waiting for you to say something." He nuzzled her cheek, a hand running through her hair. "They are a hazard to my lifestyle. Nothing I can do. However, if you are wondering if I will be faithful, I can only assure you that I am addicted to you. No one else will satisfy."

Jolie laid her head against his shoulder. His scent filled her, a sweet bourbon that created butterflies in her stomach. Her smile stretched, unhindered, and she bit her lip to stop herself from making noises in her throat. To know that a man like him was 'addicted' to someone like her was too much. She felt lost in the euphoria.

Adrik held her, unsure where this left them. There were so many things against them, but Adrik wasn't the kind to dwell on the negative. Having a mafia empire was one of the hardest businesses to own, and yet, he had succeeded. He had no doubts in himself about making this relationship work. But he did doubt if Jolie could handle it, but that was out of his hands.

"I have to go," he whispered, his lips right against her skin. She needed more time, and he had obligations to attend to before the dinner tonight. "Being apart from you is creating havoc in my head."

She giggled and nodded. "Me too."

"Oh, yeah?" He nudged her. "Tell me."

"I can't think."

"What else?"

"I look for you everywhere."

"What about at night? Do you dream of me?"

Jolie clenched her lips together as a wave of heat spread through her cheeks and down into her chest. "Yes," she admitted in a murmur.

His fingers clenched her hip, and he purposely pulled her hard against him and groaned, imagining Jolie fingering herself, with him in her mind. "You're gonna drive me crazy." Adrik shoved himself away, backstepping, and every inch placed between them was a knife in his gut.

Jolie stood, holding her arms around herself as his warmth was torn away. He walked away, only looking back once before he stepped around the trailer. She stayed against the tree, falling more for the mafia man with every second they were apart. But her happiness was being eaten away as her secret about the FBI filtered through it. Now, with her mother's acceptance, there should be nothing keeping her from diving headfirst into love, but a rope kept her tied to a wall, refusing to let her fall.

"How sweet," a voice from the bushes came.

Chapter Thirty-Three

The Past

Through the bushes, Santiago stepped out. *"¿Cómo estás, JoJo?"*

Jolie was frozen as she watched Vincent's cousin approach. Santiago was dressed in black on black, with a chain at his hip and four gold necklaces at his chest. He was heavyset, easily over two hundred, while he was her height.

Santiago pointed a fat finger. "Was that who I think it was?"

There was no way he knew who Adrik was. There was no reason for him to know. "Get off my property."

"Or?" he challenged, stepping closer.

She sneered; she could smell the cigarettes and stale liquor from the ten-foot distance between them. Jolie turned from him.

"Hold on, mama. Don't run away just yet." Jolie didn't want to stay, but she felt obligated, like she used to feel all the times her so-called friends talked crap about her. She was to blame for the loss of their star football player. There was no getting around the blame.

"Thought you knew better than to come back here. Guess my message didn't get through."

Jolie was already over his ridiculous threats. "My family lives here. You think you scare me?"

"I think you're a dumb bitch."

"Great. Well, out of the two of us, I graduated high school, so…" Jolie moved for the house again, but Santiago had her wrist. She knocked him off, taking a step back. He smelled worse up close. "Don't touch me."

"Or?" he challenged again with a cocky smirk. "Vinny ain't here, mama. And you're to blame for that."

"I wasn't the one who robbed a bank."

"But you are the one who told him how."

Jolie clenched her teeth, unwilling to expose the guilt that fell into her gut.

"Never seen anyone take a plea deal so fast."

"I didn't know he was going to actually do it!" she fought desperately. All these years, no one listened. No one cared either. They assumed that she turned on Vincent to save her skin, and maybe there was some truth to that, but he set her up first. He used her first. Everyone seemed to forget about that one heartbreaking fact.

Had she gotten any sympathy? Did anyone come up to her and say what an ass Vincent was for what he did to her? Vincent took her future in his hands when he didn't have any right to it. He nearly destroyed her life.

"I'm not the one you gotta convince, mama. If you come with me, my uncle would love to talk to you."

She chuckled, a defense mechanism to hide the bubbling panic while she stepped back. Jolie had never met Vincent's dad. In fact, Vincent never once spoke about him. "I'm not going anywhere with you. Vincent told you to leave me alone."

"You think he gives a fuck about you anymore? You left him to rot in prison for five years. Had to make sure you didn't go to the parole hearing."

The comment stayed with her. She had missed the parole hearing because of Adrik. Vincent was the furthest he'd ever been from her mind. She didn't care what happened to him now. But Santiago's comment meant something.

"You sent that person to my apartment, didn't you?"

Santiago nodded, but anger twisted his lips. "A friend of mine. Now fucking dead because of you."

"What?" Jolie knitted her brows. "What are you talking about?"

"Like you don't know. Got friends in high places now, huh? Mixed up with those Russian bastards over in Tampa. Got yourself a nice setup, right, mama?"

Jolie ran a hand through her hair. Did Adrik do something? Would he go back on his word? "He didn't. He wouldn't." She looked at Santiago. "You're lying," she determined. Adrik promised he would leave it to the cops. Not killing her attacker was the only reason she agreed to move into his house. He kept going on about being honest. Adrik wouldn't lie.

But Santiago would.

"I always told Vinny to watch out for you. You were always too fucking smart while pretending to be dumb as fuck."

Jolie shifted. She never liked Santiago, but she never believed he would hurt her. Now she knew better. Jolie backed up, moving further from the house. Santiago followed, smirking as he did so. He liked the fear in her eyes.

"*Hafe* says I got to leave you alone. But how will he find out, huh?"

Jolie sneered. "You'd have to catch me first." Jolie turned and ran to the car. The driver popped out of the vehicle, ignorant of what was going on, but rushed to open her door. She stared at Santiago from over the door, daring him to try. It was the first time she acknowledged the strength Adrik's family had.

Santiago nodded, backing up and spitting on the ground. "This ain't the last of it, mama," he promised.

The driver looked back at him. "Who is this?"

"No one," Jolie assured as she slipped into the car. She stared at him through the darkened window. Five years ago, Santiago was the loser everyone made fun of. He was the acne-covered wannabe, hanging around Vincent, if only to look more important than he was. Even with all the new piercings and tattoos, there was clearly no improvement.

But he did have the same spider tattoo as the man who attacked her in her apartment. He called them friends. Did that mean Santiago was in a gang? Adrik had mentioned the Toxins. Jolie wouldn't be surprised if he got involved in that lifestyle. Santiago was always looking for more attention than he got. Jolie used to ask Vincent why he kept Santiago around, and she could hear his reply like he was right beside her. *'He's like my bodyguard. Don't worry, mama; he's on our side.'*

Jolie picked at her nails as doubt began to filter through her head. She fell for Vincent's charms so quickly, and here she was, doing the same thing for Adrik's. Were they the same person, just a few years apart? Adrik was the older, more mature version of who Vincent would become.

She hadn't learned a thing. "Oh, God, I am so freaking dumb." She sighed.

When Jolie returned to her room at the Morozov residence, completely exhausted and ready for a long nap, a hairdresser and makeup artist were waiting outside her bedroom. Jolie tried to say 'no thanks,' but it wasn't a choice. There were six hours till the party, and she couldn't understand why they were starting so freaking early. Until she realized all that they had to do.

Now her hair was curled and pinned to the top of her head, her makeup was flawless, they managed to cover up the bruise on her arm, and her nails were perfectly cut and painted. Hours of work and Jolie despised her reflection. She looked fake. Jolie attempted to rub at it, but it was frozen on her cheeks with some type of super glue.

The dress she wore was too exposing. She didn't know how much Katia spent, but the fact that it was a designer dress meant it was over a hundred dollars. She didn't want to insult the woman by removing it, but it was too much change. Her face and hair and now her clothes? She couldn't handle it. She needed a piece of herself, or she'd go insane.

Jolie removed the dress and grabbed a simple peach-colored halter dress that went down to her feet. She kept her plain black heels, hoping that would somehow abate. But now her face and hair didn't match the type of outfit she had on. The upper part of her was ready for the Grammy's while the lower part was ready for wine country. Imposter syndrome kicked in. She didn't look like the kind of girl that hung on the arm of a mafia boss.

Because I'm not.

Katia's dress was staring at her from the bed. Should she try harder? Try to fit the mold?

A knock on the door interrupted her decision, and she whipped it open with aggravation. She blinked in surprise when Alexei stood in front of her. He wore a perfectly cut maroon suit, with a crisp white undershirt and pocket square. The only thing destroying his natural good looks were the bruises on his face. A hand went to her lips, a sound escaping her. Up close, it was worse than she thought.

Alexei smiled, his eyes running down her outfit. "You look amazing." Her look of concern didn't fade, so he touched his face to acknowledge the bruises. "I'm fine. Got in a brawl with someone. You should see the other guy."

His attempt at humor forced her to move on. She dropped her hand, smiling. "Did he insult your brother?"

His brows knitted, and he playfully wondered, "What makes you say that?"

"You'd do anything for him. Even take on someone bigger than you."

Alexei bowed his head, a slight heat coming to his cheeks. It filled him with pride to know she could see it. "I would," he whispered. Using her words, he reiterated, "Even step aside for a girl."

When Jolie made the connection, her eyes widened.

"Can I come in?" Alexei didn't wait for an invitation; he stepped in and closed the door behind him. She took a few steps back and struggled to speak, but he interrupted, holding out a small back phone. "This is for you. You and Adrik will be able to communicate without worrying about my father. Delete all your messages every time you talk, and leave it in your safe." Alexei walked over to her closet and pulled back her door. In the far corner was a black box that wasn't there before. "Make the code longer than six numbers and tell no one."

Jolie blinked, processing everything he was saying. "You're helping us?"

"Just like you said, I'd do anything for my brother. My loyalty lies with him. So, I feel I should warn you. If you hurt him—" He hesitated. Threatening her felt unnatural and wrong. "Just don't," he finished. Alexei took a breath, "Ready?"

"For?"

"I asked to escort you to dinner."

Jolie uneasily shifted on her foot, "But people might get the wrong idea."

He nodded. "That's the point. Whatever takes the attention away from Adrik. And I'll remind you, you can't look at him, can't talk to him. It's better if you don't go near him." With that, Alexei moved to the door and waited with his arm out to her.

Will it always be like this? Will Adrik and I never be able to be together in public? Or just until his father is out of the way?

Jolie took a deep breath and took Alexei's thick arm. "You smell good," she complimented, hoping to break the tension. If there was any tension. She didn't want things to be weird between them, but she was unsure how to be friends with him. He threatened to kill her but asked her out.

What if Mally was lying?

The thought would have never crossed her mind, but Mally could have lied as effortlessly as Santiago did. She trusted people without really looking at their credentials. Jolie thought about asking Alexei. Would he know what happened to the member of the Toxins? Would he admit to talking about killing her? How honest were members of the Mafia?

Chapter Thirty-Four

Dinner Party

The dinner was as extravagant as Jolie thought it would be. It was on a rooftop, with a twenty-person table, candles, and big centerpieces of roses and lilacs. The lighting and the ambiance set an elegant mood. There were couches by the edge of the glass railing and an electric fireplace in the center. A bar traced the edge, with twenty servers all standing, waiting to deliver. The menu had five items, and with no price, Jolie struggled with what to order. But as she was reminded by Alexei, it was all paid for by the Morozov family.

Sitting next to Alexei made the night a comedic adventure. With every question, he had a hilarious quip that got her several stares throughout the night. The first time she laughed out loud, she was so embarrassed she didn't know what to do with herself, except try to bury her head behind a menu.

Now, she laughed full-heartedly without a care who she disrupted.

Alexei enjoyed every laugh he received. It encouraged him to keep going. He kept his laughter silent, usually taking a drink to suppress it, but he was actually having a good time for once.

One too many times, he caught Adrik's gaze. Jealousy was an uncommon emotion in his brother, and Alexei was surprised at how much he liked seeing it. There had never been a moment in their lives that Adrik was jealous of *him.* It made him feel foolishly powerful. Which was dangerous, he knew.

Alexei slipped his gaze down the table. He was ten seats away from his father. The distance was purposeful, a way to tell Yakov he was far from forgiven. There was no going back. Alexei was done hoping things between them would eventually get better. Yakov had destroyed his pride, having beaten him like a pathetic little kid. He couldn't risk being put in such a position again, not just for his sanity but for his brother. Adrik wouldn't hold back next time. And Alexei wouldn't stop him.

Yakov walked down the line, talking to family members. Alexei took his drink in his hand, clenching it when his father rested a hand on his shoulder. It was a gesture meant to be affectionate, but it made Alexei cringe. "You enjoying yourself, Miss Bell?"

Jolie shifted slightly to look up at him, "Yes, sir, thank you."

"Yes." He added, "We've all noticed."

Jolie stuttered as she stared at her plate. "I'm-I'm sorry—

"No." Alexei gained her attention. "Don't be."

Yakov leaned into his son's ear, and whispered in Russian, ***"I thought I told you not to bring her."***

Alexei turned his head toward Adrik. His brother monitored their exchange, and Alexei raised a finger, a quiet, subtle gesture to tell Adrik he was alright. ***"I thought I made it clear I don't follow your rules."***

Yakov squeezed him harder and was about to respond when Tatianna came up behind him. ***"Did you see who came? Agent Mally. Let us greet our longtime friend."***

His father's hand drifted from his back, and Alexei watched them walk down the line, greeting the FBI agent with patronizing excitement. He stared at the back of his father's head, imagining what it would be like to put a bullet through it.

"Are you okay?" Jolie questioned, a hand on his forearm. The touch pulled him, a pleasant distraction that he focused on. He was glad she didn't know Russian.

"My father was raised in an old tradition where a woman is seen and not heard. I, however, was raised by my mother." They change their direction to see Tatianna giggling at something Mally said. "I know better." Dutifully, Alexei added, "And so does my brother."

Jolie snapped her head back to the table. Mally was here. This woman was insane. Why would she come to a lion's den? Did she have no fear? The tension that had faded over the last few days returned with a vengeance, and Jolie struggled to keep her fingers from shaking. Mally was more conniving than Jolie understood. How had she managed to come to a private, invitation-only dinner?

What if she tries to talk to me here? She'll expose me.

Jolie had to tell Adrik before Mally did. She'd be able to get him to understand that she hadn't wanted to do it, but she felt forced. It was never her intention to betray him.

Is that what I'm doing? Betraying him? But I haven't given Mally anything.

Alexei stood, cutting into Jolie's panic. "Excuse me, princess, I've been summoned." He motioned to Adrik, who was now standing with Gil and two other people.

"Oh, don't leave me." Jolie grabbed onto his hand. He had become her protector at this party, and she dreaded any moment without him.

Alexei chuckled, squeezing her fingers. "You're strong; you can handle it. As long as Katia doesn't talk to you." They both glanced toward her, and her consistent look of contempt was as constant as Adrik's scowl of envy. "Good luck," Alexei winced, regretfully slipping out of her fingers.

The smile couldn't stay off his lips even as he was accosted by cousins, hungry to know who the woman was and if he was really dating an American. The disgust and judgment they *didn't* try to hide were noticeable in their glances and lip curls.

Alexei excused himself after answering a few questions, ignoring the insults about her state of dress and her less-than-perfect features, and joined his brothers in their circle.

Gil was the first to comment, ***"Looks like you and the tutor are having a good night."***

Alexei held a drink, dodging Adrik's gaze as he stared at the liquor, swooshing it around, and carelessly said, ***"She's fun."***

"Any sparks flying?"

Adrik interrupted, ***"Enough."*** He clenched the glass in his hand, watching his brother, waiting for his attention, but Alexei was distant. Perhaps he put too much faith in his brother's loyalty. Alexei had feelings for Jolie; no amount of denial could erase the way his brother laughed.

But that wasn't a conversation for this place. Adrik turned his attention to his cousin. ***"How much are you willing to sell your stock for?"***

Jolie left the table, unwilling to sit and meet the prying eyes of strangers. Alexei had introduced her to most of them, cousins and aunts and uncles, but it was apparent none of them approved of her. The word, *americanum*, was easy to figure out. Being American was a problem for all of them. Thankfully, most of the night was spoken in English, as the younger generation wasn't as bilingual as they should be, so she was more aware of the festivities. The amount of love Yakov showed his wife was surprising. He gushed on her every chance he got, making a speech in her honor and showing her rare affection that she adored, leaning into him and smiling nonstop.

Jolie leaned against the bar, sipping her water while watching Mally leave the rooftop. The woman turned at the last minute and met her eyes, but Jolie quickly bowed her head as her heart raced.

What did Mally expect from her? She wasn't made to be a spy. Jolie hadn't brought the pen with her for multiple reasons, but none of those excuses sounded good enough for the agent. This place was probably a goldmine of information, but like every guest here, she had been searched before being allowed entry.

Jolie looked over her shoulder nonchalantly, finding Adrik. He was standing beside his brother, so anyone could think she was looking at Alexei. He wore a matching tux, and Alexei and Adrik were models on the runway side by side. Anyone passing would call them twins, but she could see their differences. Alexei viewed the world with humor, without stress or worry. But Adrik appeared with a dark cloud hanging over him. His gaze constantly scanned the crowd, eyeing people, trying to find their deception. She wondered what caused him to be so paranoid.

His blue eyes landed on her as he took a sip of his drink. Jolie quickly bowed her head to hide the flush on her cheeks and the shiver that rolled down her body. The power of his stare was overwhelming. To have a man like him desire her gave her a confidence she hadn't possessed before. Jolie lifted her head to meet his gaze, but he turned away, focusing on Katia.

Jolie's smile drifted.

Katia clung to his arm, looking at him with a mischievous smile. He leaned down and nuzzled her cheek, saying something into her ear that made her gush.

All the good feelings fled, and she turned her attention to the other brother as a distraction.

Alexei was talking to a woman, too. She was ridiculously close, the side of her fat breast touching his arm as if she didn't know. The woman giggled and reached across to caress his bicep. Jolie knew the woman was entirely wrong for him.

Without ever having a conversation about it, she already knew Alexei's type. She was his type, and it was something she was trying not to bring awareness to.

Jolie knew what kind of man she attracted in high school and college. The loners, the nerds, the acne-covered, the quiet and distant. But she wasn't attracted to them. She liked guys with confidence, like Vincent and Adrik. The fact that they weren't all that different was obvious to Jolie. But *she was different. She* was no longer an innocent teenager. She could handle Adrik's dark side in a way she could never have dealt with Vincent's.

Alexei glanced over his shoulder at her when the woman touched him, but Jolie turned away. Whether she turned from him or Adrik, he didn't know and didn't care. He removed the woman's hand from his arm and left the circle. Adrik was in a more challenging position. He couldn't leave his wife, but Alexei had no such obligation. Jolie was his priority, and the world would know it.

Alexei leaned his elbows on the bar, his jacket touching Jolie's arm. Perhaps it was slightly forward of him, but he had drunk plenty tonight and was happier than he had been in a long time, so pushing the limit to what he could and couldn't do wasn't as intimidating. She was his date; if he didn't touch her at all, it would be noticed. Jolie smiled at him, but then her gaze went over her shoulder. He could see the devastation on her face, tearing his stomach apart. Alexei clenched his teeth, fighting the urge to chastise his brother for doing this to her. He ordered another drink before telling her, "Don't watch."

Jolie shook her head and assured, "I'm fine."

"They are faking, you understand?"

"Yeah, that's what Adrik says."

"We may not be perfect, but we aren't liars. It's a pet peeve. We have tempers, and lies are a quick way to get on our bad side."

A silly smile stretched on her face, "You have a temper?"

He chuckled, sipping his drink, "Most will say worse than my brother."

"I don't see it."

Alexei shrugged, "That's because I don't brood." They glanced over their shoulders. Adrik was alone and looked tense, miserable, and ready for a fight. They chuckled, leaning into each other.

Jolie felt relaxed in Alexei's company. It made her confident enough to ask, "Do you know what happened to the man that attacked me?"

Alexei's dark brows knitted. "Someone attacked you? When? Who? What happened? Are you okay?"

She giggled as she watched every expression on his face. There was no way Alexei talked about killing her. There was too much care in his face. Jolie shrugged. "I'm fine. It was a bit ago." Alexei clenched the bar, his knuckles turning white. Jolie rested a hand on his arm. "Adrik told me the police couldn't find him. But a, um...a person I knew said he was killed. I'm just wondering what happened."

Alexei didn't need to know what happened to make the right assumption, but it was probably something Adrik didn't want her to know. The panic receded, and Alexei took a small sip of his drink. Adrik would have taken care of it, but it aggravated him more than it should have because Alexei wanted to be the one to take care of it. To be the one to take care of her.

"Come on. Before another of Katia's friends accosts me and my temper comes out." Alexei threw back the rest of his whiskey and slapped the glass on the table harder than needed.

"Oh, and I was just starting to enjoy myself." The sarcasm wasn't lost, and he cackled, resting a hand on her lower back. It gave him a thrill he didn't want to acknowledge.

They stepped inside the hotel and into the foyer of the elevator. Two guards were standing, and one pressed a button for them. Into his wrist, the soldier whispered to the guards in the garage to prepare their cars.

Adrik and Gil entered behind, and Alexei dropped his hand, feeling slightly ashamed. "After party?" Gil suggested, leaning on his crutch.

"I'm done." Alexei shook his head. "My body hurts. I need a bath."

"A bath...what a pussy. What you need is a Swedish massage."

Adrik stood on the left of Jolie, staring at her through the steel of the elevator doors. She met his gaze shyly, fighting a grin. She looked beautiful tonight, and he fought himself from approaching her the entire time. A spotlight followed Jolie, a beacon that he couldn't ignore. He struggled to stop himself more times than he wanted to admit. And every time his brother laid a hand on her, Adrik wanted to punch him in the face. This night left him bitter, but it wasn't going to end that way.

Now, in an empty hallway, Adrik was finally allowed to give her his attention. And he was not going to hold back.

Gil slapped Adrik's arm. ***"What about it, bro?"***

Adrik didn't break from her and vaguely said, ***"I have plans."***

Gil followed Adrik's stern stare and realized what he was looking at. It pissed him off. He was losing the only brother who actually liked to party. ***"No, you don't."***

The doors opened, and with a hand on her back, Adrik pushed Jolie and turned to Gil and Alexei, "Get the next one."

"Don't," Alexei hissed, trying to stop the closing doors, but Adrik winked at him, a not-so-subtle 'fuck off.'

Gil growled and snapped his head to Alexei. ***"He's out of control."***

When the doors shut, Adrik held Jolie's waist, guiding her back against the wall. She panted heavily in anticipation, and he watched every expression on her face. Adrik kissed her harshly, haphazardly, and she met every twist of his lips. Her hands gripped his shoulders, diving into his hair and holding him close. She broke from him, slightly pushing back. "Adrik, anyone can come in."

Adrik grabbed her wrists and pinned them above her head with one hand. "I don't care." This elevator was suited only to go all the way to the garage. No one could interrupt them. He kissed her neck and her naked collarbone. And then, what he thought about doing all night, he slipped her halter top down, releasing a breast into the air. His first sight of her nipple, and it was hard and ready for his mouth. She struggled, twisting, but it was all a show. She wanted it; there was no denying it. He licked her nipple once before taking her breast in his hand. It filled his palm like a water balloon, and his thumb rubbed over her hard nub.

"Stop," she whispered half-heartedly, trying to free her hands with little effort.

Adrik nuzzled her neck, and groaned, "I want you to have some ideas of what I'm gonna do to you."

The doors opened, and Adrik shifted only slightly to hide her. "It's my guards," he assured, but she still fought. He chuckled against her, squeezing her nipple with his thumb and forefinger. She gasped, pulling away while pushing into him. He adored her pathetic attempt at modesty, watching her face and all the desire that poured into it. "You fight, and yet you want it."

"Someone can see."

"No one can see," he said, leaning in, kissing her, his tongue finding hers, just as needy.

"Sir," a guard called from outside the elevator.

Adrik hated it. There was never enough time with her. He eased back, letting her go, and she quickly put her breast back in. He grinned, watching as she tried to fix her appearance, but she looked wrecked after one minute alone with him. He couldn't imagine an entire night. "I'm coming to your room tonight." He turned to leave.

"No."

His brows knitted, and he turned back to her. "No?" Adrik quickly approached, backing her up till she hit the wall. He gripped her thighs, lifting her up, and forced them around his waist as he pressed hard into her, forcing her to feel all he had to give her. "I've told you before—no one says no to me."

She struggled to speak, a wave of hunger caught in her throat. She had never been manhandled with such perfection. His lips teased her, and she closed her eyes, the nip on her skin sending shockwaves of desire through her. "I want to wait," she admitted, and even as the words came out of her mouth, she hated herself for it.

"Wait?" He ran his nose down her jaw and then stared at the top of her breasts as they heaved for air. "I've waited enough."

"Two weeks—"

"A month. I've wanted you from the first night I met you."

The confession filled her heart with warmth, and she kissed him crazily, digging her tongue into his mouth as if she could be inside him. With a dangerous growl, he thrusted against her hard before he yanked from her, dropping her to her feet clumsily.

He panted harshly and stepped back. "One week," he bargained.

"Three." Jolie adjusted her dress, keeping her back against the wall. Her legs were Jello, and she didn't trust herself to walk.

"Two," Adrik bit. "What is the point of this, exactly? Except to drive me insane?"

"I'm not gonna just get into bed with you. I was taught to wait till marriage."

Adrik sneered. "I thought you were a feminist. That rule only existed to keep women virgins because they were worth more pure."

"Sir—"

"Quiet! I know," Adrik spat, taking a step out of the elevator only to turn back to her. "Two weeks? That is what you want?"

"And three dates."

Adrik nodded once, spinning on his foot. The car was waiting for him, and he dived in. The guard shut his door. "Wait," he said to the driver. He watched Jolie, a hand on the wall as she steadied herself. He smirked, admiring the destruction he had caused. She slowly made it to her car, and as soon as she was in, he ordered the driver to go.

Adrik sat back. He didn't care about the dates, but this was his strangest arrangement. No woman had denied him in such a way. He'd make these two weeks the worst of her life. Being horny for twenty-four hours was a painful way to live, and she was about to find out.

Chapter Thirty-Five

Acting

Jolie was exhausted, spending most of the night tossing and turning, thinking about Adrik. She was trying to decide if her idea to wait was because of something she wanted or something her mother had constantly spewed into her head. She was twenty-three, and getting pregnant in high school was no longer a worry. But still, she hadn't been on birth control since Vincent was taken to jail. And her experience with condoms was always odd and uncomfortable. She was typically too dry, and it hurt when he would shove into her.

Just thinking about it eased some of the intense passion she was feeling. Jolie ended up giving herself two orgasms through the night, and it still wasn't enough to stop the intruding thoughts of Adrik licking her nipple.

Or maybe I'm waiting because I'm a piece of shit. Jolie had to face the fact that she was lying to Adrik. She was working for the FBI, and if she kept going down this path and gave information to Mally, there would be no reconciliation. Adrik would see it as a betrayal. He'd abandon her.

A knock on her door provoked her out of her room. Katia stood on the other side.

"Good morning. Would you walk with me to breakfast?"

Jolie looked down at her pajamas.

"Oh, you're not ready?" Katia mocked. "I'll wait."

Jolie almost slammed the door in her face. Sometimes, she thought Katia was sweet, and then she'd reveal herself in broad daylight. It reminded her of Adrik's warnings. Still, Jolie was desperate enough for a friend that she'd take the insults with a smile.

When Jolie exited, Katia was leaning against the wall in jeans and a T-shirt. And the look on her face said, *'Not much better.'*

"Did you enjoy yourself last night?" Katia wondered casually.

Jolie's eyes widened, and though she knew the woman wasn't talking about her self-care, it was still embarrassing. "Yeah, it was fun."

"I don't think I've seen Alexei laugh so much. It was a nice change."

It was surprising to hear because Alexei seemed to be the funniest of the group.

"You were certainly the talk of the night. Even in that dress."

Jolie knew she was going to bring it up. "Yeah, I'm sorry. I just didn't feel comfortable in the one you chose."

"Now, everyone calls you the 'thrift shop girl.' I guess it is better than being called 'the American.'"

Horror doused her. "They do?"

"Oh, yes. Among other things. How you could possibly think what you wore was more appropriate than the five-thousand-dollar designer dress we picked out, I can't understand. Perhaps, next time, you will follow my advice. If you are invited next time, that is."

They entered the dining room. It was raining outside, so the dining table was set up exquisitely. Thunder rumbled beneath their feet. They were the first to arrive, and Katia excused herself, diving down a hallway to the workers' quarters. Jolie didn't question it. She sat stiff, watching the rain pour into the pool.

Jolie hadn't intended to embarrass herself as severely as she did. It wasn't a good way to wiggle herself into Adrik's family. She would need to let some of her old tendencies go if she wanted to be in his life. And that meant following Katia's advice.

Adrik and Alexei came into the room. The smell of their colognes preceded them, snapping her head to the doorway as they walked in. They wore the same suit, nearly identical to their gelled black hair, collars open to expose the barest of their chests, and shining black dress shoes. And though they looked alike, Adrik gained all of her attention. The tattoo on the side of his neck, the necklace that rested against his collarbone, the way he touched his cuff before resting his hands on the back of his chair—his mannerisms were enough to make her fall to her knees.

"Good morning," he greeted, stiffly scanning the room for privacy.

Jolie dropped her gaze to the food in front of her. She had forgotten for a moment that she wasn't allowed to look at him. Especially with the amount of awe she was feeling.

Alexei sat in the chair next to her. "Hey, you come here often?" Jolie grinned, giggling.

Adrik wasn't going to withstand any of that shit today. He snapped in Russian, ***"Enough with the teacher."***

Alexei flicked his rebellious blue eyes up, replying, ***"Do you have something to say, brother?"***

Adrik met Alexei's gaze, a warning that he didn't want to give. ***"Your infatuation is obvious."***

Alexei sneered. ***"My infatuation? I am doing this for you. To take father's eyes off of*** **you."**

A servant came in and stopped their conversation. Adrik sat, unbuttoned his black coat, and waited for the servant to fill his mug before he sipped his steaming coffee.

Jolie questioned, "Is everything okay?"

"Fine," Adrik bit.

Alexei wasn't about to let it go so quickly. He waited till the servant left the room. "My brother is jealous because he has no sense of humor."

Adrik scoffed, rolling his eyes and shaking his head. But he found himself unable to reply because it was the annoying truth. He didn't know how to make Jolie laugh like Alexei did, which bothered him severely. He was good at everything, but the only thing Alexei excelled at was jokes. And killing people.

Alexei took a bite of a bagel, and said in Russian, ***"She is obsessed with you. Maybe because she hasn't seen your dick yet."***

Adrik snorted, dropping his head, chuckling low.

Alexei smiled and winked at Jolie, assuring her their relationship remained intact.

"Aww, you guys are so cute," Jolie gushed. "Nothing is better than siblings that are best friends."

Alexei agreed, "He is my best friend. But he's also the bane of my existence."

When Yakov and Tatianna came through, the feeling of the table drifted to anxiety and annoyance. It was crazy how someone's presence could do so much. Katia rejoined a moment after, greeting them with intense happiness that Jolie found awkward. The conversation was mainly about the party, with a contemptuous talk about Agent Mally in their midst. At least Jolie wasn't the only one who didn't like that woman.

Adrik and Alexei stood up.

"Where are you two off to?" Their father sat back, interested.

"Puerto Rico."

"What for?" their mother asked.

"To check on merchandise."

"And you both must go?" Adrik leaned over and kissed his mother's cheek. She patted his face. "Be safe."

Katia got up, and Adrik straightened as she leaned in, kissing his cheek. He rested a hand on her hip, looking down at her. "You enjoyed last night?" he whispered heavily in seduction.

Jolie's eyes widened, her fork mindlessly touching the eggs. She could feel the dread pour into her like lava, suffocating her heart. The room went quiet, and she could only hear the pounding in her ears. Her body went stiff, hot, and unbearable.

'There's nothing between Katia and I.' Adrik had assured her, yet here it was. Undeniable, unerasable. The image would stay with her for the rest of her life. How he looked at Katia had been how he looked at her last night. He used the same tone that could make her knees shutter and liquefy her insides.

Tears were pushing against her eyes, and her breath was coming in panicked pants, but she remembered she was at the table. She swallowed, shutting a door in her brain, clamping a lid on the ticking timebomb.

Jolie put a spoonful of egg in her mouth. It was tasteless, but thankfully, her body automatically knew to chew.

Katia giggled and buried her face into his neck. "I don't want you to go."

"I'll be back soon. Perhaps"—Adrik touched her stomach—"you will have a surprise for me."

Jolie nearly gagged on her food. *A baby? Were they trying to have a baby?*

Katia held his hand, rolling her eyes playfully. "Too soon, darling." He kissed her temple, and they separated.

Adrik kissed his father's cheek. "We will text when we land."

"Nothing dangerous, I hope?"

Alexei slapped a hand on Adrik's back, "Wouldn't dream of putting your favorite in danger."

Yakov chuckled, and reminded, "A parent has no favorites. That being said, if you come back without him, you might as well not come back."

Alexei laughed a dry and forced laugh. He glanced at Jolie and received a weak wave. "I'll call you," he boldly stated, glancing at his father for a reaction but Yakov yanked up his newspaper and stayed quiet.

Jolie flinched when the door shut. Her hand fell numbly in her lap. Adrik was sleeping his wife. It shouldn't sound so absurd or heartbreaking and yet, it was. She told herself it was a wake-up call. She needed to see it to fully realize what was going on. This was not a life she wanted for herself. Adrik was not husband material. He was not father material. There was nothing that could come from him but heartache.

Jolie slipped into her pocket and clicked the pen. This is why she came: to find a way to bring down this mafia family that had destroyed the lives of thousands of people. She would find something substantial that she could use so that by the time Adrik returned, she could leave.

Jolie focused her attention on Yakov. He had a scar on his chin, and the stubble refused to grow. He had a fat nose, long ears, and dark, cold eyes. Yakov read some papers, holding one up, inspecting it. He shoved food into his mouth, chewing grotesquely. All her hatred for Adrik bubbled up and directed toward him. Katia spoke in Russian, and they had a conversation that she couldn't be a part of, but she continued to sit there, hoping something they said would be relevant.

Tatianna surprised her, calling her name, "Miss Bell, you are a most wonderful girl. First, you saved my granddaughter, and now you make my son smile. We must get together and have some girl time."

Jolie met Yakov's gaze. As dead as she felt inside, he still sparked a flame of fear, but she dared him now to make a threat so the police could use it. Instead, he smiled. "Yes, I must say, it is a nice change."

Jolie couldn't stand the lie. Did Tatianna know how he had threatened her? How well did this woman know her husband?

Jolie's phone rang, much to her surprise. It was eight in the morning on a Sunday. Her mother should be at church. Jolie took up the phone, finding the number private. She almost ignored it, but something told her to answer it.

"Hello."

"Say 'hi, Mom.'" It was Adrik, and the pain she had stuffed down nearly boiled over.

The words took a moment to process, and even then, she didn't know how to make her voice sound the same. "Hey, mom."

"Excuse yourself from the table."

After a moment to find a way to move, Jolie stood. "Excuse me," she whispered, and Yakov waved a hand.

"Go down the hall to the right."

"No, I can talk," Jolie said as she hastened for the exit.

"Keep going till you see the painting of Ivan the Terrible and his son."

"Dad didn't mean it." She played along, her voice echoing.

"Turn left and go through the door."

Jolie had never been down here because it was the 'servants' quarters. She went through the door to another hallway, but it was empty. She found a storage closet and dived, leaning against the door. Tears were already in her eyes.

"You alone?"

Jolie struggled to keep any emotion from her voice. She didn't want to talk. She didn't want to hear what he had to say. It would be excuses and a bunch of bullcrap. She knew how cheaters manipulated and lied. She couldn't count the times when she saw Vincent talking to another girl, and he made her feel stupid for thinking he'd cheat on her. She always ended up apologizing for thinking the worst.

"Yeah," she murmured against her will.

"Listen to me and listen closely because I will not say it again. I did not fuck Katia."

She rolled her eyes as tears fell down her cheek.

"Katia and I are pretending to appease my father. Katia hates me, Jolie, and I despise her."

Jolie squeezed her eyes shut. Relief came so quickly, and she hated it. She believed him instantly, like an idiot. "You seemed pretty comfortable."

"You cannot fault me for being a good actor." The cockiness made her want to hit him, and at the same time, a smile broke for a second on her lips before it fell. The pain of deception still lingered. Had she learned nothing from the years with a liar? They knew what to say and how to reel you back in like a fish for slaughter.

"You doubt me?"

"I've been through this before."

"Do not compare me to your childish romance from years ago. It's insulting."

Jolie stayed quiet. Her doubts were continuous, but she knew it was a personal issue. She wasn't confident in their relationship. It was one of the reasons why she decided to wait. She didn't want to struggle with trust when trust is one of the fundamentals of a strong relationship.

"Do you think I would risk my reputation to ruin this with you? I do not waste my time, it is too precious to me. If you know anything else about me, believe in that."

Jolie nodded, but she couldn't erase all the emotions so quickly. The dread in her stomach was receding, leaving an emptiness in her gut. She was exhausted, and a headache formed in the aftermath of grief.

"Did you use my gift last night?"

"Tsk." A flush of anger and disgust spread through her, killing her sadness. "No!"

His chuckle filled her ears, warming her from the inside. It relaxed her, and now all she wanted was to curl into his arms.

Adrik sighed. "There will be many things that will question your trust in me. But being with another woman will not be one of them."

She was sucked back in with such little effort.

"Will you send me something?"

Her brows knitted. "What?"

"A picture of your tits."

Jolie slapped a hand on her face. "Goodbye."

He laughed adoringly. "See you, ***krasivyy***."

Beautiful.

Jolie pressed the phone to her chest, her smile bright and wide.

And then she remembered she had clicked the pen. She pulled it out, staring at it in her palm. Quickly, she went through their conversation, trying to pinpoint anything she could have said to alert the agent about what she was doing. Here she was, accusing Adrik of betraying her when she was doing something worse to him. Cheating would only hurt her. Trying to bring down Yakov would destroy Adrik's life. What she was doing wasn't right.

I have to pick a side. But she had already chosen, hadn't she? Jolie just needed to cross the line where she could no longer turn back.

Jolie rubbed her fingerprints from the casing and wrapped it in a fabric napkin before putting it into a thin metal garbage can by the door. She turned to leave but squeezed back into the doorway, hiding, slapping a hand on her mouth.

Katia and Gil were in the hallway.

Making out.

"Oh, crap," she cursed.

Chapter Thirty-Six

Discovered

Jolie hid in her room. She had seen Gil and Katia making out, and now she didn't know what to do. There was no doubt in her mind that Adrik didn't know his brother was moving in on his wife. But was it her place to say anything? Would Adrik believe her?

For hours, she held the phone in her hands, pacing till the exhaustion of the night before pulled her to the bed. Knowing that Katia and Gil were betraying him while she was working for the FBI felt too much for one person.

Jolie was so ready to point out Adrik's flaws, calling him Ted Bundy and recognizing all his alpha male tendencies, because she didn't want to face hers. She had lied to him. She was partnered with the FBI and didn't know how to escape it. What was she going to say to him? Because eventually, she was gonna have to tell him. There was no way around it.

I'll lose him.

The panic only increased from there because not only would Adrik abandon her, but how would he get revenge? She was playing with fire and was delusional enough to think she wouldn't get burned.

Jolie turned her head to Tae-Tae. "I have to tell him." A soft whimper escaped his throat.

Jolie's door burst open, and she sat up, clenching the blankets as soldiers clambered into her room. It was the middle of the night, but they ripped her blankets away and grabbed her arms, pulling her to her feet. "What's going on?"

They shouted in Russian, with rifles in their hands.

Jolie swung her head around, watching three other men ransack her closet and dresser drawers. They dragged her out of the room. "Stop! Please," she begged, digging her feet into the carpet, but they ignored her, yanking her along.

She was relieved when she saw Katia in the same position, her arms in their grips, being hauled down the hallway. She spewed foreign curses and then noticed Jolie over her shoulder.

"Don't fight them," Katia instructed. "They are Yakov's pigs."

Adrik's father was doing this. Was this because Alexei showed her interest? But why take Katia? No, it was something else. Something more terrifying.

Down the stairs, a lineup of servants was on their knees; they were the last two to join. The soldiers dropped them on the floor side by side, and Jolie gripped Katia's hand desperately.

"It's alright," Katia soothed, holding her.

Servants shivered and kept their heads to the ground, but not Katia; her back was straight, waiting impatiently for Yakov to come through the door. The soldiers stayed stiff in front of them, with their rifles pointed at the floor, and when they walked by Jolie, she buried her face into her knees, unable to hide her tremor.

Dressed in a black suit and with a cigar in hand, Yakov strolled into the room.

"What do you think you're doing?" Katia barked. "Adrik will tear you apart for doing this to me, old man."

Yakov put his cigar between his teeth, disregarding her as he stepped inches from a servant's hand. Jolie had nowhere near the confidence Katia had. She was a beast of a woman, and Jolie's respect for her soared.

"Adrik will forgive me," Yakov declared. ***"You, however, I doubt."***

"I've done nothing," Katia spat.

Yakov made a sound in his throat as he strolled the line. He stood before Jolie now, and her eyes widened, staring at her reflection in his shiny black shoes. "What about you, American? Do you have a secret you're hiding?"

Jolie shook her head, too afraid to speak, to move.

When his feet drifted, she let out the breath she was holding, which also triggered her tears. She rubbed her face, trying to take strength from Katia, but she was shaking like a seizure and couldn't stop.

"Shh, it's alright." Katia squeezed her hand. "You've done nothing. You know that. He needs proof for whatever he is claiming."

"Proof," Yakov quipped, "I have."

Jolie was too terrified to look up, but Katia revealed what it was. "A pen?" she cackled. "What proof is this?"

A pen.

A pen.

Jolie's eyes dilated. A wave of nausea crawled up her belly, and she put a hand over her mouth to quell it.

In Russian, Yakov explained what he found. Katia whispered in her ear. "This pen has a listening device. FBI. Found in the servants' quarters. He's gonna question all of us."

Jolie's body went cold. There was no way she would survive this. She wasn't a liar. She wasn't a spy. She was a freaking teacher. She shouldn't be here. She risked everything because of a stupid boy.

Katia ground her teeth. "You dare insult me this way? I am your daughter-in-law."

Yakov smiled, and gently assured, ***"Which is why you will be questioned last. I hope there will be no need, sweet one. Now, let's begin."*** He motioned to the first servant, and though the man struggled to his feet, the soldiers had no problem giving him encouragement by smacking him in the face and shoving him forward.

Jolie winced and shuddered. They were being hurt because of her. Because she had been so stupid to put the pen in a freaking garbage can. All the precautions Agent Mally and Adrik had taken, and she had ignored it, thinking they were overexaggerating.

They took the servant around the corner under the stairs. Jolie had thought it was an odd place for a coat closet, and now she found out what it was.

Only a second later there was a sharp smack and scream. Jolie buried her face into Katia, and the woman held her close. "It's alright. You'll be alright."

Jolie cried ridiculously into her lap, grimacing with every horrible sound. She pressed a hand against her ear, but it was pointless. She could feel it in her soul, their pain.

Fear kept her still; fear swallowed her, made her heavy, unable to dig up any courage and admit it belonged to her, but how long could she sit here and let all these people get hurt because of her? Ten innocent servants waited for her to admit she owned the pen.

What kind of person am I?

The front door opened, and for a moment, Jolie prayed it was Adrik coming to her rescue, but instead, it was Gil. He limped with a cane, skipping toward them in desperation. He went to Yakov's side, speaking in Russian. He glanced at them, at Jolie, at Katia. A hidden hand out to them to let them know he was there to help.

"Yakov does this because Adrik is out of the house," Katia whispered to her. "He will be punished for it."

It didn't matter, did it? This was too much already.

Yakov waved a hand, disregarding whatever Gil was saying, but Gil was not about to be ignored. He got out his phone and quickly dialed a number.

Jolie curled into a ball, watching with wide wet eyes. Her body trembled. It brought her back to the grocery store, where she curled up with Helina, squeezing her little body as bullets sprayed the air above them. For some reason, she found none of that confidence here. Perhaps without a child to focus on, she collapsed into a puddle of pathetic-ness. Or maybe it's because the pen belonged to her, and it's only a matter of time before they find that out, and she'd be killed.

Gil handed the phone to Yakov.

"Adrik," Yakov greeted. He listened intently for a minute before replying, "The American and your wife will be questioned like everyone else. Threaten me as you see fit." He clicked off the phone and handed it back to Gil.

Yakov sighed and took a seat. He lit up his cigar, glancing toward them, but said nothing. There was worry on his brow. Whatever threat Adrik had given him was enough for him to question his moves but not enough to stop him.

"Miss Bell," Yakov called, and her eyes flipped toward him like a frightened animal. "You went into the hallway yesterday morning for a phone call. Am I wrong?"

Jolie shook her head.

"And, Katia, you were seen back there. What was your purpose?"

Katia didn't falter. "None of your business. It doesn't matter where I go, because this is my house. Adrik lets you live here out of kindness, but that kindness can end in moments."

Yakov chuckled bitterly. "You think my son would choose you over me?"

"I believe he already has."

He cackled again, patronizing her, smoking his cigar with enjoyment. "We see things very differently."

"Yes, we do, like how I see an old man at the end of his reign, grasping at straws to stay in power. Adrik has been a king without a crown for years. Push him, and he will snatch it off your head before he throws you over a cliff."

Yakov did not like that. His smile slipped from his lips, and all playful banter died in his eyes.

The door under the stairs opened, and the servant was dragged out. There was no fight left as blood dripped from his back and face. His eyes and lips were swollen; nothing resembled the person who had entered. They dropped his body like a stuffed trash bag.

"Take Katia next."

"You fucking dirty old man," she cursed.

The soldiers came for her, and Jolie grasped her arm, but they pushed her down. Jolie cried for her, curling tighter, pressing her face against the floor.

"No marks on her face. She has a party to attend."

"Yakov," Gil called, approaching. "I beg you not to do this. As my father, as my mentor. Please do not do this."

Yakov took a drag of his cigar and looked like he was contemplating his decision. Katia stood in the arms of the guards, and they waited. Then he flicked his hand.

Jolie felt her resolve cave. They would find out it was her no matter what. She couldn't let anyone come out the way that servant did. His injuries would follow her forever. The guilt would be too much, and she'd cave. So, before all that could happen, she needed to speak.

"It was mine," Gil broke out, stopping the soldiers.

Jolie hesitated. She didn't understand what they were saying, but something had happened, and the words clogged her throat.

Yakov rolled his eyes. ***"I don't believe you."***

"Adrik interrupted a shipment of spyware to the Secret Service. Pens, pendants, earpieces, buttons, even things to put on the bottom of our shoes. I had the pen on me when I met Katia in the hallway to talk to her about Adrik's party. She asked if I had a pen, and I gave it to her."

"It didn't work," Katia murmured, latching on to the story.

Gil pointed out, ***"Which is why she must have thrown it away."***

Yakov listened, but there was much doubt in his face. ***"Why did you have the pen on you?"***

"I had a meeting with the Toxins an hour before. They speak Spanish, and I wanted to make sure they weren't double-crossing me."

"If"—Yakov emphasized the word—***"what you say is true, then you'd have another one. Let me see it."***

There was a hesitation that Yakov took as a sign. He waved again to the soldiers to take Katia into the room, but once more, Gil persisted. He shouted to one of the guards, and they ran out of the house.

Yakov snapped his fingers, and an ashtray was put in the palm of his hand. He worked all the ashes off slowly as they waited. ***"I'm curious why Adrik didn't tell me this."***

"Are you?" Gil nipped, ***"He wanted to use these things to spy on you."***

A snicker sounded deep in Yakov's throat.

The soldier rushed through the front door, with a pen in his hand. It was silver, like Jolie's, and hope formed in her gut. Where had they gotten a copy? Yakov took out his own and compared them on the desk. Jolie held her breath as she watched him, searching for any movement in his face that would reveal her future. All the pressure of the world rested on her back.

Yakov motioned, and the soldiers let Katia go.

Jolie released her breath, sinking to the ground, pressing her face into the carpet. The tension in the room eased a little, and though she didn't know what happened, she felt saved.

"You're going to regret this," Katia vowed. "Crazy old man."

Yakov held up a hand. ***"No harm done. Perhaps this is a learning experience. I may be old, but my reign is far from over."***

Chapter Thirty-Seven

Partnership

Despite how hard she fought it, Katia's motherly instincts were impossible to quell when she noticed the tutor quivering on the floor. Being in the Mafia was typically a groomed lifestyle. From the time she was four years old, Katia was exposed to guns, drugs, and naked women to the point where she envied these girls with big boobs, hoping she would have ones just like them one day. She knew what guns were worse than others. And that cocaine was supposed to be as good as ice cream.

Jolie was a twenty-three-year-old newborn, and Katia felt responsible for her in Adrik's absence. Only because her daughter loved her so.

With words of encouragement, Katia gripped the young girl's arms and got her to her feet. Jolie's body continued to tremble as they struggled with the steps. Katia knew shock all too well and didn't fault her for it, but it was still annoying. "Come on, girl," she murmured, panting as they finally reached the top of the stairs. She thought about bringing Jolie straight to her bedroom, but it wouldn't sit with Katia to leave the woman in such a state, so instead, Katia brought her into her own room. The bedroom had been trashed, and everything she owned had been thrown on the floor. She cursed Yakov some more as she moved them to the bathroom. She kicked aside all the medicines and toiletries spilled on the tile and rested Jolie on the toilet seat. Katia spun around to turn on the faucet to the Jacuzzi tub, searching the ground for bath salts.

This was the first time Yakov had done something so damaging. Would this alter their future? Would Adrik finally see Yakov as the enemy he was?

Katia moved through the mess to the side door connected with Helina's bedroom and peeked her head in. Helina remained asleep, and Katia thanked Adrik for putting in soundproof walls. Her daughter was safe for now.

When Katia found out she was having a girl, she grieved. There was no happiness for women in the Mafia. There was pretend and sacrifice. Helina's future was already set in stone despite how Adrik fought it. He had seen what happened to his sisters and wanted more for Helina. But it was a stupid hope that would only hurt Helina in the long run. The sooner Helina understood her fate, the less painful it would be.

It's like giving birth to a child with a terminal illness.

Katia's phone was ringing, but she had enough of mafia life for the time being and wanted nothing to do with any of them. She clicked it off and hid it under her pillow before returning to the bathroom.

"A bath will help you," Katia assured Jolie. "Can you get undressed?"

Jolie barely registered but began undressing subconsciously. Katia helped briefly with her pants and then aided her in climbing into the tub. The hot water sparked life into Jolie's eyes, and she moaned at the sting.

Katia smiled and cooed, "There you are."

Jolie rubbed her face with it, looking around, forcing her eyes to blink.

"Are you the same woman who saved my daughter in a gunfight?" Katia joked. If Jolie had known the things Katia witnessed and the moments where fear overwhelmed her, she wouldn't have been able to play around. There were times when Katia was embarrassed by her reactions, but time and repetition strengthened her. As she believed, one day, Jolie would be immune to such things, if she stuck around.

It made her sad for Jolie's innocence. As much as Katia hated it about her, it was also something she envied.

Jolie sat back, keeping her knees to her chest and her arms crossed in front of her. "I shouldn't be here," she finally managed to whisper.

Katia smiled, knowing the woman was talking about the house and not her bathroom. "No, but here you are."

"Is it too late?"

"Maybe," she admitted softly. Katia sat on her knees and rested her chin on the tub's edge.

"Why are you being so nice to me?"

A shrug, and the thought stuck with her about the reason. The words breached her lips without intention. "When I was a little girl," she found herself saying, "I wanted to be a nurse. I wanted to care for people. I used to carry around a briefcase full of supplies and bandage up all my stuffed animals." Her eyes drifted as she tried to remember what it felt like to want something so badly it hurt. "But I was always reminded that it would not be so. I was meant to be a wife and mother and nothing else."

"That's terrible."

She shrugged. "It is the life I've been given."

"Aren't you bored?"

Katia giggled and nodded, "Yes, immensely. But shopping helps." The words were expected of her. She's a girl, so she must love shopping. She knew how to play the role she was made for, but sometimes, she wished she was strong enough to get out.

A knock on her door sparked fear, and Katia spun her head, but then she remembered who it might be. "Excuse me." She got to her feet and shut the door behind her. With a deep breath, a shake of her blonde hair, and a forced light in her eyes, she opened the door to find Gil. The look on his face was one she couldn't turn away, and she stepped back to let him through. In Russian, she whispered in warning, ***"Jolie's in the bathroom."***

"Are you alright?"

"Yes, thanks to you."

"Katia." He reached out, gently touching her hand.

Katia closed her eyes, and though she wanted nothing more than to collapse in his arms, she stayed stiff and distant, walking away from him. ***"You didn't give me a pen,"*** Katia began. ***"So, who's pen was it?"***

Gil straightened his back, putting up his own walls to protect himself. ***"I don't know."***

"How could it be the same?"

"I don't know that either. There was a little difference. The shape of it."

Katia tried to make a connection. ***"Adrik didn't interrupt the Secret Service transport. My family did. I gave you that pen. There is no possible way another could have gotten into the house. Unless…"*** Katia shifted her gaze to the bathroom door.

Gil also glanced toward the door, whispering, ***"Do you think it was her?"***

"If it was, then she saw us."

"And she's working for the police."

Katia rolled all this around in her head. There was a benefit to it, but she would have to be careful. ***"Don't share this information. It might be helpful to me. Goodnight,"*** Katia dismissed, opening her bedroom door.

Gil closed the distance between them, a hand on her cheek even though she tried to pull away. He gripped the side of her face, forcing her eyes on him. Katia flicked her eyes over him; every second he looked at her, questioning silently if she was okay and if she needed more than she was saying, it knocked another brick out of her sturdy walls. She swallowed, hating the water stinging the back of her eyes.

Not wanting to weaken her, Gil stepped out of the room, "Goodnight."

Katia shut it, locking it, resting her head against it, and breathed, fortifying her wavering strength. She took one last breath and went back into the bathroom.

Jolie was getting dressed, slipping a shirt over her head.

"I saw your face." Katia stood against the doorframe, watching every emotion come across the girl's features. "At breakfast, when I kissed Adrik."

Jolie stared, wide-eyed, at the floor.

Katia laughed. She loved when she was right. "If you plan on staying in the Mafia, you must do better at hiding your thoughts." Katia turned out of the room, sat on the bed, and waited.

Jolie slowly stepped into the room, guilt and shame soaking in her stance.

"Are you and Adrik fucking?"

With a quick shake of the head, Katia reiterated, "Are you dating?"

Hesitantly, Jolie nodded.

Katia knew it was only a matter of time, but she was surprised at how fast Adrik moved. Usually, he played with girls like a cat after a stray mouse. But this one was different, she knew. He was no doubt in love with her. "Are you in love with him?" Katia laughed. "What am I asking? Of course, you are. You left your entire life behind to join a dangerous criminal family. No one does that for sex." The way Jolie knitted her brows and thought, maybe the realization hadn't dawned on her yet. This was the time to hit her with something else, but Katia flicked the light on before she asked, "The pen was yours, wasn't it?"

And like she knew she'd see it, the fear ignited in her gaze. If she had been looking at Yakov when he asked, he would have known it was her instantly.

"You are working with the FBI."

"No, I—" Jolie struggled with a defense. Everything could fall apart here if she didn't salvage it.

Katia held up a hand to stop her. "I'm not going to turn you in."

The chaos in her face stalled. "You're not?"

"You saw Gil and I."

She nodded sheepishly.

"So, then we are even."

Katia could see the confusion. Their secrets were not evenly matched, true enough, but Katia couldn't risk Adrik finding out about Gil. Not with what happened last time. Gil's survival meant her escape from the Morozov family.

"Are you still working for the FBI?"

Jolie shook her head.

"Why not?" But the answer was already on her lips. "Your target was Adrik." She giggled at the irony. "God loves drama." Katia shifted as her plan began to take shape. "Won't the FBI get upset with you?"

"I don't care."

Katia tapped a finger on the nightstand, contemplating. No, Katia needed Jolie to keep her connection with the FBI. Katia might need it one day. "Alexei is an easier target."

"I thought you cared for Alexei."

She snickered. "I have no care for anyone in this family. Think of me from now on as your partner. I will help you navigate the Mafia and find ways to get the information you need. And you will keep my secrets."

Jolie clenched the towel tight to her chest. "I don't want to help the FBI anymore."

"But you will." Katia smiled. "Because you want to help Adrik get rid of his father. And it might be the only way he'll forgive you."

Chapter Thirty-Eight

Dark Side

Adrik could feel the weight of his brother's stare as he looked out the window. His leg bobbed with such force it vibrated the car. Every stop sign and light was a nick at his already disintegrating patience.

When the car turned on his driveway, Adrik reached in the vest of his suit and unclipped the holster, pulling out his silver-and-gold 9mm Glock. He checked the magazine, slapped it back into place, and then pulled on the barrel to ensure a bullet was ready to go in the chamber. He rested the gun on his lap and waited for the car to weave its way along.

"Adrik."

"Don't defend him."

"I'm not," Alexei quickly stated. "But this isn't the way to do it."

Did it matter how it was done as long as it was? Adrik thought his father would step down and let him take control of the family when he was ready, but here he was, stronger, better, smarter than his father ever was, and the man continued to lead. If Yakov wasn't going to abdicate his role, then the only choice Adrik had was to physically remove him. It would cause riots. It would destroy so much of Adrik's work, but without considerable risk, there was no just reward. If Adrik got rid of his father, he could continue with expansion plans. He could dominate the west coast, from the peninsula to the Florida Keys. There was money to be made, yet his father was content with crumbs. There were so many little cartels that Adrik could take into his regime and have one of the largest families in America.

More importantly, Adrik could pursue Jolie without hesitation. He wouldn't care if Katia had a problem. He would flaunt it till she filed for divorce, and then their contract would be void. He would lose nothing, since she had violated their marriage first; everything would become his.

Adrik squeezed his eyes shut, imagining Jolie, terrified and trembling on her knees in her panda pajamas in front of his father. What damage had he done? Would Adrik be able to repair it, or would Jolie use this as a nail to their coffin? It was already cracking ice beneath their feet before his father dropped a hammer. Was it too late? Had she packed and left without saying goodbye?

As soon as the car slowed, Adrik shoved open the door even as the tires still moved. Alexei was right on his heels, and a dozen personal guards bounced out of the cars, chasing after him. The doors spread wide for him, and he pounded through the hallway. The sounds of all their footsteps rolled like thunder. Servants scattered out of their way, running for cover.

Adrik found them all sitting at the breakfast table. But he knew how forced it was, how amicable his father wanted it to feel. Adrik had been at this table enough times, compelled to play a role.

Katia put her fork down as they entered, satisfied by his presence. Jolie was wide-eyed, her hair twisted in a bun with a few strands against her cheek. The sight of her unharmed relieved him, but it also fueled him.

Yakov put down his newspaper and grinned. ***"That was a quick trip."***

Adrik clenched the gun at his side. "Katia, take the tutor upstairs."

She got Jolie up on her feet, bringing them by him. He grabbed Katia's arm and turned his head toward the woman. "Did he hurt you?"

Katia could see the swift glance toward Jolie. Though it made her sick, it appeared he was more in over his head than she first realized. She subtly replied in Russian, ***"We are both fine, Adrik."***

The words stuck out, and he caught her eye, seeing the suppressed twitch of her lip.

She knows.

Adrik released her and stepped to the dinner table, standing on the opposite end to face his father head-on. He listened till the girls' footsteps were up the stairs before he raised the gun.

Adrik's guards copied his movement, turning their rifles, pistols, and revolvers on Yakov.

But Yakov was far from alone. His guards came through as if they had been waiting for this moment. Fifteen of them filed around Yakov, with his special fighter Li-Choy over his left shoulder.

Yakov picked up his fork. *"I don't know why you are so upset. I found a listening device. I needed to figure out who it belonged to."* He took a bite.

"Don't," Adrik bit. *"You know the protocol for something like that. You do not take my wife and subject her to your bullshit! You put her on her knees next to the servants. You disrespected her, and you disrespected me."*

Yakov put up a hand. *"You are right. I apologize. So, can we move on from this? Your mother will be waking any moment."*

Adrik's arm shook, fighting the desire to end it, to put a bullet through his father's head and stop any of his manipulations. He felt his power constantly being sucked away by the old man. If he was a leech, Adrik would have no problem ripping it off and squeezing it till it popped. Why couldn't he do the same thing to his father?

Alexei stepped beside Adrik, and whispered, "Come on. Not now."

Adrik ground his teeth. *If not now, when?* He didn't know how much longer he could live under his father's shoe, allowing it to constantly press down on his neck and pretending he wasn't strong enough to get him off. He felt his manhood being tarnished in front of his men, in front of his family. He couldn't allow it to continue if these people were to be under his control.

"You will never touch my wife again. Or that tutor. She doesn't understand your games, and I don't need trouble with the police."

Yakov instantly pacified with, *"Of course."*

"I am reinstating all the changes I made when you were away. They work better. The numbers don't lie, and I don't care if your pride cannot handle it. I will give you six months to handle your affairs. Then, you will return to Russia, and I will not see you again."

Yakov fiddled with a fork, straightening his plate and looking elsewhere as he thought of Adrik's demands. Yakov waved to his soldiers, and they lowered their weapons. *"Alright. Perhaps I am holding on for too long, but it is not because I don't believe in you. It is because you are still so young. Only age gives you the knowledge that you need. But if you think you're ready—"*

"I'm ready."

A smile pushed on his father's lips. "Look at you." Yakov laughed with admiration. *"My son! Tough. Protects his wife and his family. This is my heir. Do you see?"*

Adrik clenched his teeth. Yakov tried so hard to appease, but it came out as belittling. He held out chocolate-covered poison and looked confused when it made others sick.

Alexei put a hand on his brother's arm. "No one wants this more than me, but not like this."

Adrik fired. Li-Choy's body fell backward from the jolt, and he hit the floor with a loud thud.

The silence that followed broadened the space between them. Adrik dared Yakov to say something. To move, to smile, to flinch—he didn't care what, but he waited. He waited for his father to say anything to make killing him easier. But Yakov only looked down at his dead soldier, shrugged, and went back to eating.

Adrik walked out of the room. He hit the stairs and paused against the wall, gripping the railing and digging his nails into the wood. Part of him wanted to go back and finish it. The mafia in him couldn't handle the disrespect; the line Yakov crossed could not be forgiven. Yakov disregarded every warning because he believed himself superior. It was time for that to change. Yakov needed to learn his place.

Adrik looked up the stairs. He had to calm down if he was going to face Jolie. She'd never seen this side of him, and he wasn't ready for her to see it. She would question the gunshot. She would have to acknowledge that he killed someone. Though he dreaded Jolie's response, he needed to know how she would react. This could be her first test to see if she could ever become a wife to a mafia boss.

Adrik took the stairs two at a time, slipping the gun into its holster and fixing his jacket around it so it wasn't visible. His hands shook, full of suppressed rage. The death of Li-Choy wasn't enough. He wanted to punish Yakov, but he restrained himself. Alexei always held him back, pulling him out of fights he wanted to finish, taking his gun when he wasn't done shooting, and standing in front of him when all he wanted was vengeance. Ever since they were teenagers. How much damage would Adrik have caused throughout their lifetime if Alexei hadn't been there?

He'd probably be in prison.

Adrik wanted to head straight to Jolie, but he knew the impossibility of it. There were still cameras, and his father's spies were always watching, waiting for him to slip up.

Against his desire, he knocked once on Katia's door before stepping in.

Jolie stood up from the bed.

He was frozen upon seeing her. She wore a jumper with tropical flowers and sandals. It was something casual you could wear to the thrift store, but it looked amazing on her. Her curled hair hung over her shoulder, and she played with the tips in nervousness.

Adrik shut the door behind him, putting out a hand to stop her from approaching. He needed to face Katia first.

The witch stepped out of the bathroom with her arms crossed, smug and proud. "My hero," Katia mocked. ***"Did you do it?"*** she asked in Russian. ***"Did you finally kill him?"***

He clenched his teeth, eyeing her, daring her to make a snide comment to his silence. He didn't want to hear her bullshit right now.

She snickered. ***"Of course. How foolish of me."***

Adrik clenched his fist at his side, his eyes blindly ahead as he bit, ***"What do you want?"***

"What makes you think I want anything?"

"Cut the shit, Katia. What do you want?"

Katia shrugged, swaying over to Jolie and slipping an arm through hers. In English, she replied, "We are going to the beach. We deserve an extravagant day after our night, don't you think? We might even stay at the Don."

Adrik didn't want Jolie out of sight, but he knew if he wasn't careful, someone else might spot his unnecessary attention toward her. It was better to let her go, but it was like gnawing his fingers off with his teeth.

In Russian, Katia added, ***"I'll have my list of demands ready for you by tomorrow."*** She let Jolie go and grabbed her travel bag off the bed. "You're babysitting," she threw out as she bypassed him, opening the door.

Adrik snatched the handle before she could close it, turning just enough to see her face. ***"I found him."***

The smile slipped from her lips. It was a delicious sight to see. Just when Katia thought she had won, thought she held power over him, he kicked her legs out from under her and reminded her just who he was. With her brother in his hands, her control was limited.

"Be very clear with your 'demands.'" Adrik shut the door, the sense of victory dying as he felt Jolie's gaze on him. It was stupid what he was feeling at this moment. He was a man who could stand in front of drug lords and kingpins and not cower. He had a gun pressed against his head a dozen times and still had no fear.

But facing Jolie was going to be challenging. Would she hate him? Blame him? Discard him?

Then her arms surrounded him, and her face pressed into his chest. All the tension in his shoulders drained, and he wrapped her in his arms, squeezing to assure himself she was here, she hadn't been hurt, and she still wanted to be with him.

"Are you alright?" Jolie nodded but didn't pull away. She kept her face hidden as she breathed in his cologne. "It will never happen again. I swear it."

Jolie's brows knitted. She wasn't sure he was able to promise something like that. Since she got involved in his life, she's experienced a shootout and a home invasion. More horrible things were happening to her now than ever before in her life. "I heard a gunshot," she whimpered. "Are you okay?"

He could tell her a body was being cleaned off the living room floor, but her fragility kept him silent. He was far from okay. Something in him was changing. He wanted more power, more strength, to protect her from the world he lived in. Adrik pulled back, cupping her cheek, forcing her gaze on him. Tears dripped down her face, and she tried to ignore his eyes, but he waited. "If he would have hurt you, I would have killed him."

She shook her head. If he thought that was a comfort to her, he was mistaken.

Adrik had to get her to understand. There was no peace in this life. She had to either accept it or leave. "It's fine. I'm fine," she whimpered, trying to pull away, but he wouldn't let her go.

"Jolie"—Adrik pulled her back into him—"I'm serious. I protect what's mine."

Tears built in her eyes, and her lip trembled. "He beat a man." Jolie wanted to say more and tell him it was all her fault, and she didn't know how she would ever forgive herself for saying nothing and doing nothing. What kind of person was she becoming? She didn't want to lose herself here, but the fear had been so incredible that it still left her nauseous.

Adrik gripped her, cursing his father for the damage he'd done. Jolie was as innocent as Helina. She didn't deserve what he exposed her to. But it was going to happen eventually, wasn't it? Like Helina being exposed to his world, Jolie would be, too. There was no stopping it. He could only lessen the blow. It's how the

Mafia conditioned their children. Small exposures to violence over time. Was that what he had to do for Jolie?

Jolie wiped her face. She didn't want to be this mess of a girl. She wanted to show her strength, even if she wasn't sure she had any. Jolie pulled herself back, pulling back her misery. "Katia found out about us."

The change of subject was noticed, but he allowed it. Whatever she needed to do to handle the trauma of last night was on her. "I'll deal with Katia." He rubbed the wetness off her face, kissing her lips and resting his forehead against her. "My father and I came to an agreement. He will be leaving in six months."

Jolie pulled back in surprise.

"Then I will be head of this family. I will divorce Katia and deal with the consequences."

She shook her head. "You said that your marriage keeps people from dying."

"It does, but already her brother betrayed me. How do I know her parents aren't doing the same? How do I know Katia isn't?"

Jolie's heart pounded in her chest. Katia was betraying him by sleeping with his brother. If he found out and confronted Katia, would Katia throw her under the bus to take the spotlight off her? "Katia would never put her daughter at risk."

"I'm not suggesting she did. But Katia hates me, hates my family. She has no incentive to be loyal. She is a risk not worth having. My father doesn't see this, because he sees only money. The harbor will be mine when I am through, and her family will be displaced."

Jolie shifted out of his arms, putting space between them. "Can we talk about something else?"

"No." Adrik planted his feet. "This is my life. The Mafia is my life. You will be involved in terrible things just by knowing me. Being ignorant doesn't save you." He watched her and observed the emotions she was trying to suppress. Her fingers pressed against her lips and neck until she drifted further from him, reaching for the bed. He waited till she sat and stepped up to her. "I've never done anything so stupid and reckless as being with you. My brother made me fully aware, and I cannot deny it." Adrik knelt before her. "And I have no intention of stopping. But if you can't go on, you need to tell me now." A hand slipped into her fingers, desperate to feel her. "Do you want to end this?"

Jolie's eyes were wild, flicking over his face, desperate for a path to follow. Adrik pulled her to her feet. Her hands rested on his chest as she avoided his gaze. He wasn't going to beg, but he sure as hell was gonna fight. He couldn't lose her or let her give up so soon. And though he should take this as a sign that their relationship wouldn't make it, he was too far gone to let go. He was doing shit he's never done, saying shit he's never said.

"I cannot change who I am, or the world I live in" he whispered. Adrik cupped her cheek, his thumb brushing her lip. The way the heat came to her cheeks told him that she was just as addicted as he was. "But I've never wanted anything more than I want you." He teased her, tracing her jaw, nose, and lips with his just enough to have her yearning. "Come to the dark side with me."

She shivered as those words slipped into her like a poison. It filled her lungs before it transformed into desire, settling between her legs. "Why does that sound like I'm signing away my soul?"

"You are." Adrik kissed the side of her mouth. "To me."

Jolie melted into such a declaration. She was forsaking her morals, humanity, and the goodness inside her. She was turning her back on God and her parents. All for him. She'd have to accept that he did horrible things and that she would one day witness it. But she refused to believe it was all bad. He had too much good in him to be as evil as he claimed. She could bring the goodness out of him, shine light into his dark world, and maybe, one day, all his power would be used to help the world instead of destroying it. She had to try because she was in too deep to get out now.

Jolie nodded, and Adrik captured her lips, devouring her. He pushed his tongue into her mouth, twirling hers in chaotic force as he laid her down on the bed, slipping between her legs. He parted from her lips to kiss down her jaw and neck to nuzzle the fat of her breast beneath her clothes.

"Adrik," Jolie moaned. He jerked his hips against her, letting her feel his desire pressed against her apex. Her gasp was a reward, making him smile as his teeth pinched her taut nipple through her shirt. "Please," she whimpered. There was no more waiting. She had decided, and now there was nothing left to do but give Adrik all of her.

Adrik kissed his way back to her lips. "Two weeks."

"What?" She arched, blindly begging for more.

Adrik loved it. She blinked at the realization that he was stopping, actually pulling away. She gripped his shirt to keep him there.

"Two weeks," he repeated now that she was paying attention. "When I first have you, it will not be a two-minute desperate attempt. It will be a well-executed procedure, taking hours and hours of our day till you are fulfilled in every way you have never been. Be prepared; your two weeks are fading."

Chapter Thirty-Nine

Dance Party

Spending the day at the beach with Katia wasn't as appetizing as hours of lovemaking, but it wasn't bad either. Katia was a ball of fun when she wanted to be. She knew how to spend money and didn't hesitate either. The Don was a massive hotel twenty levels high and a hundred rooms wide. They got the presidential suite overlooking the ocean. But for now, they laid out on the beach in a cabana, with a servant standing nearby, waiting to be called.

It would be easy to forget that Jolie had joined the Mafia and was instead out with a friend, enjoying the sun and waves. But the five men in black suits, with guns hidden in their vests, were hard to ignore, especially in this heat. Sweat built on their faces, and a few kept a white cloth in their hand, rubbing the wetness before it dripped into their eyes. The only reprieve from the sun was the black glasses they had on their faces.

Jolie could only imagine how uncomfortable they were, but if Katia cared, Jolie couldn't tell. She embraced her role as a mafia wife with ease and the tiniest amount of awareness possible.

This is how I need to be.

Jolie dropped her head back against the bench, closing her eyes, forcing herself not to care. It was selfish, she knew, but all of this had been. Her disregarding the FBI, becoming Adrik's girlfriend, and watching as a man was dragged away to be whipped because of her silence were all selfish.

Her conscience was becoming a ghost she couldn't escape.

"Doesn't this feel a little selfish?" Jolie suddenly found herself asking.

Katia giggled before lifting her sunglasses to the top of her head. "I was wondering when you would crack. Carrying your bag yourself. Getting your own drinks. Putting on your own sunscreen. You are a peasant in the king's castle."

"I am not a peasant. I can do those things myself. So can you."

"Yes. But you don't understand the reason why I don't. These soldiers are paid for their job like everyone else, and their job is to make you comfortable, to please you so that you are pleased with them, so they get bonuses at the end of the year that will feed their family for months. If you were to go to the hospital, diagnose yourself, and operate on yourself, don't you think the doctors would be a little pissed? If you don't need them, they have no job. So, I let them do the little things so they are needed, paid, and can provide for their families." Katia returned her sunglasses and resettled. "So, who's being selfish here?"

Jolie sloughed, hating how right that sounded. Was she wrong?

Throughout the day, Jolie noticed herself give in, allowing a servant to carry her drink back to the hotel. They sat now at the bar, and Katia took this time to make fun of her liquor abstinence. Jolie had never liked drinking; she didn't see the point, because she never needed to feel out of control, but guilt was a constant depressant. She didn't want to feel guilty for liking a dangerous man, and if she had to drown in liquor to erase the ball in her gut, then maybe it was time to indulge.

The drink went to her head faster than she was ready for, and she was dying laughing. Katia was laughing with her. "Oh, you are so much more fun this way!" She wrapped an arm around Jolie. "You know, I think if we were not pitted against each other, and you weren't American, we could be friends."

Jolie grinned and agreed. "Ahh, totally. I actually don't have many friends." It was depressing, and yet Katia only laughed at this. With one more sip, Jolie announced loudly, "I got to pee!"

When she stood, the room swayed, and she held onto the table till it passed. Two drinks in, and she could feel the tingling in her fingers and toes. It was actually enjoyable.

When Jolie got to the bathroom, a guard in a black suit peeked his head in first before holding the door out for her. She didn't understand it. She was only going to the bathroom, and no one was out to kill her.

When finished, she stood in front of the mirror over the sink. The pleasant smile on her skin drifted when she noticed Agent Mally sitting on the toilet in an open stall. She was on her phone before she looked up with a forced tight smile. "How have you been?"

Jolie turned around to face her. "What are you doing here?"

"Checking in." Mally stood, dressed in a loose shirt over her two-piece bathing suit. Her flip-flops echoed in the bathroom. She went to the sink and checked her makeup. "Want to tell me what happened to have Adrik fly all the way back from Puerto Rico in such a hurry?"

Jolie didn't want to face her. The guilt was inches underneath, and it would take only a short dig to uncover it. "I have no idea."

Mally continued to smile before she reached into her purse and dropped a picture on the counter. "Zinof Stephanov is missing. Katia's brother. Know anything?"

Thankfully, Jolie had no idea. "No."

"There is a rumor that he was in charge of the attack at Salem's. Which means Adrik would want him. Last seen?" Mally smiled. "Puerto Rico."

Jolie's heart plummeted.

Mally folded her arms and leaned against the counter. The panic on Jolie's face was so evident it was humorous. Mally felt terrible for the girl but not bad enough. Jolie was risking her livelihood for dick. It was so pathetic.

"I have been after this family longer than you've been alive. I am so close. Do you know what you're doing? You're jumping onto a sinking ship. This family is going down, and you are so stupid to think it will be a happily ever after."

Jolie moved to go, but Mally grabbed her arm, spinning her back around. "Listen to me, Jolie. If you aren't with me, you're against me. I can't promise you won't be caught in the crossfire. Are you willing to die for this man you just met? Because that is a huge possibility."

The words were caught in Jolie's throat. She didn't want to die, but to leave Adrik wasn't in the cards. He was a drug, and she was addicted.

Mally moved in, whispering, "You are just another notch on his bedpost. He couldn't care less about you."

Jolie stiffened her spine. She would have believed Mally before and perhaps even changed sides at this very moment. But the look on Adrik's face when she said she wanted to leave was still so fresh in her memory. He wanted her in his life, and despite how scary it was, as long as she held his hand, she could weather it.

"Leave me alone," Jolie ordered.

"Give me information, and I will."

The audacity that she would ask broke Jolie, "How? I can't get you anything!" There were almost tears in her eyes. Jolie wanted the woman to leave her alone, but like her conscience, it lingered.

Mally held up Zinof's picture. There was a chance he wasn't alive anymore, and Adrik knew precisely where the body was buried. "A life hangs in your hands. Find him."

Jolie returned to the bar, numb and miserable. She downed the rest of her drink before ordering another one. Katia watched her with concern but smiled nonetheless as Jolie sipped on her third drink. She ordered a round of appetizers before she asked, "Hey, you okay?"

Jolie gave a tight smile and leaned into her, "Mally is here."

Katia sank into her and hissed, "You didn't tell me you partnered with Mally. That woman is like the plague." Katia glanced around searching for the agent. The woman just came from the hallway, a drink in her hand saluting. Katia snapped her eyes to her drink. Jolie was a stupid woman for being caught in the middle of this. There was no way Adrik would forgive her. But his forgiveness wasn't her problem. Katia planned to be gone before any of *that* disaster went down.

"Do you know how long it's been since I've had fun?" Jolie asked. And though Mally was just over her shoulder in the distance, Jolie wanted to forget her.

"No, I have no idea," Katia assured.

"A long time. A looonnnggg time." The music was getting louder, or at least it was inside Jolie's head. She got off the bar stool to wiggle around. "My ex-boyfriend—you know, the one I told you about?"

"Vincent."

"Yeah, yeah, yeah." She sipped her drink. "His friends would throw these bonfire parties that were insane. Like crazy, pickup truckin', muddin' keggers in high school," she stressed. "High school. They were the talk of the town. And always got shut down by the police. There would be drugs, but I never did any of that."

"Of course," Katia patronized.

"But I danced." She shook her hips with a wild grin.

Katia smiled. "I knew this good girl persona was all an act."

"What?" Jolie screeched. "I am a good girl. I am. I was always home at curfew. I could never do what these girls did. But maybe..." Jolie leaned in, and whispered,

"Maybe I wanted to." A sudden squeal broke out as she pointed at the door. "That's a DJ. Is there music tonight?" Jolie asked the bartender.

"On the roof, it's an exclusive club. Would you like passes, Mrs. Morozov?"

Katia was hesitant. She knew what was expected of her as a wife to a mafia boss, but Jolie's exuberance was rubbing off on her. It made her wonder when the last time was *she* had fun. Jolie gripped her arm, begging.

"What do you plan to wear?"

The bartender interrupted, "It's a pool party. What you have on is perfect."

Jolie whispered, "Please, please, please."

Katia cursed internally when she heard herself say, "Alright."

"Yes!" Jolie squealed.

"But you need to eat and slow down a little. You cannot embarrass me by throwing up in the pool."

Jolie sat down and began to binge. She couldn't believe how awesome Katia was. She was caring and sweet. It made her think about why there was animosity between her and Adrik until Agent Mally's words filtered through the haze. Adrik killed her lover.

"Can I ask you something?"

"Depends." Katia smirked, glancing toward her. "What?"

Jolie paused, unsure if asking was in her best interest. Her question probably wouldn't bring happy memories. "What happened with you and Adrik?"

Like she knew it, Katia's smile drifted. She fiddled with a French fry and watched the people swim in the pool. "I broke his heart, I suppose," she finally murmured. Katia no longer saw what was around. She was back ten years when it all began. The mistakes made because of stupid love. Maybe that was why she couldn't wholly hate Jolie. Jolie was in love, a beautiful place to be. Even her goodness was something that Katia used to possess. "I was betrothed to Adrik six months before I turned eighteen. As you can imagine, I wasn't happy about being forced to be with someone I never met. I mean, we live in America; I thought I'd get freedom like everyone else. But the Mafia is a world of its own. We do not follow the rules of this society. We follow the rules of our parents." The resentment in her tone was undeniable. "No matter how hard I fought, there was no getting around it. And even though I was in love with someone else, engaged to someone else, my father told me I would marry Adrik, or he would kill my lover, Nikolas." The name said out loud brought with it all the times she had called him. She could see his face so vividly even after all these years. "So, I married. What else could I have done? I broke it off with Nikolas, but he wasn't about to give up. He found my father, got beaten, and was thrown in jail. He was a fool, and I was so desperate to be saved I didn't think about the consequences. I believed in him even though he was nothing against the power of the Morozovs."

Katia took a drink. It was a way to fortify her walls against the pain that would always be there.

"Adrik was young and so blindly wanting what his parents had. I'll never downplay how well he treated me in the beginning. He wanted me to love him, but he didn't realize I couldn't. My heart was already in the hands of another." Katia took a deep breath and then ripped it off like a Band-Aid. "I cheated on Adrik, from the very beginning. For years," she softly admitted. "One single text message I forgot to erase, and it was over. Adrik knew immediately. Every time I disappeared. Every time he couldn't reach me. The times I pushed him away or made up some excuse to get out of his bed. It all clicked, and my secrets were exposed." Katia swallowed harshly, pressing a finger under her eye to push back any wetness. Then she cleared her throat and said coldly, "Adrik killed him. Tortured him to death. Now I am without a heart, only alive to care for a daughter that should have been someone else's."

Jolie's heart broke for her, for Adrik, and for torn futures. She hadn't known it was so terrible between them. Adrik's bitterness now made sense. He had loved Katia once. He had been *in* love with her.

Jolie's belly filled with a tinge of jealousy. She didn't want to face that.

"The only thing between Adrik and I now is hatred. Remember that no matter how good we play the game."

Jolie giggled. "I did get jealous. My ex cheated on me right under my nose with so many freaking girls. I was so naive and so trustworthy. I always give the benefit of the doubt, even to those who don't deserve it. I hate that about me."

"I'm sure that's what Adrik loves about you."

Katia turned her face as she thought, *it's why I can use you, sweet girl.*

Even from twenty floors below, the music on the roof could be heard, and it shot Jolie out of her chair. "Let's go!" She took Katia's hand, squeezing her fingers as they rushed to the elevator. Two guards slipped into the steel box with them, whispering into an earpiece. Jolie didn't think she would ever get used to their constant presence.

Jolie was surer than anything that she could make Katia her friend and maybe even help the strained relationship between Adrik and herself. She could be the catalyst that allowed them to forgive, and then they could work together to raise their daughter in a better setting. Children of divorce were less likely to succeed in school and were more likely to suffer from mental disorders. She saw it too many times teaching. Helping the parents could help Helina, and that was what she was here for.

A passcode allowed them onto the roof, and when the door opened, security greeted them, checking over their invitation before leading them to the main glass door and holding it for them.

The party was in full swing. Girls in thin-string bikinis were sitting along the poolside; the DJ was set up in the corner, with a strobe light and a colorful ball that twisted around to the beat of the music. The sight would have intimidated Jolie, but the liquor kept the excitement alive.

A waiter held a tray of tequila shots, and Jolie took two. She threw the first one back and cringed, stomping her foot and twisting her body as she forced herself to swallow it. Katia laughed, unhindered. "Again, again." Katia encouraged, and Jolie took a breath, regretted it, and took the second shot. She wanted to cry as she swallowed, her tongue sticking out in disgust. When it was Katia's turn, the woman took it like a pro, only shaking her head and hissing.

Jolie took off her sundress and dived into the pool.

Katia didn't know what to make of this woman. She was utterly different from hours ago, and Katia wasn't sure if this was good. But it was going to be *very* entertaining.

Chapter Forty

Test

Adrik gripped the steering wheel of his Maserati and pressed hard on the gas. The power of the engine was hypnotic. It sang into the palm of his hand and transformed him into a god. He weaved through traffic, untouchable. But his knuckles hurt, and he had to loosen his hold.

Zinof, Katia's brother, was currently held in their dungeon. It was a small dark room they used to interrogate. Usually, they kept such things out of their house, but in some instances, with high-profile individuals, they brought them home. It was the best fortification, impenetrable from all angles. And there was no doubt in Adrik's mind that Katia's family would be coming for him. What would they bargain? He doubted it would be enough to change his mind.

Gil hung over between the front seats, too big to sit comfortably in the back, but he was smaller than Alexei, who sat in the passenger, looking like a bear stuck in a doggy door. He shifted, trying to move his legs and failing. "I hate this car. Why couldn't we take the limo?"

Adrik loved to drive. It was the power of control visibly in his hands.

"I think the girls were trying to get away," Alexei pointed out. "We shouldn't be going."

Gil fought back with, "Why should they get to have all the fun? I need a day off, too. You guys got to go to Puerto Rico. I want some Spanish pussy."

Alexei responded, "First, we were there for like twelve hours, and second, we didn't go there for pussy. Is that all you think about?"

"Dude, why isn't it all you think about?"

"Because I'm an adult."

"Oh, 'I'm an adult,'" Gil mocked. "If you're gay, just say you're gay. We won't judge you."

Alexei attempted to hit him, but the seatbelt kept him tied to his chair and frustrated him more than anything.

"I had a bisexual experience once," Gil admitted. "It wasn't as terrible as I thought it would be."

Adrik looked up in the mirror, catching Gil's humorous gaze, and fought off a laugh. Gil was constantly pushing boundaries. Where Alexei was more reserved, Gil never got embarrassed about anything. It was a perfect combination for brothers.

Alexei hid his face. "God, why do I know you?"

Gil slapped his shoulder, laughing, "Lighten up! Adrik knew it was a joke."

"Did I?" Adrik questioned. Gil having bisexual experiences wouldn't be surprising in the least.

Gil pointed, "There's the hotel. I haven't been to the Don in ages. I think the last time was for my birthday. That was a crazy party."

"And we were asked not to come back for a while," Alexei pointed out.

"Oh, they've forgiven us by now. It was only a knife fight, and no one died. Win-Win."

Adrik drowned out their conversation. He was anxious, and it showed through as he bit his nail. This was an opportunity to have Jolie in his bed, which might be his only chance for a while. If he was going to follow Alexei's rules and not screw Jolie in the house, their time together would have to be planned and staged. It wasn't the best of circumstances, but it was better than nothing, and nothing was impossible. He was losing his concentration. He knew he should be focusing on the family and figuring out what to do with Katia's brother, but all he could think about was Jolie. The moment he put his daughter down to bed, he took off with the intention of gaining access to Jolie's room. This ridiculous 'two-week' idea would come to an end tonight.

Adrik bit his lip, the desire increasing like a volcano ready to explode.

Alexei's loud voice interrupted his thoughts, "Would you stop going on about Puerto Rico? You could have come, you know?"

"I'm just saying, Spanish women fuck like porn stars. You didn't meet any girls there? You are wasting your time, Alexei. You won't be young forever. You're barely holding on to your looks."

"Oh, fuck you. I don't need a pretty face; I got muscle." Alexei flexed, slapping his bicep with appreciation.

"All those hours in the gym, and you could have been fucking." Gil slapped Adrik's shoulder. "Tell him. Tell him he's missing out. You ate some Spanish pussy, didn't you?"

Alexei snapped his head toward Adrik. They had only spent a few hours apart in Puerto Rico. And though Gil was only speculating, it wasn't a far stretch for Adrik.

Adrik felt his brother's gaze and met his eyes. "What?"

"Did you?"

"Did I?" Adrik mocked.

"Why can't you answer the question?"

Adrik scoffed, shaking his head and watching the road. Alexei's feelings for Jolie were one thing, but coming to her defense was another. It wasn't Alexei's fucking place. He didn't know how to handle Alexei's crush on Jolie. Ignoring it and hoping it went away was his current method. But was Alexei waiting on the sidelines, hoping he'd fuck up?

Because chances were, Adrik was going to fuck up at some point. Did he have to worry about his brother swooping in?

Gil cackled, coming between them, "Nah, he's too hooked to Snow White."

Alexei turned his head away, and too quickly, guilt overcame him. His feelings for Jolie were hard to quell, especially after their time together at his mother's party. He'd just have to stay away from her as much as possible. Maybe he could find a girl to take home tonight.

The idea made him sick. Girls that were easy made him think about all the dicks that had been in their pussy. He didn't know how Gil did it without being grossed out.

"I don't know how you go from Katia to her."

"Because Katia's a fucking psycho," Alexei answered for him, hoping to win some points with Adrik.

"But she's a ten!" Gil fought back.

Adrik flicked his eyes to the rearview mirror again. He studied Gil as he went on about his preferences. He was laughing and looking out the window, making ill jokes, but Adrik sensed something.

He was always good at reading people, Katia being the exception. Gil was never good at hiding, but secrets were common in the family. He didn't fault Gil for not telling him everything.

It had to do with a rumor.

A woman had told Adrik that she saw Gil and Katia arguing at the dress shop. She said that Gil reached for her hand in a very delicate manner. More of a 'lover's touch' than anything else. Adrik had blown it off, suspecting the woman was more jealous than concerned, but now it planted a seed in his head, and he was looking for the signs.

Was Gil betraying him by fucking Katia?

Adrik couldn't give two shits who Katia fucks. She was a whore, and if she wasn't the mother to his child, he'd have put her on the streets like she should be.

But it mattered who Gil took to his bed.

Gil was his brother, and his loyalties weren't up for debate.

Now, Adrik needed to test this rumor. If it proved false, he'd buy Gil a nice gift for Christmas as a way of an apology. He knew exactly what the guy wanted: his own private plane. Gil had wanted to be a pilot for the Air Force when they were younger. He wanted to 'drop bombs.' But none of them could do what they wanted with their lives. So, Gil would be happy with his own charter.

But if Adrik was right, he was still determining how he would react.

They pulled to the hotel entrance, and the valet hustled to the car, greeting him by name. "Your wife is on the roof."

Adrik buttoned his jacket, the black fabric tight around his muscles. It was a hot late September night. Living here for ten years made him expect nothing else. He walked into the hotel and was instantly bombarded by the front desk secretary, who handed Alexei the code to the elevator to access the private rooftop. He was overdressed, as he always was. It was a way to stand out from the regular drug pins, traffickers, and the like. They never took much time in their appearance because there was no one to impress, but power doesn't come from any outside force; it comes from within, like an ooze. It's why people felt inferior in his presence. It's why drug pins and traffickers struggled to keep their people in line. They are seen as equals and not as less than they were. It's what makes the Mafia different. Mafia people knew they were better and ensured everyone knew it.

They stepped out of the elevator. Gil was on his left, and Alexei was on his right as Adrik walked onto the pool deck. Katia's guards stiffened and made no sound till he questioned where his wife was. With hesitation and fear, one pointed behind him.

In the center of the dance floor, his wife and his girlfriend were dancing in their bathing suits with a bunch of hungry-looking drunks reaching and touching wherever they could.

Adrik clenched his teeth, feeling a burst of madness. He pinned his eyes on Katia because, unlike Jolie, she knew better than to make a fool of herself in front of vendors. And there were plenty here.

One by one, people stopped what they were doing. Some shifted away out of fear, hoping not to get into his eyesight. Then the DJ cut the music and the lights.

"What?" Jolie spun around. "What happened?"

Katia saw him first. The panic on her face brought a low level of satisfaction. At least she knew what she had done wrong. She swayed, catching Jolie. "Adrik. Adrik," she nipped, trying to turn Jolie around.

Jolie blinked, "Adrik?" She snapped her head this way and that before she dumbly grinned. "Hey!"

Katia grabbed her before she could greet him inappropriately in public. She quickly whispered in her ear something that sobered Jolie enough that her smile fell. Katia and Jolie, with their arms entwined, used each other as support as they stumbled and swayed. It was duel looks of childish guilt as they stared down at their bare feet.

"Adrik," Katia greeted with a fake smile. "What a surprise. We weren't expecting you."

Jolie slapped a hand to her mouth suddenly, to the concern of everyone watching. Her eyes were wide.

Katia whispered, "No, no, no, not here."

And then Jolie bent over and threw up right in front of Adrik's feet. The throw-up splashed, and all the pretzels, chips, and nachos decorated the pavement.

Jolie straightened as she rubbed her mouth. She looked at Katia. "I feel better."

"Good," Katia whimpered. "Let's get you cleaned up." She glanced nervously at Adrik, but he said nothing as they moved around him to the elevator.

Adrik eyed the onlookers, finding three of his own among the crowd. They nodded in greeting, and he looked past them. With a nudge toward the DJ, the musician quickly started the music again and got the lights going. Adrik walked over and started a conversation with one of the distributors, attempting to save himself from the humiliation the girls caused. Two of them had been invited to his ridiculous birthday party. No doubt word would get back to Yakov.

An hour later, with enough damage control, Adrik was in the elevator with Gil and Alexei.

"Go easy on them," Alexei murmured.

"Katia knows better," Adrik bit. His fists were at his sides.

Their suite was easy to find; it was the only one with a guard standing outside. Upon Adrik's approach, the guard quickly swiped a card and pushed open the door for him. He paid no attention to the extravagance. The large living room, the kitchen equipped with a waiting chef, and the dual hallways spreading to opposite sides of the floor to the bedrooms were common to his lifestyle. He bulldozed toward the only bedroom with a light on and burst into the room. Katia snapped her head toward him, putting a finger to her lips. She was helping Jolie to bed, her hair wet from a shower, her clothes on the floor, and the smell of vomit unmistakable.

Katia pulled the blanket over her and shut off the light. He left and went into the living room to wait. Alexei dismissed the chef and double-checked the rest of the suite to make sure there was no one else.

Katia was slow to approach, wearing a white bathrobe with her wet hair over her shoulder.

Adrik wanted to hear her excuse, forcing the silence between them before she finally caved.

"We were having fun," she defended pathetically.

"At my expense."

"Of course, it's about you. Everything everyone does is all about you."

"You made a fool of yourself in front of my people."

She laughed, yelling, "We were having fun!"

Adrik took a step but stopped himself. "Watch yourself."

Katia ground her teeth and lowered her voice. "I'm not going to apologize for pretending for a few hours that I wasn't part of your insufferable family. I didn't even do anything terrible."

Adrik couldn't believe her. "Men were touching you. Touching her."

"That's what it's about. *Her. She* embarrassed you, and because you are still pretending to be a good man, you are taking it out on me instead."

Adrik hastened toward her, gripping her arm, and though she struggled, she stayed. ***"Every time I give you an opportunity to redeem yourself, you fuck it up. How many times do you get before I don't bother anymore?"***

There was guilt on her face, but it was brief, and it fled quicker than it came. "I don't need to be redeemed. Divorce me already."

It was time to test his theory. Adrik gripped her throat and flicked his gaze at Gil, who stood on the back wall, pretending not to be interested. He didn't move, didn't flinch even as Adrik increased the pressure, and she grasped at his hand.

"If that's what you're waiting for, it's never gonna happen." Then he changed his tactic. He pulled her closer, his lips at her ear. ***"I still need an heir from you."*** Adrik pulled at the tie around her waist, loosening her robe. She screeched and smacked at him.

And there it was. The slightest flinch, almost undetectable, had Adrik not been paying attention.

He shoved Katia to Gil, and the man caught her arms as she held her robe together. At first, Gil just stared at Adrik, but then there was a brief recognition. Gil put Katia behind him, a bold fucking move.

Adrik couldn't believe it. All the years they'd spent together, and here it was, the bitter truth, Gil biting the hand that feeds. It was too much to process. Adrik couldn't speak at first, and Gil had nothing worth saying.

Alexei was standing between them, and he flicked his gaze back and forth, "What's going on?"

Adrik glanced at his brother before he pinned his gaze back on Gil. "Can't you tell, brother? Gil's been fucking Katia."

"What?"

Gil curled his fist. "Adrik. It's not what you think."

He could see it now. The way he stood before her like a knight. "You're in love with her." Adrik didn't know what he wanted, but the silence wasn't it. "Do you want to deny it?"

Gil licked his lips and tentatively admitted, "No. But she's not in love with me."

"Have you fucked her?"

"No."

Adrik took another step. "Did. You. Fuck her?"

"No!"

Alexei dived between them, putting his hands on Adrik's chest and pushing him back as Adrik screamed at him, "You're fucking lying! I know you, brother. I know you."

"You know me," Gil agreed. "When has Katia ever been more than a bitch to me, huh? She doesn't love me. I made advances, I admit, but she never gave me the time of day."

Adrik shoved Alexei's hands off him, pacing the room. He didn't know if Gil was telling the truth, and it almost didn't matter. The fact that Gil would even try was enough of a betrayal to leave him disgusted. The ever-present pressure of the gun in his back was pulling at him, begging him to fix it. It would be so easy and give him a temporary feeling of revenge, but it wouldn't last.

Alexei, who was always trying to make everything better, interrupted. "I think it's late. Let's deal with this in the morning. Katia, why don't you get to bed?" Alexei could see the temper in her raise, but then she thought better of it and stomped away, slamming her door. "Gil, you should head back."

"Adrik." Gil dared to step forward. "I'm sorry."

"You're *sorry*," Adrik mocked. ***"Haven't I given you everything?"***

"Of course."

"And this is how you repay me?"

"I shouldn't have to repay you if you really saw me as a brother."

Adrik fastened on him, gripping his shirt. ***"You ungrateful piece of shit."***

"How long am I supposed to be grateful?"

Adrik couldn't stop it; he punched Gil in the cheek, sending him back against the door. Alexei once more interrupted, pushing Adrik back into the living room. The pain in his knuckles was like a rush of adrenaline, drowning him in satisfaction. He wanted to do it again.

Gil touched the blood on his lip. ***"You want to act like I'm part of this family, but I'm not, Adrik. Yakov killed my parents and kept me as a consolation prize. I have always been unwanted."***

"You betrayed me, and you want me to feel sorry for you? I have no time to hear your sob story. Go find a whore to cry to."

Gil ground his teeth and nodded, quickly diving out the front door and slamming it shut.

Chapter Forty-One

Problems

Jolie felt like a train sat on her. The pounding in her head was equivalent to a hammer on her brain. She didn't want to move, but the disgust in her mouth and the tacky feeling of her tongue forced her to open her eyes. The room was dark still, with only a ray of sunlight sneaking through the sides of the blackout curtains. She was in a hotel room, a beautiful one at that.

Jolie rolled to her side, groaning, wanting to cry. She clenched her hair, apologizing to her body for doing this to it. She was better than this, she knew. Regret was piling into her as she sat up.

"You're awake."

Jolie snapped her head up, clenching her fist against her pounding temple. Katia stood from a recliner and sauntered over to the curtains. Before Jolie could protest, she slapped open the sheet, and like a vampire caught in sunlight, Jolie shrieked and threw the blanket over herself.

"Here."

Jolie peeked out to see Katia handing her Tylenol. Squinting, she sat up, holding out her hand. Katia gripped her wrist and pinned it to the bed with her knee against Jolie's forearm. She cried out in surprise until she saw a knife in Katia's hand. The woman pressed it against Jolie's palm.

"What are you doing?" she screeched, trying to get away, but Katia pressed her knee harder, cutting off the blood supply to Jolie's arm.

"Did you tell Adrik about me and Gil?"

Jolie pulled and pulled, slapping at her, but Katia pressed the point of the knife into her skin, and all her fighting stalled. "Wait, wait, stop, stop."

"Did you tell Adrik about me and Gil?" Katia asked calmly once more.

"No," Jolie whimpered. She looked up at Katia's face. "No."

"How did he find out?"

"I don't know."

Katia pressed harder, and blood puddled in her palm. She ignored Jolie's little groans.

"I don't know."

"You know what he would do to you if he found out you work for the FBI?" Katia met her eyes. "He'd do what he did to my fiancé: skin you alive. Cut you up into little pieces while you are still awake. He'd start with your toes. Then your fingers."

Jolie squeezed her eyes, slapping a hand over her face.

"This is the man you love, Jolie. You better learn to fucking accept it."

She shook her head. Disbelief was the only way to keep moving.

"Did you tell Adrik about us?"

Aggravation boiled over, and Jolie gathered all her courage and bit, "No!"

Katia watched her. She couldn't tell, really. Jolie was turning out to be one hell of a liar. It was a good trait to have in the Mafia. It was the only sign that she might survive in their world. Katia released her, and Jolie quickly tucked her bleeding hand to her chest, squeezing the blanket against her palm.

Katia cleaned the blade with a napkin. "You're lucky I believe you."

Jolie sneered, panting through her nose. "You're crazy."

"No." Katia smiled adoringly. "I'm a wife to a mafia king."

When Katia left the room, Jolie still didn't move. Her trust in the woman was shattered. All their fun last night dissolved like a dream.

Jolie stood on shaking legs, hating how her adrenaline left her feeling. She forced herself to move to the bathroom. Tears were plenty, but nausea kept creeping back in.

Jolie stared at her face in the mirror. She looked exactly how she felt: horrible. She giggled at herself, hanging her head. It wasn't one of her proudest moments. She held her hand in the sink; the blood clotted and left behind an ugly cut. It was in a terrible spot where even a Band-Aid wouldn't stick. "What am I doing?" she groaned, her legs giving out. She rested her back against the cabinets, staring blindly.

She was in Hell, trying to keep her angel wings. It wasn't possible. If she didn't surrender to the darkness, she'll be devoured.

'Come to the dark side,' Adrik whispered. And maybe that's what she had to do. She'd have to embrace every bad thing inside her. Every good instinct would have to be deleted.

I won't make it otherwise.

Then, it would be better to go.

But I can't. If I leave now, I'll never be safe again.

It was past the point of no return. She was trapped. There was no running.

There was a knock on her door, and Jolie hesitated to answer it. She looked like she got run over a few times. Her hair was in crazy wild knots, and her eyes were bloodshot. She was pretty sure that the garbage smell was coming from her mouth.

Jolie pulled back the door an inch. A nurse and a waiter stood outside. The waiter held a white box and a bouquet of red roses.

"Excuse me for interrupting. Mr. Morozov wanted to invite you to breakfast on the roof." Jolie allowed them in, and the servant placed the box on the bed and the roses on the table. "This is Nurse Julie. She will provide an IV to help with the effects of a hangover." Jolie's eyes widened as the nurse pulled in a tray, setting it on the bed. "Mr. Morozov expects you in one hour."

Jolie followed the rules of the nurse, sitting down as she set up the IV in her arm. The liquid flowed into her veins, and as the minutes passed, she felt her headache begin to ebb and her nausea disappear. Jolie eyed the box beside her, not daring enough to open it when someone else was in the room.

When the nurse was done and shut the door behind her, she felt brand new. She never knew people used IVs to treat hangovers. It must be a rich people thing.

Jolie approached the box. She untied the sash, cringing, hoping nothing was battery-operated.

To her delight, it was a beautiful sun dress with yellow flowers, a yellow hibiscus hairpiece, and white sandals. Underneath was a pair of black lace panties. Despite the misery this morning, his actions managed to bring a smile. She may be in Hell, but she was falling for a sexy, thoughtful devil.

After showering, scrubbing the horrible taste out of her mouth, and dressing up, Jolie arrived on the roof, directed by the attendant. The air was warm, and even the heavy breeze didn't ease the humidity. But the sun was barely over the horizon; from this vantage, it was the most gorgeous sunrise.

Adrik sat on a couch in the corner, on his phone. There were mimosas and a bowl of fruit on the table. He stood when he heard the door open, slipping his hands in his pockets as he greeted her with a smile.

Jolie kept herself stiff. "Is it safe here?"

He nodded and assured, "The Don is one of my investments. They are loyal to me." Adrik held a glass up to her, and she tentatively took it. He kissed her cheek in greeting before directing her to a seat. Jolie loved his care. She felt important in his presence, like her comfort mattered.

"How do you feel?"

"Good now. Thank you."

His phone rang. "Excuse me."

Jolie watched him as he sat back, putting the phone to his ear and resting his ankle on his knee. He was relaxed today. Something must have gone his way. It gave him the bad boy look, uncaring of the haters. The tattoos on his hands, along with the rings, brought all sorts of desires to her.

I want to lick his skin.

Jolie winced. Her mind has been saying the weirdest things lately.

Adrik glanced over at her, spoke into the phone, and winked. Jolie giggled like a silly schoolgirl and dropped her head. He knew how gorgeous he was and enjoyed being ogled. She rolled her eyes, hating herself for being another fan girl.

When he hung up, Jolie asked, "You seem happy?"

"I am." He watched the rising sun in the distance, enjoying the breeze. "My father will be leaving soon, and I have finally gotten hold of the man who ordered the hit on my daughter."

"Katia's brother?"

"Yes. He will pay for his sins."

Jolie bowed her head. Agent Mally had been right. Adrik found him. If she was a better person, she would take that information to Mally, and maybe she could save the man from dying. Because that's what's going to happen, wasn't it? Adrik was going to kill him?

Katia's voice broke into her thoughts. *'He'd do what he did to my fiancé. Skin you alive. Cut you up into little pieces while you are still awake. He'd start with your toes. Then your fingers. This is the man you love, Jolie. You better learn to fucking accept it.'*

"Are you—" The words caught in her throat. She could feel Adrik staring at her, waiting for her to finish the sentence, but she couldn't. She took a sip of her drink instead.

"I am not killing him if that is your question. I can't. The contract between our families forbids it. But I can make him suffer and keep him locked away for the rest of his miserable life."

She shook her head, staring at the wound on her hand.

Adrik shifted, sitting forward on the couch and resting his elbows on his knees. He followed her gaze, seeing the bandage. "What happened to your hand?"

She shook her head, clenching her fist. "It was my fault."

Adrik had no care to question further. He made himself talk about yesterday, "Did you have fun last night?"

The redirection was welcome, and Jolie latched onto it. She shoved the horrible thoughts of Adrik hurting someone to the back of her mind and slammed the door. She instead focused on his amazingly bright-blue eyes in the morning sun.

"It was awesome. I never drink, but"—she shrugged—"I needed a night to relax."

Adrik bit the inside of his cheek. He was talking to a feminist; no doubt any reprimand would be twisted into a women's rise about suppression. It was one of the reasons why he only fucked Russians. Those women knew what was expected of them.

"Your actions yesterday were not appropriate."

The defense in her was instant, and he hung his head.

"What did I do?"

With a deep breath, Adrik continued, "I am very particular about my expectations, Jolie. I expect respect and loyalty."

"I haven't disrespected you—"

"No? Allowing another man to fondle you isn't exactly a form of respect. You are lucky I didn't break their hands."

"Adrik—"

"My reputation is important to me. I control a vast number of very dangerous people. The only way that is possible is by being something to fear. If they have the audacity to touch what is mine, they do not fear me properly, and the potential to be disloyal rises. Now, these men didn't know you belonged to me; it is not their fault." He paused. "It is yours."

Jolie struggled to speak as the red poured into her vision. "So, you don't want me to have any fun?"

Adrik despised the fact it was the same response as Katia. "Is that what you heard?"

"Don't be patronizing. I was dancing. I didn't do anything wrong."

"I'm telling you, you did."

She nodded, licking her lips, getting more pissed as the seconds continued. "Naked girls on stripper poles are a 'lifestyle hazard,' but me dancing with other people is unacceptable?"

Adrik twisted the ring on his finger, watching her, disappointed in her overreaction. He was trying to be patient, but her inability to admit that what she did was wrong was chipping away at his self-control.

"Eat."

"I don't want to," she nipped back, resting the glass on the table and folding her arms.

Pouting was not a way to get his attention. Adrik leaned back and went back to his phone.

Jolie didn't like being ignored. "I'm a grown adult. You can't tell me what I can and cannot do."

Mindlessly, he responded, "I just did."

Jolie snapped to her feet. "You are being ridiculous!"

Adrik looked up at her, and very quietly said, "Lower your voice."

"Why? Are you going to hurt me if I don't?"

Adrik tossed his phone on the table and got to his feet. She took a step back as he approached, the sudden spark of fear blared on her face, and it pissed him off. "You truly believe I would hurt you? Then, why the fuck are you with me?"

Jolie strengthened against him. "You talk about torturing a man for years, and you don't want me to be afraid of you?"

To compare herself to someone who shot at his child blew him out of the water. She wasn't even making sense in her defense. "I'll let you think on my words. You are overreacting."

"This is just another attempt to control me."

Adrik scoffed, smiling despite how angry he was. "Go ask your mother if I am overstepping."

"Don't bring my mother into this."

Adrik slipped his hands into his pockets and observed her. Her defiance triggered dirty thoughts, and they roamed in his head freely. He wanted to be aggravated with her but was too turned on to care. All he wanted to do was put her in her place: on her knees or on her back.

"What?" She twittered on her feet, looking down at herself.

He shook his head, shrugging. "I am wondering if you like your ass smacked while I take you from behind."

Her face ignited in red, and he chuckled, adoring it.

"Don't make this sexual. This is a problem."

"I agree. You want respect, but you don't want to give it."

"Excuse me?"

"I respect you by keeping my distance from other women. But when I request the same from you, I'm controlling you. Talk about double standards."

The door on the roof opened up, revealing Alexei and Gil. She was relieved to see them and rushed to Alexei, gripping his arm. "Can you please talk to him? He's acting like I did something wrong last night."

Alexei glanced at his brother and slowly slipped his arm out of Jolie's grip. He gave her a reassuring smile, but that was all he offered as he sat on the couch.

Jolie scoffed, throwing her hands in the air. "I was just having fun."

Adrik had enough conversation. Nothing he was saying was getting through, and he wasn't about to repeat himself. "A car is waiting to take you back to the house."

"I don't want to go back to the house."

The rebellion was unnecessary, but it was predictable. Adrik nodded to his head guard, Dima. "I'll talk to you later."

Dima gripped her arm, and she snapped out of it. "Don't touch me." But Dima latched on harder. "Stop, you're hurting me." The sentence made him flinch, and then Dima changed his tactic, wrapping both his arms around her and picking her up off her feet. "Let me go! Help, let me go!"

Her voice disappeared into the elevator as Adrik sat down. He thumbed his lip, looking out into the ocean.

"Did you have to do that?" Alexei questioned.

Gil responded, "Fuck yeah, he did. She was being ridiculous."

Adrik snapped his head toward Gil. ***"What the fuck are you doing here?"***

Gil knitted his brows. ***"Why wouldn't I be here?"***

"I threw you out yesterday."

"Yeah, well, that was yesterday." Gil pulled out a cigarette and lit it, ignoring Adrik's glare. He took a puff before defending himself. ***"Come on, Adrik, we've been through worse."***

Adrik stood, buttoning his coat. ***"You think trying to fuck Katia is something I'll get over?"***

Gil hung his head. ***"Don't act like she matters—"***

"All she has to do is spread her fucking legs to get you on her side. She has been trying to destroy me for years, and you want to be her lap dog."

Gil snorted, glancing at Alexei for support. But he should have known better. Gil gripped his cane and stood. ***"I've been with you for over twenty years. You think I'll stab you in the back because of some chick?"***

"I don't have the luxury to wait for it."

Gil couldn't hide the hurt in his eyes as he stood there. He remained quiet, knowing Adrik better than he knew himself. No apology was going to make it better. Only punishment would do. ***"You kicking me out of the family?"***

Adrik turned his back. That would generally be the answer, but Adrik didn't want to do something he couldn't take back. Instead, he said, ***"I'm sending you to Puerto Rico, since you want to go so badly. The cartel down there isn't producing enough, and you will find out why and fix the problem."***

Gil pressed his cigarette into the ashtray. "Bullshit," he cursed. The cartels down there don't have much respect for Russians. They have never produced enough because they steal it for themselves. Sending him there was like dropping him in the ocean and hoping he didn't come home. ***"As you wish, boss,"*** he stressed. It was a word like venom on his lips. Adrik was his brother, and yet, here and now, he felt more like an employee. Gil turned away and walked to the elevator before he said over his shoulder, ***"If you ever saw me as your real brother, you wouldn't be shoving me out."***

"If you ever saw me as your real brother, you wouldn't have tried to fuck my wife."

Chapter Forty-Two

Bonding

Jolie tossed and turned all night. Aside from feeling like rocks were in her head dragging her down, she was replaying the whole conversation with Adrik over and over again and only getting angrier. Jolie wasn't the type of woman to be under anyone's thumb. She may be easy-going and not much of a fighter, but she'd never wear chains, not after Vincent.

Her phone dinged, and she clicked it on, hoping it was Adrik with a poetic apology. Depressingly, it was her mother. *'It wasn't that bad of an ask, sweetheart.'*

Jolie sneered and buried her head into her pillow.

It wasn't the request itself. Yeah, she shouldn't allow other guys to touch her when dating someone. But it was the way he did it. *'Your actions weren't appropriate.'* Saying it like she should be ashamed of herself for having fun. It wasn't right. She was a grown woman. She could have whatever kind of fun she wanted.

What other ways would he try to suppress her? Would he want her to change how she dressed, acted, and talked to people? By the end, nothing will be left of her but a shadow.

Tae-Tae rubbed his head against her, trying to pull her out of her despair. Jolie lifted her head, and he smashed his forehead against her cheek. It brought a quick smile to her, and she relaxed as she petted him.

"Am I overreacting?" she asked him.

A meow came in reply.

"I just see it. Like with Vincent. Do you remember Vincent? I forgot who I was for so long." Memories of her time five years ago resurfaced. She wore the clothes he wanted: black emo style, with black lipstick and nail polish. She pretended to like Slipknot and Korn. The only thing she wouldn't do that he tried hard was drink and smoke. It was one of the reasons she eventually gave in to sex. Something had to give so she didn't lose him.

"But I am older now," she whispered to herself. "I love who I am. I don't have to change."

The sunflower dress he bought her lay on the back of the chair. Adrik brought her clothes that she would love. He hadn't shunned her for wearing that halter dress to his mother's party. He hadn't reprimanded her for laughing and getting attention from all his family. And he wasn't even pressuring her to have sex with him. On top of it, he met her mother without being coerced.

Another beep and her mother wrote, '*Relationships are give and take. Vincent took everything you had to give, while he gave you nothing in return. Don't let this one do that to you, and you won't fall back into the same routine.*'

Her mother knew her biggest fears. She shared everything with her, except that Adrik was in the Mafia. She wondered if her opinion would change. Jolie's finger hovered over the 'M', but she was too afraid that the moment she did, her mother's support would fall away.

With renewed energy, Jolie faced the day. Tutoring Helina helped push out the fog of her brain and made her laugh. She was learning a few of Helina's phases. Her Russian was okay, but she had a long way to go to get the proper accent. She hoped to surprise Adrik one day with the ability to talk to him in his native language.

Jolie bowed her head when Katia walked into the bedroom. All their progress as friends had dissolved, and now, Jolie couldn't look at her without fear. But that fear was also tinged with resentment. She wanted to get back at the woman, but learning Katia's weaknesses was hard. The woman was a closed book.

"You look like an injured puppy," Katia mocked from across the bedroom, folding Helina's clothes and putting them in the closet.

Jolie continued staring at Helina's paperwork, helping her write letters. She clenched her hand around the bandage, the wound and fear still fresh. "I don't want to talk to you today."

A giggle. "Aww, I hurt your feelings."

Jolie clenched her teeth but didn't feed into her teasing.

The door popped open, and Jolie swung her head, expecting Adrik, but Alexei smiled back at her. She didn't let her disappointment show. "Hey."

"Hi," he greeted, glancing nervously at Katia before he continued, "Helina, want to go swimming?"

The little girl jumped up from the chair. "Yes!" A strain of Russian excitement barreled out of her mouth as she grabbed her bathing suit from the drawer and ran to the bathroom.

Jolie folded her arms. "She's got two hours left of work."

"Join us."

"I don't swim."

"Then, get a tan."

Katia looked over her shoulder, and in Russian, taunted, ***"I don't think you're the brother she wants."***

Alexei was quick to shoot back. ***"I don't think you're someone anyone wants."***

Katia giggled. "Good one."

He rolled his eyes, and announced in English, speaking to Jolie, "Adrik went to Miami for business. He won't be back for a bit. Tonight is my only free day before I have to take on his responsibilities here. And I plan on having fun, since last night was a failure. So, come have fun with me."

Katia questioned, "And Gil? Where is he gallivanting today?"

Alexei changed his tone. "Why?" he asked darkly. "What does it matter where he is?"

Jolie flicked her eyes between them. She didn't know what Alexei knew, but apparently, he had suspicions. It hit her then what Katia's weakness might be. "Is Gil okay?" she questioned for Katia. "Is he with Adrik?"

Alexei hesitated, unsure why Jolie was asking, but she was innocent in Katia's games. Helina emerged from the bathroom and ran out of the room, screaming Alexei's name to hurry. Giving in, Alexei answered. "He was sent to Puerto Rico for a job. Now, come on!"

He disappeared from the doorway, and Jolie turned her attention to Katia. She was still, her hands gripping the shirt. Instead of making Jolie feel powerful for finding Katia's weakness, it made her pity the woman. Sometimes, being a sap for love was a character flaw.

Jolie approached slowly, unsure if she should say anything at all. "Are you alright?"

The words spooked Katia into movement. "I'm fine."

The coldness annoyed Jolie, and she backed away, moving to her room, but she stopped. There were so many things in this life that were going to change Jolie, but having compassion wasn't going to be one of them. "If you need someone to talk to—"

"Ha," Katia shoved a hanger into the closet before turning to her. "Are you this dense on purpose? You're one of those people that if a dog bites you, you make excuses for it."

"Dogs have bad days like the rest of us," Jolie defended.

Katia's eyes widened, before her hands went through her hair. "Oh, God. You're hopeless." Katia snatched up another shirt. "The thing with Yakov and the FBI is off. I can't trust you. Your foolishness is going to get me killed because it's going to get you killed." She spun on Jolie, approaching. "Do you understand, girl? This isn't a magic kingdom. You don't get happy endings and sweet forgiveness. We don't hope for the best and hug at the end of the night. This world you are invading is bloody, and violent, and scary. What are you trying to do here? What do you think you'll get out of this? Love?" She scoffed. "It's not enough, Jolie. We'll destroy you. So, please, get out. Run. Escape before you can't anymore."

Jolie backed away. The desperation in Katia's face was too much, too pure, too uncharacteristic that it was terrifying. She locked the door to her bedroom and sank to the floor.

Jolie laid on a lounge chair in shorts and a tank top. It took her time to recover from Katia's outburst, and she still felt shaken inside, but Helina had come to her room and begged her to come down. The sun was blazing, warming her, and the panic receded more every passing minute. On the pool deck, dozen men in shorts were drinking and laughing nearby. Women in string bikinis walked on high heels and strutted from one end of the pool to the other for no reason whatsoever other than to get attention. She felt completely out of place, like a nerd at a frat party. But Helina and Alexei played in the pool, and she forced her attention on them, even when her gaze drifted.

This was Adrik's life. Men with guns exposed at their waist. Women showing off their bodies and getting their butts smacked by random strangers. Drugs lay on the table with children around. It was surreal, sitting here, knowing she wasn't one of them.

'Run. Escape before you can't anymore.'

Jolie appreciated Katia's advice, but there was no walking away. She was already in the middle of the jungle. What she needed to do was get stronger, educate herself on the dangers, and learn how to navigate them. There was a point to this. Katia believed that love wasn't enough, but love was the only reason to endure hardships. Love was the only reason to fight back.

A young man approached her. He was staring at her, and his eyes drifted down her body with obvious intent. She pulled her legs into her chest. "Hey, I'm Trevor." He sat beside her, holding a beer out to her.

"Trevor," Alexei called from the pool.

They both turned their gaze toward Alexei, and with only a slight tick of his head, Trevor excused himself and left her alone. Jolie relaxed and let her legs fall back down. A soft smile on her lips as she thanked him. It hit her then why Alexei wasn't with Adrik, considering they typically traveled together. Adrik made his brother stay behind to watch over her.

Her stomach filled with warmth. It was something so silly, something probably not worth a thought, but it meant something to her. Even angry, Adrik thought of her well-being. It was something Vincent had been incapable of. He left her on the side of the road once after he kicked her out of his car because he was pissed about something she said. She needed to stop comparing. Adrik was in a league all of his own.

A phone on top of Alexei's shirt rang, and Jolie got up to hand it to him. He pushed himself out of the pool with his bad arm tucked into his stomach and sat on the edge, dangling his legs in. Jolie averted her eyes. There was no doubt that Alexei had a good body. Though currently there were terrible bruises, it didn't hide the muscles in his arms. Alexei may not have a six-pack like Adrik, but it didn't matter. He was thick, like a Viking. How these women weren't flocking to his side, she didn't know.

He's more like a bear, Jolie thought, recalling Katia's cat analogy.

Jolie leaned down, pretending to play with Helina, hoping to find out who was on the phone, but Alexei spoke in Russian, and nothing about what he said was familiar. Would Adrik ignore her till he returned? Her secret phone was in her pocket, with no messages. She wasn't the kind of woman that sat in anger. She liked to get it out as soon as possible. But she doubted Adrik was that way.

A tap on her arm, and the phone waited for her. Jolie's eyes widened, and she grabbed it. "Hello?"

"Don't say anything," Adrik said. "Only listen." He waited for an 'okay,' but she was smart enough to stay silent. "I'm dealing with coke heads in the south for a few days. Don't do anything without telling Alexei. My father should stay away from you, but if he does anything, you let my brother know. And stay away from Katia. Give the phone back."

Jolie's brows knitted at his complete disregard. She wanted more from him; she wanted him to fix the ache in her chest, not make it worse. She numbly handed it over and sat staring at the water.

Alexei tossed the phone back on the chair and glanced at her nervously.

Jolie didn't want him to feel obligated to talk to her, so she burst into conversation. "You dated any of those girls?" It was a pathetic attempt to keep his attention off her.

His brows knitted in disgust, and he pointed to two girls. "My cousins." Then he pointed to two more. "Cousins." Three more. "Wives of cousins."

"Oh," she whimpered, glancing toward them. They were beyond gorgeous and intimidating, but knowing they were family took the edge off a little.

"Most of them were at my mom's party."

Jolie bowed her head, embarrassed. There were a bunch of people, and they were fully clothed. She couldn't possibly remember who was who.

Alexei fiddled with the water. "I told you before I'm picky."

"You're young, gorgeous, and a millionaire. Didn't think it would be a struggle."

"Well, first, she's got to be Russian, so that deletes like ninety-nine percent of the population."

Jolie rolled her eyes. "Of course, how could I forget."

"And she can't be family, obviously, so that takes out like half of the people I know. Then she has to be okay with drugs, guns, drunks, druggies, violence, strippers, and blood."

Jolie nodded with wide eyes. "That's a lot."

"Then she'd have to be cool with being alone eighty percent of our life because I'm always fucking busy. And when I'm out, I'm typically in the audience of"—he pointed to the nearly naked women—"that. So, if you know anyone—"

She laughed, hanging her head. When he put it that way, it didn't sound like something Jolie would be good with. But it was something she would have to figure out. If she wanted to be in Adrik's life than she would have to accept his life.

Alexei smiled. Her happiness caught him in a trance, and he stared at her longer than planned. He forced his eyes back to the water and brought up his brother. It was the only way to remind himself that she would never be his.

"You and Adrik are fighting, huh?"

Jolie sighed and shrugged. "Yes. Everything you just pointed out is a struggle. I feel like we're doomed."

Alexei agreed silently. Not only did they have completely contrasting lifestyles, but their personalities were on opposite ends of the spectrum. It's one of the reasons why there was a slim chance that Jolie would one day realize Alexei was more suited for her.

But that's an asshole's hope.

"Adrik's had a tough life," he began, glancing around them, ensuring no one could hear him. "When we were little kids, my father was hard on me. I would take on the family, so he was merciless in training. I was beaten many times and was never allowed to fight back. It was to condition me to pain."

"That sounds more like *you* had a tough life."

Alexei yearned for her sympathy, but if he was a lesser man, he might have dived for more, but this wasn't about him.

"When Adrik turned ten, he came between me and my father. He took on every beating. He took on every terrible thing my father could invent. He even took on the family so I wouldn't have to. Adrik is one of the most loyal, dedicated, amazing men I know."

Jolie loved how much Adrik cared for his brother. It's the type of care she knew he was capable of, and wanted for herself.

Alexei held up a hand. "But," he added, "he's not the best boyfriend. He went through girls like crazy in high school. You can only imagine when my dad told him he was getting married. But like I said, he's loyal and dedicated, so he swallowed all his doubts and completely gave in to Katia. And he was so good to her." Alexei shook his head, thinking back to it. "She wanted for nothing. He changed, became a good man, and gave her his full attention. And she fucking destroyed him."

The words came out bitterly, as if Adrik's pain was his. "Katie told me." Katia should have ended things with her boyfriend or at least told Adrik what was going on. He might have understood.

Just like how I need to tell Adrik what's happened with Mally. Jolie bowed her head, feeling the small bubbling guilt in her chest.

Alexei continued his story. "Adrik went right back to the guy he was before and got a little colder. Waiting six months to find out if the child she was carrying was his or the other guy's really fucked with his head. He put everyone at a distance, even me." Alexei leaned back on his hands, watching Helina jump in the pool. "I'm telling you this because even though I know he can be distant and maybe a little heartless, Adrik's worth the trouble. He'll be good to you. And if I didn't fully believe that—" Alexei paused, and he got to his feet, squatting beside her with his elbows on his knees, his hands hanging between them. Alexei met her gaze. Did she even know how beautiful she looked in the sunlight? "I would be trying to steal you away."

Chapter Forty-Three

Choice

Jolie stared out the window of the limo. The bright-blue water stretched forever as they approached the beach. A surprise invitation by Tatianna to join her on the yacht had come this morning, and Jolie couldn't say no. Six days of waiting for Adrik to return had resulted in misery on top of misery. Jolie was avoiding Katia like the plague. And though Alexei invited her to parties every night, she dutifully declined. His confession at the pool made her weary of his friendship. She didn't want him to think there was anything between them. She enjoyed being with him, but she couldn't risk him making a pass at her. Adrik loved his brother. She couldn't imagine what damage it would do to their kinship.

The limo drove by fishing charters and sunset cruises, and then, as the car kept going down the line, her gaze came upon the largest yacht on the dock. The limo stopped in front of it. Her mouth fell open.

Jolie quickly typed, *'I'm going on a yacht.'*

Her mother instantly replied, *'Why didn't you invite me?'*

Jolie smiled, adoring her mother. Heather was the rock these last few days, her only form of entertainment. And though her mother still didn't know what exactly was going on inside the Morozov household, her advice and affection was still very much needed.

The driver opened Jolie's door, helping her out. He dutifully took her bag, directing her to the ramp. It squeaked with each step till her feet landed on the hollow deck of the ship.

"Jolie!"

Helina ran down the side of the ship and jumped into her arms. "Hi, baby girl!" Jolie squeezed her, kissing her cheek.

"Miss Bell!" Tatianna greeted Jolie from the second floor. She had a drink in her hand, oversized sunglasses on her face, and her flowered sundress waved in the wind. "Come up! We'll be leaving shortly."

Jolie followed Helina, taking her around the front of the massive ship. She took her inside where the stairs were. There was a living room with a flat-screen TV, three bedrooms, and three different levels. She couldn't imagine what kind of price tag this thing had. Helina revealed that Adrik was on the ship, sleeping.

"Your dad's here?" The words slipped out, too hopeful, but thankfully the little girl didn't notice a difference. Jolie touched her hair and glanced at herself in the hallway mirror, suddenly more self-conscious than ever. She should have gotten a better bathing suit that didn't look like an eighty-year-old grandma would wear. Her hair was in a messy bun. With no makeup, she was sure she had bags under her eyes from the lack of sleep these past few days.

But at least I shaved.

With Helina pulling her hand, she was brought to the extravagant breakfast table where Tatianna waited. "My favorite person! Come sit next to me." Jolie slid into the booth, and Tatianna kissed her cheek in greeting. "I'm so glad you could make it. Eat, please; I can't possibly finish all this. My cooks love to impress."

Jolie adored Tatianna. She spoke of random extravagances, like dinner parties in Paris and her sixtieth birthday in a Russian ballroom. She wasn't trying to brag; it didn't feel like that to Jolie. She only wanted to share the greatness of her life, and Jolie loved to hear it.

It was an hour later when Adrik strolled through the door. He wore swim shorts and flip-flops, exposing his chest and belly, full of decorative tattoos. The light from the windows ignited his blue eyes like little holes to Heaven. A smile bloomed on her face. Any thought of being mad at him disappeared, and she shifted as if to get up and hug him.

Thankfully, Helina beat her to it.

Adrik lifted her, holding Helina against his hip as he approached the breakfast table. His gaze didn't even glance in her direction. The complete lack of acknowledgment derailed her. Adrik set Helina in her chair and greeted his mother in Russian, picking at the bacon and eggs.

"Manners, Adrik," his mother reminded. "Speak in English."

He sighed and then glanced at Jolie dutifully. "Good morning."

Jolie forced a tight smile. "Morning."

Adrik sat across from them, piling food on his plate. "I'm starving."

"You look too skinny," Tatianna chastised. "Are you eating?"

"There is no time, mama."

Tatianna scoffed. "Then you make time. You are in charge, and your health is important."

Adrik chewed without really hearing. "Where's Alexei?"

"He had plans already. If only Gil was around." She sighed.

Adrik eyed her over his plate of food. He knew she was upset that he sent Gil to Puerto Rico, but she would get over it. Adrik pointed. "Why is the tutor here?"

Jolie kept her eyes down at her plate. His disregard was like being tossed out with the garbage.

Tatianna sipped her cocktail with a smile. "I wanted to get to know Miss Bell, since my son seems to like her. I haven't heard Alexei's laugh in so long."

Heat spread out over her cheeks. The dinner party was still being discussed, and Jolie wished it could be forgotten. She didn't realize how much these people love to gossip.

"Papa wasn't too impressed."

"Oh, who cares?" she said flippantly. "Love is love."

Adrik snorted, and said under his breath, "I doubt it's love."

The insinuation that Alexei only likes her because he wanted to sleep with her unnerved her. And the way they talked about her like she wasn't there pushed her over. "Excuse me." Jolie left the table.

Adrik chewed his bacon, staring at his food.

"What was that?" Tatianna chided in terse Russian. ***"I didn't raise you to be disrespectful. Go talk to her."***

There was hesitation, but he got up and kissed Helina's forehead before whispering, ***"Stay with grandma."***

Adrik went out into the hallway but had no idea which way she went. He wasn't about to chase her either. He jotted down the stairs and thankfully found her hanging onto the railing as the yacht went out to sea. It weaved through the harbor slowly, with the morning light shining on the city buildings. There were still too many ships this morning, with too many spies. He couldn't risk touching her till they were deep in the gulf.

Adrik called her, and though she was refused at first, she thought better of it and crossed her arms as she approached. He held the door open for her and shut it tight. He stood in front of her, observing all the walls she had in front of her. He took a step back to make room for it. Adrik had hoped her temper would have abated by now. "Have you thought about my words?"

She stood silent, with a pout.

"I'm not good with this kind of shit," Adrik admitted. "I knew you'd start with that feminist crap, but I thought you'd also see reason. Having men touch you will never be acceptable."

Jolie bit out, "I get it."

"You do?"

"Yeah, but it's the way you're treating me that I'm pissed at."

Adrik clenched his fists. If it wasn't one thing, it was another. "My mother is very perceptive. What did you want me to do? Make out with you at the breakfast table?"

"No phone calls?"

"I couldn't even call Helina. Larger things are going on than us. I don't have time for it."

"Then, maybe I should leave."

He turned from her with a scoff, cursing in Russian. There were too many things happening, and on top of it, he was starting a new relationship, one that needed proper attention, but how was he supposed to stretch his time? This was why he never dated, and he hated himself for doing it during one of the most crucial moments in his career.

"I'm not an afterthought, Adrik."

He faced her with knitted brows. "Is that what you think?"

"What am I supposed to think? You are barely around to begin with. You show up whenever you want, and I'm supposed to be waiting around for you, hoping you remember to stop by. It sucks."

"I'm running an empire, Jolie. This is not a nine-to-five, Monday-Friday type of job. I don't get to go to every birthday. I don't get to go to every dinner. My success is based on what I put into it."

"That sounds sad."

Adrik slipped his hands into his pockets. "That's funny coming from someone broke their whole life."

"Oh, now you want to attack *my* lifestyle?"

This was getting out of his control. He wanted to make up with her, not make it worse, yet here he was, going down a slippery slope. But backing down from an argument wasn't a talent Adrik possessed. "When have you ever worked hard in your life? Too busy watching sunrises and babysitting. But it's money that makes this world, and I mean to have plenty of it."

Jolie shook her head. "And all this money, will it be holding your hand if you get sick?"

"I won't need anyone to hold my hand. I'll have the best doctors in the world and survive."

"Then, why am I here? If you have all this money that can take care of you, you certainly don't need me." Jolie spun to go, but Adrik latched onto her wrist.

She fought it, but he caught her eyes, keeping her still. "I don't need you," Adrik affirmed.

The words were painful to hear, and Jolie nearly cracked, but Adrik brushed his fingers through her hair. "I want you. And I hope you appreciate the difference."

"What's the difference?" She wiped a tear from her cheek.

Adrik stepped before her. "Needing someone means there's no choice. It's a miserable thing not being able to pick who is by your side for life. But wanting someone"—Adrik touched her cheek—"means out of every woman I've ever met, I chose you." She dropped her head and tears flowed down her cheeks. He hoped it was because of relief and latched onto this moment of vulnerability with eagerness. "Be honest with yourself, baby; you don't need me either. You can take care of yourself. You could go on and do amazing things without me. But here you are, enduring, struggling, accepting this life, because you are choosing me."

Jolie kept her head down, staring at his chest. The tattoos were vibrant, some more dull, some with color. Her fingers rested on his pectoral, over his heart. The touch was a soothing balm on his temper. He swallowed it down, allowing her to bring out the softness in his voice.

"My time is sparse. But know that any second I have free, I come to you because you are where I want to be. So, enjoy today with me. You can hate me tomorrow."

A smile teased her lips. "I don't hate you."

"No? Even though you think I'm a misogynist?"

A giggle breached her throat. "I can fix that."

"I'll let you try." Adrik stepped forward, and the walls that separated them burned to ashes. Her hand spread on his chest, and he wondered if she could feel the heavy beat of his heart. He leaned down and kissed her. Softly, hesitantly.

Jolie broke from his lips and hugged him. He sighed into her touch. A silly hug wasn't sexual, but it was everything he wanted from her.

"Is everything better now? Are you back for good?" she wondered.

Adrik didn't want to tell her he had been back in town for three days. He stayed an hour away at a hideaway house. He had too much on his plate, and he knew that going back home with Jolie there would only distract him.

"No. I only have today, and then I have to return tomorrow."

"Is it because of Zinof?"

Her interest pleased him. Adrik wanted her to be curious about his life. One day, he could get her opinion on matters, and they could be a team, like his father and mother in their younger years. But he wouldn't mess it up like his father had. He'd be faithful, for one.

"It is." Adrik leaned back against a bar top, pulling her hips to him. "Katia's father, Boris, sabotaged some shipments in the harbor. Killed a few of my men." They were low-tier members that Adrik didn't have names for. But the sign left above their heads, *'Give back what's ours,'* was more important.

The police were in a rage, and Agent Mally was coming after multiple members, interrogating and threatening. The situation was slowly increasing daily, and it wouldn't be long before a war ignited. Adrik dreaded something like this because of the bloodshed that would follow, but he also looked forward to it. It would give him just cause to divorce Katia.

Today, he refused to take a phone call. There were a few 'managers' that Adrik left in charge, including his brother Alexei. He pretended that he hadn't known where Alexei was when he had given him a specific job to keep him off the boat this morning.

Adrik was done talking about business. Other things were on his mind, and he couldn't hold himself back any longer. "I've missed you."

A warmth spread over her cheeks, and Jolie nodded. "I missed you, too."

He leaned down and barely touched her lips with a soft kiss. "Date number one," he whispered. "This boat is under my command. Have no fear of guards here. Any time my mother or Helina appear busy, sneak away with me."

Jolie bit her lip, sinking into his body like Play-Doh. "Oh, yeah? And what are we going to do in those moments?"

Adrik captured her lips with his to show her.

Adrik directed Jolie back to the breakfast table, much to his mother's delight. Tatianna greeted her with so much excitement Jolie couldn't stop smiling, listening to her go on. Adrik wanted them to spend more time together because he hoped to reveal soon that he was dating Jolie, not Alexei. He wasn't quite sure how his mother would respond. 'Love is love' was a great saying for people who could do whatever they wanted, but she understood his responsibility to the family just as much as Adrik did. Would she be against it?

Would it matter if she was?

It took an hour to get to the middle of the gulf, without an eye on them. It was a blank canvas aside from the three-speed cruisers that followed them. His guards watched from a distance. There were ten soldiers on the ship, but he didn't want Jolie or Helina to be overwhelmed by the mass of soldiers. It was paranoia that kept them close. Boris was being more forceful than Adrik thought he could be. He couldn't take the chance that someone came upon them while he was out on the sea.

Adrik spent the morning playing with Helina. It was much needed after so many days away. He basked in her attention, sparing no moment to make her laugh. She was getting smarter, and her ability to speak English increased daily. Small words, small sentences. But impressive, nonetheless. Jolie was good at her job, as he knew she would be. Jolie was dedicated and not one to turn away from hard work. She would make a perfect mafia member if she let go of her angelic morality.

When Helina looked sleepy, he carried her to his mother's room, where Tatianna was already napping, and snuggled her in. He put a guard outside their door to tell him when they woke.

Jolie was sitting on the leather couches in the living room. She wore a bathing suit with a loose, see-through beach dress. Throughout the afternoon, there were spare minutes of slipping into a hallway or a closet and making out with her, touching her in random places before she slipped out of his arms, giggling as she went. He felt stressless here. It was slowly becoming one of the best days of his life.

Adrik approached, and her gaze caught him with a smile. She was a beautiful woman, and keeping his distance from her was getting harder and harder. But for now, he didn't have to. The space between them disappeared, and he kissed her harshly, desperately, pushing her down on the couch as he climbed over her. The seriousness freaked Jolie out; she giggled and tried to push him away. "Adrik, your daughter."

"They're sleeping. Don't worry." Adrik kissed her neck, holding himself above her between her legs. He rubbed himself against her, groaning into her skin. "I want you," Adrik whispered. "So fucking badly." He nipped at her throat before lifting to her lips again. His tongue found hers, and he swirled it with hers till they struggled to breathe. Her hips met him with every rocking movement he made, and it only pushed him out of control.

Adrik shoved himself off, panting, sitting beside her as he calmed himself. He felt like a pubescent boy in her arms, already so close to exploding.

Jolie watched with a heaving chest, red cheeks, and eyes full of want. "Don't stop." There was no option but to stop. They were still days away from the designated two weeks, and he was being as respectful as he could by honoring her wishes.

She sat up, sitting against his side. She gripped his jaw, forcing his head to her, and kissed him gently. Her hand slithered down his chest, her palm sliding over his nipple. Further still, her hand descended till she touched the rim of his swim shorts.

Adrik smirked into her lips. "Touch it," he tempted, leaning back, allowing her full control. "I dare you."

Chapter Forty-Four

Teach

Jolie's fingers slid along the hem of Adrik's shorts. Her heart pounded in her chest as she watched his face. He rested his head back on the couch and waited, the dare hanging in the air as she struggled with the desire to touch him. She had imagined moments like this, and she ended up with her hand between her legs every time. This powerful man was weak at the hands of a schoolteacher.

"Come on, Jolie, do it. Grab my cock." The words were sinful and made her body shiver. She let her fingers crawl toward the lump in his shorts and grazed it, panting, terrified, and exhilarated. Adrik lost his patience. He pulled the top of his pants down and pulled out his hard dick before resting back and letting go. He presented it to her like a trophy and admired her face as she observed him.

Jolie swallowed, staring at him with no reserve. She was relieved it wasn't as enormous as the dildo he bought her, but it was still intimidating and worried her. It was thick and pulsing, with the tip dripping with a sheen of precum. Adrik took her wrist and guided her to it. He wrapped her fingers around him and groaned. "Go ahead," he encouraged, keeping himself from thrusting into her hand.

Jolie watched his face as her hand rose and fell. His skin was smooth aside from the vein up the middle. His dick stood tall and proud with every reason to be. He bit his lips, his eyes closing, basking in her attention.

Adrik wanted more. "Put your lips on it."

Nervousness set in, and she shifted uncomfortably. "I'm not very good."

He pulled her to his lips, kissing her, encouraging her. "That's why I'm gonna teach you. Get on your knees."

Jolie shivered. The order sent a thrill through her that she didn't want to admit to. His dominating ways were a double-edged sword. She wanted to be controlled. She wanted to be manhandled, but her pride was difficult to surrender.

She slid down to the floor and moved between his legs. Now his cock was right in front of her face, twitching with his heartbeat. Jolie could see the veins running through it with such clarity she could take a pen and trace them. Tattoos ran along his thighs and pelvis, but his penis remained unsullied.

Adrik grasped his cock and tugged it once before her. "First, you lick it."

Jolie couldn't believe she was doing this. She had only given oral to Vincent for his birthday and Christmas. Each time, Jolie felt so disgusted with herself, she would gag before it got to the back of her throat and accidentally bit him. She didn't want to embarrass herself in that way. But there was a difference between then and now.

Now she wanted to do it. Jolie took hold of the base of his cock and licked the tip. His sharp hiss was the only encouragement she needed before she pressed her tongue against the base of his cock and rode it up to the top. He cursed and bit his lip, bucking in her hand. "Now," he panted. Adrik took a handful of her hair and pulled her closer. "Suck it."

Jolie took his girth into her mouth. The first time she went down, she only took in an inch.

"More," he instructed.

Jolie went down again, taking in two inches. She could feel the resistance against his hand as he kept her where she was.

"Come on, Jolie," he insisted.

The next time she went down, four inches filled her mouth. Up and down, she sucked on his dick. Listening to his heavy breathing and soft moans filled her with confidence, and the stress in her shoulders began to ebb. But then he pushed her down too far, and she bucked, her teeth nipping his sensitive skin, and he hissed, flinching.

Jolie leaned back, pressing a hand to her lips. "I'm sorry,"

Adrik reached for her head. "Don't stop." Jolie took him in her mouth again, surprised he didn't respond angrily. "Bite my balls," he whispered and then added, "Gently."

Jolie sat back on her heels. "You want me to bite them?" With a gentle hand, she lifted his shaved ball sack and nibbled on it. He twisted and hissed, provoking her hand to jerk him off as she teased his sensitive skin with her teeth.

"Good girl," he praised. "Now take them in your mouth."

Jolie sucked and ran her tongue over his balls, but she didn't stay there long. She wanted another chance to suck his cock. She pulled his tip into her mouth, licking the slit, tasting the precum.

He dropped his hands to the side, giving her complete control. It gave her all the power to go as deep as she wanted. With a deep breath, she sucked his cock, her head bobbing like a bouncing Ping Pong ball, going lower and lower till she could feel him in the back of her throat.

"Oh, fuck," he groaned, digging his nails into the couch. Adrik gripped her hair and pulled her off him. She was panting as she sat back.

"What, did I hurt you?"

He tried to smile but was too busy focusing on control, stopping the approaching orgasm. He sat up and pulled Jolie into his lap with a brutal yank. Their tongues swirled. He slipped his hands under her bathing suit, gripping the fat of her ass and pushing her against his erection. All that was between them was the thin material of her bathing suit. Adrik trailed his lips down her jaw and neck. He nuzzled the fat of her breasts and fingered her nipple through the fabric. "You want my cock, baby?"

Jolie bit her lip, closing her eyes as she felt his hard dick press against her clit. Her hips were wiggling on their own, trying to ease the pressure building at her core. Pushing the fabric aside and sliding him into her would be so easy. She imagined it over and over within seconds. The words were in her throat, ready to give in.

A hard knock on the door turned Adrik's attention.

Through the one-way glass windows of the ship, he found a row of soldiers lining up along the front of the boat. Adrik moved her off, double-checking her attire to ensure she wasn't exposing anything as he pushed his dick back in his pants. She was confused and looked around in a daze.

Adrik pulled the door open. ***"What is it?"***

In Russian, the soldier reported, ***"Sir, four speedboats are headed our way from the north."***

"Is it Boris?"

"They sent a message." He handed over the paper, and Adrik tore it open.

'Give back what's ours.'

He cursed, looking back at Jolie. The concern was in her eyes. He knew what was coming. Adrik grabbed his soldier, Dima, by the collar. ***"Take her to the safe room. Stay outside and guard it."***

"Yes, sir." Dima approached, reaching for her arm and helping Jolie to her feet.

"What's happening?"

Adrik lifted the seat to the couch, revealing a row of weapons tucked into the crevices. "A war," Adrik responded, taking out a 9 mm. He checked the bullets. "They think I have Zinof on the ship. Probably thinking I'd throw the fucker overboard." Adrik darted for the stairs. "I have to get Helina and my mother. Get to the safe room. No matter what you hear, you don't come out." He paused halfway up and looked back at her. "Jolie, do you understand?"

The severity of his voice made her speechless, and she nodded. She was still in a whirlwind of confusion. They were making out, about to have sex, and now the feeling in the air was tense and frightening.

Adrik rushed up the stairs while Jolie followed the soldier into the ship's lower levels. All the servants were now carrying guns, shouting orders to each other as they ran in different directions. Three floors they descended before getting to the engine room. It was hot and stuffy and terrifyingly loud. She wouldn't be able to hear anything down here. The soldier pushed aside a fake water heater, and behind it on the wall was a keypad. He typed in the number quickly and then grabbed Jolie's hand.

"You are the only one that will be able to open this door once it closes," Dima told her. "Wait for Helina and Mrs. Morozov."

Stepping inside, it was a square box. Against the wall was a cabinet full of guns, a phone glued to the wall, a small refrigerator with food and water, and a small bathroom with a sliding door. Fold-up chairs were laid on the floor, and she picked one up to sit. Jolie clenched the chair, her knuckles white in their hold.

Nothing wrong with this, she whispered to herself. *Just a typical day dating the king of the Mafia.*

Chapter Forty-Five

Attack

Adrik pressed against the wall, panting, slightly bleeding on the arm. He kept his gun close to his body, listening for footsteps and signs of life. The body of one of his men was at his feet, but it phased him little.

Their opponents were strong and plentiful. They came on four speedboats, with a dozen soldiers on each. It should have been like shooting fish in a barrel, but their enemy was prepared. They had mirrors to blind them and tear gas that they shot from over-the-shoulder cannons. But their arrival had been a diversion. A team of sea divers went under the boat and boarded from the other side, taking Adrik and his team off guard.

Now, they were searching the hull of the yacht, and Adrik had the means to kill every last one. But his numbers were decreasing as the minutes passed.

This boat had never been breached. Thirty million went into this ship, now being reduced to splinters. The failure would eat at Adrik at another time, but right now, he needed to focus on his target.

In his ear, Adrik wore a small Bluetooth and could hear the other members of his army continuing to fight. Adrik didn't want to put himself between the safe room and their enemy for a simple reason. They would know he was protecting something, and they would only try harder. So, he left the safe room to Dima, who sat in hiding, watching the room's safety. He listened every moment for Dima to tell him if the girls were in danger.

Adrik pretended instead to be protecting the upstairs bedroom, and that's where the stalemate was.

A shout called in English, "We only want Zinof."

"He's not here, you fucking idiots." Adrik hollered back in Russian, if only to spite them. But even if Zinof was here, Adrik would still fight with the same amount of zest. They dared come onto his boat; now they must face the penalties.

"Hand him over, and no one else has to die."

"Fuck you," Adrik yelled, and then he shot down the hallway with only his arm out. Immediately, his opponent fired back, and the bullets stuck into the floorboards and walls.

In his ear, he heard Dima. ***"Sir, there's someone coming."*** Adrik pressed his back against the wall and closed his eyes. 'Someone coming' didn't mean they knew where the safe room was. But even if they did, they couldn't breach it, not without a bomb or Jolie's hand.

"Sir," another voice came on the line. He was whispering and clearly out of breath. ***"In the back of the ship, there's a crew of four. They're sawing into the side. They're breaching the safe room from the outside."***

Adrik ground his teeth and smashed his head back against the wall. A tangent of curses rolled through his head. This group of mercenaries had a smart leader. Adrik touched his earpiece. ***"How long?"***

"Five, ten minutes tops."

"How many are on the ship?"

The count went out, and it came to seven. He ordered someone to the stairs to help clear his pathway. Adrik entered his bedroom and threw the mattress off the bed to reveal a safe. He typed in a number quickly, listening behind him for any footsteps closing in on his position. Inside the safe was money, drugs, and two grenades. He snatched the two dark-green balls and put one in his pocket. Then he tossed the other down the hall. The yells were humorous, and the bomb vibrated the ground at his feet. Gunfire followed, but from the bottom stairwell.

"Clear!" his soldiers called.

Adrik stepped out of the room, and a gunshot hit him in the shoulder. It pushed him back a step, and he looked down at the wound seeping blood. Then he fired his gun five, six times into the mutilated corpse on the floor. How the soldier managed to get half of him blown off and still survive, Adrik didn't care to know. He was dead now. Adrik vaguely touched the bullet wound on his shoulder, but the adrenaline kept him from feeling most of the pain.

Pulling all his soldiers together, they arrived at the back of the ship. There were two opponents on the top of the railing as lookouts. They wore sunglasses and body armor. Adrik couldn't see the others, but he could hear the drilling, even feel it in the bottom of his bloody feet. So much glass dug into his soles, but he paid it no mind.

Adrik tossed the bomb and watched the two soldiers try to dive off the edge, but it blew them up into the air, and they fell into the water. He stepped out as his soldiers ran to gun down the crew on the side of the ship. They sat in little swings, trying to dive out of their seats, but it was too late. Bullets rained down on them from up above.

"Adrik," Dima's whisper was a siren in his head. His hearing had dulled because of the bombs, and now, in a moment of clarity, it came back to him. "She opened the door."

His brows knit, confused first before his eyes widened. *Jolie opened the door.*

Adrik ran to the front of the ship and darted through the living room. The team kept up with him, trying to calm him, to stop him, but he wouldn't. He threw himself down a flight of stairs, barely catching himself from falling. It felt like hours till he made it to the boiler room and shoved his way through the door. He finally arrived, but the sight made his heart stop.

In the safe room, Jolie sat on the ground with Helina tucked into her side as they watched Frozen in Russian. The words were rough, coarse, and difficult for her to work her lips around, but she tried her hardest to pay attention to the little girl as she went over sayings.

Jolie's mind was on something entirely different and terrifying, but she pretended for the child. She smiled and laughed, watching Helina get annoyed with her inability to speak Russian properly.

It was over an hour now that they were in this safe room. With soundproof walls and the movie blaring, there were no hints of what was happening out there. Jolie watched Tatianna, hoping for support, but the woman was fixing her makeup with a small glass mirror. Tatianna was as sweet as sunshine, but emotionally, she was empty. Was there nothing that bothered her?

Is Tatianna my future?

Jolie wanted to ask the woman thousands of questions about marrying into the Mafia, but she didn't dare in case she accidentally leaked that she was dating the *other* brother. Instead, they sat quietly, listening to the Russian voices of actors.

A weird sound rang in her ear, like scrapping metal against metal. "What is that?"

Tatianna shook her head. "I never know. It will be over soon. I hope this doesn't ruin our afternoon."

Jolie snatched the iPad and turned it off. Helina hollered at her, but Jolie quieted her, and they listened. The sound was a continuous vibration, and soon, the sound became familiar. It sounded like a tool her stepfather used on weekends when he built her a swing set. A saw. She got up on her feet, searching. "They're sawing through the ship."

Tatianna giggled. "No, sweetie, what would they do that for? They would have to know about the safe room, and only a few people know about it."

"Do you trust those people?"

"Adrik took the proper precautions, I'm sure." The sound stopped. Jolie put her hand against the wall tentatively before she pressed her ear against it.

Two inches from her face, the saw broke through.

Jolie jumped back, pulled Tatianna out of the chair, and picked up Helina. The little girl clung to her, once more spouting Russian. It brought the memories from the shootout fresh into her thoughts, and she gripped the little girl's head. This time, Jolie was ready with soothing Russian words. They were choppy and felt odd on her tongue, but she nonetheless whispered, ***"You're okay, princess."*** Jolie went for the door, but Tatianna gripped her arm.

"What are you doing?"

Jolie flicked her eyes between the woman and the sparks shooting out from the wall. "We can't stay here!"

"My son is coming. Just wait."

"They are breaking down the wall!"

Tatianna touched Jolie's arm. "I understand it is scary. But be patient, sweetheart."

The woman was out of her mind. Jolie was quite sure there wasn't a human in her. She was a shell of a woman, only acting like she was alive. Jolie ripped her arm free and placed her hand on the keypad. The door clicked as it unlocked, and Jolie pushed it open.

The door was pulled out of her grasp, and two black men stood before her. They were giants, grinning like fools, with guns in their hands. The first one reached for Helina, and Jolie resisted, pulling her back, but when a barrel pressed into the side of her forehead, her muscles weakened. Helina was pried out of her arms, her little fingers trying to grip Jolie's clothes, but the man peeled her off.

"On your knees," the left one ordered. Jolie wasn't paying attention; she was watching Helina, trying to soothe her. A sharp hit to the side of her head dropped her to the floor. She moaned, trying to push the dizziness from her brain.

A bomb went off from above, vibrating the ground. Jolie blinked, focusing on the noise, and she pressed a hand against the floor, feeling the movement. The drilling behind them stopped, and shouts weren't too far behind. But it was only a minute before the sound of a dozen bullets broke through the crack in the soundproof wall, and screams followed.

Jolie stared at the floor, her heart pounding, her breath coming in crazy pants. If she had waited, Adrik and his people would have saved them, and they would have remained unharmed in the safe house. Guilt barreled on her heavier than gravity. She squeezed her eyes shut, trying to wrap her brain around everything, but she was lost. This was too extreme. She might have killed them all.

Helina shivered and whimpered as the man placed his hands on her shoulders. "Don't do anything stupid, and we won't hurt you. You understand?"

Jolie clenched her teeth, but it was painful. She forced out, "She only speaks Russian."

The mercenary flicked his eyes to her. "Then, translate," he bit back.

Tatianna whispered to her with a sweet, calming voice, and Jolie sunk to the ground in shame. She was criticizing the woman for not responding like an average person, yet she now saw Tatianna's attitude as more of a strength. The woman was impenetrable. She didn't whimper and shake. To her, this was a momentary misunderstanding.

If only I could tell my heart that, Jolie mused.

A shadow shifted in the backwall. “Dima!” Helina cried, but it was the worst thing she could have done. The man in front of her wasted no time, spinning around and firing into the darkness. Bullets ricocheted off pipes and hissed, sending out a stream of white smoke. “No! Dima!” Helina wiggled and kicked at the man, but he had one good hold of her shoulder and it was all he needed. Dima collapsed, his gun falling inches from him. He struggled with movement, trying to push against the ground to drag his body, stretching for his gun. Another shot to his head and the arm slapped against the ground.

Jolie clenched her eyes tight. *Don't look, don't look, don't look. It's fine. He's fine.* The words were illogical; even she knew that, but she kept repeating them.

"Dima!" Helina tried to crumble, but the man wouldn't let her go. Tatianna desperately spoke to her, asking her to calm down and not look. Helina buried her face into her hands, her shoulders shaking with tears.

"Get ready," the mercenary said. "He'll be coming."

"All part of the plan, right?" the other replied. Keeping his gun on Jolie, the man took out a walkie-talkie. "We got the package. Bring the boat to the front of the ship." There was a pause, but no one responded, and the man repeated it. When there was only radio silence, the two of them glanced at each other. "Not part of the plan."

"Fuck, Mic, this is your fucking fault," the other said, tightening his hold on Helina.

Moments later, Adrik and six soldiers were running toward them. Jolie flinched, wanting nothing more than to go to him. But Helina called out, "Papa!" Any of Jolie's wants didn't matter. Only Helina mattered. Could she somehow help? Or was it better to just let Adrik handle it? He knew how to get out of these situations, didn't he? He's had more practice. He was made for this; she was a bumbling bird caught in a storm she couldn't weather.

Adrik slowed as he approached, a hand up to stop the six men behind him from making any rash moves. His daughter, mother, and girlfriend in the hands of an enemy was his worst nightmare. But his focus remained solely on Helina. In Russian, he whispered, ***"I'm here, baby. Don't move, okay? Wait for me."*** Her little whimper was the only reply.

The leader instructed, "Put your guns down."

Adrik ground his teeth and shifted his focus to the man holding her. He tossed his weapon on the floor while the others dropped theirs. Though he had another in the back of his pants, there was no way to move without being noticed. "Zinof is not on this ship."

"But you know where he is."

Adrik fisted his hands, staying silent. He studied their faces, trying to pinpoint who they were. They weren't the run-of-the-mill mercenaries. They were too structured, with an abundance of money. They had to be from a cartel or family. But Adrik knew all the local leaders.

Mic snickered. "Don't make this harder."

Was there an accent? From the northern states? Why would a mafia family from the North come down here? Adrik ran his eyes over their tattoos, but they were shrewd. They were covered in long sleeves and gloves. But they couldn't disguise the fact that they were black, and there were only three black mafia families in the United States. That's if they were mafia, but they had to be, right? This was too well organized to be a random gang or cartel.

"Who do you work for?"

With a small shake of his head, the man smirked. "I'm not at liberty to say."

"I can give you double whatever they are paying you."

A scoff. "The moment I let these bitches go, you'd shoot me. I know your history." The leader nudged his head, and Mic ordered Jolie and Tatianna to their feet. "We are taking them with us."

"You're not going anywhere. You will not make it off this ship alive."

The leader clenched Helina's shoulder, making her wince. "Big words when I hold your daughter in my hand."

Adrik shifted, but the man casually laid a gun on her shoulder, but by not pointing it at her head, he was saying something. Whoever ordered him here gave an explicit instruction not to harm Helina. But Adrik wasn't willing to risk that theory.

"Let us through."

Adrik clenched his teeth and then flicked his eyes over Jolie, over to his mother. In Russian, he asked her, ***"Mama, what do you think?"***

She smiled sweetly. ***"It might be best to listen, honey. They seem very upset right now, and we don't want any accidents."***

He was hoping she would have a plan or some sort of encouragement. But to just give in caused the rage to build. Every bit of him wanted to lash out, but there was too much risk. Someone was going to get hurt, and he couldn't have a single one of them caught in the crossfire. This mercenary had found a trifecta of weakness. It was a learning moment that Adrik would not soon forget.

Any threats were hollow. The words 'If you hurt them' died on his tongue. Adrik was going to get his revenge, no matter what. They were already dead in his eyes. It didn't matter if they treated Helina like a princess; he would torture them just the same. “Zinof will be dropped in the middle of Hyde Park in one hour.”

“That’s where we’ll be. One hour.”

Adrik grit his teeth and nodded. It took every ounce of control to step aside, but he did it. His men parted, allowing the leader and Helina to walk through first. Words of comfort speedily came off Adrik's lips, trying to assure his crying daughter that everything would be alright. But it twisted all his organs, making him sick to let her go.

Tatianna passed. ***"I'll look after her,"*** she assured.

Mic stood behind Jolie, with a hand on her shoulder and a gun at her temple, walking backward to keep Adrik and his people in his sight.

Adrik finally met her gaze. Blood was knotted in her hair on the side of her head. Her panic and fear were just another block on his shoulders. "Follow their rules," he told her, shoving down everything he wanted to say. He wanted to tell her he was in love with her, that she was everything he ever wanted in a wife, and that even barely knowing her, he wasn't far from putting a ring on her finger. But instead, he was silent. He didn't want the mercenaries to know just how important Jolie was to him.

"I'm sorry," she whispered, and the terror in her voice nearly made him move to her. "I should have waited for you."

Adrik took a step, stopping himself as the man tightened his hold on her arm. He clenched his fists at his side, dying with every inch she moved away from him. He wasn't angry about any of that. How could he be? It was his fault for not teaching her how dangerous his life was.

Mic smirked from over Jolie's shoulder. "Don't worry. I'll take good care of your whore."

A single bullet fired, and Mic twisted his head around to see his brother's body smack into the wall. A grief-stricken scream caught in his throat, but Tatianna turned and put a bullet through his forehead.

Jolie screamed as Mic's body fell on her, and they both crumbled. Hot blood splattered her face, and she could taste the metallic substance in her mouth. It froze her like a sheet of ice encasing her.

Adrik stared wide-eyed at his mother. She stood in the center of the dead bodies, with a small six-inch handgun. Tatianna waved it around like a flag, and a hint of the woman she used to be sprang to the surface. ***"Didn't I say this the other day?"*** she nipped at Adrik. ***"They never check the women. Am I so helpless that they think I can't even hold a gun?"***

Chapter Forty-Six

Over

Adrik sat on a bench on the front of the ship, with his elbows on his knees. A glass of whiskey was in his hand. The sun was setting, but no one paid attention to it as bodies were dragged to the front, one after another. Ten of his own were lined up in body bags that would eventually go into big freezers. Another fifteen of his men were sitting against the side, tending to wounds, some more serious than others. Two were missing, presumed overboard, while their enemies were wrapped up with stones tied to their feet and flung out into the ocean, never to be found.

The SOS call brought fifty of his people out to sea with a doctor. Adrik's arm was already patched up; the bullet had gone right through. Only now that he was relaxing did he feel the burn of it. But it was a welcome distraction.

Helina and his mother were back in their bedroom, tightly guarded.

Failure was creeping on him. Not only had he failed to stop mercenaries from gaining access to his boat, but Helina was once more in danger. The worst of the guilt was the fact he was here; he was with her, and he still hadn't been able to stop her from being subjected to violence. Five years old, and she's seen too much. The hope for her future was drifting. And he didn't know how to stop it.

Adrik turned his head, and through the cabin's open door, he could see Jolie sitting by herself on the couch. She'd been motionless since his people pulled the body off her. Blood splattered on her face and soaked her skin. She had been given an ice pack for the bruise on her head, but it sat in her hand on her lap as she stared blindly at the floor.

There was no recovery from this. Adrik lost her. He didn't need to talk to her to know she was done with this life. The trauma she faced today would dissolve any lingering hope that they could be together. And maybe it was better that way. Having another person in his life that meant as much to him as Helina was draining. He felt himself pulled in too many directions. If he had been smart, he would have kept them separated at all times so something like this couldn't happen, but he never imagined anyone could do what these invaders had just done.

All this time being a powerful mafia figurehead, and it meant nothing. He nearly lost everything because he wasn't good enough.

When the ship docked, Adrik didn't move. He watched them team up and carry the big square freezers into a waiting truck. The bodies were sent to a family-owned morgue, where a doctor would diagnose them with some common illness, and no questions would be asked. They would be given proper funerals, with closed caskets, over the next few weeks, and their families would be compensated. It would all look normal, and the police would never know what happened here.

But it would be something Adrik wouldn't forget. Or forgive. Someone was going to pay.

Footsteps approached, and he already knew who it was. Adrik closed his eyes as he downed the rest of his whiskey, letting it burn his throat and chest. Yakov stood in front of him. He had a cigar in between his lips and a smugness about him that Adrik couldn't stomach, and he looked away.

"***You know,***" Yakov began thoughtfully, "***I think I will stay on a little while longer. As much as you think you are ready, there are still things in this world, boy, that you can't handle. That's why I'm here. I've seen everything, and I know what's best.***" With a slight slap on his bad shoulder, his father walked away.

Adrik watched Yakov as he strutted along the skiff, delegating. As much as he despised him, Adrik couldn't find the will to fight against it. Yakov was right. There were so many things that Adrik could use help with. And now it appeared he was about to start a turf war with a mafia family from the North. He'd need his father to help guide him through it.

A car slammed on its brakes, and Alexei popped out. He wobbled on the ramp and up the stairs, with panic in every step. Relief ignited over his face when he found his brother. Adrik stood as Alexei slammed into him, hugging him fiercely. "You alright? God, what the hell happened?" Alexei breathed, stepping back and looking around.

"Dima is gone." Adrik said, sitting back down. His knees were weak.

Alexei ran a hand through his hair, a momentary grief keeping him quiet. Dima had been with the family for many years, but death in their world was common. Dima had survived longer than most.

"This is insane," Alexei bit, looking around. The deck had been washed already. A second team would come in the morning and bleach the whole ship. Inside the cabins was a different story, left untouched. There wasn't time to fix it, but with private glass on every floor, there was no way any of Agent Mally's spies could see into the rooms.

Adrik was numb, staring past the blood and out into the water. He was still trying to wrap his head around how this happened. He had been prepared for Boris, but this wasn't his wife's father. This was someone else.

"Could you, um—" Adrik nudged his head to the living room.

Glancing over his shoulder, Alexei found Jolie. A curse whispered under his breath at the sight of her. "What the hell was she doing here?" Alexei glared at his brother, but he could see the defeat in his shoulders and let it go. "Yeah, yeah, no worries."

Adrik shook his head, a hand burying into his hair. "It's probably over," he acknowledged. "She's not meant for this."

Alexei could not disagree. "No, she isn't."

Adrik nodded, sinking further. He never did well with sadness. It was a calling card to the darkness inside him. Instead of crying like a bitch, he channeled it like any real man to violence. He clenched his teeth. "I'm gonna find out who did this."

Alexei reminded him, "You can't attack Katia's family. We need the harbor, or we'll lose sixty percent of our supplies."

Adrik hated being told what he couldn't do. It was a trigger to do precisely that. But his brother was right. He couldn't hurt Zinof or Katia or her parents. But there were other things he could do. Ways to smoke out who had the balls to come for his family.

Adrik took one last look at Jolie. Was there a way to salvage it? Was there any point? He couldn't promise that it wouldn't happen again. He couldn't promise he wouldn't let anything bad happen to her. He lived in a violent world. If he couldn't keep his own daughter out of the shit he bathed in, how could he keep Jolie?

Adrik walked away.

Alexei took a deep breath as he stepped through the doors. Jolie was covered in blood, and she stared with a dead gaze, shivering in the unbearable heat. The shock was sinking into her.

He'd seen people break before. Usually, when he's torturing them. He didn't mind it then because anyone who wasn't family didn't affect him, but Jolie had become family. Seeing her hurt was a nail in the hand.

Alexei stepped in front of her, and her gaze finally shifted off the floor, traveling up his legs like a slowly moving train. When they landed on his face, the disappointment that flashed derailed and burned in his chest. Alexei ground his teeth and bowed his head. He should have told Adrik to go to her, to be the one to console her, but selfishly, he hadn't.

He told himself it was for the best for both of them. Their relationship wasn't going to last. Alexei knew his brother and how he worked. Girls like Jolie didn't put up with shit as much as average women. She knew her self-worth. She knew what she deserved. Alexei could give her that, but Adrik had too much pride.

Jolie curled in on herself, crying, and Alexei kneeled down. He had only to reach out for her to fall into his lap, her face buried into his neck. He clung to her as her body convulsed, sobs that twisted his gut and made him sick. He whispered softly, "You're okay. I've got you," as he ran his fingers through her hair. "You're safe." Alexei closed his eyes and breathed in her sweet perfume. A fire ignited in him, wanting nothing more than to protect her from every danger.

Even if that danger was his brother.

Chapter Forty-Seven

Resign

Jolie sat on her borrowed bed in the Morozov household. Her cats lingered around her, rubbing against her back, but she felt nothing except emptiness. Three days ago was the worst day of her life, brought on by her stupidity and ignorance. After mourning, she had to face her choices and try her best to undo them. There was no way to continue on here, in this place.

It was over. The moment Alexei stood in front of her on the boat instead of Adrik, she knew.

Adrik blamed her. And instead of facing her and telling her how stupid she was, he chose silence. She felt guilty enough for leaving the safe room; she didn't need his passive-aggressive anger.

Underneath the guilt was the desperate need for comfort. She had gone through something traumatic, and Jolie needed Adrik. Instead, she got Alexei. She wasn't dating his brother. She didn't want Alexei to comfort her. Even if Adrik was so pissed at her for coming out, he could still hold her and gripe her simultaneously. If she was going to live in this hellish world, then she at least needed to know that Adrik would be there with her.

But he hadn't been. Maybe he was too much his father's son. Something that Katia kept hinting at during their endless days together. She knew Adrik's weaknesses better than anyone, and Jolie was foolish not to listen to her.

With a letter in her hand, Jolie stood with a straight back. She wore black, mourning the lives that would never be spoken about. Even villains deserved justice, but this family took it upon themselves to be judge and jury. And Jolie had enough.

At the breakfast table, the family sat. Yakov at the head, with a son on each side. Katia was next to Adrik, a place that would never be hers. And Tatianna on the opposite end, eating and chatting, unburdened.

Jolie approached slowly, shaking. She no longer guessed what they were capable of. Now that she had seen what they could do. They were perfect for each other, this family of murderers.

She would never belong.

Yakov greeted her with a smile. "I'm so happy you've joined us."

Adrik shifted, his head to the side, but he didn't look at her. He was a coward, and she despised it about him. All the confidence and pride trying to cover up his most obvious flaw.

It's why Jolie handed Yakov the letter. Since he was clearly in charge.

"What's this?"

"My resignation. I'm sorry, but I cannot continue on here."

She turned to go, but Yakov called her back. She wanted to refuse but knew better. Yakov got out of his chair and instructed her to follow. Alexei stood, suddenly nervous, but she gave him a small smile for reassurance. Adrik continued to ignore her, and her gaze lingered on the back of his head, begging him to turn around.

But he didn't.

Jolie entered Yakov's office, and he sat in a wingback leather chair and gestured to the opposite one. Jolie hesitated.

"Indulge me for a moment, Miss Bell."

With a clenched jaw, she sat.

"I'm sorry about what happened. I can't imagine what that was like for you."

Despite the empty words, it was more than Adrik had given her. It brought tears to her eyes, but she didn't want to cry in front of him. She sniffed and hardened her gaze as she stared at Yakov.

"Can I ask what you were doing on the ship? I'm a little taken aback by your presence."

"I went for Helina."

"Ah. Teaching even on vacation? Such dedication."

Jolie crossed her legs, unwilling to be intimidated by him anymore. She was too numb to feel anything.

Yakov smiled. "Do you know when I realized you weren't courting Alexei, despite the efforts you went through to deceive?"

Jolie felt a little jolt to her heart.

"After the pen incident. Alexei was too desperate to calm Adrik, when they both should have wanted some retribution. But Alexei does have feelings for you, doesn't he, Miss Bell? How you managed to ensnare both of them is a curiosity, since they typically have different tastes." Yakov watched her, waited for a response, and was annoyed when he received none. "Adrik normally obeys me; he knows what I want is best and follows my rules. So, you must understand that your presence on his yacht was disturbing. Now, his disappearance these last couple of weeks is beginning to add up. And I wonder if I were to look back on all the security footage and the documents, would you happen to 'disappear' at the same time?"

Jolie didn't care. It didn't matter. She was leaving. She remained impassive. After the boat, nothing he said could affect her. Not when she was still trying to get the blood out of her hair.

"It may not seem like it to you, but I am very protective of my children. I cannot have some young slut try to come between them. This is why I will not only take your resignation, but I implore you to leave this state. Get as far away from here as possible. Because if I see you again near my sons, planning an accident is one of the main things I learned to do before I was ten."

His threat woke something in her, set her heart back to beating, and pulled her from the coma she'd been in. It wasn't fear. It was adrenaline.

She found herself without a filter. "You're a horrible man."

He smirked and shrugged. "Yes. I am. But I get what I want. Adrik and Alexei needed a little reminder, and now, things should return to where they were. All that's messing up the equation is you. I didn't know it before, but now it's very clear. Nothing makes a man fight harder and more desperately than for family. Whatever they saw in you sparked that rebellion. But without you, they'll fall back in line."

Jolie clenched her fingers around her dress. She didn't know what kind of person Adrik and Alexei had to deal with, and now it was slowly coming to light. Yakov was a terror, and though he was portrayed as a good father, he was a manipulating narcissist. What had he done to Adrik and Alexei to 'remind' them of their place?

Alexei's bruises. Would Yakov physically harm them?

It was an easy answer.

The phone rang, and Yakov held up a finger as he answered it. It was all in Russian. When she got out of this hellhole, she never wanted to hear another person speak the harsh language. Jolie wondered if she could leave, but she was sure she needed to be dismissed. But what did she care about his rules? She was never going to see him again. Jolie stood.

The door burst open. "Yakov!" An old black man in a black suit entered. The soldiers at his side were constantly trying to pull him back, but they were clearly trying not to upset him. "Yakov, where are my sons? The last time I spoke to them, they said they had a job from you, and that was days ago."

Yakov slowly stood, tucking his phone back into his pocket. He pointed a finger at one of his soldiers and said, "Please take Miss Bell out. And help her pack." The soldier latched onto her bicep, pulling her out of the room. She stumbled as she watched the older gentleman. There was something familiar about him that she couldn't pinpoint. His face was familiar.

The intruder kept yanking his arms out of the soldiers' hold. "Where are they? Where are Luke and Mic?"

The door shut, and the floor beneath her feet faded. She floated as the soldiers dragged her back to her room like a tethered ghost.

Mic. The name of one of the soldiers on the boat. Why would Yakov know them? Unless he was the one who hired them.

A hand pressed against her mouth. It was only a theory; she had no proof, but it was too much of a coincidence. Should she tell Adrik? Would he believe her?

The soldier shoved her on the bed. Jolie tried to make a run for it, but he tossed her back on the mattress and dared her to try again.

Esfir came in to delegate the packing, ordering a bunch of servants around. This time, they were less than gentle, taking a drawer and dumping it in a box. They took armfuls of clothes from the closet, shoved them in, and then dumped her shoes on top.

Yakov betrayed his son. He put the lives of his wife and granddaughter in jeopardy for what? To prove a point? He was mentally unhinged, and if she didn't help get Adrik away from him, what other horrible things would he do to keep his sons in line?

Box after box was stacked against the wall. When it was over, a soldier stood at the door. "Yakov has given you until tomorrow morning while Esfir finds you a place to live. I will be back at seven in the morning to take you." The door shut, and she was sure she heard it lock.

Jolie got to her feet. Her cats meowed in concern, jumping from box to box, sniffing around. Her fingers reached out for the doorknob, but it didn't move. They had locked her in. Her head pressed against the wood.

The moment Yakov had disappeared down the hall with Jolie, Adrik got to his feet. He wasn't going to sit there and torture himself over some woman. Jolie made her decision. He wasn't raised to be a simp; if she expected some emotional plea, she was an idiot.

Everything he imagined for his future was gone. If he couldn't have it with Jolie, he wouldn't have it with anyone. Accepting this life was the only thing that was left. Accepting the fact that his daughter was going to be used for the family, going to be auctioned off like some fucking animal, was becoming more realistic than not. There was no hope left. His father had been hinting at it for years, and now, Adrik stopped fighting it. His father was right about everything.

Alexei was on his heels. "You okay?"

"Fine," he snapped back.

"Because you don't look okay."

Adrik kept going down the stairs, ignoring his brother. They twisted through the bottom level of the house, typing in a password to get into the deepest floor. A guard was on the other side, tracking who was coming and going. Down here, there were no cameras. There would be no evidence that could ever be leaked.

When they turned the corner, Adrik faced Alexei. "She wants to go; she can go. I'm done."

"Have you even talked to her?"

"I don't need to. I can see it."

"Oh, well, that's a talent."

"I don't need your shit right now."

Alexei snatched Adrik's arm, but Adrik retaliated with a quick fist, punching his brother hard in the face, and he fell back against the wall, holding his cheek. Adrik cursed and ran his hands through his hair, pacing for a minute.

Alexei clenched his jaw; the pain was nothing new. He didn't know why he was putting up a fight about this. He should be happy. Relieved even. But here he was. "All she wanted was you. When she saw me standing in front of her, it devastated her. Why can't you live for yourself for once? Why do you have to do everything Papa says?"

Adrik stepped up to him with a finger in his face and screamed, "That's what I've been trying to do! But you don't understand. He's everywhere, Alexei. I can't escape from him."

"Then, stop trying to. Face him." Alexei watched Adrik turn away, scoffing, as if the very idea was impossible. And then words escaped him. "Kill him."

Adrik snapped his head toward his brother. He stared at him, observing Alexei trying to piece together the statement, processing the words as if they were foreign. They repeated in his head like echoes in a cavern, but instead of getting distant and quieter, they got louder and deafening.

Adrik leaned around the corner, finding the man still sitting at the front entrance. He had earphones plugged in as he watched TV on his phone. Adrik turned his attention back to Alexei. "What did you say?"

"You heard me."

Once more, the words replayed, and Adrik shifted on his foot, fear creeping into him. And underneath that fear was a slim ray of hope.

"How long have you thought of that?"

"Years," Alexei admitted, daring to look at him. "I don't have the same love for him as you do."

Adrik backstepped, and Alexei reached for him, but Adrik put a hand out to stop him. It wasn't that Adrik never thought about killing their father, but it was a stupid fantasy. Like running away. Like faking his death. They were thoughts that were better left unsaid. Because speaking them aloud gave it potential, and nothing good could come from killing Yakov. If anyone found out, they'd be hunted down by cousins and uncles. Their own grandfathers wouldn't be able to look away.

And if they somehow made it appear like an accident, they would be looking over their shoulders every day for the rest of their lives, praying no one figured it out.

There was no peace in murdering their father.

Despite how much they wanted it.

Adrik didn't understand. "You always stop me."

"Because it shouldn't be you," Alexei whispered. "All you have to do is tell me yes. You won't know anything else. Not when, or where, or how. You'll be safe."

Adrik knitted his brows. Alexei was serious. But there was no killing Yakov. How could he think that would ever be a possibility? And then to assume that Adrik would let Alexei handle something so horrible on his own? It was too much. Adrik backstepped further and further. Alexei begged him to stay, but he couldn't. The world was crumbling beneath his feet; he needed some control. And that control came from violence.

Chapter Forty-Eight

Revenge

Adrik stepped into the room that's become a torture chamber for a few high-rated victims. It used to be a gym. There was glass on the walls and cold marble flooring. But it was too far from the main house, being at least a hundred feet by tunnel, so they moved the gym to the other side of the property. Now, it was the 'torture chamber,' as Gil liked to call it. There was a single working light in the center of the room, and it shined down like a spotlight. It kept Adrik in darkness as he circled Zinof like a predator in the night. He watched as his soldiers took turns punching Zinof, slapping him, poking him with an electric taser. They laughed as Zinof screamed.

"Bring Katia," he ordered to the open air, and someone quickly left to do his bidding.

Zinof turned his head, searching the shadows. He was bleeding from every spot. His ears, his nose, his eyes, his lips. There were whip marks on his back. He sat in only underwear. Someone had cleaned up Zinof's shit recently. The room didn't smell as bad as it typically did.

"Adrik," he panted. "My father is gonna kill you."

Adrik smiled. Threats were humorous coming from someone trapped in his house. A soldier came to him, holding up a baggie of cocaine. Adrik pinched the white powder, placing it on the back of his hand before he sniffed it. The burn was instant, and he rubbed at his nose till it passed. It took only moments for the drug to work into his system, and he closed his eyes, enjoying it. He hadn't had a hit since Jolie came into his life. He had been trying to be something he wasn't. And look where that got him.

But there was no escaping the Mafia.

It wasn't long till Katia was shoved into the room. She fought the soldier at first, but then she froze upon seeing Zinof. Pain flashed over her face, and she found Adrik in the dark. "What are you doing?"

"Giving you justice."

She shook her head, trying to back up, but the soldier remained behind her, blocking her path. "Please."

"He tried to kill Helina," Adrik reasoned. "Do you want mercy?"

She shivered, and her gaze returned to her brother. "Zinof, why did you attack my daughter?"

Zinof curled his lip. "All of them deserve to fucking die."

A soldier shocked him with a small jolt of electricity. And though Adrik enjoyed it, he watched Katia's expression. She tried to hide her face, covering her mouth to suppress any screams.

"I want you to tell your father something," Adrik said to Katia. "I can keep him alive for years. Or, if he would rather, I could send the body to him tomorrow. It is his choice."

"What do you want?"

A divorce, Adrik nearly said. It would have been the perfect opportunity to get it. He could withdraw from the contract, and their families could go their separate ways peacefully. The war would be over before it even began. No one would die, and Agent Mally could have her peace.

But without Jolie, what was the point of it? There were other things he could bargain for, things that would make him more powerful. Things that could bring him millions. And maybe by doing so, he could save his daughter from the violent future of mafia life.

"The harbor."

Katia's brows knitted. "You think Zinof is worth the harbor?" She scoffed. "I love my brother, but I'm not an idiot."

Adrik shrugged. She was right, of course. But it didn't matter. He wanted Zinof dead, and if they didn't comply with his demands, then he had every right to kill him.

Adrik nudged his head to one of his soldiers, and they continued their torture. A punch to the gut, a slap to the side of the head, a quick electric jolt that made his body shudder.

"Stop!" screamed Katia, turning her head away. The soldier behind her gripped her arms, forcing her hands down and making her watch. Katia's tears dripped down her face as more blood spilled on the floor.

A knife shined in the spotlight, and too soon, they pressed down on one of his toes, and blood splattered as it pulsed out of his foot.

Katia gritted her teeth. "It was supposed to be you!"

Adrik held up a hand and stalled the movements of his people. He approached her, the tap of his shoes echoing underneath the whimpers of his victim. "What did you say?"

With twisted lips, Katia lifted her head and bit, "It was supposed to be you."

Adrik gripped her arms now, forcing her up. "You planned it?"

"Katia," Zinof huffed, twisting in pain, "don't." A soldier was quick to gag him.

"I want him to know," she barked. "I planned it. We were at the wedding for your cousin. You promised Helina to get candy. But you were too busy fucking a bridesmaid in her car when you should have been with Helina."

Adrik's brows knitted. "You would risk our daughter?"

Tears dripped down her face. "I would risk hell to get rid of you."

Adrik smacked her hard, and she fell to the floor. A hand covered his mouth, devastated by her. He never allowed himself to doubt Katia because of the simple fact that she was a mother. He trusted in that simple fact, and it fucked him.

Katia held her cheek. "She was supposed to be Niko's," she whimpered.

Adrik stood before her. The name was a trigger that brought red. All the years they were together, five years of building a life, of struggling with infertility, of learning how to love each other, he was stuck back in the same pain she caused him all those years ago.

Adrik had been merciful before.

But there was no mercy left.

Adrik unbuckled his belt and ordered his soldiers. "Take off her clothes."

Panic ensued, and Katia struggled and screamed, but it did nothing to him. He was dead. The mother of his child tried to kill him and their daughter. She was nothing now. She wasn't family. She was a corpse, already buried. But if she wanted death, he'd do everything in his power to keep her alive.

They ripped the clothes from her back, and once naked, they laid her on her belly, pinning her to the floor. Zinof was bucking in his chair, cursing and spewing threats through the towel in his mouth.

Adrik pulled his belt from his waist. "You owe me a son."

With her face pressed against the floor, she tried to find him, her gaze to the far right. "Does Jolie know you're a rapist?"

She used that name to plague him, and he despised how it worked. The blind rage was doused in ice water, and his fingers froze. There was a part of him that knew the relationship with Jolie was over, but if he forced Katia, there could never be a revival. And despite how he believed they were done, hope still existed deep down inside him.

Adrik turned suddenly and attacked Zinof, his belt sliding down his face, his chest, and thighs. Welts ignited from every lash, and he screamed and cried. Blood rained on Adrik, covering every inch of him. It took several minutes, but Zinof's screams died away when his face was unrecognizable.

The belt fell from his hand. Adrik panted and could taste blood on his lips. He spit it out and turned away from Zinof's dead body. Katia remained pinned to the floor. He nudged his head, and his soldiers lifted off her. She curled into herself, crying and bitter, glaring at him from her knees. A soldier dropped a towel over her, and she clung to it.

"You aren't to leave this house," Adrik said. "No phone calls. And you will not see Helina again."

Katia sneered. "My father is going to tear you apart."

Adrik leaned down to get even with her. He wanted her to see up close the blood of her brother dripping down his face. "Let him try."

Chapter Forty-Nine

Surrender

Jolie hugged a pillow, facing the phone propped against the blankets. She watched her mother tend to a flower bed, and she mindlessly talked about the bugs and what fertilizer worked and what didn't. The stress in her voice brought peace to Jolie. Something as silly as bugs on her mother's flowers. It brought reality back. *This* was normal. Not shootouts on a thirty-million-dollar yacht. Not shivering in a safe room as someone drilled a hole in the wall.

And though it was boring and uneventful, Jolie yearned for it now.

All her life, she always wanted more than what her parents had. She wanted to buy gifts for Christmas without worrying if she could afford to eat. But more importantly, she wanted to reach the lives of children and ensure that poverty and misery weren't all they were made for. It was possible to get out of the tar of life and find something worth living for.

If she had never been deterred from that desire, she'd be in school, teaching children full of hope, and she wouldn't be here, regretting every day Adrik came into her life.

She sniffed and rubbed the tear off her nose.

Why, then, did she yearn for him? She hated herself for it. She hated that all she wanted was for him to knock on her door, tell her how sorry he was, and beg her to stay.

But his pride was more significant than that. Nothing would get him to stoop so low. This relationship was doomed from the start. Jolie knew it, yet she still wanted to try because she believed it would have been a fantastic adventure if they could make it work.

Jolie popped her head up. She swore she heard a soft, barely there knock from Helina's door. The cats verified it, approaching the door, meowing with the hope someone else would give them attention. Jolie said goodbye to her mother, clicking it off before getting to her feet. Her heart pounded, but she didn't want to hope. It was probably Alexei again, once more replacing the spot where Adrik should be.

Jolie rubbed her face and approached. "The door's locked," she told whoever was behind it.

There was a latch undone from the other side. Jolie unlocked her side and pulled the door open.

A gasp escaped her.

Adrik stood in front of her, covered in blood. There wasn't a spot on him that was clean. It had dried on his skin, stiffened his shirt, and squished in his shoes. He kept his blue eyes on the floor, unresponsive as she called his name.

Jolie tentatively reached for his hand. She didn't want to touch him, but she couldn't let him remain in case Helina returned. She pulled Adrik through the door and locked it behind him. "What happened?"

No response. Jolie leaned down to get his eyes, but Adrik avoided her. At least she knew there was something inside him left.

Words she never thought she'd say came out of her mouth. "Who's dead, Adrik?"

Was it his father? Why did she hope it was?

"Zinof," he whispered.

Her brows knitted. "I thought you couldn't kill him."

The silence sunk into her. She shivered and wrapped her arms around herself. What had he done? This was irrefutable evidence that he was a murderer. A wave of nausea went through her, and she just stood there for a moment. Jolie wanted to leave, return to her parents' house, sink into her mother's warmth, and live in mediocrity. She wasn't meant for this type of lifestyle. Everyone knew it, and they all warned her.

But there was something else there that she acknowledged.

Despite being covered in blood, it hadn't changed the way she felt about him. Jolie had, at some point, come to terms with what he did for a living. And she decided what he did wasn't who he was.

I'm choosing him, Jolie realized.

Jolie ran to the bathroom and twisted the knob for the shower. She took out towels and put one out on the floor. Then she went back to him. Jolie wanted nothing more than to care for him, to ease his pain. "You need to wash off; you'll feel better."

Adrik didn't move. He couldn't force any action as he stared at the floor. His arms were heavy, and he could still feel the clench of his fingers around the leather of his belt.

Jolie touched his wrist and pulled, guiding him into the bathroom. She observed the emptiness in his face and the lack of emotion, as if he couldn't allow himself to feel. She took hold of his shirt and lifted it above his head. His eyes came to hers at that moment. She smiled as she saw the light ignite in his eyes. "You're okay," she assured.

Under Adrik's scrutiny, Jolie removed his shoes and helped him with his pants. She squirmed and sneered at every piece covered in blood, tossing it on a towel. What had he done to make it splash on him? The question seeped into her consciousness, but she forced it away. It wasn't that she was ignoring his actions. Instead, she found herself excusing them. Like he had reasons to do what he did.

Jolie opened the shower door and directed him inside. But he wouldn't let go of her hand.

If she turned him away, Adrik would know that they were finished. He'd accept it, and though it would kill him, he'd take whatever pity was forcing her to help him.

But if she stepped into the shower with him, the small flame of hope burning inside him would become an inferno. His desire for her would devour him, and he wouldn't hold himself back.

They stood in silence as the water poured over his chest. Adrik made his position clear. He wanted her here, but he wouldn't force her to stay.

Jolie lifted her shirt over her head, and Adrik released the stress on his shoulders.

Her breasts were free, her nipples hard and perfect. Adrik didn't care how embarrassed she got under his gaze. He traveled along her tight stomach as she pushed down her pajamas and panties. She kept a hand over her privates, trying to twist out of his stare. He held out his hand and pulled her in, flushed against him.

The water rained over both of them. It was a light pink as the blood washed away. He leaned in to kiss her, but Jolie pulled back. Adrik flicked his gaze over her face, trying to figure out why until she grabbed the body wash and held it up. He didn't reach for it. He wanted her care. He needed it, so he surrendered to her ministrations, hoping she could fix what had come undone inside him.

Jolie poured the soap over him and ran her hands along every limp, scrubbing the stains away. He closed his eyes and clenched his jaw, enjoying her touch and compassion. Being vulnerable had become an impossibility over the years. He never trusted anyone. Not because he was afraid to but because none of them had proven faithful. Everyone he'd ever known had an agenda. They talked to him for their own gain. They spoke to him for status, money, and opportunities to improve their lives.

With Jolie, the good in her shined like the sun. He trusted himself with her. She wouldn't betray him or hurt him. She would never cheat on him or lie to him. There was nothing for her to gain. She was not selfish or self-centered.

The urge to ask her to marry him clogged the back of his throat. He knew how ridiculous it sounded to want to marry a woman he just met. And if he believed she'd say yes, he might have asked. But Jolie was more logical than he was. She'd say no only because it was expected of her.

As he watched the water drip off her lips, Adrik couldn't hold himself back any further. He leaned down and pressed his lips to hers, capturing them like a bucking dragonfly. She surrendered, falling into him with her hands buried in his hair. He parted from her to kiss her jaw and neck, lowering still till he took a nipple into his mouth. She moaned, holding his head to her.

Adrik turned her to the wall, pressing her against it. All the hours he spent thinking about this moment, and it was here. He was eager to devour her but knew she wasn't ready. He needed to go slow.

Adrik took her hands in one of his, pinning them above her head as she wiggled beneath his lips. His tongue flicked her nipple till she was whimpering. His other hand drifted down her side, past her hip, and landed in the center of her pelvis. She had shaved, leaving a smooth vagina for his fingers. He slid them along her lips, touching her clit, and she bucked against him, gasping, her legs widening on their own.

"Adrik," Jolie whimpered.

Adrik slipped his middle finger inside her, curling it, and she broke from his lips to moan. He clenched his teeth to keep his own moans at bay. She was tight, warm, and wet around his finger. He could only imagine what it would feel like around his cock. He watched her, her mouth open, her eyes clenched shut. Every bit of her screaming while she remained quiet, stifling moans he fiercely wanted to hear. His finger slid in and out, slowly, torturously. Adrik slipped another finger in, biting her shoulder as he did so. He was losing control, his dick pulsing against her hip.

Adrik pulled his fingers away, watching the disappointment when she opened her eyes. He let her hands go and stepped back into the water spray, running his hands through his hair, removing all the soap and any lingering droplets of blood. The aftermath of Zinof was fading, but Katia's words still clung to him like a poison in his veins. He couldn't wash it away. It wasn't betrayal, because he never trusted her since she cheated on him, but it was disappointment. How would he create a good life for Helina with a mother who tried to kill her? It would be better if it was something Helina never learned.

Adrik could feel the depression slipping back into his head. The horror of his actions was coming at him, reminding him of what he had almost done. The blind rage was over, and all that was left was the aftermath. How terrible of a person could he become in those moments? He almost found out. Were there no limits? Did he have no sense of morality? How much of his father was in him?

When he opened his eyes, Jolie was hypnotized by him, watching every inch of the water descend his body. Her desire was a fire, eating away the world outside. She was his salve, his solution, his cure. He put no other thought into what would happen with Zinof, with Katia, or his future. All he wanted was Jolie.

Adrik shut off the water and led Jolie out. He wrapped a towel around her before taking one for himself. It was a pause, another chance he gave her to run, to change her mind. He was going to dive into the deep end, and he needed to know she was there swimming with him.

Jolie pushed up on her toes, kissing him. He smiled into her lips before slipping his tongue through, barely touching her, teasing her. It exhilarated her. She was eager for his touch, just as he was for hers.

He brought her back to the bed, and she sat on the edge, with a towel clinging to her form. She stared up at him, waiting for him to take charge. She was unconfident, and it showed in her wide, deer-in-headlights look.

Adrik leaned down and lifted her feet in the air. She squealed as she fell back on the mattress. Jolie clung to the towel and covered her exposed privates with a hand. "What are you doing?" she scolded.

Adrik slipped his fingers between her tightly knit thighs and forced them apart, squeezing himself between her legs as he lowered to his knees. When he kissed the inner part of her thigh, realization dawned on her. Jolie clamped a hand tight over her entrance. He kissed closer to her pussy, watching her breathing increase with every touch. Adrik pulled the towel off to expose her breasts to the air. A hand clamped on one, pinching her hard nipple. She stared at him over her heaving chest, excitement shining in her lust-filled eyes. He nudged her hands with his nose, a gentle caress to encourage. He needed Jolie to want him, to beg him, to trust him.

Her hands fell away, surrendering.

Adrik kissed her center, and she bucked. Anticipation and fear swirled like a violent storm. He graced her clit with the tip of his tongue, and her body flinched. Then he licked her, a full flat-tongue lick that made her quake.

After that, it was erratic, his tongue working her pussy. She tasted like honey, and he was a bear diving into a hive. He licked every nook and cranny, focusing on her most sensitive area. The clit was full of nerve endings that had her dying. Jolie kept her hands over her face, suppressing every sound, but he knew when she got closer. She breathed in deep and held it longer and longer. Her muscles tightened in her thighs. With his hands spreading her thighs wide, Adrik shook his head with his tongue stretched over her, her juices smothering his cheeks and chin, but he loved it. His tongue worked harder than it ever had, and when she climaxed, her body shivered, and her legs clamped down on him, trapping him, while her hand pushed on his head, trying to get him out.

Adrik pulled back, and she curled into a ball, breathing, enjoying the last remaining waves. He had never felt so proud. He was going to enjoy every orgasm he could squeeze out of her. It was time to completely erase her ex-boyfriend from her memory.

Adrik used the towel to wipe his face. But he wasn't going to let her rest. He took hold of his erection and rubbed it between her wet folds. He watched her, giving her the opportunity to push him away, but she was lost in ecstasy. Adrik positioned himself at her entrance and pushed. Just an inch at a time, watching as her eyes widened. "Oh, God," a whisper escaped her, and Jolie dropped her head back on the bed. Her fingers pressed against his chest, fearful it would hurt. But with his care and the wetness of her pussy, he slid in without resistance. He heard every hitch of her breath, every groan and moan. The slowness was killing him.

He wanted to pound into her without control, but he ground his teeth and took his time, allowing her walls to relax so he wouldn't hurt her.

Minutes it took till her legs lost their strength.

Standing on the floor, Adrik placed her feet on his chest as he shoved his dick inside. The gasp was pleasure-filled, and she slapped her hand over her mouth to quiet herself. He stayed still inside her, basking in the wet heat around his cock, pressing in till he was fully inside. Adrik pulled at her wrist and waited for her dazed gaze to land on him. "No one can hear you but me. And I want to hear all of it. I want to make you scream." He pounded her hard, and a small whimper escaped. "More," he ordered, thrusting harshly. A sob was released. Jolie clenched the bedsheets, gritting her teeth as she watched him move inside her over and over, rocking her tits. Still sensitive from her last orgasm, it took barely any effort to make her cum again. Her back arched off the bed, her noises louder but still reserved.

Adrik put his knees on the bed, sitting back on his heels. Her legs laid useless on the bed, dropped open, welcoming him to do as he pleased. His thumb swirled around on her clit, slowly enticing her back to reality. Her eyes opened, meeting his. If he could paint a picture of her, this would be it, the one he'd put above his bed. Her wet hair was a mess, her legs wide, her pussy bare, his dick buried in deep.

Adrik put his hands on the bed next to her face, leaning over her. He stared at her, and she couldn't take her eyes off him. Everything he wanted to say to her was loud between them, without either of them making a sound. He could feel the love Jolie felt, and he prayed she could feel his.

Adrik kissed her softly, over and over again. He moved but with patience, barely making her move as he gently thrust into her. He had never made love before, but this had to be it. There was nothing else that could describe the connection. It was tangible, thick like molasses, and drowned him.

Jolie's hand rested on his cheek. Her attention was like heaven. She was forgiving him for leaving her on the boat. He knew he should have talked to her, but he was too worried about his father finding out. It was time to put things into perspective.

Jolie was now his family.

Adrik paused in his movements, burying his face into her neck. "Stay," he whispered against her skin. He didn't want to see any sorrow or hear any words that would hurt him, so he didn't wait for any. He thrusted, and Jolie gasped into his ear. It was a beautiful sound. He increased his pace a little until he was pounding so hard into her that the bed shook. But he could only keep that pace for a minute before his orgasm approached. He yanked away, panting as he calmed himself. His dick shined with her juices. He grabbed his cock, rubbing it, watching her as she lay on the bed, already exhausted from a ten-minute fuck. She was the most beautiful thing he'd ever seen. The way the light struck her was divine. Every curve, every dip, he wanted to bask in all of it.

Adrik grabbed her legs and dragged her toward him. She giggled, trying once more to be modest, but he flipped her over on her belly. Her feet hit the floor, and he stepped up, resting his cock between her butt cheeks. His fingers roamed down the curve of her back, squeezing the fat of her ass. Adrik slapped her softly just to see her reaction. Then he did it a little harder. She made a quiet cry, but her ass shifted toward him. He slapped her again harder, and a red imprint quickly formed. He soothed it, admiring her round cheeks. She worked hard for their perfection.

"Do you have a condom?" Jolie whispered into the sheets.

"A little late for that," he pointed out. "You think I've been with anyone else since I met you?"

A smile twitched on her lips. "I don't want a kid yet."

The way she said 'yet,' like it was a possibility, drove him crazy. He slipped his cock inside, groaning at the same time she did. "I'll get you the morning-after pill." Adrik pulled her up, resting her back against his chest as he kissed her neck. His hands were on her tits, twisting the nipples, and though she tried to stop him, the effort was minimal. "From now on, you're mine." He shoved hard into her, and she gasped. "Everything is mine, and I'm gonna cum in your pussy," he warned her. His hand drifted down her stomach and cupped her vagina. A finger pressing strategically against her clit. "You gonna stop me?"

Jolie's head rested on his shoulder, submitting wholly, and a moaned sigh escaped. "No."

Adrik smirked against her sweaty skin. He dropped her on the bed and pounded hard and fast into her. Her cries were unhindered, finally free and loud. He enjoyed every noise, digging deeper, wanting to see if there was more she was smothering. He wanted all of it, and he always got what he wanted.

Chapter Fifty

Stay

Jolie stared at Adrik as he slept. The sun was rising just beyond him, telling her they'd been in her room for more than eighteen hours. They've been in and out of sleep, waking up to make love. And though her vagina felt like it's been beaten with a bat, she didn't want to say no. She didn't know if it was his size or how he used it, but he reached pleasure in her she didn't know existed. It was like every nerve ending in her was on full blast. Every movement he made nearly triggered an orgasm. She's had more avalanches of ecstasy than she ever had in her life.

Jolie's fingers danced on his chest, tracing each tattoo, putting them to memory, questioning what made him get them. Some were nicer than others. She didn't appreciate the naked women or the devil, but they were choices he made without her. There were random scars covered by dark ink, and she teased them, trying to guess where he got them from. There was so much about his life she didn't know about, and yet he didn't feel like a stranger. She felt like she had been waiting for him her whole life.

The gunshot wound on his shoulder had opened during their lovemaking. Band-Aids proved ineffective, but thankfully, they had a small first aid kit in the bathroom, and she wrapped gauze over it. He was immune to pain, not caring as it bled when he tried to have sex with her on the bathroom floor.

Food was brought to her by Esfir as Adrik hid under the covers. Lunch and dinner, but it was only enough for one. They shared, but now she was starving. She was unbelievably thirsty, but she didn't want to move. She didn't want the peace between them to be over.

Adrik moaned as he woke, his gaze on her through the haze of sleepiness. "You okay?"

She nodded, trying to smother her smile but was terribly unsuccessful. "Happy Birthday," she whispered, kissing his chin.

Adrik smirked as a hand danced along her cheek. They spent so much time together, and it wasn't enough. He didn't want the day to start. He wanted to stay wrapped in her bedsheets forever. "You thought that was it," he joked, recalling when he came inside her for the first time. She got up and cleaned her pussy, then tried to put clothes on. He had picked her up and sat her on the dresser. The confusion on her face as he shoved his hard dick back into her had made him laugh. "You should have seen your face."

Jolie defended herself. "How was I supposed to know you can do that?"

"You read enough books."

"And it's typically one and done."

He chuckled. "Then, the women writing them aren't as lucky as you."

Jolie giggled. "You're so full of yourself." She curved her body around him, a naked leg over his. His fingers drifted up and down on her arm. She was floating in a cloud. Conversations between them had all been playful and sweet, with naughty talk sneaking in. She learned all his favorite things and saw every kind of smile. The bubble of happiness she was floating on couldn't be popped.

But she knew they still needed to discuss some things. Now that the day was just beginning, she wanted to start off on the right foot. Sex wasn't a balm; it wasn't going to make all their problems better.

"I'm sorry," Jolie began.

Adrik turned to her with knitted brows. "Sorry? For what?"

Jolie avoided his gaze. "I opened the door on the ship. You told me not to, but I got scared when they were drilling in from the other side. Your mom told me to stay, but I grabbed Helina and left. And they were waiting on the other side. I'm sorry. It's my fault you almost lost her."

Adrik rolled on his side, a hand propping his head up. "Baby, I wasn't mad at you."

The tears in her eyes hurt him, and he touched her bruised skin to assure her it was alright. "Then, why didn't you talk to me?"

He didn't know how to say his worries out loud. He wasn't typically a sharer. But Jolie wasn't like Katia, who saw emotion as a weakness. Jolie needed his words to soothe her. "I thought you would tell me it was over. I'm honestly surprised it isn't." He leaned into her ear, and whispered, "I'm starting to think you like a little danger."

Jolie giggled, pushing him away as he chuckled. But her smile fell after that. "You asked me to stay," she whispered. "And I want to."

"But?" he added, hearing it in her tone. He dropped on his back and stared at the ceiling. There was always a 'but.'

Jolie sat up, holding a blanket to her chest. She stared down at him, and his blue eyes avoided her. He didn't want to hear it, but she wasn't going to keep quiet. "I was terrified on the ship. I needed you, and instead, I got your brother. You use your brother to fix things. You can't do that. I don't want your brother. I want you."

Once more, she proved different. Adrik was beginning to realize his preconceived ideas of all the women he knew didn't apply to her. Adrik shrugged. "Alexei knows what to say."

"I don't care. His words aren't your words. His presence isn't your presence. In a relationship, we need to learn how to support each other. You can't rely on him to make me feel better. It puts him in a vulnerable position. It's misleading."

Adrik sat up. "Did he come on to you?"

"No," Jolie quickly corrected. "But"—she took a deep breath—"I think he likes me."

"I know he does." Adrik threw the covers off and put his feet on the floor, stretching. "But he knows his place."

"Adrik, that's not the point."

Adrik knew she was right, but Alexei was always the communicator. He knew how to deal with certain situations, usually with women, because Adrik didn't have the patience to deal with hysteria. He was not polite when met with crazy. But Jolie wasn't being crazy. She was communicating her needs, and he needed to listen.

He snatched his phone off the nightstand and turned it on. The agonizing seconds it took, with Jolie staring at him, was a new torture. Thankfully, dozens of beeps took away his attention the moment it activated. Being absent from his business for so long without letting anyone know was a good way to cause panic.

Jolie laid back on the bed, her heavy sigh distracting for half a second. He didn't want to deal with his supposed imperfections this early in the morning. It was his birthday, after all; didn't he deserve a break?

"You're right," he forced out after several minutes. He dropped the phone on the bed and lay down to face her. Jolie was scrutinizing him, her eyes slightly watery. He didn't like such a look. "Katia and I were married for ten years and hated each other for over half. I'm not used to dealing with shit like this."

A smile slipped on her lips, and her eyes sparkled with happiness. "And here I thought you were good at everything."

Adrik shrugged. "I am no god. But I am close."

She curled into him with a giggle. "All I want is for you to try."

Adrik touched her cheek and kissed her lips. "All I want is for you to suck my dick." He pulled at her head suddenly, and she squealed, yanking back, and rolled away. He snatched her at the waist, pulling her against his chest, tickling her sides, and she giggled and wiggled, trying to escape him.

Adrik got between her legs. "You think you can go again?"

"One way to find out."

He smirked as he held himself above her. "That's what I want to hear." With a hand on his cock, he pushed himself inside her. She hissed and knitted her brows, watching him as he sunk into her. Adrik nuzzled her neck. "I'll give you a break. Just this once." He pulled out, laying down beside her with a sigh. "I've destroyed your pussy."

"Shut up. Don't act so proud."

He rolled off her and stood. "I need to go."

Jolie sat up, suddenly desperate to keep him. "Stay."

"I can't. I've done something that will have repercussions, and I have to get ahead of it. With the birthday party tonight, I need to move fast." Adrik leaned down and kissed her. "You would be safer with your parents."

Adrik disappeared into the bathroom, using the toilet and brushing his teeth. Jolie curled on the bed as Ming and Tae-Tae roamed around her, meowing for food. She didn't want to leave him, but she might not have a choice.

Adrik came out, tying a towel around his waist. He winced slightly and folded his arm against his chest, checking on the bandage on his gunshot wound. The effects of the drug had worn off, and without the adrenaline of fucking Jolie, he could feel the pain radiate. As he looked up, he noticed Jolie drinking in every move he made.

Adrik smirked as he walked up to her. He took her chin in his hands. "If you look at me like that, I'll have no choice but to bend you over and fuck you from behind."

Her face ignited in red, and she slapped his hand away. How could she still be shy after all the words he unleashed last night? He enjoyed it, but he also couldn't wait for her to talk back.

Adrik motioned to the boxes around the room. "What is this?"

Jolie sighed, and admitted, "Your father is ready for me to leave."

"I'll deal with him."

Jolie bit her lip. The memory of yesterday, leaving Yakov's office, returned to her. She didn't know how to politely say his father tried to kill him. Would he want proof? Would he believe her?

"Adrik," she whispered, getting his attention. "I think your father staged the attack on the ship."

Gravity slammed him back to earth, and Adrik stood frozen. There were times on the ship when that terrible thought pierced him, and he gave it no time to build because it was so insane. But the pieces gathered together like a puzzle. The enemy was gentle with Helina. They knew where the safe room was on the ship. They never threatened his mother or daughter. The only person they pointed a gun at was Jolie.

'I think I will stay on a little while longer. As much as you think you are ready, there are still things in this world, boy, that you can't handle. That's why I'm here. I've seen everything, and I know what's best.'

"Why?" he breathlessly forced out of his lips. "Why do you say that?"

"When I was in his office, another man came in. He looked like the two attackers and even called one of them by a name I heard. Mic. He was looking for his sons."

There were no coincidences in the Mafia. Everything was connected, and it was all about finding those hidden lines. And here it was, exposed.

Adrik nodded. It was the only thing he could do as his future began to solidify.

The lock on the front door was unlatched, followed by a sharp hard knock. Adrik tightened the towel at his waist and glanced at Jolie as she hugged a blanket around herself. He put a hand, keeping her in place. "Cover up." He pointed to her exposed thigh.

Adrik faced the door like he was facing his father. It was time to go head-to-head with Yakov. His father had lost all his love, years and years' worth of betrayal. Adrik kept forgiving, but now, nothing left in him could wash away the vileness of Yakov's actions. He threatened not only his daughter but his girlfriend and his mother. It was clear he had no care for family, despite how much he claimed it was so important to him.

Adrik opened the door.

"Mr. Morozov?" Yakov's soldier greeted awkwardly.

"Tell my father Miss Bell is not going anywhere."

The man stuttered, going to leave before he stiffened his feet. ***"I'm here to bring Miss Bell to the car."***

Adrik purposefully replied in English, "She won't be leaving. In fact, send someone up to help her unpack. And tell my father—" He paused, a fist clenching at his side. So his threat wasn't lost in translation, Adrik said in Russian, ***"He's officially worn out his welcome."*** Adrik looked over his shoulder at Jolie. "Stay in your room." Adrik shoved past the soldier, and the door shut, leaving her.

Jolie stared after him, sinking into the bedsheets covered in their sex. A smile twitched on her lips. There were so many unknowns, things to fear, and the future was still unpredictable, but it was clouded by excitement. She could only see the positive in this new adventure. Adrik could protect her and keep her from his world. He'd let her feel the rush of the dark side without becoming part of it. It was like being caught in a tornado with no fear of death. Adrik opened up an entirely new world, and she couldn't wait to embrace it.

Jolie's smile faded as she stared out at the rising sun. There was still another secret she had yet to tell him. One that could destroy the world they were creating. Did she continue to pretend she wasn't betraying him? Or did she face him and pray he showed mercy?

The image of Adrik's blood-covered body flashed in front of her eyes like an omen.

The Morozov Series

Continue reading Adrik and Jolie's story:
Book 2: Embracing the Dark Side: releasing January 20th, 2025
Book 3: Becoming the Dark Side: releasing June 20thth, 2025

Prequel:
Yakov and Tatianna-(Standalone) Releasing TBD

The Daughters of Morozov Mafia:
Luerna
Nadia
Anya
Kira

The Morozov Children:
(interconnected and to be read last) TBD
Helina Morozov: TBD
Rurik Jr. Morozov: TBD

Find more information about releases at mcrivera.net

Special Thanks

There are multiple people I want to thank for helping make this series a possibility, but first a little backstory.

I have been writing for twenty years. My mother was the first person to realize my writing addiction. I used to write in a notepad until she bough me my first labtop. My first story was a horror and it was basically a bunch of people dying. It was terrible, but as a twelve-year-old it was amazing. I got the courage to post stuff on fanfiction when I was fifteen, and my stories did well enough to give me enough confidence to keep going. For fifteen years I wrote random things. I created my dystopian thriller, My Name is Scream. I wrote a Epic fantasy called War in Heaven. I wrote and read nothing for a few years. Then at 29 I found Wattpad and Inkitt. It took my erotica, My Wife's Desires being deleted from Wattpad to learn about self-publishing. I learned from a friend that she was making money publishing books, and I knew then I could do it too. I published without any thought to what I was doing. It wasn't so successful, but thankfully My Wife's Desires had a following from Inkitt, so I got a taste of potential.

I learned, I watched, I grew. And I knew I could do better.

One day, my husband was searching for a business to invest in. And I boldly said, 'Invest in me.' It's been a few years since then, but every day I am living up to that moment. He agreed and every spare dollar was put into my author business. Now I'm on my way to retire him. Soon. Because no matter what I'm going to be a best seller. If not this book, then the next. I thank him every day for helping make my dreams a reality.

Next, I have to thank is Joneyda, my sister-in-law. She is my go-to. I have spent hours drilling her brain, searching for ideas, ways to improve the book, and have taken her thoughts and molded them into my own. It's her opinion I cherish when I'm stuck with imposter syndrome, and I lack confidence. She believes in my work and wants me to succeed for no reason. Her selflessness is a rare quality to find, but I've been lucky enough to receive it.

All my family that's helped babysit my kids deserve my gratitude as well. If not for them, it would have taken me years to get to this point.

To the many booktokers on Tiktok that liked, commented, shared, and encouraged me, you are without a doubt the reason I write.

I have an amazing team of ARC readers and can't wait to hear what they have to say. Thank you to everyone that's taken the time to review.

Please follow me on Tiktok @mcriveramafiawriter and watch me grow.

www.ingramcontent.com/pod-product-compliance
Lightning Source LLC
Chambersburg PA
CBHW010356050826
48979CB00052B/2819/J

* 9 7 9 8 9 8 8 0 5 0 0 9 4 *